Return to Poughkeepsie

Debra Anastasia

Omnific Publishing
Los Angeles

Omnific Publishing
1901 Avenue of the Stars, 2nd floor
Los Angeles, CA 90067
www.omnificpublishing.com

First Omnific eBook edition, December 2013
First Omnific trade paperback edition, December 2013

Library of Congress Cataloguing-in-Publication Data

Anastasia, Debra.
Return to Poughkeepsie / Debra Anastasia - 1st ed.
ISBN: 978-1-623420-76-5
1. Poughkeepsie — Fiction. 2. Contemporary Romance — Fiction.
3. Kidnapping — Fiction. 4. Organized Crime — Fiction. I. Title

10 9 8 7 6 5 4 3 2 1

Cover Design by Micha Stone and Amy Brokaw
Interior Book Design by Coreen Montagna

Printed in the United States of America

T, J, and D, it's always all for you.

PART ONE

1

A True Friend

The SUV Beckett had stolen idled while he made his decision. This part should be easy—he was sufficiently soused, and the gun was so powerful they might find bits of his brain a mile down the road. If anyone cared enough to look. Which they wouldn't.

It was a nice last view, if you got to pick one. The winding road was a snake in a beautiful clump of fall trees.

It was fall again. One full year since he had loved Eve enough to leave.

And yet.

And yet.

And yet she was all he could think about. When he was feeling gracious, he pictured her snuggled in a warm sweater under some lucky fuck's arm. And when he was feeling jealous, which was most of the goddamn time, he pictured her naked under some nameless three-pump chump. Being a girlfriend or a wife.

God, please not a wife.

The pistol lay between his legs, the liquor sat in the seat next to him like a true friend.

Do it, you pussy-headed motherfucker.

But the sky was too blue. And his hand kept shaking.

He took another swig from the bottle, mentally listing all the reasons his life was over. First, no Eve. Second, his brothers were far safer without him. Third, *he* was the only thing he needed to protect his loved ones from anymore. So was he man enough to take care of the problem? Because he had no doubts he was the problem.

But he wanted her. He craved her. All of the loose-assed whores he'd fucked since her smelled like eggs, moaned like tramps, and never, ever dared him to be anything but an asshole. His brothers were tucked into perfect worlds with perfect girls. Christ, he couldn't set them up sweeter if he tried. But he hadn't tried. He'd only made shit worse and crazy dangerous.

He was the oldest of the foster brothers, but he certainly wasn't leading the way toward happiness and fulfillment. But Beckett's approach to life had been the only thing he could come up with back in the day. As a kid, he'd been really good at watching. He'd seen other foster kids age out of the system and hit the streets—homeless, minimally educated, and desperate to find a foothold in a society that didn't even know they existed. He knew his troubled brothers would need protecting, and by the time he aged out ahead of them, he'd figured out a way he could do it: become the scariest motherfucker in Poughkeepsie.

He'd killed more people than shy folks probably talked to in their lives. And he'd gotten his hands dirty with everything from weapons to drugs to whores. But when Blake and Cole were cut loose from the foster care system, Beckett Taylor's name in their mouth bought them protection from the worst of society's evils. No one dared cross him. Cole had found his way by working at a local church, but Blake had remained a concern because—despite the money Beckett could provide—he chose to be homeless and his mind didn't always seem clear.

But that was all in the past now. When the McHugh girls, Livia and Kyle, had barreled into his brothers' lives, everything fell into place for them. Only Beckett was left behind as king of the bloodiest mountain, both ruler and prisoner now of all he possessed.

Despite all the times he'd used them, Beckett was afraid of this gun. It was more final than time. It wouldn't erase the pain, and he was afraid that after his body was wasted, the only thing left would be fear. And he fucking despised fear. The gun had been his tool. His ladder. His friend. His medal of valor. Now it mocked him from between his legs. It was heavy. After clenching and unclenching his hand, he finally touched it. He lifted it and let the safety go. Beckett put the pistol back in his lap, with the muzzle pointed straight at him.

That's better. To be serious, you have to get serious.

Would death be something he'd feel? He was going to hell—Christ, he'd always been going to hell. His first memory as a child was hearing the word *hell.* It had bound him to the place like a rope.

He took another drink.

Here, in the bowels of suburban America, he would be no one. Just a down-on-his-luck bastard passing through town. He had no identifying papers with him. He looked at his singed fingertips. No prints to be found. He'd also yanked out his two fillings with a pair of pliers and thrown them in the trash by the CVS. He was his own best murderer. He could do it better than anyone else.

He should be deep in the fucking woods—where no one but a pissing bear would find his body. But he was here, facing the fact that he absolutely hated the thought of being alone. If his soul stayed stuck to his body like Velcro, he wanted to at least be in a grave with some other fuckers. Maybe he also wanted his brothers to know he was gone. To have them say, "Thank you, oh great big brother Beckett. You saved us from your-fucking-self." *Or maybe I want Livia, sweet little Whitebread, to come with her red, flushed cheeks, sobbing, to lay flowers on my grave. That would be okay.*

Selfish son of a bitch. Beckett picked up the gun and set it to his temple. *Do it! Do it! You're nothing without them. Be gone. Go away.*

His hand shook, and he could feel the muzzle imprinting a circle right where the bullet would pierce his skin. He started to sweat and worked hard not to piss his fucking pants. He squeezed his eyes shut. He willed his finger to have the guts. Sweat rolled down his face.

"*Fuck me!*" Beckett tossed the gun aside. The shaking overwhelmed him. Teeth chattering, he did go ahead and piss.

Her. He'd be sending a message to Eve by letting his body be found: *See? See what leaving you did? I gave the fuck up.* He looked at the pistol on the floor. *I'm a selfish bastard. That's why I'm doing this. I don't want to nut up and do life without her.*

Beckett didn't bother to wipe his face as his shivering turned to sobbing. His breathing made a racket. When he saw himself in the rearview mirror, his whole face was puffy. He leaned his head back against the headrest, feeling his warm urine start to cool.

A tapping noise on the driver's side window caused him to open one blurry eye. The speedy fluttering was so bizarre. The little bird tapping on his window had mistaken a flower decal for the real thing. It just hovered there like a helicopter, tapping on the window as if it were trying to get his attention.

Another hummingbird came along and tried for the same pretend flower, pecking at the first in anger. *Eve's right. These things are little assholes.* The two birds decided to get in a birdy pissing match, diving and trying to outmaneuver each other. They tumbled away from the window, out of Beckett's sight. *Fucking hummingbirds. They couldn't leave each other's ass alone? It's like they* wanted *to fight over their flower. Little knights without a queen to defend.*

Then it was so obvious, it was almost funny. It was like he had a pair of glasses on his heart: Eve was a hummingbird, and so was he. They'd rather fight each-fucking-other than drink together from a boring old flower. She came to him then, for a moment—a vision on Cole and Kyle's wedding day with her hummingbird brooch.

Beckett put the stolen SUV in reverse and weaved his way down the winding road. He was amazed, considering how drunk he was, when he made it back to his hotel. He left the vehicle sort of where he half-remembered taking it from, somehow stumbled to his room, and passed out on the bed.

When he woke a good fifteen hours later, his head was cracking open with whatever he had drunk the night before. But he knew where he was going.

Today, he was going to win the Big Fucking Humping Pussy Award and go back to Poughkeepsie. He had no plan beyond that. Maybe stalk the fuck out of Eve.

It took him two days to get back to Poughkeepsie, where it all had started. He'd driven these streets as a king. A man to be feared. And now he was twitching at the cop cars and bright lights, pulling his hat down low and trying not to act like the fucking suspect he was.

Beckett could see the lights on in Blake's apartment. He parked in a spot and closed the door of his paid-for-in-cash Lincoln quietly. If the police were still searching for him, Blake's place should be first on their list. But he was going to get to see his brother's home—his first real home. The thought stopped him mid-stride.

Thank you, God. He has a home inside, in a building, in a girl's arms. I don't think you're taking my calls anymore, but take this: Thank you.

Back when Eve was still his and she was helping Blake deal with his sun thing, she'd told him about the apartment in detail—like they were a SWAT team about to attack. He knew where every piece of furniture should be, where the windows were, but he was dying to see it. With his own eyes he wanted to see his brother standing and breathing and happy.

He knocked softly on the door. He listened as two locks clicked and watched the knob turn. Livia's arms were around him as soon as the door flew open. She had enough sense to not say his name out loud.

He mumbled into her hair, "Don't you look in the peephole before you open the fucking door?" He could feel warm wetness on his T-shirt and knew she was crying. She was happy to see him. He put one thick arm around her back and walked her into the apartment, closing the door behind them.

"Beckett, I missed your crazy ass." Livia put her hands on his shoulders and looked into his eyes.

"Mrs. Whitebread, you look as fantastic as anyone could in a pair of polar bear pants." Beckett smiled for her.

"You just missed Blake. He left for work. Let me call his cell and tell him you're here." Livia let go of him long enough to retrieve her phone from the end table in the living room.

Beckett covered her fingers as she began to call. "Wait, babycakes. Work? He has regular work?"

She was like metal in a microwave, she lit up so instantly. "I should let him tell you."

Beckett raised an eyebrow. "Say it. Spit it out."

Livia took a deep, smiling breath. "Okay, so he's been working at the piano bar? He took over for the full-time guy, and he's been a big hit. Of course, right?"

Beckett nodded. "Of course."

"Well, just yesterday an agent stopped by and wants Blake to make a demo. In a studio. With microphones." Livia's voice went up an octave with every sentence. Beckett was pretty sure she now hovered a few inches above the floor.

"That's fucking amazing news, I can't even tell you. Look how great you guys have been doing with me gone." Beckett wanted this to be a compliment, but Livia's eyes widened, then narrowed.

"Oh, no. You don't get to say that. He misses you so much. Things that remind him of you? They just stop him in his tracks. He even wrote a song about you." Livia put her hand on his arm.

"As fucking gay as that is, it chokes me up like a bitch." Beckett laughed but covered his mouth with his fist.

He took a moment to look around, finding touches of his brother: two glasses in the sink, a pile of music paper, a picture of Blake and Livia in front of a Disney castle stuck on the fridge with a magnet, an extra pair of his shoes by the door. An extra pair of *Blake's* shoes by the door. *Fuck yeah.* It was better than he could've ever imagined. On the coffee table, he saw a brand new pair of baby socks and a teeny, tiny hat.

"Wait a minute, is your sister knocked up? Did Cole do this?" He pointed at the pile of hope. Livia shook her head and put her hand on her own belly.

"You? You! Oh, baby, come here." He gathered her again in his arms, patting her back. "You and my brother are having a kid?" Beckett kissed her on the forehead.

She smiled even wider now. "We just found out on our belated honeymoon last week. The honeymoon you paid for, by the way. Thank you."

Beckett brushed away her thanks. "That's you guys' money. I'm glad you did something cool with it."

He let her go and picked up the impossibly small baby clothes. Winnie the Pooh was printed happy and fat repeatedly on the fabric. "Kids start out this freaking small? Holy crap."

Livia nodded. "Yeah. I've got to say, I'm a little scared. I've never even *held* an infant."

Beckett put the hat and booties down as if they were made of glass. "Whitebread, I can just picture you, hair in a ponytail, spooning some glop into an adorable kid. You'll be amazing." The whole sight of Livia, glowing and smiling, made him think of Eve and everything he'd taken from her. He needed to find out if she was happy.

"Thanks, Beck. I sure hope so."

"So, is Eve married yet?" Beckett looked at his feet, but he knew he'd tipped his cards. Women were so fucking intuitive.

"Ahh. I see. I'm glad you're looking for her." Livia sat on the couch.

Beckett shook his head and sat next to her. "No, see, I'm just checking on my people. So they're not pregnant, but how're Fairy Princess and Cole?"

"They're doing really well. Cole has gone back to college to become a teacher. He's going for his special education degree. His church congregation has provided him with the first-ever Riverside Church College Scholarship. Kyle is still at Mode, working her fashion magic, and the owner has made her a manager. Kyle and Cole also spend a lot of time hiking and volunteering at the church."

Beckett ran his hand through his messy hair. "What does 'special education' mean? Who'll Cole be teaching?"

Livia took his hand but waited until he looked at her to speak. "He can teach anyone, but his focus will be emotionally disturbed students. The ones who only have anger to respond to feelings. The ones who have big hearts, but big fists as well. He'll be teaching them how to love without pain."

"Kids like he was? That's perfect." Beckett could easily picture Cole driving to a school in his grandpa car. No kid would get one over on him. Cole knew all their tricks already.

Livia curled Beckett's hand into a fist. "He says, and I quote, 'I want to be there for the kids like Beckett. I want to be for them what I couldn't be for him.' He's so proud."

Beckett took his fist from her hand and stood. They were all doing great. Coming here was a selfish mistake. He didn't even trust himself in the room with her, with a little baby in her belly. God, what if one of his old enemies spotted him and took aim through the window? He had a flash of her beautiful hair tangled in blood, lying on the floor, a bullet putting an end to all this perfect. He moved so fast, she gasped as he pulled all the curtains closed. Slapping light switches off, he pulled her to the safest place in the room.

"You have to promise to take good care of yourself. Good care of that baby. Good care of my brother. Okay? I've got to go. I need to go. I need to leave all of you here—in this storybook ending in my head." Beckett hugged her again and headed for the door. He could feel his poison spreading through all he'd found.

Livia spoke harshly, "Beckett. You will not leave now. I need to know what the hell is going on. Why do you look like shit? Why are you acting paranoid? You show up after a year? I want answers. Blake will demand answers, and if I can't give them to him, he'll quit his job and go find you. Do you want that?"

Beckett paused with his hand on the door.

"Livia, please let me leave while I can." He waited.

Livia grabbed her cell phone again.

Good, baby. Call the cops. Get me out of here.

She scrolled until she found what she wanted. She handed him the phone:

Lollipop's Ladies: 702-555-1354

"We haven't seen Eve since before the wedding. She calls from this number once a week to talk to Blake about the sun. She refuses to give him any information about what she's doing. But Blake says he's heard people calling her January."

Beckett stared at the phone and smiled an evil smile. "Lollipop's is a strip club—a skin shop outside of Vegas. She's taking her clothes off for money. Which makes no fucking sense, because I paid her enough to live two comfortable lives."

He was beginning to rage. Livia hugged him. "Beckett, I want to know what you've been doing."

Livia was in front of a window again. Though the curtain was secure, Beckett had another flash of her being shot in his arms, so he pulled her back to the couch where they could sit in the semi-dark. He handed her back her phone.

"You want to know, Whitebread? Well, I can't tell you most of it. Honestly, I wouldn't even try in your delicate condition." But the minute the words were out of his mouth, he knew she would be anything but delicate as a mother. She would be fierce and devoted and tireless. "I've spent a year wishing," he finally said. "Wishing the best for all of you. And looks like I got my wish, right?"

He looked at her. It was her deep gray eyes that made him tell her. "I was this fucking close to blowing my brains out a few days ago."

She nodded, waiting for the rest.

"I wanted to make my absence permanent, because I can't trust myself. I want to be close to my family. I'm too selfish to leave forever."

He held his head and looked at the floor, ashamed to be admitting his weakness to his brother's wife.

"No. No." Livia turned his face toward hers. "You love us too much to take away someone we love. Beckett, please, your life is dangerous enough. You don't need *you* as an enemy too."

"Don't make me out to be something worth saving. We both know I'm a waste." His voice was so quiet.

"I wish I was better at telling you why you have to stay here. I wish I could put into words the part of my heart that has your name written on it. That part hurts right now. You have to be here. You love life too much. You're so important. I wish I could make you understand this."

He tried to smile at her valiant efforts.

"I would keep you if I could. You can sleep here, right on this couch. Beckett, I will let you hold this baby when it comes." She touched her stomach. "Does that tell you how much you mean to me? It's the only thing I can come up with."

He shrugged.

"Mouse would be disappointed. He'd feel like he didn't do his job if you died...Eve loves you. Wherever she is—in this strip club—is that what you've been wishing for?"

Beckett shook his head.

"No, right? She loves you. You can't kill someone she loves. You just can't." Livia's earnest efforts filled the room.

Really? I already did that, baby. Twice.

Livia bit her lip.

Beckett picked up her hand and kissed it. "Thank you. I'm sorry for bothering you." He stood.

"Please promise me you won't try to hurt yourself again. Just promise me that, and I'll let you go."

He loved that she thought she could stop him from doing anything. He knew she would try. "You tell my brothers they'll hear from me again and to keep up the good work. I'm so fucking proud of them. Tell your sister I told her to get knocked up too."

"And? For me?"

In that moment Livia looked exactly like the wife every man should want: flannel pants, little booties on the table, love written all over her soft skin like it was a newspaper. "I won't hurt myself on purpose. I promise you." Beckett turned to leave but didn't miss the tears on her cheeks. "You lock this door behind me," he added. "And name that kid Beckett."

Just before he closed the door he heard her retort, "But I already named the plant Beckett!"

He waited until he heard the locks click back into place. *Safe again.*

He wanted to go listen to Blake. He wanted to pound Cole on the back. But he needed to find Eve. If one more dude saw her tits, his head might explode. Livia *had* said something that changed his mind. He would keep his promise to her. He wouldn't blow his own head off.

"She loves you. You can't kill someone she loves. You just can't." If Eve loved him still, even a little, he couldn't kill yet another person she loved.

2

Frankentits

Lollipop's was no candy store. Sin and debauchery rolled off the place in waves. But it was upscale, if you considered low-scale a cardboard box and a flashlight. Beckett had dressed the part: jeans, combat boots, and a black T-shirt. He waited in line and kept his head down, paying his entrance fee like the rest of the slime with hard-ons. The bouncer reminded him of Mouse a bit. He wore jeans, a Lollipop T-shirt, and, absurdly, a bowtie. But when Beckett looked him in the face, he saw none of Mouse's intelligence.

Inside, the music was loud, the waitresses were topless, and mirrors reflected every bad choice the people inside made. Beckett slid onto a faux leather couch. He knew from experience that pleather was a great material. With just a few swipes it wiped clean of alcohol, jizz, and blood. Upscale.

January. He waited for January in the middle of October. Two scumbags plopped themselves at a table in front of him, obscuring his view of the stage. Normally he would have removed them, protecting his personal space like a tiger with a kill. But not tonight.

A waitress bounced up. Her welcoming body language and glittered skin couldn't entirely offset her dead eyes. "Hello, handsome. What can I get you?"

Beckett looked her up and down. The fluffy tulle skirt was meant to make her semi-nude body seem playful, but her nipples were too large, and he could easily see the scars from her last boob job even in the dim light.

"Whiskey. Just bring me the bottle." He turned his attention to the back of the scumbags' heads.

"Sorry, sir. We only sell it by the glass."

"Listen, dollface, you get me the fucking bottle, and I'll tip you so big you can get those frankentits fixed and get your ass up on stage to make some real money." He pointed at the offending mammaries with two fingers.

Without a word, Frankentits disappeared into the throng of sweaty men.

The spotlights began whizzing around the club, their operator careful not to focus on any particular patron's face. Shortly, a partially dressed chick in a French maid's costume began to prance around onstage, using her duster in a variety of crazy ways. Beckett looked around, but he'd seen it all before: the panting men trying to pretend they weren't watching the girls, then getting too soused not to ogle.

Frankentits arrived with his bottle, and he slid a wad of cash into her tutu. She scrambled off to count it in such a way that made him believe she would be shooting it up as soon as she could.

French maid, nurse, naughty schoolteacher—every fantasy played out on the stage. As the time ticked by, Beckett tried not to picture Eve demeaning herself in front of these assholes. *Would she be the dominatrix? Of course.* He was going to grab her and get the fuck out of here before any man saw her. He would keep her covered. Still, he drank like it was his purpose in life. For some reason he had to.

Finally the music rose to pounding, and the lights flickered on and off. Alternating strobe lights prepared for the big reveal. Beckett wished he was wrong, but as the club went pitch black, he knew he would see her. A spotlight cracked through the darkness, and at center stage, a black-leather-clad goddess stood with her back to the men. She cracked a whip with a flick of her wrist. She began to turn, and Beckett got to his feet, finishing the last guzzle of the whiskey.

The two fools in front of him started moaning. "January. Oh man, my dick's so hard. Just watch her work. Ah…"

Beckett looked down at them and contemplated cracking their heads together like pool balls. He situated his hands behind their skulls. Then he realized they weren't looking at the stage, but toward the bar. The dominatrix now turned to face the crowd, and she looked nothing like Eve.

The assholes started grabbing their crotches and moaning, "January."

Beckett followed the direction of their lust. Two drunk guys were being handsy with Frankentits, and now security came in the form of Eve/January. She wore a version of the bouncers' gear: short daisy dukes, red heels, T-shirt, and a bowtie. The men had Frankentits backed against the bar, and a crowd had formed around them. Eve confidently used a barstool as a stair. She hopped onto the bar and waltzed along as if it were a sidewalk.

She kicked one drunk's head like a soccer ball, and he went down with a thud. The other looked up past the miles of legs to her face, beautiful even when angry. The assholes in front of Beckett groaned and stood on their chairs to get a better view. The music ground to a halt.

"That dude's going to die. She'll kill the fuck outta him," one said to the other.

Eve slid off the bar and had a knife to the man's throat, but she'd started to smile. "Offering me money? What's this? A dollar? Did you think I would take my top off?"

The drunk nodded.

"Eat your dollar." Her eyes sparkled.

The crowd started to chant "Jan-u-ar-y!" over and over.

Beckett stood on a table to watch her. The drunk did, in fact, eat his dollar.

The bouncers from the front door had made their way to the ruckus. Eve nodded as the men removed the drunks. She had no comforting words for Frankentits. She just slipped her knife back in her hair. The crowd clapped and whistled at her. She had no reaction.

As the cheers faded away, Beckett kept clapping. A slow, mocking cadence. "Hey, January!" he called. "What do I have to do to get you all up in my business?"

Eve stopped, her back to him. There was a low mumbling in the crowd. No one had ever dared taunt her, of that Beckett was sure. He jumped off the table. "How about this?" He swiveled and cold-clocked one of the assholes in front of him, who was still holding his penis.

She faced him, looking furious, which made Beckett angrier. He gave the other asshole a three-punch combination. He, too, went down like a sack of rocks. She stood glaring at him as he closed the distance between them.

"I leave you to start a life, I live without you, and this is my replacement? You're a freak for them to cheer about?"

She closed her eyes. He was being cruel, and he knew it.

"January? Do you have such a taste for blood that you couldn't walk away from it? You're that much of a fucking vampire?" He was close enough to touch her now. But he didn't.

The crowd was paying attention. Beckett figured she was an enigma to them. The most beautiful chick in the world, doing a man's job in a strip club. He would love it if he didn't hate it.

"They're mocking you, *January*. They're not really afraid of you. You're as much of a show as that piece of trash." He pointed to the stripper onstage.

She opened her eyes. "You know what? This is what I do. If you're trying to shame me, you're wasting your breath. I never killed you—that's enough shame. Go, Beckett. I don't want you. Don't come back."

Eve turned and exited through a door behind the bar.

Beckett just stood there, wiping his mouth. All the wrong words had come out.

Eve, please be next to me, 'cause I don't think I can stand on my own.

Eve, be with me, because at night I shake and only your warm skin can heal me.

Eve, don't leave, because I have nowhere else to go.

After a moment he followed her, with no one making a move to stop him. Above the club there was a crappy hotel. He heard her heels hitting the last step and knew where to go. From the skeezy hotel's hallway, he imagined her silhouette dancing across the sheers in her room. Her shape would be sharp, the light soft. She'd pace, agitated—probably steaming mad, actually. Beckett bit his lip and cracked his knuckles. He needed to taste her.

He didn't bother knocking. He didn't call to her. He approached the door like it was already open. His combat boot hit the door's sweet spot, and it crashed, releasing its hold on the night. Eve already had her gun in one hand and was pulling her knife out of her hair with the other. That made him hard. He didn't slow down, just swatted the hand with the gun and grabbed her by the throat. He slammed her against the wall.

She made no noise. She was far too tough for that. He should explain, but he didn't have a taste for words. He had a desire to swallow her moans. To be everything she wanted. Even if she said she didn't.

"Kill me now," he screamed at her. "*Do it!* Do it, or I fucking take what I want. I'll give you a count of three." He meant it—either he would be dead or he would have her. "One." He loosened his grip. She tightened hers on her knife. "Two." Beckett licked his lips. She put the knife to his throat. He bent his neck to give her access to his jugular. They waited, tension rippling between them. "Three."

Eve threw the knife, and it lodged in the headboard across the room. Through her half-slit eyes, he saw lust.

"You're mine now. You gave up. Know that. You could have killed me. Now nothing will stop me."

Eve turned her head. Letting him. Beckett grabbed her neck again. With his other hand he grabbed her waist and threw her. She landed in the middle of the bed. She pulled herself backward, her eyes on his, already panting.

Beckett smiled as he grabbed her ankle and pulled her to the edge of the bed. He pulled off his shirt and stood, penetrating her first with fear. How far would he go? How much would he take?

Eve set her fuck-hot red hooker heels on his bare chest. The danger in her face was an alarm to any man who dared get this close. She could easily slam a pointy heel between his eyes.

He pulled her shoes off, declawing the tiger. Her ridiculously tight denim shorts were in the way. Beckett retrieved the knife from the headboard, silently cursing her for how deeply it was lodged. When he turned back, she hadn't moved. The door hung open, jagged, from its hinges. Pounding bass from the club made the floor beneath his feet vibrate.

He returned to his spot between her legs. "You want this. You want me here. Say it, Eve. 'Cause I'm the only motherfucker with the balls to do this to you. Fucking say it."

Her voice was raw. "Do it."

Beckett used the knife to cut away the fabric, sawing so close to her pussy that she gritted her teeth. He watched her face as he cut her loose, and when he was done his knuckles were wet from brushing against her. She was so hot inside, she could probably melt the knife into a silver puddle. He repositioned the blade and held it like a psycho killer. She found herself moaning. Beckett brought the knife down hard and fast, burying it in the mattress up to its hilt, right next to her face. Eve turned and stared at it, tossing under her own touch.

Beckett grabbed her wrists. "Stop that. You'll come for me and only me."

She snarled at him. He could tell she hated that she wanted him so much. He let go and grabbed the center of her T-shirt, ripping it to reveal her breasts. They were rising and setting like two fucking suns. His fingers dug into her neck. She slapped him across the face. Again. Again. He pulled her to a sitting position.

"Find my dick and put it in your fucking mouth."

Eve punched his stomach and undid his buckle, the button. The zipper to his pants was hard to loosen around his erection, but she managed. He could feel the air and waited for her gorgeous red lips to take him. Eve slapped his cock across its head.

"Son of a bitch." He tightened his grip on her neck.

Her lips had a blue cast to them, and blue lips were sexier than red as she wrapped them around him. Instead of tongue and humming, Eve tortured him with scraping teeth. Every third rake up and down, she released to slap him in the cock.

He let go of her neck and crawled on top of her, angry with need. "You'll suck my dick, or I won't fuck you with it." He used his most threatening gangster voice.

"Make me." Eve licked her traitor lips, so plump.

He kicked off his pants and boots. Beckett climbed her body so his cock was all she could see. When he pushed it to where her mouth should be, he was met with her tongue, then her hands. Exquisite. She was so fucking good at this. Finally she turned her head, and his aching dick hit nothing but scratchy comforter.

He rolled off her and stood.

Eve wiped her mouth. "I'm taking good care of you, but fuck you. Fuck you, Taylor." She got off the bed as if to leave.

"The hell you're leaving." He had to move quickly to catch her. The crazy bitch walked out the door, her shorts hanging like a skirt. Beckett grabbed her by the hair and reached around for her breast.

He spoke to her neck, licking it in between words. "This is where you want it? Where everyone can see you?" He pinched her nipple. Beckett kept his fist tangled in her hair. He dragged the other hand down her stomach, around her hip, and underneath the ragged denim. She was more than ready. He stuck three fingers into her without warning.

Eve grabbed the railing that kept the drunk motherfuckers from falling off the second-floor walkway. Her knuckles were white. He moved his hand at lightning speed, letting his pinky rub her, and she rocked into him with pleasure.

"More? You want my dick? Eve, you whore, you want it?" Beckett bit her neck.

All she could do was moan.

"Say my fucking name. Now." Beckett stilled his hand.

She panted. "I hate you."

He yanked her hair and forced her to look at him. He took the hand from between her legs and held her jaw tenderly, the smell of her sex between them.

Her blue eyes filled with tears. "I love you."

His forceful manner slipped. His voice caught on the emotion in his throat. "I know. I'm sorry."

They kissed deeply, lovers on a balcony, until Beckett broke the kiss. "Say my name." He rubbed his length against her back, reminding her what he had to offer.

"No, asshole. You say mine." Eve adjusted her hips, and he bent his knees.

All the way in on the first thrust.

Beckett had taken Eve from her now-exposed former place of shelter. He'd registered them brazenly with his given name in a fancy hotel on the other side of town, far from Lollipop's. After a night of fucking everywhere they could prop themselves up, they'd fallen asleep together.

The next morning, Eve lay in the soft, crisp, monochromatic hotel sheets, seemingly exhausted. Beckett moved so very slowly—she was always quick and ready to kill. But to see her lie in the gentle feathers of morning sunlight was a treat he'd never expected again. The white light had not a hint of gold, and her pale skin grabbed and absorbed it. He propped his head on one hand, and the other itched, wanting to touch her. *Is her skin warm from the sun?*

She looked just like the Eve who'd laughed and joked with the little girl at the safe house more than a year ago. Here, in his bed. Her face's little slopes created such loveliness. Beckett allowed just the smallest part of his fingertip to skate over her skin. It was warm. He indulged himself in the feel of the nape of her neck. He had choked it so often to bring her pleasure. Under her eyes were marks left from the dark that stayed with those who had seen too much of the night. She'd slept poorly without him.

Instead of feeling a cocky pride, he ached for her, for this peaceful Eve. A sight this fucking magnificent added to the world, gave it peace, made the sky more blue. He traced her breast, smiling as her nipple reacted in her sleep. Reflexes—things she couldn't control, like him. She loved him, and it hurt her. He traced her radiating skin, possessive, refusing to let the blaze of the sun have all the claim on this Eve. He slowed to trace her navel.

She sighed in her sleep and turned toward his touch. He slipped his arm under her head, letting his bicep be her pillow. She snuggled deeper, trusting him. Sleeping with him. Beckett hugged her closer. *Protection. Family.* The words still stirred something inside. But as his greedy hand traced her hourglass shape, he saw something for the first time: Her hip—this spot that drove him crazy, drove him with the need to bury his dick in her—was more than just a grip. It was the perfect spot to prop a chubby little kid. A baby would hang like a koala, using this gorgeous hip as a notch to stay closer to Eve.

He traced her shape back up to her face and lay his hand on her cheek. *I love her. So fucking much. I'm going to give her everything. Everything she never even knew she needed.* He rolled her off his arm to lay on her back again. He positioned himself between her legs and slid slowly into her center. Rocking gently, pushing slowly, so different than any other time. She sighed again in her sleep. He paused in his gentle, sexual alarm clock to kiss her forehead.

Eve's eyes fluttered open, like Snow White waking. In an instant she had the gun she kept under her pillow pointed between his eyes. Soft Eve became deadly in less time than it took to exhale.

Beckett continued his slow, methodical thrusts while smiling at his venomous lady. "I love you, Eve." He watched as the white light and his own revelation confused her. She latched the safety back on her pistol and slid it under the pillow. He saw the sneer begin to form as she readied herself for their violent screwing.

"I want to make love to you, without pain," he said. "I want to make love to *you*, the woman I just watched dreaming."

Instead of turning her hands into claws, she flattened them on his chest. "Love?" she said, with cautious, skeptical eyes.

Beckett just nodded and slowly moved in and out of her.

She looked above his head.

"Look at you," he continued. "I want to build things for you, give you a reason to be soft. Give you a reason not to reach for a fucking gun when you open your eyes." He increased his tempo.

She blinked, her eyes clouding with tears, but she looked at him. Instead of twisting her like a pretzel, he gathered her closer, bringing her against his chest, kneeling while she straddled him.

Eve buried her face in the hollow of his neck.

He leaned his cheek against her head as he moved in her. "You don't have to say anything. Just feel me inside you."

Together they moved, so different, so soft.

Eve's tears finally spilled. Beckett waited until they were both spent, rearranging their bodies so he could cuddle her back against his chest. He didn't want to see her reaction to his next words. Though limp now, he remained surrounded by her warmth.

"I think you love me with your hate. I want you to love me from the same part of your heart that loved David." He expected some arguing, but she was still, frozen in his arms. "I'm asking too much—I know that. I'm not worth your heart yet, but I'm gonna be. Eve, the next time you see me, I'm going to be a man worth it." Her turned her head and kissed her now salty lips. "Just don't fuck anybody else."

He reluctantly pulled from her and began to dress. He skipped the shower so he could still smell her skin on his body. She stayed curled in the mold he had made for her, not getting up to stop him. He could tell she wanted this too. She wanted him to be part of her normal, no matter how fucked up it was going to be. He was almost to the door when she spoke. He could see her reflection in the mirror above the dresser.

"Just make sure you come back, Beckett. I'll go crazy if you don't."

He smiled, though she couldn't see it. "You'll be underneath me again. I promise."

3

My Left Nut

It was a nice fucking day—and not just because of how his morning began. Beckett was trying to look at the world with new eyes. If he was going to be a different person, there were two men he needed to talk to. So back into the Lincoln he went for another ungodly thirty five hour drive. He pulled his cap down low and adopted a thuggish lean. He needed to get in and out of Poughkeepsie one more time. Which was stupid, but that seemed to be his modus operandi of late.

When he finally rolled in, his ass vowing never to forgive him, he called Blake, but Livia reported he'd gone for a walk. She didn't need to say anything more. The spot in the woods where Blake had almost taken his last breath was also his favorite place in the world.

By the time Beckett arrived, it was twilight. The sun dusted the tops of the trees with the last of its energy. He parked in the lot at Firefly Park as Blake emerged from the trees. Beckett just watched his brother for a minute. Blake turned toward the fading sun and nodded, like one man would to another. Acknowledging. Beckett covered his face briefly to make sure his suddenly watery eyes wouldn't spill over onto his cheeks.

When he glanced back up, Blake was coming toward him. Of course he'd noticed him. Blake was so fucking observant. Beckett tried his door before realizing it was locked. He damn near ripped off the button in his haste to get to Blake. He got the thing open just as Blake closed in. They pounded each other on the back vigorously.

"Beck? What the hell?" Blake pulled away to look at his face, as if making sure he was real.

Beckett disentangled himself to hold up his arm in their standard greeting. Blake nodded to him much like he had the receding sun before wrapping his forearm around Beckett's, drawing their matching tattoos together.

"Brother. I've missed you. Damn it." Blake looked close to tears himself as he pulled Beckett into another pounding hug. "This is not safe at all. What the hell are you doing here?"

"Baby, I got to change some shit, and you're one of only two people in the world I want advice from." Beckett slapped Blake's shoulder again. "But say the word and I'm gone."

Blake shook his head as if the thought pained him. "Let's get out of sight."

They climbed into the car, and Beckett eased them into the thickening night. They kept smiling stupidly at each other.

"You look like crap. Wow. What the hell's going on?" Blake looked worried.

Beckett ignored the question and kept his eyes on the road. "Can you text Cole in a way that keeps this quiet?"

Blake pulled out his cell phone and typed a quick message. He flashed it in Beckett's direction before hitting send:

Listening to the Ave Maria in the car.

Almost immediately Cole's response chimed through:

I'd love 2 join u. Get me at the church?

As he read it over the center console, Beckett flipped on his right turn signal.

"So you stopped by to see Livia?" Blake didn't sound thrilled. Beckett couldn't blame him. He was a time bomb strapped to a landmine.

"I won't do that again. Don't worry." Beckett tried not to feel the walls of his isolation narrow beyond where he could breathe.

Blake nodded. "So you know about the baby."

"It's going to be okay. There's no way in hell you'll be like your mom—just so you know." Beckett gave Blake a side-glance. He'd guessed right. Considering Blake's alcoholic mother and series of tragic foster homes, he had no good role models for being a parent—particularly a dad.

"She's so excited, and I am too, don't get me wrong. But crap. We know what happens when you do it wrong, you know?" Blake made a fist on his lap.

Beckett shook his head. It was going to be a long blob of months for his brother. "I know a few things. Not a lot, mind you, but a few things. And one of those is that a kid who gets raised by you will be honest and kind and able to survive in the wild for months at a time."

Blake laughed, and Beckett tried not to be obvious as he drank the noise in.

They stopped at a red light—all slow like, no cause for attention. Beckett turned to his brother, this shattered man so whole now, and looked him up and down. "I would've given my left nut to be raised by a man like you."

Blake held out his arm and Beckett grasped it so their tattoos touched again. "I feel the same way about you," Blake said.

The light changed, and Beckett smiled at Blake before returning to his task. Two quick turns and Beckett killed the headlights as he approached the dark church. Cole rapped with a knuckle on the back window, and within seconds the car was rolling again. Beckett managed to drive as Cole bear-hugged him from the backseat, but barely. He held up his arm and his brothers wrapped theirs around it in an awkward, but exuberant celebration.

"What's going on? Is everyone okay?" Cole squeezed the back of Beckett's neck and pounded Blake on the shoulder.

"We're good. Beckett just wants some advice, right?" Blake looked over at him with those trusting green eyes.

"True." Beckett glanced in his rearview mirror. "How's the home front? Please tell me Fairy Princess will soon be knocked up with triplets you're naming after the three of us."

Beckett pulled into an empty driveway. The economy had taken its toll on almost the whole block, and each house in the row showed the abuse of abandonment. He threaded the car around some overgrown bushes and onto the paved patio behind the house.

"We're really excited about becoming an *aunt* and *uncle*," Cole said as Beckett parked the car. "Let's leave the parent thing to the professionals. Kyle's already got enough baby clothes to stock a store, even though we don't know what sex it is, right?"

"Not for a few more months, according to the books and all." Blake shrugged and looked nervous.

Wives and babies. Perfect concerns for his brothers. Beckett silently cursed himself for showing up here. He sure as fuck wanted their opinions, but not enough to put them in danger.

Blake opened his door, stood, and stretched. Beckett followed so he could watch the surroundings. Cole exited as well, and the three relived their greeting more properly. All had huge smiles. After a moment Blake motioned for them and popped the lock on the abandoned house's back door. Beckett closed it behind his brothers. They sat on the floor, backs against the empty walls. The room was meant to be a dining area attached to the kitchen. As his eyes adjusted, Beckett could see the walls displayed the previous occupants' displeasure at leaving. There were paint splatters and some holes from an angry foot or fist.

"They're still looking for you." Cole's serious eyes found Beckett's.

"Ah, somebody's always looking for me. That's the price of infamy." Beckett tried not to be obvious in his joy. His brothers. *His* brothers. Safe, happy. He'd expected to be dead when this time came. He'd expected to be on a spit roasting down in Hell. And he should be—or at least he shouldn't be here. It was selfish. Best to move it along.

"I saw Eve," he began. "I made some promises to her, and I'm not sure how to live up to them. So I brought my sorry ass here. To look at you guys." He stopped and looked at his hands. There was so much blood on them he was surprised they weren't permanently red.

His brothers waited.

"I told her I was going to become a man worthy of her. And I don't know how to do that. It sounded awesome as the money move walking out the door—and I did mean it—but how does a wanted felon, someone with my history, turn straight? I don't want to go to jail." The abandoned house creaked and groaned as the wind outside picked up.

Blake winked at him and smiled. "Congrats on that. That's big damn step. What've you been doing while you were gone?"

Beckett shook his head. "I was here and there...trying to find something to live for. Money makes disappearing easy, and Mouse had my shit set nice. He was a fucking genius. But I haven't done anything worth getting a medal for in the last year. And for Eve, I need to do better. Be better. I've done such...fucking evil."

Cole seemed to process the information before answering. "Living with previous sins is tough, and making choices is hard for you without resorting to anger. You know, if you can fly over an ocean in a plane, why swim it?"

"Not sure I'm following." Beckett knew there was no easy answer, but at least they hadn't laughed at the thought of a clean Beckett.

Blake cleared his throat. "Can I be blunt? I mean, I don't want you to take it the wrong way."

Beckett nodded. "Brother, there's not a single thing you could do to me, including punching me in the face, that I would ever take the wrong way."

"All right. You did a lot of bad things. We're not even going to pretend. But that was a quick way to the top of the heap, yeah? You decided to make sure Cole and I were safe, and you did it." Blake stood and paced.

Beckett nodded again.

"We were young, right? What the hell are eighteen-year-old kids supposed to know about the world? But that's how you got things done. And I think you got used to that. Changing who you are? That's hard. Like, when I had to go out in the sun? For Livia, I could do it once, twice. But I had to do it for myself if it was going to last. There were habits Eve made me break. Or better, she made me realize what I was doing and told me I needed to make a better choice." He paused. "This seems weird, I know."

"No, I want your advice." Beckett braced himself.

"What I'm saying is, it'll have to be a battle for you. It'll be hard not to take the easy way of solving a problem. Not that fighting is easy, but it's the way you know, and I imagine for you it's easier than listening and sometimes letting things go. I think you just need to try to live day to day like a guy who doesn't kill for a living. Let things unfold after that." Blake looked a little worried as he finished.

"Yeah. That'll be hard," Beckett said slowly. "I mean, this last year it's sort of just been me making the same choices I used to make because I was protecting you guys…only now, punching a guy is just hurting him. There's no higher cause—and I'm not saying I haven't done lots of things just 'cause I fucking felt like it over the years, but at least I started for a reason." Beckett sighed and ran his hands over his face. "Since I left I've basically been running, trying to stay under the radar, and fucking failing over and over." He shrugged. "It just feels wrong. It's not what I really want to be doing."

He paused to look at each of them. "Have things here been all right? Has anyone crawled out of the fucking debris I left here to mess with either of you?"

Blake shook his head. "It's been fine. We miss you. Eve checks in, by the way. So you know, when she calls she asks all kinds of weird, pointed questions, and I know she's trying to figure out if any of your enemies are angling on us."

"I should've left someone here to protect you." Beckett rubbed his forehead with the palm of his hand.

Cole shook his head. "Beck, we're men. As much as we love you, we do have a set of balls. And neither of us was a bottle-fed kitten growing up. It's okay for you to live your life, do what *you* need to do."

The only sound for a while was the wind howling. Beckett sighed. "I just don't know where to start. I mean, what do I do to be someone different?"

"You have to be you," Blake said. "But maybe try an experiment. Find a safe town where no one knows you, get a freaking job, and see. See what it's like to just be."

Cole stood, and Beckett rose from his place on the floor. Blake came and patted him on the back. "I could always use a backup singer down at the bar."

"Hey, did that guy come listen? What'd he say?" Beckett knew it had to be good news, because Blake's immediate excitement was mirrored on Cole's face.

"He was impressed—his words. So, yeah, I'm going to meet him at a recording studio in town next week, actually."

Beckett hugged Blake hard, slapping his back. "Damn it. I knew he'd freak out over you. If he tries to feel you up, let 'em. You're a handsome motherfucker."

They all laughed a bit and tried to avoid the obvious. Cole and Blake took out their phones to text the various McHugh women and let them know they'd be home soon.

Beckett put his hands on top of his head, procrastinating.

Cole looked at him sheepishly. "Do you mind? Can I pray?"

"Of course. You know I love when you and Jesus dance."

Cole grabbed one of Beckett's hands and then the other.

"If we kiss now, I should tell you, I think I need a mint."

Cole closed his eyes for a moment. "Blake got to give you his advice. This is how I give mine. Ready? And pay attention, no drifting off."

"All right, now that you got me all ready for my First Communion, hit me with it."

Cole took a deep breath. "Lord, this man before me is known to you. Beckett's soul is littered with sins that he committed to protect Blake and me."

Beckett interrupted. "Some of those sins were for the sake of my horny penis."

Cole squeezed his hands hard.

"Motherfucker. You've got a tight grip. Must have been all those years of masturbating. You've got Voldemort's handshake, baby."

Blake covered his laugh with a cough.

"I'm going to test it out around your neck in a hot minute," Cole replied calmly.

"Proceed." Beckett winked at Blake.

"Despite his sins of lust..." Cole gave Beckett a harsh look before closing his eyes again. "This man needs your guidance. He seeks a new life filled with nothing more exciting than reading the newspaper and maybe getting a dog. He took the blame for some of my worst transgressions, and never once has he asked for any repayment. All I have to offer this man, my brother, is your spiritual guidance. Please see to him in this time of need. As I pray for him every day, I hope the umbrella of your love finds him wherever he may roam." Cole made eye contact. "Amen."

"Every day?" Beckett tried not to choke up.

"Every damn day. Every time I hear of a shooting, anything that sounds like a mob hit—you know those guys hate you. Every time I see Blake play and know you wish you were there. I pray for you and about you all the time. You were meant for more than pain, Beck." Cole released his hands.

"All right, thank you. Thanks so damn much. You make me believe I have a shot."

Blake stepped forward. "It's us that should be thanking you. Not a day goes by that Cole and I don't remember you've given your life for ours. Your heart is good. You are the man you seek to be. Never forget that. If it's getting rough, think of what you've already accomplished. Trusting you got Cole and me the lives of our dreams."

Cole nodded. "And no matter your sins, your brothers will never forsake you."

They lingered longer than they should have, but in the end, they sent him off alone in the Lincoln. No one said it out loud, but bringing Beckett home to the women was a bad idea. They needed protection from the likes of him. And it hurt. Damned if it didn't hurt. But his brothers had given him advice, and Beckett was about to start taking it. He gripped the wheel a little tighter and turned toward the highway.

Driving out of Poughkeepsie felt like a winning loss, if there was even such a thing. He was on his own, but seeing his brothers, having seen Eve, made everything better. He felt a little less paranoid, and Cole was right—they weren't boys. They were men capable of taking care of their own. It came down to him wanting to do their dirty work for them. But they were good. They'd be fine. Instead he needed to work on getting the violence out of his system. It was his go-to drug. He actually couldn't think of a conflict he hadn't fought or killed his way out of. To stand in front of Eve again, he needed to handle himself differently.

He'd almost crossed out of the city limits when a sign caught his eye. It was an animal shelter. Although he'd teased Cole about his prayer, he'd listened to it. Committed it to memory. And Cole had mentioned a damn dog. What's better than busting one out of jail?

Beckett slid his leather jacket on and approached the door. He reached it just as a pretty little lady was about to switch the lock into place. She sighed and cracked it open.

"If you're looking for your pet, please come back in the morning. The only dog we're putting down tonight has been here for months. Did you lose one recently?"

She had on scrubs decorated with puppies. Her pink lips should have been advertising Chapstick or something, not pronouncing a dog's death.

"Hello, gorgeous. I didn't lose a dog. I'm looking for one." He gave her his best dimpled smile.

She was frustrated, not charmed. "We're all out of puppies. We've got old ones, ones that eat furniture, and ones that crap on the floor. You in the market for any of those?"

"You suck at being a saleswoman." Beckett bit his lip.

That brought around a smile. "You're right. Sorry. I just…this is a tough night. I was really hoping Methuselah would get adopted. We've had him here for eight months. Three weeks ago was supposed to be his last night, but we keep putting it off. Police just found a hoarder, and we're going to be swamped tomorrow. We need his cage."

"Sounds like I just found my dog."

Hope bloomed in her eyes. "Wait. Really? You haven't met him yet."

"If the thought of putting him down makes you that sad, he's got to be awesome." Beckett put on his most pleading face. "Can I come in?" He watched as she ran though the possibilities.

"I really can't. We're closed. There's a whole process." She was crestfallen.

"What's your name?" He smiled encouragingly. It was his panty-dropping stare, and he watched her soften.

"Kristen." She opened the door a bit more.

"I'm Mouse. It's nice to meet you. I'm on my way outta town, but something brought me here right now. I'm hoping it's to save the life of that dog." He waited.

She looked over her shoulder and raised a finger in the universal one-second-please hand gesture. She went behind the counter and turned off the security camera.

Beckett hated that she did it. She shouldn't be putting herself in danger. He knew he was a charming fuck, but if he hadn't been such a nice bastard, she'd be in trouble starting right…

Kristen opened the door and locked it behind him.

Now. "Well, Kristen, if I'm not mistaken, Methuselah was supposed to be the oldest human to ever live. So how long has my new dog been around?" He watched as she tinkered behind the counter, pulling up computer files and writing things down.

"Actually, the vet thinks Meth is only about four years old. He got the nickname because he's been here so long—and we all hated the name he came in with. Let me see…Yup, I'm sorry. We can't do this now. He hasn't had his shots, and he needs to be neutered before we send him out the door."

"That worries you. Tell me why." Beckett leaned against the counter so he could see Kristen and the door at the same time.

"Well, I've seen people change their minds so often, and I hate today. I hate the thought of putting him down, but I don't want to have this same day tomorrow when you don't show up." She tapped her pen.

"I won't be here tomorrow," Beckett confirmed. "I'm leaving tonight for good. I can't come back. What if you mark him down as dead, and I take him out of here?" He tried to get a sense of where this dog that caused her so much angst might be. He could hear barking in the distance. The whole place seemed to have an otherworldly echo. "What name did he come in with, by the way?"

"Pussy. The previous owner had him in dogfights. But the dog was a lover not a fighter. Even when they cut off his ears, he couldn't bring himself to fight." She didn't even tear up. He had to give her credit for being tough.

"I'll get him the best vet care in the world." Beckett realized he was making promises to this girl about a dog he'd yet to meet. But she was starting to consider illegally slipping him this dog, he could tell.

"You'd *have* to get him neutered. Overpopulation is a huge part of the reason we have overcrowding here at the shelter."

Beckett nodded. "Sure. No problem."

"You're going to get his nuts removed?" She looked like she didn't believe him.

"Oh. That's what that means? Sure. As long as doesn't hate me afterward." Beckett looked over his shoulder, worried about staying in one place too long.

"If I find out you put this dog in fights, I will actually neuter *you*. And I grew up on a farm, so I know how to do it." She pointed at him with her pen.

"Noted. He won't fight for anything. Ever. We can rename him Gandhi." Beckett smiled again.

"I like that." She looked over her shoulder too. "Crap. Let's do this."

Beckett hopped over the counter and followed her through a set of swinging doors. She nodded at a nondescript door on the left.

"That's where we put 'em down." She tapped the door with her finger as they passed. "Meth, excuse me, *Gandhi* is here." She opened a different door, and curled up in a ball on a soft blanket was the ugliest blob of fur Beckett had ever seen.

"Wow. That's a dog?" Beckett closed the door behind him.

The fat blob of fur frowned at him from his place on the floor. Enya played softly from a cell phone on a nearby counter. A plate was set with a hamburger, fries, and a bowlful of what looked like chocolate shake.

Kristen ignored Beckett's surprise and went to her knees. The fur wiggled around and made horrible retching noises.

"You're such a good boy. I know, baby, I know. He's a good one." Kristen hugged him hard around the neck, and Beckett watched as a sort of face emerged. "I'm going to give him his last meal. Now it can be the first of his new life."

He watched as the "dog" opened half its head to gulp down the meal on the plate. "You do this for all the dogs?" he asked. She obviously loved this animal. He couldn't imagine the guts it took to march down the hallway to kill it.

"We do. We want them to spend a few hours as somebody's treasured pet." Kristen lifted the now-empty plate as Gandhi licked his ginormous chops.

Now that the dog was looking at him, Beckett could make out its face more clearly. His nose was smooshed in like someone had slapped him with a frying pan. And he made a lot of horrible noises that sounded like a combination of choking and puking.

Kristen wiped her hands on her pants. "Give me your phone."

Beckett handed it to her. She pulled up his contact list and added her number, then called her phone to register his number there. "For serious, I want a picture a week and a picture of all his shot records. If I don't hear from you, I will find you and reclaim this dog."

"You love him. Why haven't you taken him?" Beckett squatted down to get a closer look. He could've sworn the dog gave him the finger.

"It's not an option for me. Listen, I have to set that alarm in four minutes. You better wait in the parking lot. Take him."

She slipped a leash around the dog's short, plump neck, handed it to Beckett, and rushed out. Gandhi fought the leash as Beckett tried to get him out the door. Kristen obviously had a few closing-up routines she was expediting. "Just pick him up and carry him!" she hollered on a pass near the room.

Beckett watched Gandhi as Gandhi watched him. Both were uncomfortable as Beckett wrapped his arms around the fat dog's middle. He was heavy—super heavy like a sack of bowling balls. Beckett walked around the counter, backed out the door Kristen must have unlocked, and set the dog down outside, still holding his leash. She came running out and slammed the door just as a warning beep from the alarm sounded.

She inserted a key and turned it. "Just in time." She took a deep breath and turned to face him. "Okay, here's your crash course in bulldogs. Listening?"

Beckett nodded.

"Well, Gandhi here is a bulldog mix, so he's stubborn and could possibly have health problems down the line. You need a relationship with a vet. You have to clean the folds of his face and not let him get too hot. Get good food from the vet, your new best friend, that has meat listed first in the ingredients."

Beckett nodded again. He was still trying to count the folds on this dog's ugly mug. There were a lot.

"He breathes mostly through his mouth, so he farts and drools a lot. Get rid of his balls and buy him a harness before you take him on a walk. It's better for him. Any questions?" Kristen leaned down and handed Gandhi a stuffed school bus.

The dog wagged its stump of a tail and made a horrible woofle noise.

"Um. Why wouldn't anyone adopt him?" Beckett had a sinking feeling because although the dog was hideous, he seemed sort of cute.

"Well, partly because of the dogfighting background, even though he wasn't good at it. The clipped ears make people reluctant, and he's a humper." She began scratching Gandhi's hindquarters. He sounded like a wet motorcycle starting up.

"A humper? Like actually humps stuff?" The dog had his school bus in his mouth while he enjoyed the love Kristen threw at him.

"Oh yeah. He'll hump other animals, pillows, blankets…That might taper off after you get his nuts hacked."

Beckett grimaced at the thought.

"But now it's a learned habit and a personality trait, so he might be a forever humper," she concluded. Kristen grabbed the dog's face and kissed the top of his head. "Oh, I almost forgot: his nose doesn't stay wet enough, so you have to get cream for that. You can always text me with questions. If I don't know the answer, I'll find out for you." She boldly opened the back door of the Lincoln. She picked up the dog easily and set him in the back. She hugged him and kissed him again. "I knew I'd break rules for you, silly pup."

The dog responded with more horrible noises like he was talking to her. She closed the door and took a deep breath before facing Beckett again.

"Okay, Mouse, quick review: tell me what you have to do." She looked like a serious schoolteacher.

"Um, get a harness, a vet, lose the man bags, clean the cheese out of his folds, and don't let him get hot. Smear some shit on his nose. Was that everything?" Beckett shook his head in disbelief. This night was getting weird.

"And…" She tapped her foot.

He snapped and pointed at her when he remembered. "Text you pictures."

"Good. And I will stalk you and find you if this dog doesn't have the most amazing life." She turned and blew a kiss to Gandhi before patting Beckett's shoulder. "Congratulations. You just became a daddy."

Having resolved the issue of the dog's future happiness, Kristen went to her crappy car with a bounce in her step. And despite how much Beckett knew he needed to get out of there, he sat for a moment, just watching her go. When her taillights had disappeared into the falling darkness, he took one last glance at Gandhi and pulled the Lincoln out of the lot.

His drive through the night seemed longer than it was, but that's probably because he had no idea where he was going. And after a while, he couldn't take the car any more. "I could do Vegas and back, but now I can't take five hours," he informed Gandhi. "You've made me a wang-rocket already." He pulled off at the next exit, and by the time he'd settled into a dog-friendly hotel, he was physically and mentally exhausted. His snarfling furball seemed to be as well. The freaking dog was like a rock all night long in the center of the bed.

It was lunchtime by the time Beckett and Gandhi emerged for their morning walk and hotel checkout. Beckett threw his duffle bag and the damned stuffed bus back in the car and drove down the street to a gas station. The sun was high, and his new dog had settled into the back, apparently for a nap, despite sleeping like a freaking baby all night. Gandhi grumbled and harrumphed his disapproval when the car stopped again so soon. Beckett laughed as he walked into the station and grabbed a crappy coffee before prepaying in cash for the gas. On his way back out he sniffed the air, finding it filled with fresh sea salt. He was accidently in a beautiful little town. As he leaned against the car while it filled, he tried to come up with a reason this shouldn't be his new home.

He couldn't come up with one. He loved the goddamn ocean, and this place had enough stores not to feel like a deserted old man's crotch but not so many that he couldn't see the fucking stars at night. He could see the bridge he'd crossed to get to this little town in the distance. It was a million stories up and only had those cement highway dividers as a wall. It was scary and pretty all rolled into one. *Kinda like you, you handsome bastard.*

He looked in on his new dog. The freaking thing looked like Jabba the Hutt's dingleberry. So damn ugly. His impulse decisions were super impulsive. As if his name were Beckett's Disappointment, the dog looked up and half smiled. Beckett nodded in his direction. "What about it? You like this place?"

Gandhi wiggled his butt in response. Maybe this thing would be okay after all. Beckett slapped the gas dispenser back in its holster and turned to take one more look at his new pet. Gandhi was wildly humping his stuffed bus.

"Wow." He slid behind the steering wheel. "We could've just high-fived. You are so getting your nuts chopped off. And soon."

The dog fell off the seat in his amorous state and gave Beckett a shocked glare.

He couldn't help but laugh. "You are a silly damn thing."

They had to cool their heels outside a real estate office for almost an hour until the entire staff came back from lunch. By then Gandhi had relived himself robustly several times and now seemed to be enjoying sitting in the car, tongue lolling out. Beckett didn't really have a plan, just an assload of cash and a hope for a better life that would somehow include Eve again someday.

Part Two

Five Years Later

4

Poseidon

Ryan Morales rolled his head on his neck, trying to release the tension. It didn't work. He was pretty sure his entire body had a headache, and he was so, so exhausted.

When he opened his apartment door, he went from tired to on-the-job in a breath. He drew his gun and assessed the exits, sliding against the wall to protect his six. His apartment was almost completely empty—of everything. After a quiet assessment he holstered his weapon. He recognized this type of destruction. Ryan closed the door behind him and didn't bother to throw the lock. He went to the fridge and found a single beer instead of the twelve-pack that should have been nice and cold.

"Bitch." He took out the beer and popped it open on the countertop. "But, if you left me a beer, that means breakup sex is on the table. Right, Poseidon?" Ryan toasted the fish bowl and noticed his beta was belly up and floating.

He looked closely at the water and shook his head. The crazy whore had filled the bowl with hand soap.

"Well, now *I'm* taking breakup sex off the table." He toasted his dead fish again and drained the beer before scooping him out of the bowl. As he flushed the fish, he noticed she'd left him not one sheet of toilet paper.

He sighed. By his count this was his fifth failed romance since becoming a Poughkeepsie police officer a little over six years ago.

They say the job makes you a bachelor, and he was certainly proving *them* right.

"Whoever the fuck they are," he mumbled as he walked the apartment to note what else she'd left him. She'd had the good sense to leave his expensive Sleep Number bed and his huge flat screen TV, but pretty much everything else one insane woman could carry by herself was gone. He'd have to get his stuff back from her, maybe threaten to file a theft report…though his work buddies would make his life hell the minute he put in the paperwork.

He undressed and disarmed. He'd been looking forward to cuddling up with Trish, er, the psycho bitch tonight. It'd been a vicious one. Another domestic, which had to be his least favorite. The haunted eyes of the kids as they absorbed the conflict like a sponge always chilled him. He desperately wanted a shower, but she'd taken all the towels. He was due for a trip to Walmart in the morning.

He lay down, then immediately sat up and adjusted his sleep number, which she'd set absurdly high, making his mattress like a slab of cement. He closed his eyes and made the best of his one limp pillow.

He was a few hours into not sleeping when he indulged. He tried not to let his memories sneak up on him, tried not to wallow in them, but his fish was dead so he figured he deserved it. A little refueling was due anyway.

Just closing his eyes brought back the day, even though it had been seven years. His uncles had always been everything he wanted to be. They were tall and seemed to know exactly what they were doing. As a kid, he'd felt like he was in the presence of kings. When they showed up his mother was always flustered, thrilled to see her brothers. She'd fussed over them, made the most of their time together, because then they'd disappear for weeks.

Nikko and Wade had loved to roughhouse with him when he was little. It was almost like they were trying to mega-dose him with male attention because most of the time it was just him and his mom. "So he comes at you, right? This is what you do." Wade would make Nikko hold still so he could show Ryan how to do the moves. And when it was time for Ryan to practice? They were both ready: willing and dramatic victims. He'd loved being with them. He could still hear their laughter if he tried. They'd thought he was hilarious. Every joke and story he told about middle school, Wade and Nikko seemed to love. They'd hung on his every word.

It still hurt to replay these memories, especially because back in the day their presence had meant relief for his mother. When they weren't around, his mom struggled to pay bills and concoct enough meals. When Nikko and Wade returned, their cars were always different—and full of clothes, electronics, and frivolous stuff like dancing stuffed animals. He never quite understood where they'd been, and no one ever answered his questions. "Workin', kid," they'd tell him. "We've been workin'."

His uncles had liked to drive him and his mom to the grocery store and treat her to a restriction-free shopping trip. She could get the expensive cuts of meat, the name brand paper towels, and there was usually a stop to get him a new pair of sneakers as part of the deal. As he got older, he would haunt his mom, always asking when they'd be back. And he cringed now as he recalled the times his asshole teenaged self had criticized her for not providing the way they did. But the older he got, the less Nikko and Wade came around. They made it to his high school graduation, and that was really the last good day with them Ryan could recall. They'd all gone out for a fancy dinner, and his mom had glowed with happiness.

After that he'd gone off to SUNY New Paltz to study political science, and he was ashamed to admit he hadn't thought much about his uncles at all. He barely kept up with his classes and checking in on his mother. The day she found out Nikko was dead, Ryan had been packing up his laundry in the living room, headed back to school for the second half of his junior year. Her screaming made him cry by reflex. The policewoman who delivered the news tried to comfort her, but Nikko wasn't just gone, he'd been murdered. And Wade couldn't be found.

He was still missing, though Ryan now knew he was dead. He'd known that first day, if he was honest. He'd had a cop's intuition even then. He realized his mother had really considered her brothers to be her children, not to mention her saviors and providers of the male influence she felt Ryan needed. The three had only had each other for a long time, as Ryan's grandmother had succumbed to cancer before Ryan was born, and his grandfather had left years before that.

Ryan had been pretty good at cheering his mom up in those early days of her debilitating depression—of course he hadn't gone back to school—but she suffered a break the day she learned Nikko had bled out. She began to have conversations with Ryan about her theories on what happened. She didn't believe the man who'd killed

Nikko was innocent like he claimed. "*Beckett Taylor never defends himself*," she used to say. "*He's just a murderer.*"

They'd gone to court the day Taylor was released — not guilty on account of self-defense. When she came home, she spent her time drawing the tattoo she'd seen on his arm. "*This is the sign, Ryan*," she'd told him, over and over. "*Watch for this sign. If a man wears this, run. Run fast and far. He's the devil.*"

Joining the force had finally been the only thing Ryan could think to do to offer her hope. "I'll find him, Mama. I'm going to get a badge and gun, and I'll make him tell me what happened, where Wade is. I promise." His mother had patted his cheek. He'd turned his back on political science and college and gone to the police academy so he could pack some heat and get his hands on folders that contained information about his uncles. He had to give her some peace and closure.

Ryan sat up in bed and really wished he could shower. *Stupid Trish.* A man has a right to wash his ass at the end of the damn day. He stretched and went into the bathroom. Under the cabinet he found a bottle of body wash Trish said was too harsh for her skin. He smiled at his find, and as he set the water temp, a floating bit in the toilet caught his eye. Poseidon had been kicked back by the crapper. He cursed as steam filled the bathroom. He grabbed the plunger and prepared to do the dirty deed when the fish flopped.

"Poseidon?" Ryan reached into the bowl and cupped the fish in his hands. It flopped again. "Shit!" He ran into the kitchen and awkwardly filled a bowl with tap water while clutching his pet in one hand. Once the fish was in water again he pulsed a few times before starting to swim.

"You're alive, motherfucker! No way!" Ryan's exuberance was dimmed by the lady downstairs banging on her ceiling with a broom. "Well, Mrs. Clarke might think this Lazarus shit is too much, but I'm damned glad to see you, buddy." He sprinkled in some fish food, which Poseidon greedily ate. "Now that's something."

He went back into the bathroom and stepped into the shower, savoring the steam as well as the water. He was glad Trish was gone — saved him the trouble of breaking up with her. She'd been pressing for a wedding, leaving little hints about diamond rings and tuxedoes. And he didn't have time for it. He was closer than ever to finding out more about his uncles' deaths. The tattoo his mother had been so obsessed with had made an appearance in a case at work.

Ryan turned off the water and sighed at his sopping wet body. He wasn't looking forward to drip-drying. He wandered over to the fogged mirror and drew the tattoo, his go-to doodle. The water beaded up around the lines left by his finger. The knife, cross, and music clef was actually a pretty sweet tat. He'd recognized it as if it were his name when he saw it on a colleague's report. With a little prodding, he found out an undercover officer had sent a warning to the Poughkeepsie PD about escalating crime and potential efforts at organization in their town.

As he left the bathroom in a puff of steam and looked for a sweatshirt to sacrifice on behalf of his stolen towels, Ryan recalled the conversation he'd overheard between the prosecutor and another beat cop: "*Man, I thought we were done with this. Once Taylor was history, things got small time. Last thing we want is another infestation of crap.*" Taylor's name was a gift Ryan didn't need. He already knew the tat was related to the man he'd joined the force to catch.

After he was as dry as he was going to get using his sweatshirt, he slipped on boxers and went back to bed. His girlfriend was gone, his fish was alive, and he'd recently gotten his first lead on Taylor since strapping on a gun. Things might just be looking up after all.

5

I'd Do Anything

Red. Kyle never thought she would hate a color. Until now she'd only worried about whether the hue went nicely with her skin. But red and white ruled her moods now. The toilet paper was either stained with failure, or its pristine surface gave her soaring hope.

How many times had she abused this part of her body? So many. She'd treated it like a piece of equipment—her trump card in the game of sex. Now she wanted it to perform, create, and believe.

But this morning there was red again. Her period was back. Every month her dreams took flight and crashed, like a kite on a short gust of wind. It had been nearly four years now. The days piled on top of one another, making permanent her punishment of being barren.

Cole had learned not to ask. She knew her crippling, crying depression must be impossible for him to bear. They just left the gaping hole unspoken in the middle of their lives. She had been to the doctor. Cole had submitted to a thorough examination. They were both healthy and young. *Stress* was the pretend disease the specialist offered her, though they both knew it was just so Kyle didn't leave completely empty handed.

Kyle crammed a tampon roughly inside her. She let the water run after she washed her hands. She'd perfected sobbing quietly. If she clenched her teeth and refused to take a deep breath, she could get away with it. Cole wouldn't know she was dying inside.

Little did she know her efforts were for naught, as her husband often fought his own quiet battle on the opposite side of the bathroom door. He would keep one hand resting on the door, the other clenched in a fist at his side. Cole wanted to fix it, or hold her hard until something in her healed, but he couldn't. Instead he prayed, his reflex for pain. He cursed, his response to helplessness.

Kyle would pat her face until it was no longer pink and puffy. Cole would step softly away from the door on the carpeted floor, careful to avoid the squeaky spot. He didn't want her to know he'd been hoping with her, for her. Then they'd greet each other in the kitchen as if the crack in their foundation didn't exist at all.

Kyle wished her husband a good day with his students and kissed him goodbye at the door, even though she'd called in sick at work. She was dedicated to the new store's success, and lying about her health didn't sit well, but this had been the last time she was prepared to face an empty womb. It was too much. She needed something. She needed anything.

She dressed warmly and drove her car a ways before parking it at the very edge of a wooded lot. As she walked in the direction of the church, the crisp air kicked her monthly cramps into high gear. She moved with purpose, like she had an appointment, but she didn't. She was in a hurry to go nowhere.

There was more to life than babies. She knew that. Intellectually, she knew. But her heart kept trying to wrestle her head to the ground. When she and Cole had decided to have children, it was the bow on the gift that was their love. *A baby.* Kyle had happily flushed her birth control pills, and for the first few months, it was fun just trying. Then she became a scientist of intercourse, spending time on the Internet and stocking her bathroom with various tools to tell her exactly when to pounce on Cole. Lately she had been a like a junkie, jonesing for ovulation.

And him. God, Cole was everything he should be and more. She knew she was being a bitch. She knew she had turned their sex life into a science experiment. But the baby clothes were so tiny. And wherever she turned, there was a mother with a perfect child propped on her hip. Did they even know what they had? If she could only taste that moment...holding her very own child.

She drew closer to the church. Maybe coming back to the beginning was good luck. She wasn't beyond trying weird things—potions, positions, and strange-tasting foods. Soon it would get medical. She knew she would press Cole into helping her with fertility treatments: injecting her, navigating her mood swings, comforting her as she packed on the pounds. Cole would do whatever she asked, over and over. That thought made her want to hug him — but worse, it made her hope for twins.

She opened the huge front door. There was no Mass today, and what she thought an empty church could solve, she didn't know. But the surroundings felt nourishing. Cole had left this place for her. He'd loved it so much, and now she'd reduced him to just an ingredient for what she wanted. She wasn't adequately grateful for the gift of him right now, but her hungry soul was unrepentant. *A baby.*

"Mrs. Bridge, to what do I owe this pleasure?"

Kyle spun quickly, wrenching herself out of her pain and gasping as Father Callahan's voice filled the church.

"Sorry, Father, you startled me." She stepped into his comforting arms, and he gave her a fatherly pat.

"Have a seat, dear girl. My old bones need a rest today." They settled next to each other in a pew, facing the tableau of religion at the front of the sanctuary. "This isn't a social call," he ventured after a moment. "Tell me why you're here instead of at work."

Kyle let her hands follow the wood grain of the pew. "I need to think. Here is where it started, you know? I met him, and everything fell into place."

The priest settled in to listen.

Kyle felt her worries spill over and splash onto the church floor. "I can't get pregnant. We've done it every which way. We're having sex all the time. It's not even fun anymore. It hasn't been fun in a while." She clasped her hands in her lap. Talking to an old, celibate man about her vagina suddenly seemed like a horrible idea.

"Kyle, so many times have I heard the lament of a lady — prayers from the wanting, cursing the unwanted. Women are responsible for bringing life into the world. I've often thought it a tough row to sow." He made no move to get up.

Kyle focused on one of the stained glass windows. Each piece of glass held the sun like a lover. "I just want my body to do what it was built for. I don't know why that's too much to ask."

Father Callahan let the silence sit in their laps like a cat for a while before he disturbed it. "You know, God asks too much from us.

Really, He does. All these trials, tribulations, He knows it won't be easy. I've often heard before 'God doesn't give you more than you can handle.'" The old priest snorted. "He does, Kyle. At least more than any of us wants to handle. You will face pain—that's a given. Do any of us need it? I don't think so...But maybe it's just the age talking."

She had stolen this church's future, their lifeblood, in the young Cole. She had no right to seek solace in this building. She looked at the tall, vaulted ceiling. She wondered if hopes rose like hot hair. *Were there millions of wishes and prayers bouncing around up there, trapped like balloons?*

"I want a baby so bad, Father. I feel like that's all there is. It's eating me. I can't..." She started tapping her feet, unfulfilled, unsatisfied.

"Sweet girl, I don't have answers, but I do sympathize. Here's what I've learned, and only time can teach this lesson: sometimes the hard times are preparing you to handle the next important thing. Pray, my child. Hold on to the love you *do* have." Father Callahan patted her hand. "Look for a sign. He will tell you what might be on the horizon. Keep your heart open."

The priest stood. Kyle followed suit. She didn't feel better. She knew nothing but a positive pregnancy test would silence her need. But a sign was something maybe she could hold on to. Father Callahan opened his arms for another hug, and this time Kyle was surprised at how slight he felt.

"Another thing, young lady, don't push Cole away. It's these times when you have to respect your vows the most."

Kyle thanked him and turned to leave. She passed the spot where Cole had knelt before her so long ago. He would take anything she doled out to him, whips or feathers. Suddenly she wanted to be in his arms, listening to his heartbeat. She opened the door knowing she had to let him hold this burden with her. Together.

The drive back home seemed endless, but when she finally arrived the house was still waiting, perfect and exactly as she'd left it. She kicked off her shoes and headed up to the bedroom, where she found a letter propped on her pillow. Only one mailman had access to this room. She left her jacket on as she tore the envelope away, ripping and pulling until the letter was revealed.

It took a while to get through it because her eyes kept blurring. She sobbed out loud a few times, crumpling the edge of her jacket in a tight fist.

Dear Kyle,

I see you crying when you don't think I notice. I do. I see your eyes — red and glassy with the tears you swallowed because I came in the room.

I can't give you the baby we want. Our love should be enough, but I feel it too. There's a hole in between us when we hold hands. We're feeling the loss of someone who has yet to even exist. Your smiles are getting smaller. When you look at me, I want to give you more, I just don't know how.

I remember when I first found your eyes, when I first realized you existed. I could hardly make my tongue work. My words were fuzzy, wrapped in cotton. When you were taken from me, I had so much rage. I would have killed a million men to get to you, just to rest my hands on your face. Kissing your lips, remembering you safe in that hospital bed is a waterfall of relief for me still. And our wedding? Everything blue makes me want to touch you, taste your lips, see your skin wet in the shower.

How can something that isn't happening come between us? When you're reluctant to walk past a stroller, when you change the channel to save your heart the sight of a chubby baby, I know you're aching. You're building a wall, and only you fit behind it. How can I show you I love you so much anyway? Will you ever understand that you're just as important as a woman who can have a child? I'll make love to you whenever you demand it. I'll hold you tightly when you cry.

If it's just us, Kyle, if that's all there is, it's enough for me. And if that thought makes you sad, I'll move heaven and hell until you see a future you want to be in, smiling, with me. Whatever you need, just step into my arms, let me be there with you.

You're not protecting me from your pain. I feel all of it, except I feel it alone when you won't let me help. Come to me. Let me kiss your hair. Let me make love to you for no reason at all.

I'm yours forever,

Cole

He got it. There was no need to describe it to him. He knew when she cried. He knew what she wanted. He loved her always.

Kyle dug her cell phone out of her pocket, hitting the send button twice, the shortcut for the last call dialed. She could trust that his name and picture would pop up on her screen.

He answered his phone: "Baby, I love you." Not *Hello?* Not *What's up?* He got her.

"Please, Cole. Please." She bit her fist, unable to tell him she needed his weight on top of her to hold her steady, to keep her from floating away.

"I'm coming home. Keep the phone by your ear."

She heard the rustling noises of Cole rearranging his schedule, talking softly to his colleagues so he could attend to her needs. Every few minutes he would check, "You still with me?"

She answered from her forever. "Always."

His car started, and she listened as he turned off his radio. The engine grew louder or softer depending on where he was in traffic. All the way he kept the line open, finally appearing in their bedroom door, handsome and worried.

He still had the phone to his ear. "I'm here."

She wrinkled her nose and said, "Thank you," into her phone. They ended the call at the same moment. And like all hell breaking loose, her words flew at him.

"What if it's because I'm a whore? What if it's because I used up all the good I ever had? What if I wasted it all on bastards for a quick high? What if I broke everything? You shouldn't have to have me. This. I can't even make a baby for you."

Cole was in front of her in two quick steps. He knelt before her, holding the tops of her arms. "No one calls you a whore. Not even you. *Ever*. You got that?"

She nodded, the motion causing tears to trail down her cheeks. He released her arms to wipe her face dry.

"I'm wasted. I'm wasted, Cole." She began choking on his name as she slid from the bed. Kyle balled herself on the floor, sobbing. It was primal, guttural, and pure desperation. She felt him cover her with his body, like he was protecting her from gunfire. They stayed until her anguish subsided into gentle whimpering. Then he gathered her body in his arms, his own face wet and red.

"If I could fix this, I'd do anything, Kyle. I'd do anything."

6

SHARK

Eve could see New York City past her reflection. There was a love song on the radio, and she could almost hear it without thinking about him. Beckett had been gone for five years. *He's dead.* She looked down at her shoes. The patent leather heels showed her what she looked like in their smooth surface. That's what she was now—just an image of her real self. People could see what she looked like, but no one knew who she was. Waiting for him was over. It had to be. She fussed with her low ponytail, and her office door opened.

"January, the fiscal results are in. You wanted them?" Eve nodded toward her desk but didn't acknowledge her coworker. This import-export company was huge. Even when you'd climbed the corporate ladder as fast as she had, you were still one of thousands of employees. It was a great place to hide.

She picked up the file after he'd left, but didn't have the energy to compare the figures. It was crazy how similar the work she'd done for Beckett was to the work she now did for Silver Force Systems. She had to make sure products got delivered and people paid their bills—although she hadn't killed anyone in years.

Eve turned off her computer and locked up her files. She slipped on her trench coat and left the plush office without a backward glance. Normally she took the elevator down to street level and walked to her apartment building, but today she hailed a cab to a different destination.

When she was feeling particularly numb, she would train. More specifically, she would train others. Through her remaining connections, she knew a few people looking to hone their deadly skills. She slipped cash to the cabbie and got out in front of a warehouse. After punching in the code, she entered a space dedicated to the fighting techniques that kept evil people alive and rich.

A quick change in the makeshift locker room and Eve was ready. It was quiet tonight—she had to slap lights on as she went. She stretched and went to the knife-throwing area. The blades were already sharp, and they were gorgeously weighted. One after another she landed her mark: the dead center of the outline's chest.

She sensed him before she heard him, felt his breath on her neck.

"Nice shot."

"Sneaking up on me is a quick way to die." She ignored him and retrieved her knives. When she turned, she was armed to the teeth. But he held a hand grenade. If they'd been playing poker with weapons, he won.

"That's not what everyone thinks, apparently." His gaze traveled over her.

He was stupidly good looking—so much so that most women would miss the sharkish look to his eyes. Eve knew his face and ran through her memories to figure out who he worked for. She couldn't even pull up a name.

She put the knives back on their platform. "Why are you here? I don't have the energy for puzzles and riddles." She picked up a jump rope and began her cardio workout.

"I'm here to exercise, baby. Just like you." He tossed the grenade in the air, pin still in. She didn't look his way.

After three sets of thirty, he was still watching, waiting. She narrowed her eyes. "What?" She tossed the rope and made her way to the punching bag.

"Just watching the view." He bit his full lip. He'd perfected the five o'clock shadow, as well as the placement of tattoos to highlight his muscles.

Punching and kicking, she did her best to ignore him. Finally getting up a decent sweat, she switched again to the treadmill. The pounding of her feet and the sound of the machine were all she could hear.

Still he waited. She could tell he was trying to unnerve her. It didn't work, or at least she'd never let him see it. The minute she flinched or showed human emotions, it would be over. After her run, he remained, tossing his hand grenade from hand to hand like a tennis ball.

She walked into the locker room. It was really just a place in the center of the warehouse with plumbing, divided by what looked like a long series of bathroom-stall doors. He followed her—obviously daring her to change in front of him or leave in her sweaty gear. Eve didn't hesitate as she pulled off her clothes and started the shower. His gaze crawled over her body. She forced a shiver from her spine. She took her shower, taking time to shave her legs and condition her hair. She could tell he was still in the room.

She dressed in jeans and sweatshirt and pulled her wet hair in to a ponytail. He was right behind her, looking in the mirror with her.

"That was quite a show. Thanks. I bet Beckett loved getting that all the time." He smirked.

She thought about Beckett constantly, but she knew she'd closed her eyes at the unexpected mention of his name. She spun, and her brush clattered to the ground. She snagged his grenade mid-toss from one hand to the other. Holding his pants open, she pushed it inside and slipped her pinkie under the pin.

"Speak. Tell me what you're doing here." She finally met his oily eyes, and in that instant his name came to her: Shark. It should have been so obvious.

He rotated his hips, and she felt his penis pressing against her hand and the weapon.

"Well, now there's two explosive things in my pants. Feel free to get creative." He smiled.

"You're wasting my time." She pulled her hand out and tossed the grenade, pin still in place, back to him. He caught it, but fumbled a bit. She felt better since they'd both made mistakes now. She'd feel spectacular if she could remember who he worked for. Instead she grabbed her bag from her locker and walked past him.

Before she could get to the main door, he caught her arm. She faced him, nearly nose to nose.

"Did it ever occur to you that I'm here to help you?" He was perfect, even up close. And he smelled amazing.

"No. Because you're not." She wrenched her arm free just as two more "patrons" entered. Neither of the burly men seemed inclined to get involved in Eve and Shark's tense situation.

"Now I'm hurt. After the striptease I thought for sure we were best friends." He licked his lips.

Eve ignored him and stepped outside. There were no cabs to be seen, and it was dark—later than she thought. She'd have to walk. Glad she wasn't burdened by high heels, she started off at a quick pace. He stayed right next to her.

"We'd make a stunning couple, you know. My dark and your pale? Half the time we could be killing each other, the other half screwing our brains out."

He'd never know, but he'd just described her relationship with Beckett to a T.

After three blocks, he seemed to realize she was never going to start a conversation with him. And he felt compelled to fill the void.

"Okay, I'm just letting you know there's some movement on Poughkeepsie. And I know it's Taylor's but…"

She stopped and turned to look at him. "Who?"

"I'm proposing we work together and get Poughkeepsie organized before it gets absorbed by someone else. There's some lucrative deals to be had there." He winked at her, smirking the whole time.

"Why not go alone?" She didn't like how this was going—or anything about this guy. He knew way too much.

"Well, you have the connections already. The respect." He shrugged his well-built shoulders.

They both looked around, assessing the situation.

"I think you're fishing for information, and I'm not helping." She spotted a cab and hailed it.

He got in behind her. The cab ride to her apartment building was silent, save for the crackle of the radio, which wasn't quite tuned in. The cabbie didn't seem to notice.

Shark paid for the trip, and they stood in front of her building, staring at each other as the cab drove away.

"Unless you have something useful to offer, I'm going to kill you," she breathed.

He tilted his head. "I know. I'm not your friend or your lover, but I'm smart enough to find you, to find where you work out. Aren't you at least a little interested in who my angel is?"

She looked toward the sky, hazy with the lights from the building. "What do you want?"

"Just a little information on the two-way street. Taylor still alive?"

When Eve looked back at him, shrewdness had crowded out any playfulness in his eyes. It was a hard choice, right there on the sidewalk, to decide which answer would be the best for Beckett, for his brothers, for Poughkeepsie.

"He's been dead for four years, thirty eight days, and four hours." She looked Shark in the face and gave no tells.

"So specific. How can you be sure?" He shifted his weight.

Eve noticed his shoes were Italian and expensive. "That's two questions, and yet you've told me nothing." She stood as still as a predator, filing away everything she could about him. She'd stalk him later.

He leaned in close—close enough to stab her or kiss her. "The Vitullos are coming that way. Looking for information. Stirring things up. Evidently there's money to be made there."

Eve didn't tell him she'd light every bill in the world on fire if it meant saving her loved ones.

"So how do you know for sure he's dead?"

"That's a stupid question," she said.

"You did him?"

She forced herself to shrug and look at him knowingly.

"He was a tough bitch to crack."

She didn't answer, letting his imagination fill in the blanks. "Give me a number, and I'll think about it," she finally said.

He pulled out his wallet, and she handed him a pen from her bag. He scrawled a number on a hundred-dollar bill.

She left him and walked into her lobby without another word. This wasn't good. How did this random asshole have more information on her town than she did?

She didn't get more than a few feet into her apartment before her cell phone rang. Blake was on the other end.

"Hey, are you sitting down? Your dad's in the hospital. He's alive, but he's really injured. I think you need to come home."

"I'll be there in forty-five minutes." Eve ended the call and put the phone against her forehead.

In spite of all the time she'd spent building her new, placeholder life, she'd always known she'd eventually get a phone call like this: one that would drag her right back.

Blake waited for Eve in the hospital parking lot. A sleek sports car caught his attention, and he wasn't surprised when she stepped out of it. He hadn't actually seen her in years. She looked hollow. He silently cursed Beckett for leaving her for so long.

"How bad?" She was composed, but barely.

"He took a real beating. The kind I used to see back in the day." Blake didn't need to say more. They were speaking of Beckett's sins and Eve's talents. Her steps faltered a bit.

He reached out quickly in case she tripped. She shook off his questioning hand.

"Okay, I understand. Come with me?"

When they made eye contact, he knew she was coming undone. Blake took her hand in his as they entered the hospital. They were cousins. She'd helped him with his rehabilitation. And now he would be here for her.

Blake explained who Eve was to the duty nurse and led her to her father's hospital room. Blake stopped her before she stepped through the open door. "It's rough," he warned.

She nodded and exhaled. As they walked around the curtain giving Dr. Ted Hartt a bit of privacy, Blake put one hand on Eve's lower back. She swooned a bit before shoring herself up and proceeding. Blake had been with Ted since shortly after the phone call from the hospital, and he still wasn't accustomed to the sight. Ted was covered in bruises, abrasions, and worst of all, burns. The doctor on his case had been surprised to find he had no broken bones.

Eve gently touched her father's unmarked hand, then his cheek. Blake watched as her jaw tensed. Her father opened his eyes, heavy with pain meds.

"Who did this, Dad? What happened?" Eve's jittery hands belied her cool, confident voice.

"I was walking and…fell. I fell." Ted closed his eyes again, a wave of medication taking him under.

"Hello, Eve." The doctor on call swept into the room. "Your father's on a powerful sedative. His condition is stable."

Blake's eyes widened for a moment before he realized the doctor knew Eve personally. Considering Dr. Hartt's prominent place on the staff, this shouldn't have surprised him.

"Is this all superficial? The wounds?" Eve crossed her arms in front of her.

"Yes, for the most part. He lost a lot of blood, and the burns will take a while to heal—he'll have to be fastidious with his bandages. He was brought in unconscious." The doctor scrolled through the chart on his iPad and nodded, as if approving his own facts.

"Who brought him in?" She glanced at Blake, who shook his head.

"Ah, your father arrived as a John Doe by ambulance. He was found on the side of Ritcher Street by the bar. When we were finally able to bring him around, he insisted he fell and that no police be called. And he didn't want you called either, but one of our nurses had already called Blake so…"

"Okay, thank you." Eve nodded to the doctor, giving him his cue to leave.

The minute the door closed behind him, Eve put her hands on her head and squatted, quiet sobbing noises escaping her. Blake came around the bed and put his arm around her.

"I'm sorry." He tried to pat a comforting pattern on her back.

Eve wiped her tears and stood, her moment of humanness over. "Listen, go home. Tell Cole to keep his head up. If either of you see anything out of the ordinary, call me immediately. You watch the girls and the baby like hawks. Until I know what's happening, I need you both to check in three times a day. Make sure someone knows where you're going at all times."

Blake nodded. "This about Beck?"

Eve leveled her cold blue eyes on him. "Right now? It's about me."

She leaned over and kissed her father's head. "Dad, don't worry. I'm gonna take this burden from you," she whispered. She stood and smoothed her blond hair. "There'll be security here soon, so Dad will be fine. You don't come back. Stay with your family. That's your only job. Got it?"

Blake nodded as she brushed past him and out the door.

Eve started her car and pulled away from the hospital. Whatever happened to her father, it hadn't been an accident. What had they wanted? Money? Information, like Shark said? Had they connected him to Blake and Beckett, or just to the hospital? Maybe his skill as a surgeon had caught someone's eye, and the next time he saw them he'd be expected to help. Or maybe knowing her had been his downfall.

She'd gotten people's attention the same sort of way for Beckett, once upon a time—back when she was a monster. But now five years had passed since he'd left her in a hotel room, naked and hoping for a better life. After weeks in limbo, she'd realized she had to do something, be something while she waited for his return. Vegas was over for her, and Poughkeepsie was just too much. There her role was labeled and marked. Too many people wanted her to replace Beckett, and she had no desire to be him. So she kept her distance and did her best to disappear—just sneaking in and out to visit her father for holidays.

Clearly, Beckett was either trying so hard to be different that he'd found another life entirely or he was dead. So many years later, she wasn't sure what the hell was going on. But not being near him, memories of the time she'd spent enforcing for him—all of it hurt. Damned if she'd show it. If he was still alive, she could find him. Yet she hadn't even tried. It mattered that he came to her. And maybe he'd found someone else. He wasn't a damned priest, after all. Her heart hurt thinking about him.

Her new life had come together nicely, but the longer she worked in New York, the more she felt herself drifting with no real purpose, no idea of her future. Nothing seemed real, and none of it was what she really wanted. Her mind was always on him.

And now she would have to go back to her previous life, face down an incoming enemy—one that had targeted her father—without him. And without Mouse. She had nothing. Or worse than nothing.

She pulled out her phone and hit Shark's number. Instead of hello, he just laughed his knowing, sexy laugh. She bit her lip until he was done and then delivered her instructions: "Meet me tomorrow at five. I'll be at the river dock in Poughkeepsie."

Shark was waiting at the river the next evening when Eve pulled up in her Audi 8. It was a place she hadn't visited in a long damn time, and she wished she were here under better circumstances now.

While setting up security for her father, Eve had tapped Midian, a little spitfire down at the courthouse, for some inside info. Mouse had trusted her, and she had ways of finding every slippery bastard in the business. Shark was an easy find for the woman, and turns out Mr. Dax Aaron was not the most trustworthy. Shocking. He seemed to have worked a little bit for everyone, with no real loyalty anywhere. With Midian's help, it was all coming back to her now. She'd never done business with him without Mouse, but now she didn't have much of a choice. This whole situation sucked.

Leaving the car running, Eve got out and left her door open. She wasn't even armed—well, not with weapons anyway. Her father's condition had rattled her, and she had to acknowledge it. Brutal honesty was the only way to live through this encounter.

"Evening, ma'am." Shark gave her an I've-got-you-where-I-want-you shit-eating grin.

She didn't look at him. Watching the choppy Hudson River, she waited until her silence became awkward for him.

"You called me, in case you don't remember." Shark leaned against the low brick wall by the boat launch.

"Why are the Vitullos in Poughkeepsie?" She still wouldn't look at him.

"I think we need a little tit for tat. Last I checked I sought you out. Now I'm here at your beck and call. What have you done for me lately?" He pushed away from the wall and approached her.

Every nerve in her body sprang to high alert, and she monitored him using only her peripheral vision and hearing.

He wrapped her ponytail around his fist, leaning close to her ear. "I'm never opposed to sexual favors as payment."

"I'm too exhausted to kick your ass. Drop my hair. You know better." Eve waited for him to release it.

"Maybe you've gotten soft these last few years. I might want to try my luck." He turned her head with her hair so she looked him full in his handsome face.

As soon as her gaze was level with his, she replied. "I think Mackenzie is a beautiful name. Ten is such a fun age."

Shark let go of her hair like he'd been burned. His eyes widened before his stare sharpened. "Bitch."

Eve just shrugged and resumed looking at the river like she hadn't just threatened to kill this man's little girl. He couldn't know she'd never hurt a kid — never in a million years. But her stop at the storage unit where Mouse had kept some encoded files had given Eve the edge she needed on this particular contact, once she had his real name.

Shark prided himself on his anonymity. He wanted you off guard. If he appeared in your bedroom, he wanted you scared shitless and not sure if he was hired to kill you or help you. How Mouse had found that tidbit about Mackenzie, Eve didn't know, but it had worked.

"You tell me what I want to know and what you need me for. I don't have time to see how much bigger my dick is than yours." Eve pulled out her phone and saw an update from the security she'd hired for her dad's hospital room door. He was doing fine, sleeping.

"All right. The Vitullos are in weapons, and they've been based in New York for years. My job is from Mary Ellen, the daughter, which is new. She seems to have big plans for this area, maybe wants to squeeze out some other players. She's gathering info at this point — the hard way when she has to. Apparently it's personal. That's all I know." Shark seemed on edge now, lighting up a cigarette with a fidgety hand.

"And from me you need…?" She pulled his smoke from his fingers and tossed it in the river. It barely sizzled before floating.

"Well, Sunday night they're having an audition for new girls. I need one of them to know this same information I'm giving you." Shark pulled another smoke out and lit it, this time keeping it far away from Eve.

She nodded.

"They want classy chicks. Ones that don't actually slut it up." He took a quick drag from the side of his mouth. "You've got four days to get ready."

Eve raised her eyebrows. "That's it?"

"Yeah. That's it." He pulled out a twenty with an address written on it.

"Eight o'clock is the time. Dress sharp. Your name is still January. Find Micki and tell her everything I just told you." He used his lighter to ignite the bill.

"I never said I wanted to get into a weapons ring." Eve watched as her breath turned to mist.

"You want to be there. Trust me." Shark headed for his car.

"I don't trust anyone. Give Micki the message yourself." Eve turned toward her car as well.

He stopped her door from closing, and she allowed it. He looked panicked. "They're looking for Beckett."

She gave him a look that clearly said she didn't care. "Killed him. Doesn't matter."

"They're looking for anyone with the same tattoo he had." Shark gave her a knowing look before slamming her door shut.

She waited until he'd pulled away before pounding her steering wheel. "Shit!"

She'd be damned if anyone was going to punish the people she considered family. Shark knew about the brothers, and this Vitullo woman knew about the brothers. Granted, they weren't the biggest damn secret, but why now, after five years? She'd hoped they were long off the radar. And that no one would fuck with Beckett. Ever.

7

Nourishment

Blake liked the crunch of fresh snow under his boots, and little clouds of his breath led the way. The trees were barren fingers pointing at the gray sky. He could smell more snow in the February air. *Perfect.* And she was with him, so snow or no snow, the afternoon was a grace. A blessing.

Emme stuck her mittened hand in his big warm one with barely a glance. Instinct, maybe. She liked to hum while she walked, but she did it quietly, barely alerting the wildlife. Blake liked to tease her that she was like Snow White, just to watch her stomp her foot. *"Daddy, that princess was a wuss,"* she'd say. *"I woulda fought that bad witch. And you don't take food from strangers. Everybody knows that."* Walking in the wintery woods with his daughter was a simple pleasure. He loved to hear what she said in the quiet, just him and her.

"Wait, baby, let's sit for a minute." He took another glance at the sky. It was just about time, if he was gauging correctly. She climbed into his lap, and he wrapped his arms around her middle, loving this puffed up, dressed-for-cold-weather version of his little girl.

"I'm not a baby. I'm a big girl, Daddy." She rested her hooded head under his chin.

Blake wanted to protest. He wanted to show her he could still toss her high to hear her laugh. But he respected her independence. "Of course. You're huge. Gigantic. You, little girl, are a giant."

Emme's laugh finally did scare a skinny squirrel, sending it scampering up the trunk of a nearby oak.

"Daddy, why does Kellan cry so much?" She tilted her head back so her solemn green eyes could watch his face while he answered her.

Stunning. She was absolutely breathtaking. Blake gave her the smile he'd felt on his face since the first time he held her. He had expected to be nervous. He had anticipated all the fears he'd have as a new father. But as the nurse laid a freshly wrapped Emme in his arms, the world connected to his heart. Her tiny baby face had soothed him. He couldn't take his eyes off of her. *"Hello, little girl. Welcome to the world. I've been waiting for you."* Livia gently teased him because Emme had wrapped herself so quickly around his soul.

"Kellan cries because he's brand new. You cried just as much, and maybe a little more." He kissed the soft skin of her forehead. She smelled like angel's wings and Livia.

Emme bit her lip and seemed to think for a moment. "I love you, Daddy."

She always said it. She would stop in the middle of playing to get up and cuddle him around the neck.

"I love you too." And he did. So big was his love for his little girl, it nearly overwhelmed him. It should have had him fretting for her future, especially now, but she made it all so much easier. Her small voice brought him peace.

"Ready?" he asked. He motioned for her to look to the sky.

She'd been on enough long walks with her father to know it was time to open her mind. Their times in nature usually held a secret surprise. It could be anything, really—a rainbow touching the snow or heart-shaped shade cast by a pair of trees. Anything. Today, the gift was being outside the second it started to snow.

"Ooh, Daddy! Look, it's like a salt shaker!" She stuck her tongue out for the newborn snowflakes.

Blake followed her lead. Snow tasted sweeter with Emme around.

She hopped up from his lap and twirled in the misting of crystal rain. He tried to take a picture with his senses: Emme's snow boots squeaking in the snow at her feet, her hood falling off her head, her laughter making it hard to keep her tongue out.

When she was full from the experience, Blake put her on his shoulders so they could get home quickly. In half the time it had taken them to get to their spot in the woods, they'd returned and unlocked the door to John's house. *Our house,* he amended mentally. He was still trying to make the adjustment. Livia's father had sold them the house for an obscenely low price, claiming he and his new bride, Kathy, didn't need all that space for themselves. *"I hate yard work, son. You're doing me a favor, not the other way around."* He and Kathy were now settled in a condo about ten minutes away.

As they entered, Livia looked up from her rocking chair. Kellan was blissfully asleep, evidently having passed out while nursing.

"Our boy's eating *again?"* Blake smiled at the sight of them.

Livia nodded and raised her eyebrows. "Shh..."

Blake looked in the hallway mirror to see what Livia was indicating. Sure enough his long, steady steps had lulled Emme to sleep. She had her arms crisscrossed on his hair with her eyes shut.

Livia maneuvered Kellan to his playpen and slowly laid him on his back. After his limbs twitched with complaint at the loss of her warmth, he settled into a deep nap, mouth still moving, clicking on occasion, soothing himself with the memory of his feeding.

Livia held up one finger and disappeared. Blake waited, knowing what was next. She reappeared and took a quick slew of pictures with their camera. He smiled for her, and then pretended to be asleep while standing. Finally, Livia reached up to remove Emme from her perch. Blake stretched his neck. Supporting her that way was getting tougher, as she was almost five years old now.

Livia efficiently removed Emme's snow clothes and tucked a Mouse-knitted afghan around her on the couch.

Blake watched his wife as he removed his own coat and boots. Livia got on her knees and warmed Emme's cold cheeks with her hands. He tiptoed over and held out his hand to help Livia up. She glanced at both her children, then snuggled into his arms.

He tilted her face toward his as he walked her back to the living room, letting her see his pride. It almost choked him at times, there was so much of it. *His* house, *his* woman, *his* babies, all of it was everything.

She shook her head and whispered into his shirt, muffled. "I can't kiss you. I haven't brushed my teeth."

He kissed the top of her head. She often forgot to take care of even the most basic things for herself. For Livia, being a mother was a calling. She said it was instinct, but he knew better. She revolved around her children. Whether it was folding the children's laundry and stacking it in drawers, or yanking her knotted hair into a ponytail instead of styling it so she could hold Kellan sooner, he knew she worked constantly at the job of motherhood.

She spoke into his shirt again. "I didn't take anything out for dinner."

He whispered in her ear, "I'll handle it."

"No, I've got it. I have to pick up first." Livia stepped away from him and bent down to straighten the toys.

Blake placed a hand on her back. "Hey, gorgeous, can you come with me for a minute?"

She sighed and looked at the strewn things. He could tell she really wanted an organized living room, but she followed him upstairs anyway. He left her in their bedroom and went into the bathroom to turn on the shower.

"It's ready for you," he announced as he returned. She opened her mouth as if to speak, but instead just nodded gratefully as she closed the bathroom door.

When she was finally done, she pulled back the curtain. Sitting on the bathroom vanity was a folded towel and her favorite, very not-sexy pajamas, both warm from the dryer. Livia dried herself and put on the offerings her husband had snuck into the bathroom.

When she opened the door, the bed was made and the laundry folded. Blake sat on the edge of the bed with a grin that told her he knew she'd be impressed.

"You know I suck at that." He pointed to the clothes he'd wrestled with while she showered. Sure enough, the piles were a bit askew.

"You totally suck at that." She twirled her damp hair into a knot, then picked up the baby monitor.

"They're both still napping. I just checked," Blake told her. "And yes, look, their feet are covered by a blanket."

"Well, it *has* been more than six weeks," Livia sighed. "We should get this over with."

Blake rolled his eyes. "So sexy. Just what every man wants to hear." He patted the top of the bed, and Livia got in as he slid back to the pillows, the mattress creaking with their arrival.

She curled into his arms again, smelling his chest and smiling. He was her home.

"How long has it been since we've been in this bed alone?" Livia closed her eyes and sighed.

"I think it was three weeks ago." His chuckle rumbled in his chest.

Livia put her hand on his heart, waiting for it to beat. It did, over and over.

Blake pulled the comforter around her shoulders, and she snuggled deeper into his arms. He began stroking her hair.

"You're going to put me to sleep." The warmth, the shower, and his arms were forcing her eyes closed.

"That's the point, my love. Take a nap."

Livia's mind whispered thanks, but the words didn't make it to her lips.

When she woke three hours later, she was disoriented. She looked to the monitor first, and it was off—no comforting green light assuring her the world was still on axis. Listening closely, she could hear the TV on and Emme's playful voice. Livia tossed off the covers and headed downstairs. Every light was on. Emme had an elaborate fort set up with bed sheets over chairs.

Blake was walking with a fussy Kellan. He looked grateful and pleased with himself as he saw her panic slide into knowing. He had let her sleep. Now she was unbearably turned on. *Dear God, that nap was better than money, sex, and more money.* Her kids looked cuter. Her life seemed brighter. It had been a wonderful rest.

She sat in the rocking chair, and Blake passed a wriggling Kellan into her arms.

"Did we wake you?"

Livia grabbed a fistful of his hair and held his face close to hers. She peeked in Emme's direction—she was deep in her fort. Livia smiled and turned her attention back to his mouth. She whispered, "If we were alone, I would have you right now." And she kissed him until he moaned.

His eyes full of lust, he backed away to let her feed the baby. "Are you hungry? I ordered pizza." Blake turned toward the kitchen.

"That'd be great." Livia put her head back and enjoyed the feeling of the baby releasing her milk.

Emme peeked her head out from under the flower-patterned ceiling of her fort.

"Mommy! You're awake. Kellan was getting hungry, and I told Daddy to let him eat pizza, but he said no, and I said, 'Daddy, put the pizza on your chest and let Kellan suck it,' and Daddy just laughed, but I bet Kellan would love pizza. Hi, Mommy."

Livia watched her daughter emerge from her fort. She had a stuffed dog tucked under her arm. Livia used her free hand to pull her little girl close, kissing her cheek over and over noisily. "I want to eat you. Forget pizza. I'll eat you with no teeth!" Livia tickled Emme's armpit and gently nibbled on her.

"Mommy! You are too silly!" Emme leaned into the love, letting the attention fill her.

Blake returned with a warm slice of pizza and a tall glass of ice water.

Livia knew she had it made. This was it. She'd daydream about these glory days as an old woman. She hoped she'd still be able to dream up the details, years and years later. She prayed she'd never forget Blake's wild hair, sexy and careless. She hoped she'd remember exactly how lopsided Emme's pigtails were when she demanded Blake do her hair instead of Mommy because he was "less ouchy." In a perfect world, whenever Kellan's nose wrinkled up, she would remember what it felt like to be so connected to him, to be his nourishment.

8

Mary Ellen

Eve looked in the mirror of her Mahopac hotel room—her home away from home now that neither New York or Poughkeepsie seemed like a good option. Staring back at her in this dinky little dive was a new woman. A few subtle changes and a different hair color made a world of difference. Her long blond hair was now bluish black. Her eyebrows were thinner with a new arch. The effect made her blue eyes pop, and she'd used liner to make her lips appear a bit bigger.

Soon enough, January was ready for her audition. She grabbed her purse, which included no weapons—she wasn't even taking her favorite hair knife—and called a cab to take her to the mansion in Somers.

When they arrived, the cab driver wouldn't take her up the driveway or accept any money for the ride. As he squealed away, she knew she was in the right place. Walking up the long driveway, she surveyed the dense trees she passed before she reached the gate. She hit the intercom and a very clipped voice asked her for her name and purpose.

"January. Audition." The less she said the better.

She was told to wait, and soon enough a limo pulled in from the street. The door opened, and Eve got in. There were four other women in the car and two bodyguard types. No one was smiling. This was a somber affair, despite the party atmosphere when they arrived at the house. Twinkling lights lined the paths and music played from unseen speakers as they were lead inside and into a waiting room.

The draperies alone probably cost what a middle-class family made in a year. In total Eve counted twenty girls in the room—some in very suggestive clothes, others like her who were tasteful in their black dresses and pumps.

She made sure to stand close to the tall blonde with close-cropped hair. Micki would have a mole like Marilyn Monroe, according to Shark's last text a few hours ago. After she asked Micki for a mint and confirmed her identity, Eve passed her the message and wandered away.

When it was time to move, the ladies were told to form a line. Eve made a point to be last. She needed to see as much of the situation as she could before she was in the room. The hallway was set up like a makeshift airport security gate, and each girl was thoroughly searched before she entered the room beyond the checkpoint.

The first few passed through without incident. The fourth one leaned in to the bodyguards suggestively. The ladies following her then tried to out-do each other with flirting. Eve watched as Micki went through without making a fool of herself. Eve half wondered if she'd just condemned the woman to death. Shark never told her if he was saving either of them. She could easily be walking to her doom. Why a weapons business would have a call for prostitutes and want them to act the opposite was puzzling.

When it was Eve's turn, the bodyguards smiled.

"Hey, baby. You're last in line. Lucky you. The caboose gets the body cavity search." The closest one reached his hand toward her skirt.

She bared her teeth.

"Whoa! Rules are rules, honey." The one on her left slid his hand across her ass.

Eve stomped her foot, scraping her heel down his shin and grinding it on his toe. "Touch me and die. The metal detector will tell you everything you'll ever get to know about my body."

She expected a fight, but the other bodyguard just motioned her through. They looked through her purse as she passed under the detector's scan. Eve took her bag back on the opposite side and the bodyguards assumed a quiet, almost respectful demeanor—only one of them now stood on one leg. Eve turned and entered the room. *Ballroom*, she mentally corrected.

After giving the large expanse a onceover, she stood again at the end of the line of girls. Suddenly a clacking of heels echoed in the room as a woman appeared at the top of the staircase. She was slight and dressed in a pastel blue shirt-and-coat combo. Her black hair bore a distinctive gray stripe, which she wore like an elegant badge of honor. As she slowly descended, like this was her wedding or something, Eve struggled to get a bead on her age. She noticed that each of the woman's pumps had a delicate bow made of diamonds at the toe just about the time she determined her to be perhaps a bit past fifty.

When the woman finally reached the end of the staircase, she smiled a loving schoolteacher's smile. But her eyes were the giveaway. This woman, whoever she was, had the most soulless eyes Eve had ever seen.

Some of the other girls made the mistake of scoffing and whispering. Eve could make out mumblings of *mobster's wife* and *prima donna*. The woman cleared her throat and patted her chest gently, her femininity over the top—Southern belle dipped in syrup and rolled in sugar. It was all for show, Eve was sure of it.

The woman moved to the center of the room, facing the women in line to audition. "Hello, girls. First, let me thank you for coming here and submitting to the guards and detectors." She looked from one to the other and smiled. Some girls responded, others did not. Eve returned the woman's gaze evenly.

"Do you pick out hookers for your husband?" came a voice from somewhere down the line. Nervous giggles rippled through the room.

"I'm *Ms.* Vitullo, but please, call me Mary Ellen. This evening I'll just need to speak with you for a few moments so I can decide if you're right for this job. I'll let you gather your thoughts." She twirled and made her way to a nearby table. A bodyguard ran over to pull out her chair. She sat and sweetly thanked him. And then they waited. Mary Ellen gazed out one of the floor-to-ceiling windows as the women chatted nervously.

Eve watched her for tells. She didn't like what she saw. This woman was manipulating them. After a weird amount of time had passed, the room settled into an awkward silence. Only then did Mary Ellen turn and beckon for the first girl in line. True to her word, she had a brief, quiet conversation with the auditioning prostitute before shaking her hand and pointing to a table on her left. Girl after girl endured the encounter, and each was sent to the table on the left. Micki was next, and when she was through, Mary Ellen pointed to another table on her right.

The chatter halted at the left-hand table. Suddenly it was clear some evaluation was going on. A few more girls were summoned, and three of them were sent to the right. Last was Eve. Mary Ellen beckoned coyly, almost flirtatiously to her.

After Eve took her seat, Mary Ellen smiled indulgently. "I noticed at the check-in you were unwilling to submit to the search by my guards. Care to tell me why?" She batted her lashes.

"Not particularly." Eve crossed her legs.

"Well." Mary Ellen raised a perfect eyebrow, or at least part of one. Botox seemed to have rendered a good portion of her face immobile. Her eyes were so brown they were almost black. "Name?"

"January." Eve didn't fidget and tried to avoid a staring contest with the woman. Her vibe was intense.

"Last place of employment?" Mary Ellen gently bit her finger.

"Lollipop's Ladies, and then I went solo." Eve sat back in her chair and waited to see how this information would be digested.

"What's your best skill, Miss January, wouldya say?" Now she was folksy, like they were best friends.

Eve wasn't sure what story to make up. She decided to go with the truth.

She leaned in and spoke in a whisper. "I can tell you're going to kill every single girl at that table." She pointed to the left.

Mary Ellen's eyes widened just a tiny bit in surprise. "And if I sent you to that table? What would you do?"

Eve stood. "Try me."

Mary Ellen stood as well and looked up at Eve. "I'll need you to go sit down." She motioned with her head to the table on the right.

Eve nodded and sat down next to Micki.

"Boys? Can you show the ladies to the left their new view, please?" Mary Ellen looked every bit the gracious host.

The girls from the other table lined up, clearly excited at the thought of living in this huge mansion. Mary Ellen came to sit at the right-hand table, across from Eve. She waited until the rest of the ladies were out of the ballroom, gazing at the spectacular view of the mountains just beyond, dotted with house lights.

She turned to the small group of women at the table. "So, after that group is done, I'll have the boys show you your view."

As the first gunshot popped, eyes widened all around the table. Most of the women seemed confused, curious, but Eve knew it was a .48 Magnum with a silencer. The second and third shots drew their attention. Eve knew if she looked she'd see the girls falling boneless to the stone patio. She didn't look. Eve watched Mary Ellen instead. Horrified screams now came from the remaining girls on the terrace. Eve bet they were starting to run, trying to escape.

With each shot, Mary Ellen's mouth crawled up into a larger smile. When the last shot sounded on the patio, she was grinning like she'd just won a puppy.

9

It's Okay

"Motherfucker." Beckett threw his Keno ticket on the floor. "I swear one day I'm figuring this shit out." Then he stood and picked up the damn ticket. He slid his sunglasses on just as Chery opened the front door to the liquor store. The morning sun felt like knives in his head, even with his sunglasses on, and he cringed.

She was flustered, dropping her keys as she began apologizing. "Sorry, boss. I'm late—I know I'm late. My sister was late to the program, and I'm late, and I'm sorry."

"Settle yourself, baby. It's okay, baby! Monday morning is not a hot time for liquor. I've been playing the fucking Keno game, and I swear on my left, slightly hairless nut that this damn thing is rigged."

He picked up a few receipts that had fallen like leaves from her messy purse. Chery was wearing a turtleneck on an unseasonably warm day. She did that a lot, actually. At first he'd thought her boyfriend was a sucker—got off on leaving his open-mouthed mark on his woman. But the last two times Chery was late, she'd worn thick makeup as well. The lights of the liquor store worked like an x-ray, and he could see the bruises she'd tried to cover. Didn't take a genius to know Chery was getting knocked around by her "man."

"Just get behind that thing and make sense of the sales I forced it to take," Beckett said, sliding away from the register. "You're good. No worries, baby." He made sure Chery gave him a smile before he whistled through his teeth, and Gandhi snorted himself out of his deep snores. "I'm going to sort out that shipment in the back."

Chery nodded and his ugly dog followed him, passing gas with every step. Beckett shook his head and slid his glasses off, hooking them on the back of his T-shirt. "I used to be cool. I had some swagger before you came farting along, G."

The dog gave him an open-jawed smile, his tongue lolling out.

Beckett's office was in the back. G had a nice fluffy bed, which he immediately curled up in. Beckett grabbed the inventory list and began sorting the booze. His mind drifted with the manual labor…to Chery. He was desperate every damn day, trying to be a better fucking guy. It was like an addiction, his need to bust people's freaking skulls for being assholes. This girl he had on the payroll was a hot mess when she'd applied for a job about eight months ago—nervous and shifty during the interview. She had huge gaps in her resume. Just the type of person he tried to hire.

He didn't need the goddamn money. Mouse had set him up so sweet he didn't need a damn thing. This liquor store had been an impulse buy. It was a sack of shit. But it was his church now. He collected people: patrons, employees, the local hookers. They found their way here, and he tried to give them a damn chance. Loan them money that didn't have their blood on the note. He was shocked how damn grateful the misfits of this little town were. And how often they surprised the shit out him.

Chery was a test, though. In the past, Beckett would have just killed her boyfriend—or at the very least broken enough bones in the man's body to make him see God. But this new Beckett, this guy he was trying his damnedest to be, was all about letting people make their choices, find their way. Trusting them a little.

And it was because he didn't kill the boyfriend that Beckett learned about Vere. Chery was the only provider for her older sister, who had autism. In a few quiet moments when he listened, he heard about how Vere was Chery's only family. They were fiercely devoted to each other. Their mother, who had seen to it that Vere had all she needed, passed from cancer years ago. Chery had come home from college and vowed to keep Vere's schedule as close to the same as possible. Vere participated in a program four days a week, doing jobs in the community with the help of an amazing staff. There were also the horseback riding lessons Vere loved. An old horse had made a connection with her, a lady who lived inside her head so much. Chery teared up when she described Vere's rare shows of emotion around the damn horse. The therapist wasn't cheap either, and their mother's medical plan had expired with her life.

Chery's boyfriend was also her landlord. They never got very far into discussing her relationship with him, but Beckett had an inkling Chery put up with the man at least partly to keep things stable for Vere.

Slowly, quietly, Beckett had been able to go behind the scenes and donate things to help Vere. The horseback riding lessons were now free: the farm's owner loved getting a brand new John Deere tractor in exchange. The program that took Vere for her job in town had received stunning donations. They were now able to take their participants on even grander adventures. And the final piece had been when Beckett was able to get Chery a medical plan. She contributed a pittance from her paycheck, and Beckett supplied her with insurance that would take care of her and her sister for their entire lifetimes.

And on the days when Chery came in all excited about a new development with Vere, it was all worth it. Helping her had been a rush. Maybe adopting Gandhi had been the starting point, but there had been a kindness avalanche since then.

It was work though. He wanted to kick the shit out of Chery's landlord/boyfriend/asshole so damn much. And he wasn't ruling that out. The man had stopped in to buy alcohol once. Chery had disappeared instantly into the back of the store, and Beckett had stood at the cash register with his arms folded. The guy's name was Jared. Normal-looking fucker. He tried to offer money, but Beckett wouldn't take it. He looked at the man without his nice-guy filter, and it took only his stare. He'd squinted into the bastard's soul. Jared had immediately dropped the money and the whiskey and left.

Beckett twirled a box cutter in his hand, trying to put some thought into his decisions. Working with the type of people he now sought out, he knew he couldn't fix everybody's everything. And a lot of damn times ladies who took a beating would side with their men, no matter what. If that happened he'd lose his connection to Chery.

It was tough. He prayed sometimes. To Mouse. Which probably made Bibles spontaneously combust, but whatever. He asked for patience and clarity, and damn it if once in a while he didn't feel like he was getting a shot of just that.

He looked over the bottles and cans he'd unpacked. There was a chick on the side of a particular six-pack of beer who looked like Eve. Stupid. He ordered the damn stuff religiously even though the beer never sold and tasted like shit. He was thinking about her again out of fucking nowhere. That's always how it was. He'd be doing something boring and normal, and then it would be her. The way her damn blue eyes would see through all his crap. How damn gorgeous she was, but used her looks only as another weapon.

Years. He'd been gone years. He'd been gone so long, it was crippling now. She'd expect so much more than what he'd accomplished. He should be saving people from fires every day. Or finding missing kids. But all he had to offer as evidence of being a better person was running the worst liquor store in a little out-of-the-way town by the water.

He sliced through the last box and put the last few six-packs in the cooler. He heard the bell on the front door and Chery's welcome to Nolan. The guy'd been out of prison for ten years—he had grandchildren now, for crap's sake—and no one else would give the poor bastard a freaking job. He was a great guy who'd made a bunch of stupid choices as a kid.

Beckett woke Gandhi and grabbed his keys. Chery would manage the front for most of the day, and Nolan would take over at night and lock up. With his employees in place, he was out. He slapped the older man on the back on his way through the store. Chery blew Gandhi a kiss, and Beck was out the door. He felt good, but he had no idea if the simple shit he did here would ever be worthy of Eve.

Kyle took another huge breath and forced a smile as Cole stuck the needle in her stomach. He was decent at making it not hurt too much, and she was trying to be a good sport, but these fertility treatments were a freaking joke. Between the bloating and the imported hormones she felt more like a water balloon than a woman.

"There. All done for today. You okay?" Cole stood and rubbed her stomach.

"I can't even begin to think about this. How's Ted? What's it been, a week now since he was hurt? Did Eve come home? Tell me something else." Kyle sat on the bed and watched Cole meticulously put away the syringes and vials of drugs that contained her hopes and dreams.

"It has been a week, and Blake said she came by pretty much just long enough to set up security for her dad. Her parting words were 'protect your family.'"

Kyle pulled her knees to her chest. Her stomach burned, and there was an odd metal taste in her mouth.

"Livia said she had the alarm people out the other day. But I mean, is the concern Beckett's enemies or what?"

Cole turned, and she indulged in staring at him. His skin was the most gorgeous color, and it made his clear eyes sparkle even more. He could still look mysterious even though they'd been married for years now.

"Or what. No one's heard from Beck in years. I don't think it's related. It's bad news, and we have to be careful, but it doesn't necessarily have anything to do with him." Cole crawled onto the bed and wrapped his arms around her.

She traced the *Sorry* tattoo on his forearm. "You don't think he's dead, do you?"

She could feel him shake his head. "No. I think I'd know. Blake and I think he's trying to turn himself around, and that might take a while. I hope, anyway."

"I think he's still alive too." She sighed and left the conversation at that. Speculating about Beckett was an exercise in futility. Her eyes landed on her "fertility kit" where Cole had placed it on the dresser. She hoped it wasn't the same type of thing.

10

Vindictive

Ryan looked at his phone in the Wednesday-morning Starbucks line. Christian Grey was calling. He answered somewhat timidly, "Yo."

"Morales, I need you at the station in thirty minutes." John McHugh's voice was unmistakable.

"Sure, boss. You want something from 'Bucks?" Ryan handed his frequent-caffeine-binger card to the barista and added the captain's order to his before hanging up.

While he waited for his coffees, he scrolled to the contact page on his phone. Angry Trish had changed all his contacts to characters from *Fifty Shades of Grey*. He knew this because Al's Auto Shop, usually listed first, was now "50 Shades of Grey gave me more orgasms than you." After that he had Anastasia Steele and A helicopter. Worst of all, his mom—whose number he could thankfully remember—was listed as The Red Room of Pain.

He didn't bother fixing it. His order was ready for pickup. God love Starbucks. They made a breakup go down smoother.

When he entered the precinct, Kathy took a break from filing her nails to wave at him with the phone propped on her shoulder. He nodded and rushed past, kicking himself for not getting her her favorite latte. McHugh was waiting for him in the conference room, and Ryan closed the door with his foot. His boss looked serious.

"Here's your drug of choice, Captain. What the hell's going on?" Ryan tried to make sense of all the old files scattered on the table.

McHugh sipped the drink and kept scanning the files. After a beat he spoke. "I've got a real delicate situation I'm dealing with here, and I think you're the man for the job. You fit the profile."

Ryan waited him out. His captain was a methodical cop. Usually his files were arranged just so. This mess would normally lead Ryan to believe the man was drunk, but when McHugh's red eyes met his he could tells his boss was fighting some demons, but not the bottle.

"We're getting some escalating crime. Some beatings, some reports of people being harassed. There's a bit of a method to it. Someone's looking for something, and trying to be stealthy about it. I haven't dealt with this for years." McHugh tapped the crime photo of a man stabbed over and over, to death.

"So the party's over. What do you need from me?" Ryan took the last gulp of his coffee.

"They'll likely be buying cops. That's how this happened." He tapped the picture of the bloody murder again. "The cop guarding this man's door was on the take and left his post. Beckett Taylor went in and did him."

Ryan snapped to full attention. "I thought we never had him for anything."

"We didn't. We still don't. All I have is motive and opportunity. But if he's back in town, we'll see a lot more of this type of crap." McHugh shuffled the picture under another file. "I'm proposing that we let you get bought. And then we can find out more about what's going on. Say no if you can't. This is no joke. These people are subhuman. I don't know how serious you and Trish are— "

"She dumped me." Ryan set down his empty cup and grabbed the file and the picture underneath it.

"Sorry to hear it," McHugh added gruffly.

"Don't be. She's apparently pretty vindictive. I'll do this." He glanced at the name at the top. Chris Simmer was the name of the dead body in the picture. The weapon had been determined to be a small sharp. Hell of a way to go. "Is his throat sliced? Damn."

The captain added to the horror. "So he wouldn't scream as he died. I have to be honest with you, I knew this boy. He was briefly engaged to Livia."

"Wow. I'm sorry. That's shitty." Ryan mentally reviewed his comments, hoping he hadn't insulted the man.

"Don't be sorry. The kid was an asshole. Tried to kill Livia and damn near killed my son-in-law. It was complicated, but regardless, Taylor's signature was all over his murder. I will not allow that man back into my city or anywhere near my children and grandchildren." McHugh pulled the files into a big pile.

"So you want me to be undercover by being a cop." Ryan nodded. He liked the plan so far.

"That's the best I've got. These bastards are shady and it's like nailing Jell-O to the wall. There'll be crazy temptations. This assignment is really horrible—although it could also start you on your way to detective. We'd have to stay in touch the whole time, and you'll have to be honest with me." McHugh looked like he was reconsidering even as he explained.

Ryan had to have this assignment. It had to be him. It was fate. Kismet. "Sir, I'd be honored to help protect the city and your loved ones. As long as we're on the same page—I'm a cop, not the bad guy, no matter what goes down—I'll start today. What do you want me to do?"

"For starters..." McHugh handed Ryan an old-school map. "Your new beat is all Taylor's old stomping grounds. I want you to slack off there. Pretend to sleep. Talk to hookers. Ignore crimes. Be approachable."

"I can handle that." Ryan began plotting ways to seem like more of an asshole than he already was.

McHugh extended his hand. "Thanks. I feel a lot better having you on this. It's a service to me, as well as to the public."

The men shook hands, and before Ryan could leave McHugh handed him another picture, almost as an afterthought. "You might as well see what the devil looks like."

Ryan nodded, but waited until he was in his patrol car to look. Beckett grinned in the picture. He wore a T-shirt and cammo pants, and it was easy to see the tattoo on his forearm: a cross, a knife, and a music clef intertwined.

Ryan's brain did a fist pump. This was a hundred steps closer to Nikko and Wade's killer then he'd ever been.

Two days in on his new assignment, Ryan texted The Red Room of Pain as he walked to his truck: Yes, he was fine and yes, he'd be by for Sunday dinner.

This evening he planned to go drinking in one of the bad parts of town, but one look at his vehicle and he knew his plans had changed.

"Trish, you hosebag."

Super-glued to the passenger side of his F-150 was what had to be fifty dollars in quarters, forming the gorgeous proclamation SMALL COCK. He shook his head and slammed his palm against his forehead. He shouted into the fading sunlight, "I don't have a small dick! You have a large vagina!"

An older couple walking their cocker spaniels gave him a disapproving look. He kicked the side of his truck. He called his insurance company, which helpfully suggested he call the police to report the vandalism, then tried picking the quarters off with his keys. There was no way in hell he'd call the precinct and report *small cock* vandalism. He silently gave Trish credit for her diabolical plan. She knew he'd never press charges for this. He would've called her to confront her, but he wasn't sure if she'd deleted her number or renamed herself after a sex toy on his phone. *Bitch.*

He stomped into his apartment after re-parking his truck so the penis-libeling side wasn't visible from the road. As far as he was concerned, his love snake was just fine. He changed clothes, improvised on his plan, and hailed a cab. He had the driver stop at a pawn shop frequented by Taylor's people back in the day. He asked the cab to come back in an hour.

The pawn shop was hardly what anyone would call busy, and Ryan walked straight to the antique guns. It took enough minutes for the shop owner to make his way over that he had no doubt customer service was not paramount—or even remotely essential.

"You got anything more modern? With a bit of a kick and a dick?" Ryan pulled out his phone and let his badge slip onto the counter. "Sorry. I've been drinking a little. Really, I just want to buy something of my own. Sometimes the service weapon doesn't cut it, you know?" Ryan did his best to look fuzzy.

The pawn store owner gave him a sharp look before shaking his head. "A cop? Shit, you should have your pickings of the evidence room."

"If they've got their eye on you, you don't get to touch shit. Never mind." Ryan gathered up his badge and phone before giving the shop owner the finger. "Fuck you very much."

The message was sent. Ryan had made his first official appearance as a slightly crazy cop.

11

Sweet Treasures

"How's Ted?" Livia finished wiping down the counters on Monday afternoon.

Blake burped Kellan before settling into an easy sway. "Your father reported he left the hospital and he's home. I want to go check on him."

She leaned against the now-damp Formica. "At the very least I'd like to slip him a few dinners. Have you heard from Eve?"

"It's been two weeks. Not a word." Blake shifted the baby so he could cradle him.

She paused for a moment, captured by the sight of Blake's bicep flexing to protect Kellan's head. She was sure her hormones were a giant bag of crazy, but Blake was hot holding the baby, simple as that.

Livia came close to kiss the baby's head and then Blake's lips. "Thank you."

"For burping him?" He leaned forward to kiss her forehead.

She shook her head. "For fighting for this. For us. Every day."

"It's an honor, Mrs. Hartt." Blake shifted back into his easy sway, keeping the baby locked in his slumber.

"When was the last time we slept? Do you remember?" Livia went to the fridge. She knew she had some items that were long past their pitching date.

"Define sleep? Like in a bed and closing your eyes until you're done?"

She smiled. "Now that is ridiculous talk. I mean like four hours drooling in the rocker."

"I think I indulged in that pleasure on Wednesday of last week. Someday they'll want to sleep, right? That happens?" Blake smiled as Emme bounded into the kitchen wearing a unicorn outfit.

She saw Kellan asleep and spoke in an exaggerated stage whisper, "Daddy, baby brother Kellan is asleep. Don't sneeze!"

Blake mouthed, "I won't."

"Mommy, today at school a man said hello to me. I told him he was a stranger and I don't talk to his type." She proceeded to drag a chair over so she could climb onto the counter.

Livia felt herself pale and watched Blake stop mid sway. "Where was Miss Jenny?"

Emme got herself a package of fruit chews from the cabinet. "Frank bumped his head and there was blood. I was playing frogs with Sawyer, and it was my turn to run away. I was by the woods fence." She used her teeth to rip into the package.

Livia held herself back. All at once she wanted to gather her girl up and beat the hell out of her teacher. It was irrational — the teacher at Emme's preschool was excellent.

"What did he say to you, exactly?" Blake asked, resuming his sway.

Emme was too smart to be played. "Am I in trouble? Mommy?"

She searched her parents faces, big green eyes filling with tears.

"Of course not," Blake said. "But you were right, he was a stranger so your adults need to know what he said."

Livia went to Emme and cuddled her up, kissing her head. "Tell me what happened with the stranger. We're proud of you for doing the right thing."

Her daughter clutched the fruit chews like a stuffed animal. "I'm sorry. I'm sorry."

Livia pulled Emme off the counter and hugged her hard, forcing her own tears back with superhuman strength. "No. You did great. Shh."

She carried the sniffling girl to the rocker and sat, humming her favorite lullaby. Emme began out and out crying. Blake laid Kellan down in his playpen and began to help Livia comfort their girl.

"Hey, look at me, sweetheart. It is so okay. I'm so glad you told me and Mommy. That was really brave." He patted her back and kissed her cheek.

Through hiccups and sniffles, Emme gave her version of the events. "Well, I was being a frog, and Sawyer was the frog catcher, so I ran to the fence, and I stepped in the No Zone just for a minute. Just for a second. And that's when the stranger said, 'Emme.' And then he asked me if Daddy had a drawing on his arm, and he showed me a picture of this." Emme turned Blake's hand until they could all see his brothers' mark. "He had a long mark under his eye, like an old boo-boo. And then I told him he was a stranger, and I left."

Livia hugged Emme closer. "It's okay. You're here. I've got you. I've got you."

She began humming again and rocked the chair out of habit. Emme sniffed herself to sleep. Livia rested her head on her daughter's. Blake shook his head and looked at his tattoo. Livia raised her hands and shrugged, asking him what the hell they were going to do without actually saying the words.

Blake pulled an ottoman closer and sat, placing his hand on her back. Her sleeping breaths shuddered from time to time, her body still crying just a little.

"I'll tell your father. I'll find a way to tell Eve. And Emme's not going back to that school." Blake looked ready to defend them all with just his anger and fear.

Something her father had told her a million years ago trickled up Livia's spine and into her consciousness: *"Do you know what we call Beckett Taylor down at the precinct? The Bloody Bastard."*

Livia loved Blake with all that she was. He was an amazing father and husband, but there was no way she was putting her children in danger. And she was scared they were already there.

Eve added diamond earrings and stepped away from the mirror. Technically this was her room at Mary Ellen's mansion, but in her nearly two weeks of official "employment" she had yet to spend the night. The girls weren't imprisoned, so to speak, but strongly encouraged to remain.

Eve had refused. She had things to do. Fortunately, one of them was not currently going to her job at Silver Force Industries. They'd generously offered her a leave of absence when she'd explained her father's sudden illness. But she did spend time checking on him. Well, actually she checked her updates from the security she'd hired. If Mary Ellen's people hadn't put two and two together yet, she wasn't going to help by leading them to her father's door.

She looked at her reflection dispassionately. The dress was a designer number—probably cost more than the expensive drapes. She fastened her high heel's buckle, also diamond, before double-checking the knife in her garter belt. Carrying a gun to this shitfest wasn't a smart move.

Earlier that day Mary Ellen had called the chosen ladies into the ballroom for a meeting. Each girl sat as Mary Ellen smiled benevolently. "Ladies. My sweet treasures. I have your first outing planned, and I wanted to give you some pointers!" She leaned forward and patted the closest woman's hand.

Eve folded her arms and waited. All this woman wanted to do was play games. There'd been no talk of Beckett, Poughkeepsie, nothing. It was fashion and playtime. There were now ten girls who "worked" for Mary Ellen. Five were old timers with plenty of experience.

"Tonight I need all you new recruits to watch how my girls work a room. They're part geisha, part Mary Kay lady. Tonya is a particular one to watch, January. Promise you'll do me that little favor?" She leaned forward and smiled.

Eve nodded once to acknowledge she'd heard Mary Ellen but didn't commit to anything.

"I have some business to discuss with the gentlemen attending tonight's gathering, and having gorgeous women around makes the boys more amenable. Please don't actually gratify any of them until Tonya gives you an all clear. We need sexual tension. Men don't understand that the person who willingly puts their testicles in her mouth owns them, not the other way around." She shrugged and clapped at her own observation. "In your rooms are your Cinderella outfits. You may dress and wait for your stylist to appear. We have three hours to become divine. Off you go!"

The stylist hadn't spent long with Eve—gave her the jewelry she was wearing and added a few thin braids to her hair before leaving.

So Eve now sat down to contemplate the conversation she'd had with Blake in the Poughkeepsie woods a few days earlier.

"Did John find anything?" She'd leaned against the large oak next to one of Blake's wood shelters made from sticks and leaves.

"A few people reported seeing a man in camouflage on foot, headed in the direction of the school a few days before Emme was approached. She noticed a scar under his eye when she talked to him." Blake jammed his hands in his pockets.

"So he'd been lying in wait for the perfect moment. Fucker." Eve closed her eyes and tried to make sense of her swirling emotions. "I'll get you security. Someone will be near all of you at all times."

"And John will grill the hell out of anyone you hire. Will they pass his inspection?" He ran a hand through his hair.

"I'll find people who do." She pushed away from the tree. Hanging with the pastel princess was turning out to be huge waste of time. *This* was where she was needed.

"We've got it right now. But Livia and I were both really freaked out." He came to stand next to her. "Your hair is...different. Everything okay?"

She turned to face him. "Everything is far from okay. Your family was targeted. A man I fully intend on killing talked to my niece. Alone. I wish Be— " She bit her tongue.

"You don't know if him being here would make it worse or better." Blake touched her shoulder gently.

"He's still causing us trouble five years later. Loving him is a life sentence." She patted his hand awkwardly.

"I gotta believe loving my brother is the right thing to do. I've got my family safe. You worry about living through whatever it is you're doing."

Eve began stepping backward as he did the same. "I'm in a dragon's lair, cousin. And I'm going burn it to the ground so no one else gets hurt."

She'd spun on the heel of her boot then, as Blake gave her a final wave. She looked down now at the frou-frou shoes Mary Ellen had chosen for her. Ridiculous, and impossible to work in.

Just then one of the bodyguards knocked and in the same motion opened her door. He was so stoic. She knew now when he'd hit on her at the audition he'd been acting a part. She almost felt bad that she'd scraped all the skin off his shin.

He rubbed his nose with his hand before issuing Mary Ellen's latest decree: "Miss January, I'm gonna have to frisk you. I'm sorry."

She stepped up to him and spread her arms and legs. He patted her down very clinically and found the knife on her thigh. His hands stilled.

They made eye contact, and Eve said nothing. She wasn't going to apologize for being *lightly* armed. He nodded and waved her past him.

She met the other women in the lobby. Turned out they all had matching dresses—like billionaire bridesmaids. Mary Ellen arrived in a white dress tailored to show not one inch more of her skin than her conservative suits did. Eve glanced at her own cleavage, which was barely contained, and the slit on her right leg was almost to her hipbone. Mary Ellen nodded appreciatively.

"And this, ladies, is why no one ever turns down an invitation to meet with me. You look stunning." She flounced ahead, holding her hand out like a princess for her bodyguard.

They all followed her out, and each girl had an SUV with a driver. Their caravan left the mansion like a parade. By the time they'd reached the city, Eve had to acknowledge that Mary Ellen was insane but possibly a genius. She'd been to many tense meetings when she worked for Beckett. A parade of gorgeous women in low-cut dresses ready to please the participants would do a lot to turn the tide in your favor.

One at time, the ladies left the cars and paraded into a fancy building with a doorman. No backroom meetings for Mary Ellen. When it was Eve's turn, she exited and made sure to put a little vamp in her step. She spotted four snipers within shooting distance. There were surely more hidden from view.

She took her driver's offered arm and walked through the revolving doors. He walked her into a huge event space and brought her to stand behind the center table. Each of Mary Ellen's girls stood like pillars: equidistant apart in a perfect circle, and the drivers stepped behind them.

The men seated at the tables in the room were either pointedly gawking or pointedly ignoring the show in front of them. Mary Ellen smiled like Mother Superior before addressing the men.

"Gentlemen, I asked you here this evening as a courtesy, and because I'd appreciate your input so very much. I'd like to let you know my plans. I'm interested in learning about what's happening in Poughkeepsie. And of course you can make your own decisions, but in a related matter, I'd be very pleased if you stopped doing business with Sevan Harmon immediately. Consider this a heads up, because if I have my way, he'll soon be out of business altogether."

Eve worked not to show her surprise. Mary Ellen had just broken every rule of a meeting like this. You never stated your ultimate purpose. Some of the men rolled their eyes. Others stared at her slack-jawed. Still others looked bored.

Mary Ellen smiled widely.

"Mary." Eve traced the voice to a man she was pretty sure was a mob boss from New Jersey. "Are you having some sort of spasm? What the hell are you talking about?"

"No, sir. And please, my name is Mary Ellen, address me as such. I'm just interested in your thoughts on what's happening in Poughkeepsie these days." She smiled again.

Eve had to remember not to act too interested. She was arm candy at best.

A charmingly handsome man spoke. "Sweetheart, we appreciate the heads up." He put air quotes around the words. "But none of us is looking for business advice from you." The other men laughed and agreed.

Mary Ellen put a finger to her lips and smiled around it. "Dan is it? Dan, you have dealings with Mr. Harmon, do you not?" She had to speak loudly to be heard.

"Discussing specifics in this company is ill advised," Dan shot back. "Did you not find Daddy's How to Run the Business handbook?" That comment earned him a healthy round of laughter. "Mary Ellen, I know Rodolfo has had one hell of a stroke, but does he have any idea what you're up to? It's hard to take you seriously when I still remember you as the only one without a date to the Prom. Where the hell is Primo?"

Mary Ellen lifted one hand and motioned to the circle. Each of the ladies took the cue and stepped forward. Eve was closest to Dan, so she stepped up and leaned down, giving him a 3D view of her cleavage.

"My father is just fine and well on the way to recovery already. My brother is involved with other business this evening. But did I mention that I brought gifts? Boys, these ladies are highly trained in the art of pleasuring a man. They've spent years perfecting their sexual skills." Mary Ellen clapped twice.

Eve looked to Tonya and watched as she slid into her mark's lap. Eve did the same.

Dan made a pleased sound. "Sexual skills? Did you get a degree? A BA in hand jobs?"

Eve smiled. "I'll be happy to let you discover my specialty." She licked her lips and straightened his tie.

Mary Ellen clapped again, and Eve matched Tonya's graceful escape. She disentangled herself from Dan's searching hands and stood in front of her driver again.

"Now, before we get on with the fun part of your evening, I'll need your cooperation. I'm going to be doing some organizing in Poughkeepsie—just a small parcel of land in the big scheme of things. And quite the power vacuum these days. Does anyone object?"

Eve closed her eyes briefly. Finally she might learn something.

Dan spoke up again. "That's Taylor's. I wouldn't fuck with it."

"Yes. Beckett Taylor. He's fairly infamous, am I correct?" Mary Ellen leaned forward on her elbows.

The men kept shifting in their seats, sliding glances toward the girls.

Another man cleared his throat before speaking. "Taylor's dead."

Eve's heart beat faster.

"Really?" Mary Ellen purred, her eyes wide. "What else can you gentlemen tell me?"

"Heard he had a brothel out in Arkansas. That shit legal there? He always had a way with pussy," a different slimebag mused.

"No, sir," offered another. "Taylor's gone straight. Has a huge weed farm in California. Medicinal, my ass."

No one knew anything, of that Eve was now sure. Beckett had reached epic, folkloric proportions.

Mary Ellen's eyes sparkled. "It seems he's no longer concerned with Poughkeepsie then. I'll make sure to cross all my Ts and dot the Is. Anyone else have thoughts to share?" She addressed them like she was at a PTA meeting, looking from one man to another.

No one added anything. This woman was out of bounds and out of order on so many levels. Eve would be surprised if she lived through the next hour. And why was she asking these questions? Surely her father, Rodolfo, would have this information. And if he was ill his people would have this information. They must be shutting Mary Ellen out.

"Very well. Drinks?" Mary Ellen held her hands out, palms up, and the doors to the room were flooded with waiters. Tuxedoed bartenders wheeled in three bars. Music began, and the lights went down. It was like a freaking wedding. "We worked. Now, shall we play? Please, pick your favorite poison, gentlemen." She pushed herself out of her chair and gestured to the bars, the food arriving on trays, the ladies, and finally to a drug bar.

Mary Ellen stepped away from the table and snapped. It was then Eve realized what the couches were intended for. Dotted around the room, they were soon covered by a long circle of silk to create semi-private quarters.

The man sitting in front of Micki smiled. "Don't mind if I do." He signaled over the waiter and Micki at the same time. "You. Blow me." He winked and pointed under the table. As Micki swallowed her pride and tried to make crawling under the fancy tablecloth look sexy, the man pointed to various foods on the tray and demanded a scotch.

As he stuffed a small crepe in his mouth, his eyes headed skyward. "Oh, yeah. Damn, Mary Ellen, you weren't kidding. Jesus." He slid further down in his seat and did his very best to drink and eat while being serviced.

Eve watched as each of the men signaled the woman behind him. Some began dancing with their lady, others demanded a striptease, and still others took their woman into a silk room.

Dan stood and headed for Eve. He was tan enough that she bet his skin was still warm from a tropical location. His eyes were a collage of clears: green, blue, gray. They looked like magic.

"Your name?" He put on the charm and smiled.

"January."

He took her hand from her side and kissed it. "Are you always this chilly, January?" He stepped around her and tugged her toward the silken circle.

"Yes," she said as they entered a room. She waited as he reclined on the couch.

"For a girl with a martial arts belt in men's orgasms, you sure have a lot of clothes on." He lifted an eyebrow.

The curtain parted, and Eve's driver cleared his throat. "Excuse me, sir. Miss January? Mary Ellen requests your presence."

Eve winked at Dan. "You stay right here. I'll be back."

As she left the love nest, her driver spoke in her ear. "Mary Ellen likes female company when she uses the restroom."

Eve shrugged. This woman wants to organize Beckett's territory but needs to hold hands in the little girl's room? *Fine.*

One of the other ladies joined Eve as they crossed the room. Mary Ellen smiled at them from the far side of the room as they approached. "Let me apologize, ladies. You'll be able to get back to the party soon."

Eve glanced around. In a few short minutes, every woman she could see had been stripped. Micki was on top of the table in front of the man who'd had her along with his appetizer, and several others had gathered. She now writhed as the men threw food at her. The first man laughed when a cracker smeared with something landed on her skin and stuck. Cash was tossed on the table.

They were betting on Micki.

Eve closed her eyes briefly and inhaled. She had to let it roll off her back. She focused on Mary Ellen, who was chattering away about how well the party was going. Every door and window was a danger. If someone was moving against this woman, this would be the perfect place to take her down. Obviously this event had been prepared in advance. Her enemies would know she was here.

The bodyguard led them down the hall to the ladies' lounge.

"We checked it, ma'am. You're good." He opened the door for them and let it shut.

Eve didn't like the set up at all. There was a sitting room with couches and plush carpets before another door that opened into the opulent marble bathroom. There was a huge, frosted-glass window that Eve was sure had their silhouettes dancing on the other side.

Mary Ellen stepped into a stall, still yammering on about the party. Eve stood just outside while the other girl fluffed her hair in the huge mirror.

A creepy feeling settled itself in Eve's stomach. Something was off. She looked to the ceiling. It was some sort of mock texture, but looking past that camouflage, she could see drop tiles. And the one next to the heating vent was just a few centimeters askew. Trying to seem nonchalant as she swept the room, she thought she spotted at least one hidden camera. Whether it was piping feed to Mary Ellen's people or someone else was the question.

"How many of the snipers were yours?" Eve asked suddenly.

"Excuse me?" A flush sounded as Mary Ellen opened the stall door.

Mary Ellen pushed past her to get to the sinks. She turned a gold handle as Eve watched the tile above her head move infinitesimally.

Eve made a quick choice. She didn't know nearly enough about what was going on in Poughkeepsie to let Mary Ellen die yet. So whoever was coming from the ceiling was going down. Eve slipped a hand to her thigh and pulled out her knife. She walked to the mirror behind Mary Ellen and pretended to fix her hair. When she caught her eyes, Mary Ellen stiffened.

Eve whispered, "Hide under the sink, understand?"

Mary Ellen nodded. At least she wasn't hysterical.

Eve kept her body directly behind Mary Ellen's as a gloved hand appeared through the now-open tile holding a handgun with a silencer. He likely had a mirror angled for aiming. In one movement she threw her knife, which stuck in her mark—the nerves in the wrist that controlled the hand, and pushed Mary Ellen's head down like they were playing a vicious game of Duck, Duck, Goose.

The woman scurried under the marble sink and covered her head. Eve turned and dove for the pistol. She flipped on her back as she landed and emptied it into the ceiling, sending bullets through the hole and all the surrounding tiles. She tossed the spent gun aside and motioned for Mary Ellen to stay put. The other woman had joined her below the sink. Eve heard gunfire outside the restroom as well.

She emerged to help Eve drag a couch from the sitting room to give her a boost up into the hole the attackers had made. Eve still had to jump twice to get a handhold and pull her body up. She scrambled and waited a second for the dark hole's shapes to make sense. The tunnel was larger than an air vent should be.

There were three dead bodies and beyond them a long shaft to traverse. One of the men moaned. Eve pulled her knife from the dead man's wrist and tucked it back in its holster. She turned and popped her head through the hole, motioning to Mary Ellen. The other woman gave her a boost, but Eve's arm still screamed with the strain as she hauled Mary Ellen up. Then Eve popped the tile back in place.

"What about Lena?" Mary Ellen didn't look as horrified as she should have at the dead bodies.

"You're my priority. Do you know any of these guys?" Eve stole a flashlight from a still hand. After seeing each of the faces, the woman shook her head.

"Let's go." Eve crawled over the men, one moaning a last time, stole their weapons, and handed a gun to Mary Ellen.

After they'd crawled a short distance, they heard the gunfire.

"Were you expecting this?" Eve turned her flashlight on Mary Ellen's face.

"I think in my line of work this is always an option." She nodded for Eve to continue.

They reached a place where two air vents connected. Eve felt the vibration of someone else crawling in the vent.

She motioned for Mary Ellen to go up the ladder to the next level. Despite their high heels, they managed two stories before Eve tapped Mary Ellen and motioned her onto a new floor. They crawled through this much smaller tunnel until Eve found the first air grate. She pulled out her knife and used it as a screw driver. After a moment the vent dropped onto a desk below, somewhat muffled by the large amount of paper the messy person had left on their desk. The sounds of at least two men ascending the ladder echoed as Eve lowered Mary Ellen into the room.

"Hide." Eve whispered as she jumped down after her. There was no way to reattach the grate in the time she had, so Eve backed herself into a corner to wait.

The men who entered the room were obviously not as prepared as the first crew. A huge man jumped from the vent hole onto the desk. He was dressed in complete black, almost like a SWAT team member, and the only thing that stopped Eve from killing him was the fact that he'd let her keep her knife earlier in the night. These were Mary Ellen's men. Another man came in after him and startled at the sight of Eve.

"Ma'am?" he called, looking around.

"She's in the closet." Eve tried to listen for more attackers.

Mary Ellen came out and hugged the closest bodyguard before slapping his arm. "Where were you? If she hadn't been there I'd be dead right now. What do I pay you for?"

The bodyguard started apologizing. "Everything was crazy after you left— "

Eve hushed them. "We need to get her out of here." She unclasped her shoes and gathered her dress so she could run. She slung an AR-16 over her shoulder and stuffed the pistol in her cleavage. "Let's go. You two bring up the rear. You have cell phones?" The bodyguards nodded. "Text for more people. Have cars as close as possible in every direction. You guys have a helicopter?" Again they nodded.

"Two, actually." Mary Ellen smiled at Eve in the way she hated.

They were three stories off the ground. The bodyguards began texting. The fall was doable, but the snipers would be waiting for that. "Get them in the air. You never answered me. How many snipers did you have?" Eve turned on Mary Ellen.

"I believe we have six."

"Four of them will be dead. Too obvious. Find out if you still have anyone in position."

Mary Ellen extracted a phone from somewhere in her ensemble, and Eve tried to recall her brief view of the outside as she'd entered this sitting-duck party. There was a walkway between the two buildings on possibly the eighth floor...and that would be the first place she'd put someone to keep Mary Ellen contained if she was running the other side of this show. Even if they got to the roof, the helicopter would be vulnerable the whole time. She formed a half-assed plan and checked the hallway. The minute the door to the office opened, an audible alarm sounded. *Shit.*

Eve motioned the bodyguards and Mary Ellen to the stairwell. Then she grabbed Mary Ellen's arm and yanked her up five flights of stairs. The guards shot the security cameras as they went, and as Eve pulled Mary Ellen back into the main building, one of them kept going. She could hear glass breaking as the fire door closed. When Eve turned back to her, Mary Ellen was out of breath. "You're bruising my arm," she panted.

"Shut up." Eve picked an office and shot the lock. The door popped open and she dragged the desk close to the air grate in the ceiling. This one was much larger. She let it flap open before pulling herself into it. She felt no vibrations, but at best they had only seconds with all the noise they were making. She pulled Mary Ellen up as the remaining bodyguard hoisted her. They were able to walk, though hunched over, through these larger ducts. The bodyguard pulled himself up to join them, and Eve could hear helicopters in the distance.

They moved along quietly until the ducts changed from a shiny silver to a dull one. Eve hoped this meant they were in the adjacent building. She found a vent and popped it out: conference room. She hopped down and checked the exits. This was definitely a different building. The guard dropped Mary Ellen down just as gunshots rang through the vent. The bodyguard returned fire. Eve grabbed Mary Ellen's arm and ran with her as alarms raged in their ears, and the sprinklers went off, drenching them.

Eve could feel their attackers getting closer. She hoped they wouldn't be tapped in to security in this new building. Mouse would have done that for Beckett, but not everyone has something even close to a Mouse.

Eve took Mary Ellen straight to the opposite side of the building. This hallway had a long window, and the next building over seemed crazy close. Eve shot the corner of the large pane of glass, then fired two more times until the glass crumbled. Mary Ellen finally looked as scared as she should have all along.

"Watch our backs." Eve grabbed an extension ladder from a nearby conference room that seemed to be undergoing renovations. She swung it around and settled it on the open window. It was sturdy. And if it could span the distance between buildings, they would have a chance.

Eve took a moment to shoot out the opposing window. It shattered, glass tinkling to the ground far below. She set her pistol down and held the ladder tight while sliding it across the divide. Finally it caught, and Eve settled it on the other building's façade. The wind was insane, whipping through the windows and ripping at their wet hair.

She motioned to Mary Ellen, then pulled out her knife and cut the woman's skirt right off her body.

"Excuse me? What the—?" Mary Ellen tried to grab her skirt. Eve heard a door open nearby.

"It would be like a sail out there. Go." Eve held end of the ladder. "I've got you."

"I'm not going out there." Mary Ellen crossed her arms.

They heard men shouting. "In here!"

Eve gave Mary Ellen an exasperated look. "Do it, damn it, or I'm shooting you."

Mary Ellen climbed out onto the ladder. She shakily started across the chasm just as Eve abandoned holding their bridge steady to climb out herself. Eve turned, set her bare feet on either side of Mary Ellen, and faced the men entering the hallway they'd just departed. She fired her gun again and again, unable to see more than shadows.

The wind caught Eve's dress and pulled her off balance. She took a knee, but still inched backward. The unusual movement shifted the ladder—one wrong move and Eve and Mary Ellen were plummeting to their deaths.

Mary Ellen crawled over the glass-strewn window ledge and into the next building. Eve stepped on the ledge and pressed her back against the façade, barely missing the ladder as it fell from underneath her.

Mary Ellen began firing, giving Eve cover as she came inside. They were running as soon as Eve had her feet on the floor.

"Call one of the 'copters and tell them to go to the roof. Tell another car to meet us in the alley."

They ran past an elevator, and Eve slapped the down button. After what seemed like an eternity, the doors opened. Once the elevator was moving, Eve motioned to Mary Ellen's shoes.

"Kick those off. Be ready to be under fire when these doors open. I'll go high and cover you."

They could hear the helicopter approaching the roof. Mary Ellen barked the orders Eve requested into her phone before sliding it back into her cleavage.

"Why are we going down?" Mary Ellen managed to look regal in just pantyhose and the top part of her dress.

"We're buying seconds. Ready? The doors are opening." Eve rolled her head on her neck and swung the AR-16 forward. But there was nothing. Silence. She pushed Mary Ellen forward and ran into the foyer of the fancy skyscraper. To her left she saw the red exit sign, and they ran for it just as the front door exploded with gunfire.

The alarms were still blaring, so opening the fire exit went unnoticed. Eve crammed Mary Ellen into the backseat of the waiting SUV, then jumped in and slammed the door behind her. "Go, go, go!" She slapped the driver in the back of the head.

He put the SUV in reverse and careened out of the alley. He ignored the rules of the road and took the least obvious path to the center of the city. Whoever he was, he was an excellent driver.

"Pull into a parking garage. We've got to toss this car." Eve leaned forward and watched as the driver ignored the ticket that came spitting out. She picked a minivan as her target.

"Right here, pull in next to it." She motioned to Mary Ellen. "Give me a second."

Eve had her gun ready to blow out the window as she tried the handle. But it was already unlocked. Mouse had taught her to always check because, damn it, some things are easier than they appear. In an instant she ripped the plastic panel out of the way and had the van purring to life. Eve moved into the driver's seat as the driver and Mary Ellen jumped in. They were moving before the driver could even close the door and she busted straight through the arm at the exit. She bounced onto the main road and commenced driving as normally as possible.

She heard Mary Ellen exhale.

Eve looked at her passengers in the rearview mirror. "Where can I take you that's safe?"

The driver spoke up. "Fifty-Ninth Street. I'll let them know we're coming."

"I'd rather go home. Take me home." Mary Ellen raised her chin.

"That's the first place they'll send people. In fact, the people there are probably already dead." Eve sat at a light, watching the pedestrians as well as the vehicles around her.

"Sir, yes. We are requesting admittance. Three." The driver ended his call. "We can go."

After a short drive, Eve turned onto 59th Street. A garage opened, and she pulled in. The minivan was instantly surrounded by armed men.

"Now I have to deal with Primo, in my father's house." Mary Ellen sounded scared *and* annoyed as she wrapped the driver's jacket around her waist.

Great.

12

Fast Food

Beckett watched the game with his dog snoring next to him. The beer was delicious — a sample dropped off by a local home-brewer. Damned if he wasn't going to order a nice batch of this shit tomorrow.

The game was interrupted by a harried newscaster. She had hair poking out all over the place. Looked like she'd just been fucked properly by someone. "Bummer that you have to be on the air now, eh, baby?" he asked her with a laugh. It was almost time for a piss break. As he got up and stretched, the newscaster got down to business.

"This is breaking news. We have some alarming updates from New York City. There's been a helicopter crash, and we have reports of a gunfight erupting in the streets." The screen filled with the remnants of the helicopter, and the soundtrack was various pops of gunfire. "Obviously, police are refusing to let the media in, but we have a cameraman filming from a nearby building. We'll report as soon as we have anything more." The newswoman had smoothed her hair while the clip was shown.

Only scumbags had firefights in the street after hours. *What on earth could be causing this kind of movement?* Back in the day, this news item would've had him on high alert, planning and plotting. He could never let his guard down. For now he was just glad it *wasn't* Poughkeepsie. He snickered as he remembered the time Eve blew up his fucking strip mall. Then, like a punch in the stomach, he missed her even more.

He sat back down with his iPad and hit all the local news websites. It was way too early for even them to speculate. He looked at his cell phone, itching to call his brothers. He felt this way any time he thought about freaking Poughkeepsie at all—for any reason. It was an addiction worse than any of the others he'd kicked in the last five years, so fucking hard to ignore the longing for them. And for her. And that's when he remembered he was selfish. If he appeared on the scene, that would make things worse instead of better. He brought shit like he was seeing on TV right along with him. He was poison, a loaded gun.

There was a frantic knocking on his front door. Gandhi twirled and slobbered himself into a frenzy, barking and rushing and falling over himself. Beckett tried to get him to quiet down and failed. He turned on the porch light and saw Chery and another woman. When he opened the door Chery pushed her way in, pulling the other woman, who refused to look at him, with her. She closed the door and locked the deadbolt as Beckett picked up Gandhi. She looked everywhere but at him, so it was a moment before Beckett could see Chery's face. Gandhi ceased barking and tried to lick the women from his place in Beckett's arms.

"Did Jared do this to you?" Beckett felt his anger surge.

Chery ignored him and turned to the other woman. "Vere? Listen. Look at me. Vere, look at me."

Vere reluctantly moved her gaze from the dog to her sister's face.

"I'm going to get your clock and your book. Tonight you sleep here and wake up here. Then I'll take you to work tomorrow. And tomorrow is a horse day, right?"

Chery waited until her sister nodded.

Vere finally spoke, her voice a bit higher than Beckett was expecting. "My boots."

"Yes, I'll grab your boots too, okay?" Chery looked at Beckett. "Is it okay for Vere to play with Gandhi? I've told her all about how he likes the store and loves to play fetch."

Beckett played along with Chery's feigned happiness. "Sure." He set the dog down so he could sniff the ladies and wag his stump. Beckett grabbed a tennis ball out of his spoiled dog's basket and tossed it down the hallway. Gandhi ran and slid to get it and brought it back. He dropped it at Beckett's feet. Beckett held the ball out to Vere. "Would you like to try?"

Chery gently touched her sister's shoulder. "It's okay."

Vere took the ball from Beckett, careful not to touch his hand. She threw it gently, too softly, but Gandhi went after it all the same, then dropped it at Vere's feet.

After a few tosses, Beckett offered them both a drink. Only Chery accepted, and she followed him into his kitchen. He filled a glass of ice water from the dispenser in his fridge and lifted an eyebrow as he handed it to her.

"My face is bad?" She put the glass up to her bruised cheek and winced.

Beckett saw only red. He closed his eyes as adrenaline became a pounding force, making all his choices for him.

"I'm sorry. I'm sorry I know where you live, that I burst in here with my sister. I can't have her see him like that. He scares her. You're disgusted. I'll leave. I'm sorry." Chery put her glass on the counter.

"Please don't apologize. You're safe here. I'm glad you came." Beckett was sure his words sounded awful and insincere, as they had to pass through his gritted teeth.

"If Vere could stay tonight, I'm going to go get her stuff real quick. She loves dogs, and I won't be more than a half hour. Is that okay?" She ran her hand through her hair, hitting so many knots she gave up.

Someone had dragged this woman by her hair, Beckett would bet on it.

"No." He exhaled. "You're making a list, and I'll go get what you guys need."

"I couldn't ask that. Thank you but…" She put her hand to her split lip and looked at it. There was blood there.

Beckett handed her a paper towel. "Here. Do you need to go to the hospital?"

She shook her head. "He's just not right tonight. It's mostly my fault. He hates chicken, and I made it because it's what I had left, and then I burnt the edges on the grill. I'll just pick him up some Wendy's and grab Vere's stuff, and then I'll be back." She looked toward the door to the hallway as Gandhi slobbered past, focused on getting the ball. "She's wanted to meet your dog for a while. It was the only way I was able to get her here."

"Chery?" Slowly she looked at him. She had a pretty face normally, though her sweet hazel eyes always looked a little sad despite the makeup she applied. "You're not going back there tonight." He held up a finger to stop the protest on her lips. "You're making a list, and I'm going to get that stuff for you and Vere. I have a nice upstairs bedroom and bathroom. Go take a shower. Get your sister settled."

"Beckett, he's mean right now, and I know you're a strong guy and everything, but he can be…unpredictable on a night like tonight." Chery hugged herself. "I need to go back or it'll get worse." She looked seriously spooked, and damn if she was hundred pounds soaking wet.

"Do you love him?" Beckett watched Gandhi fly down the hall again.

Her answer was quiet. "Sometimes."

He nodded. Damned vicious circle. He'd seen it before. Hookers that came from asshole pimps. She was fighting a battle in her head between what she wanted and what she needed. Sometimes any attention cranked up to a desperate level felt like love.

"Can you please make a list? I won't make it worse. Okay?" Beckett got her a pad of paper and a pen.

Chery looked toward the dog and then to the paper. "You think I'm stupid to put up with this."

"No. I think you need some things from your house to get through tonight. And once that's settled, you can process. I'm not going to ask you to leave him, to make anything different. I just want to make sure tonight that you and Vere are safe." She was still a bit hesitant, but he wasn't sure that would ever change. "He can't hurt me. Okay?"

She exhaled and wrote down the things Vere needed and then her address.

Beckett slipped on his boots and leather jacket. "I'm setting the alarm, okay? Don't let Gandhi talk you into walking him. He's fine."

"I'm having second thoughts about this. Never mind." Chery held out her hand for the list.

Beckett took her offered hand and held it. "You listen to me. I can do this. I have a few hidden talents I'll be using for your benefit tonight."

She shook her head, and her eyes filled with tears. "See, he'll accuse me of sleeping with you and then…And I've got Vere to worry about."

Beckett gently touched the side of her face that didn't have a bruise. She still flinched. "Just breathe. You worry all the time about everyone else. I've got this. You can just breathe."

Beckett left through the back door, locking the ladies in and setting the alarm from his key chain. He took his Challenger this time, and although he had weapons tucked all over the car out of habit, he didn't plan to use them.

A little ways down the road he pulled around the Wendy's drive-thru and got the hugest hamburger he could order with an equally huge Coke. The entire rest of the ride to Chery's house he reminded himself not to kill the motherfucker. It was going to be hard. And honestly, he was having trouble promising himself anything. The thought of that asshole using Chery as a punching bag lit something on fire in him. When he pictured her beaten, coaxing her sister out of her little happy den with the promise of his dog, something broke open in him that he'd had sealed shut for a while.

He pulled up to a rundown brick house with all the lights off. His headlights bounced off a smaller building in the back as he swung in the drive, then focused on the porch. He left them on because they illuminated Jared.

The asshole had a rifle sitting on his lap and a cigarette dangling out of his mouth. Beckett could almost taste the blood he wanted on his tongue. He got out of his car and turned to grab the monster bag of food.

"Hungry?" Beckett held up the meal.

"You're the asshat that's fucking my girl." Jared stayed seated on his front porch.

"She burned your chicken. And you don't even like chicken." Beckett walked up to Jared as if he were an invited guest. "Can I sit? Thanks."

"You're trespassing. I'm gonna call the cops." Jared took another puff from his smoke.

"Sure. You wanna borrow my phone?" Beckett smiled. "Here, take the sandwich. I got you a drink too. You like those?"

"Ya probably poisoned them. I'll tell you what—you leave now and I won't give you a brand new asshole with my rifle. But I am fucking hungry," he added after a moment. Jared took the hamburger out of its wrapper and took a huge bite.

Beckett waited while the man chewed noisily and swallowed.

"And this is better than the shit she tried to serve me. Too busy with that sister of hers." Jared went to take another bite.

Beckett moved so quickly Jared was probably already pinned to the porch with his rifle threaded between his arms before he knew anyone had moved. Beckett kneeled on the rifle with one knee and with the other kept Jared's legs immobile.

"The fuck? Get off me!" Jared was incensed.

Beckett just smiled as he peeled off the first layer of the triple-decker burger. The next time the man opened his mouth to protest, Beckett shoved the burger in, hard. Jared's eyes widened.

"You've some learning to do. Understand?" Beckett waited.

The hamburger gagged Jared, who now actively worked to prevent himself from choking.

"You will treat her like a queen for as long as she wants you. Her sister is your king. She needs it? You do it." Beckett watched as disobedience flashed through Jared's eyes. He shook his head. "We're off to a bad start. Let me rephrase that."

Beckett picked up the huge drink and squeezed it a bit to pop the lid off. He tilted Jared's head and hammered the hamburger down deeper into his throat. When Beckett started pouring the soda in Jared's nostrils, he watched the man get as close to his maker as he'd probably ever been.

He stopped and let Jared cough out the burger to get a deep, wet breath. After he gasped back to life, Beckett tilted his head. "I'm curious how fucking hardheaded you are. Now tell me how you're going to treat Chery and Vere." Beckett readjusted his weight to dig the rifle harder into the soft parts of Jared's arms.

"You're insane. I love Chery and…"

Beckett pulled off the second layer of the burger and looked at Jared. He clamped down his jaws and tried to lock them in place. But when Beckett found the soft tissue near Jared's ear and pressed, the man's jaw popped open. When the food was crammed in place and he started with the soda again, the man grew frantic.

"Can you see Jesus yet?" Beckett allowed the man to cough up the burger again. He turned Jared's head to the side just as he puked up the contents of his stomach. "You're disgusting. Now tell me again how you're going to treat Chery and Vere." Beckett sat back on his haunches a bit, compressing Jared's legs enough to likely render them numb.

"Chery's my queen and the retard is my king. Right, right? Wait, no. I'm Chery's queen?"

Beckett looked into the night and exhaled. He began muttering, "I will not kill him. I will not kill him. I will not kill him. Aww, fuck."

Beckett took the last layer of burger and fought Jared until he'd inserted it into his windpipe. "I *hate* the word retard," he told him. "If that word was a person I'd kill him."

Jared's eyes tried to apologize. Beckett picked up the soda, which had just a few mouthfuls left, and brought the cup to Jared's nose.

"You know, they say fast food's not good for you."

13

Rose-Petal Soap

Eve got out of the minivan in front of a strangely nondescript building and put her hands up. The armed men frisked her and took both her knife and the gun she'd tucked into the top of her dress. The driver was disarmed as well. Then they were hustled into the entry area, where one of the men handed Mary Ellen a pair of sweatpants. She slipped them on under the driver's jacket.

"Follow her," a guard instructed.

Eve nodded, and she and the driver trailed after Mary Ellen. As they passed through a few different sets of doors, it became apparent that Mary Ellen's father owned the whole building and he was using it as his residence. This man had the kind of money that ruled small countries.

"Mary Ellen! Is this you? You did this?" The man headed at them wore a velvet robe, monogrammed with PV. He pointed at an enormous television where a picture of the building that had hosted Mary Ellen's gathering filled the screen. The place was a wreck.

"Primo, listen, it's been a long night. I don't want to talk about it." Mary Ellen tried to brush past her brother.

Eve stood back and surveyed the scene. Primo was an incomplete kind of handsome. If his father had put in just three more thrusts, Primo would have been movie-star gorgeous. But instead he was just shy of getting laid like a rock star.

"Father is going to have *another* stroke when he finds out about this. What the hell were you trying to do? What did you think would happen?" Primo twirled and sat in an expensive, high-backed chair. He spread his legs enough for Eve to shift her gaze away. Dude did not have pants on.

"He won't find out about it, *Primo*. Why would you intentionally upset him that way? And anyway, who's to say this wasn't part of my plan? Please. I had an exit strategy. January and Leon are professionals, and I knew they'd get me out. Everything went according to design." Mary Ellen went to the bar in the luxurious living room and poured a glass of wine.

Eve kept her face neutral, not letting on that Mary Ellen had been in a giant clusterfuck of crazy and barely gotten out by the skin of her tits.

"January? She looks like one of your showgirls. And I know Leon's a good driver, but did you see the mess? That's half of midtown shut down, and dad's helicopter is ashes, twatness. What if they track that back to us? How many of your guys got arrested?" Primo stood and stomped over to grab her wine glass.

Panic ran across Mary Ellen's face briefly, but she dug deep and recovered. "Since when do you care at all what I do, Primo? Since when do you care about anyone but yourself? While Daddy is ill, someone needs to be thinking about the future of our business."

"Is that what you think you're doing?" he countered. Mary Ellen gave him a curt nod and he opened his mouth to speak again, but then abruptly closed it. He appeared to think for a moment. "You know what? You want a whack at running dad's business? Have at it. Go nuts. We all know who will carry on his legacy. That'd be me. *His son.*"

Having said his piece, Primo turned and looked Eve up and down like she might be a prospect for his evening.

"I didn't ask for your opinion," Mary Ellen announced. "And I will not allow you to upset our father's recovery by sharing your speculations. Just keep them to yourself and try not to piss Daddy's money away in the casinos." With that, she turned on her heel and waved everyone out of the room before stomping upstairs.

Eve nodded and followed Leon down the hall to the guest quarters. They walked into the suite—two bedrooms with an adjoining bathroom and shared living room—and Leon closed the door.

"You're a decent driver." He took his tie off.

Eve glanced around the room, seeing plenty of places where audio and video equipment could be hidden. "Back at you."

Mary Ellen knocked on the door, still in her mismatched outfit. "I suggest you lock the door if you don't want a visit from Primo later," she told Eve. "I'll expect to speak with you again first thing in the morning."

Eve just waited. Mary Ellen was still putting on an act. Obviously she knew the place was wired.

"Thank you." Eve would have said, "fuck you" with the same amount of venom. "But I'm leaving. Have one of those guys show me out. I have places to go. And I want my knife."

Mary Ellen shook her head. "No, I want you to stay."

"I've got some loose ends of *your plan* to tie up. I want to make sure none of your people turn on you." Eve stepped around Mary Ellen and opened the door.

The woman whispered, now that Eve was so close. "I don't trust you."

Eve turned and looked her full in the face. "That's the smartest thing you've said all night."

As she anticipated, she was met in the hallway by guards. "Just get me to street level."

"No, miss. We're instructed to get you far from here before letting you out." The two burly men escorted her to a much larger garage where an extremely convincing replica of a city cab waited with the door open, its windows treated with dark tinting. She slid in and one of the guards handed her back her knife before he closed the door. The driver looked at her in the rearview mirror.

"Can you take me to Poughkeepsie?" Eve closed her eyes and massaged her temples.

Mary Ellen stood in her room at her father's house. She'd waited until this very moment to let the panic flow through her. She sank to the floor and almost convulsed with shivers as she ran through the close calls she'd endured tonight.

It was a good half hour before she got up off the floor and went into her bathroom to shower off the fear and adrenaline. The water was perfect, but as she lathered up with rose-petal soap, memories assaulted her. It had been months since she spent time in this house, and the last time she was here it was with him. Sevan: the love of her life and the man who'd torn her heart to shreds. It felt like just moments ago she'd been meeting him for dinner.

It always took her forever to decide what to wear when she knew she'd be seeing him. That night she'd settled on a pale purple pencil skirt. She'd tried on quite a few, but this one seemed to flatter her eyes the best. The maître d' nodded and welcomed her warmly.

She touched his arm as he moved to place her menu on a center table, where she normally preferred to sit. "I'm expecting company." She discreetly pointed instead to a secluded table in the corner.

He nodded and made the change, holding out her chair for her. She thanked him demurely.

Sevan was late. With any other man Mary Ellen would have left—and possibly asked Daddy to have the gentleman disciplined for her disappointment. But Sevan was different, so different he sounded every single alarm in her head. And his dark eyes and quick grin sounded all the alarms she had below the waist.

She forced herself not to look around the restaurant, searching for him. She didn't want to appear eager. She slid her phone out of her purse and checked for texts. She had none. Sevan had turned her into a sniveling schoolgirl.

Her view of her phone was obscured by a single white rose. She recognized his strong forearm and inhaled her relief. The rose smelled wonderful. She felt him press his lips to her cheek, and she smiled.

"Mary Ellen." His voice was perfection, so deep and inviting. He stepped around her and winked.

"Mr. Harmon." She took the rose from him and nodded.

"So formal. What have I done?" He simultaneously took his seat and control of the table, signaling the waiter. "Two glasses of Dom Perignon and an order of calamari." He turned his attention back to her. "Were you afraid I'd forgotten? That I found myself in the arms of another? Surely a woman as lovely as you would be so very confident."

He bit his lip as he looked at her, as if he were admiring art. It was a practiced move, and she saw right through him, but found herself blushing just the same.

After the champagne was poured, Mary Ellen held up her glass for his toast.

"To your beauty."

She tapped her glass to his, locking eyes.

Her father had warned her against falling in love. Her brother said he'd heard horrible things about Sevan. But Primo was always saying things like that, looking for ways to make her unhappy. Sevan couldn't be all that different from her family, she told herself. After all, he'd come into her life through a business deal.

Based in South America, Sevan had approached her father with a request for weapons to be used by his personnel working in the United States. "Protection," he explained simply. And he needed a professional like Rodolfo Vitullo because his employees had passports from every country under the sun. This made things...*complicated*, and he needed help...*streamlining* the process of getting them outfitted. Mary Ellen recalled how her father's eyes had narrowed for a moment as he listened to Sevan's request. But rather than ask any questions, he just nodded and escorted the man into another room, leaving her behind. As always.

Still, Mary Ellen found ways to cross Sevan's path whenever she could. She arranged to bump into him after his meetings with Daddy. Sevan's ardor was intense, and she fell hard for every bit of it. He was ambitious. She knew that from how hard he worked at courting her.

Sevan was tall enough that she'd had to crane her neck to look at him when they walked together, and he was young enough to know all the latest fashions and unheard of bands. He made her feel alive and naughty. They often walked the streets of Manhattan after their dinners with Sevan's arm thrown around her shoulders, like the lovers they were. Like young lovers.

She didn't miss his appreciative glances at other women. He sometimes turned his head to catch a particularly enchanting receding figure. He would notice her attention and always have a quick compliment.

"She has nothing on you, baby. Nothing on you." He would brush his lips across her forehead.

She knew he'd marked her as his. He took her to event after event, paraded her around. Her father took notice and offered warnings. Her brother ignored her.

But with Sevan, her heart raced. In his bed he pleased her more than she'd known was possible. Just thinking about the orgasms she'd been treated to at his hands was distracting. It made her angry with the other lovers in her life, those who hadn't known how her body worked. But he knew. How much she needed, how deep it had to be, the praise, the dirty talk—everything about him worked for her. Her love now mixed so completely with lust she knew she'd never tell them apart.

As the months went by, they'd grown closer, and Sevan began to talk with her—as if she understood things, as if she were an equal—in a way her father and Primo rarely ever did. She learned that Sevan's business was *importing pharmaceuticals*, as he liked to call it. He was always so suave and polite. But he couldn't help but brag a bit as he explained how he'd developed an elaborate system over the years to filter his products into NYC without a big base operation set up there. Poughkeepsie was the gem of his route because it was perfectly situated: just far enough from the city to stay out of the spotlight, but connected to it by any form of transit you might want. "*And*," he liked to say, "*there are just enough lowlifes there to keep the cops busy with other things*."

As they became more entwined, Mary Ellen had confided in Sevan, the only one who seemed to understand her at all. She'd told him her deepest fears about being left out of the business as her father grew older, how he sometimes favored Primo even though he had no head for business at all. Sevan was always sympathetic, always encouraging. He forced her to realize her father's confidence in her—the way he allowed her to introduce herself to clients. Sevan urged her to build on that, to become more of a presence in the office, demand to be a part of her father's business meetings.

But even as he reassured her, there were signs: missed dates, unexplained absences. There were steps she knew she should take with Sevan, ways she needed to protect herself. But whenever she broached the topic, he would melt her with his delicious lips and strong hands. Still, she'd refused to tell him how much she loved him. And he never uttered anything but praise that was one size fits all.

The day Daddy had his stroke, Mary Ellen had felt she'd had one as well. But at the hospital, just after hearing the dire news, Sevan had appeared. He'd kept a comforting hand at her lower back and asked questions she'd not had the forethought to ask. He brought her water. Lover's actions, all of them. But at the time, they'd barely registered.

Her concern for her father was more than just his health. His empire was a huge, towering nightmare, and she could not imagine what would happen if. . .Not that Daddy wouldn't recover — of course he would — but decisive action needed to be taken. It was then that Sevan had planted the seed: She should take this opportunity to make some adjustments so she couldn't be cut out of the business any longer. Otherwise Primo would take over — maybe sooner rather than later — and she'd be out forever. Primo wasn't about to share with her, to let her have a say in anything. He'd always hated her.

Empowered by Sevan, Mary Ellen's mind had begun to turn. Along with keeping the company in line, her show of strength would surely impress Rodolfo once he'd recovered enough to understand her reasoning. And either way, he'd have no choice. If she held access to the money, she'd have to be part of the decision-making from now on. So, with Sevan's guidance, she'd managed to move several chunks of money into new accounts.

When the last transaction cleared and Mary Ellen had assured Sevan she could not access any more of her father's fortune, her lover had stopped coming by, stopped checking on her and her father. She refused for a week to even consider that Sevan had betrayed her. But when she finally rang the bank to check on the accounts, they all had the same horrible number as a balance: zero. Nothing. He'd taken every last dime.

It hurt so deeply to know that her trust had been plundered, and her father's money as well, but it got worse. So much worse. When Sevan finally contacted her, instead of an apology, his lips spilled over with blackmail demands. He wanted her to do whatever he said, get him whatever he wanted, or once Rodolfo recovered, he'd tell him she tried to make a move on the company while he was critically ill. And the paperwork would support his story. Even worse, Primo would be beside himself, preening and gloating over her demise.

But in that moment, something inside her shifted and Mary Ellen knew she would never cave to Sevan's threats. She cried — sure, she cried — but her tears fell on words she wrote: a master plan to ruin

Sevan's business and get her father's money back. And she would do it all before Rodolfo returned to work.

She stepped back, out of the overhead stream for a moment, and forced her hand to unclench its death grip on the handheld sprayer. She'd been busy in the ensuing days, snooping through Daddy's lists of contacts and plying all her charms and skills to serve her purposes. And tonight should have gone perfectly, would have gone perfectly, but Sevan had tainted it. She'd recognized two of the dead bodies in the bathroom air vent. Sevan's bodyguards had stood like two gargoyles outside their boudoir so many times during their affair, their faces were almost as familiar as his.

Of course there were ways to fix this, and she had gained some valuable information this evening. But as she stepped out of the shower, all she could remember was the time Sevan had taken her on the bed she was about to lay in alone.

14

Dancing Dongs

Beckett got everything on the list, then went to Chery's room and got her some damn clothes too. And makeup. She'd want to cover her shiner the way she always did after nights like this.

On his way out, he looked at Jared's limp body on the porch. The fuck knuckle was still alive...well, at least last time he'd checked he was. Beckett tossed the stuff in his car and went back just to make sure he didn't have to smack him back to life. The woman-beater was boneless. Beckett took Jared's rifle, now unloaded, and set it in his backseat before finally checking that the shit was still breathing. He was. Beckett pinched him in the armpit until the man came to. When Jared's eyes finally focused, fear shaped his whole expression.

"I didn't kill you," Beckett said. "Remember that. I made that choice tonight. Now say thank you, you filthy motherfucker. Before I change my mind."

Jared burped and seemed to try to make sense of things. "What? Yeah. You're welcome? No. Thank you?"

Beckett stood and walked back to his car. As he pulled out, he smiled and waved at the jackass. On the ride home he congratulated himself on not killing the sperm bucket, and he took a quick detour to launch the wiped-down rifle into a crappy, muddy lake. Then he mentally reviewed the injuries he'd inflicted on Jared. He might have bruising on his arms where the rifle had pinned him down, but for the most part Beckett had been a clean convincer. Not quite as good as Eve, but not bad.

A few minutes later he pulled into his driveway and heard G barking his little ass off. He hoped Vere wasn't spooked. After disabling the alarm from his keychain, Beckett walked in with their bags of things.

"I grabbed shopping bags from your kitchen. I couldn't find luggage. Hope that was okay?" Beckett watched as his dog offered Vere his tummy.

Chery stood and nodded. "Can you help me take them upstairs?"

"Sure." Beckett scooped up the bags.

Before following Chery up the stairs he added, "My dog's fallen in love with you, Vere."

The woman froze and looked at the floor.

Chery turned. "Vere, please tell Beckett what you think of Gandhi."

Finally the woman put her stunning blue eyes on Beckett, just a little shy of meeting his gaze. "I like the dog. Thank you."

Beckett nodded. "Awesome."

Chery went the rest of way up the stairs, and Beckett followed her into the guest bedroom.

"Are you okay?" she whispered.

"I'm fine. Here's your stuff." Beckett put the bags on the bed.

"Was he…mad?" Chery covered her mouth, like even mentioning that Jared got angry was a secret she was sharing.

"He and I came to an understanding. He knows you and I are friends, and that's going to be okay." Beckett waited.

Chery exhaled. "Leaving can't be that easy."

"It probably won't be. You've got feelings for him. But if you decide you're done? It will be that easy. I'll make sure of it." He turned toward the door.

"Why are you doing this?" Chery hugged herself as suspicion showed in her eyes.

He got it. She was probably not used to a guy just being a human being. "I used to be a bad guy—not a woman-beater like drizzle nuts over there, but not good either. I'm trying to be different. You and your sister are safe here, if that's what's got you worried." He walked down to the main floor and reset his alarm. He could sense Chery drifting back downstairs behind him.

"Ladies, I'm off to bed. Chery, text me if you need anything, and feel free to eat anything in the kitchen." Beckett walked down the hallway to his bedroom, and Gandhi reluctantly tore himself away from Vere to follow.

He normally didn't call it a day this damn early, but he wanted to give them some privacy. He put the dog on the bed and sat next to him with his laptop. Tonight had been like a hit on a crack pipe. Doing the right damn thing felt wonderful, but getting to use some physical methods to accomplish it had felt so fucking good he could just cry like a pussy.

He missed his brothers. *Damn it.* He brought up Google and punched Blake's name in. The first link was a birth notice. He clicked on it, knowing he was weak. There was a picture of the baby, who looked like a smooshed-up old man, and then Beckett read the words: "Blake and Livia Hartt and big sister Emme welcomed Kellan Beckett Hartt on December fifteenth. He weighed eight pounds, two ounces, and was twenty-two inches long." He rested his head against his headboard and closed his eyes. Good God, that kid was already a couple months old. He missed Poughkeepsie so damn much.

On Saturday morning, Ryan woke up early and surveyed the drying tampons on his ceiling. Trish still had his key, which was turning out to suck, but he didn't want to deal with his annoying landlord to get his lock changed. God bless Trish—she was as inventive as she was crazy. Last night she'd brought at least ten boxes of tampons into his apartment and wet them down. Then she'd transformed the cathedral ceiling in his living room into a *tamponscape*. He didn't have a ladder, which she knew, so the tampons would be there until they dried up and fell on his head. *Awesome.* That ruled out getting lucky with any other chicks until the feminine products were gone.

In the last ten days he'd visited as many crapholes as he could find in Poughkeepsie without being too goddamn obvious. He even did some tongue jousting with a fairly filthy hooker on a major street. He turned on the TV and watched a helicopter burning as it crashed in New York City. As a cop, his first instinct was always to think terrorism when he saw smoke and buildings. But after listening to the report, it seemed more like a crazy gun battle. If that was Poughkeepsie, he'd be all over it. Instead he just watched the flames peter out while the newscaster sensationalized everything.

One of his "special" cell phones rang. He'd purchased a few disposable ones at the start of his assignment. The number was unavailable, but he answered it anyway, expecting another telemarketer.

"You need to stop dicking around or you're going to get all of us fucking killed." The voice sounded computerized. It had been altered somehow.

"Suck my ass." Ryan waited to see where disobedience got him.

"Cops like you don't last long." The voice sounded disembodied.

He couldn't glean any emotion or background noises as clues. "Says who?"

The laugh sounded more like a bark with the distortion. Probably a free fucking app. "Just leave."

"I'll go wherever I fucking want. I'm above the law, and I sure as shit don't listen to coward-ass vaginas who can't even use their real voices." Ryan didn't hang up.

"She's not my boss, but you best listen." The call ended.

"That was weird." He'd have to let the guys at work analyze this phone. He got up to check the notes on his computer. He wanted to track which places he'd given out that particular phone's number, but as he neared his desk, he stopped in his tracks. His screen saver was dongs—hundreds of them bouncing across his monitor. And worse, each dick had either his or a member of his family's face on the tip. Dancing Dongs would make a great band name. It was less delightful as a screen saver. He wiggled the mouse to make the picture go away, only to see Trish had set a particularly veiny one with his mother's face on it as his wallpaper.

"Bitch." Ryan pulled up his spreadsheet. At least she'd left Poseidon alone. He'd left his ammunition out next to the fish, hoping to send her a clear message.

He smiled to himself, proud to have one-upped her at least on that, when he felt the wet slap of a tampon coming loose from the ceiling and landing on his head.

15

Insane Bitch

When Eve returned to Mary Ellen's house in Somers a few days after the debacle, she was surprised to see it still standing. Security had been beefed up even more, but she was buzzed through anyway. She wore jeans and a T-shirt under her coat—simple, non-threatening clothes. Still, she was surprised when she wasn't frisked.

On her way through the foyer, she noted ten new men. One directed her into the freaking ballroom, which was apparently where Mary Ellen preferred to do business. The room had flickering candles on every table despite the lack of an actual event. It was the middle of the day.

"January. Welcome home. You and I have quite a bit to discuss. Ladies, please go to your rooms."

As they passed, Eve noted that Micki was among them, though she seemed to have some wounds on her arm. There were less than a handful of ladies left now. Eve crossed her arms and waited to see what was next from this insane bitch.

Mary Ellen sighed. "I do suppose you deserve some credit for what you did the other night. But how about money instead?" She sent a quick text on her phone and one of her guards entered with an envelope.

The man handed the envelope to Eve. She didn't bother to open it, but she examined him as he turned to leave. He had a scar under his right eye—one so obvious, even a scared little girl would notice it. She marked him as an enemy in her head. Someday she would make him pay.

Mary Ellen smirked. "I'm sure you'll be pleased. Go ahead, count it."

Eve stepped to the nearest table and held the envelope over the candle's flame. The paper blackened before catching. Mary Ellen's eyes widened in surprise. Eve let the flames lick her fingers far past what was sensible before dropping it on the floor and stamping it out. What had been a sizeable stack of money was now black ash.

"I don't want your money." Eve crossed her arms again.

Mary Ellen tapped her first finger on her lips. "So I can't trust you, and I can't pay you. What's keeping me from just eliminating you?"

"As I've mentioned before, try me." Eve tilted her head a bit.

"Burning that money is an act of war. Surely you know that." Mary Ellen stood and stepped closer.

"Or an act of loyalty like you've never seen before. Perspective is everything." Eve smiled. "We have a common enemy."

An odd shadow passed over Mary Ellen's face, but she quickly composed herself. "Okay. I've an assignment for you. We'll let the outcome of that decide your fate, shall we?" She went to the table again and picked up a manila envelope.

Eve did rip this one open and scanned the information. *Finally.* The file was on a Poughkeepsie cop. She studied the papers and pictures for a moment, then slid them back into the envelope. She walked back over and lit it with the same candle that had destroyed the money.

Mary Ellen was furious. "Do you have some sort of mental problem? Or a death wish? Both?"

Eve shook her head. "Are you an amateur? Never keep hard copies." She took a deep breath and rattled off Ryan Morales's address, social security number, and badge number. "He's been on the force six years and has been known to frequent pawn shops, strip clubs, and four known drug dealers' houses. He likes brunettes and has type O-positive blood. Did I miss anything?"

Mary Ellen narrowed her eyes. "Fine. Seek him out. Become his girlfriend. I want pictures of the inside of his apartment, details on his favorite sexual position, and information on anyone he loves. We're buying him. You're— "

Eve interrupted, "Providing insurance. I know how the game is played. I'll be in touch." She turned and wondered if she'd make it out the front door without a bullet in her back.

Ryan stood in line at Starbucks to get his usual fix. He should've been preparing to spend his weekend in the worst parts of the city, but damn it, he was going to speak fake Italian and feel like a yuppie douche for a few freaking minutes first. He dug through his wallet to find his gold card and nearly dropped it when an iPhone damn near exploded at his feet. As he bent down to retrieve it, he noted two very promising black high heels. He said a silent prayer that the picture his mind had drummed up to match the sexy shoes would prove accurate.

The legs were long and shapely, and just past the beautiful knees came a black skirt—an inch shorter than sensible. He almost moaned. Her white shirt had one too many buttons open, and the face waiting for the now-broken iPhone? Even his imagination wasn't active enough to come up with a face that damn gorgeous.

She was shaking her head. "I took it out of its case for two seconds to clean it. Now look at it." She held out her hand and winced. "Sorry. Didn't mean to throw my phone at you."

"It's okay." Ryan was thrilled to find his voice still worked.

The barista interrupted. "Next, please?"

Ryan gestured. "Can I buy you your coffee? Make up a little for your destroyed phone?"

"I couldn't. Plus, I'm a total wuss and get hot cocoa." She smiled at him and Ryan's pants felt like they were on fire. Her long black hair swept forward and covered one stunning blue eye.

"I'll have a venti Caramel Macchiato and a venti hot chocolate." Ryan turned to her. "Is that okay?"

She laughed. "Thanks."

Ryan gave his name and waited with the gorgeous woman for their order.

"So, I hope you have your boyfriend's number memorized." He pointed at the shattered phone in her hand.

"You're smooth." She smiled like she wasn't offended.

"Sorry. That obvious?"

She nodded toward the counter, and he found the barista had called his name and he'd not even heard it. He grabbed her drink and a coffee sleeve for her. He bare-handed his piping-hot cardboard so he'd look tougher.

"Can we sit? Do you have somewhere to be?" She motioned to an empty table.

"Yes—I mean, yes we can sit. And no to having somewhere to be. I mean, other than work, and that can wait." He put down the drinks and pulled out her chair just in time for her to sit.

She smiled. "So where do you work?"

He looked her up and down. Her outfit said expensive business-woman. He hoped she wouldn't look down on his profession. "I'm a cop." He waited to see if she would be crestfallen.

"Really? Wow."

He couldn't read her. She took a sip of her drink.

"And you do?" he asked. *Me. Please say me.*

"I'm in import and export, which sounds pretty exciting. It's not. I'm in town to visit my dad." She looked out the window, concern passing over her pretty face.

"So how's ol' dad holding up?" Ryan tried not to choke on his coffee and pay attention to her answer. She'd hugged herself, and her cleavage now monopolized his line of sight. *Don't look. Don't look. Fuck. Looked. Stop looking.*

"He's recovering. Almost all the way recovered. Scared me this time." She bit her bottom lip.

His copness helped him ask the next question, thank God. "Was he ill?"

"No, he was attacked. Won't tell me by who. He's the nicest guy. It doesn't make sense. He's insisting he fell."

She leveled her gaze at him. He felt like he was being analyzed.

"Here? In my town?" Ryan really looked away from her boobs now.

She shrugged. "I'm assuming. He doesn't want me involved."

"I don't blame him." Ryan sat back in his chair. He'd seen no report of an older man being assaulted recently, and he'd been watching for shit like this.

Fire flashed in her eyes before she closed them. "Listen, didn't mean to dump my concerns on you. You just have that kind of face, I guess. Thanks for the hot cocoa." She stood.

Ryan stood as well, trying not to scramble in surprise. *She's leaving.*

"Hey, I didn't mean to offend you. Seriously. You're concerned. Is there any way I can help?" He waited as she seemed to try to make up her mind.

"Maybe you could to talk to him? See if he'll tell you what happened?" She covered her mouth as if she couldn't believe she'd asked.

"Sure. How about now? You busy?" Ryan held her hot cocoa out to her.

"Not with anything that can't wait." She looked excited.

He followed her out the door to her sweet Audi.

She opened her door. "Do you want to just follow me? Although, having a police officer follow me makes me nervous—will I leave my blinker on? Am I going too fast?" She wrinkled her nose when she laughed.

He took a breath and looked her dead in the eyes. "It's okay. I'd never let anything bad happen to you."

She looked away, and his cop radar went up. This lady was working through something, but she slid immediately back into an upbeat mood.

"Listen, it's right across town," she said, no trace of strain in her voice. "He's going back to work tomorrow, and I just want to keep him safe."

"Sure. I'll follow you..." He left the sentence dangling and held his hands palms out.

"Eve." She rolled her eyes at him.

"I'll follow you, Eve. Just don't run any lights." Ryan pulled out his keys and turned toward his truck. "Crap." It was covered in bright yellow Post-it notes.

Eve came to stand next to him. "Wow. Is that your ride?" There was laughter in her voice.

"Yeah. Just give me a second to peel those off."

She followed him over to his car, and he wanted it to explode all action-movie style when he saw that Trish had scrawled helpful little tidbits on each note: *Momma's boy. Afraid of lobsters. Pissed his pants in third grade!*

"You know what? How about you give me your dad's address and I'll meet you there in like ten minutes?" Ryan watched as her eyes slid over the notes.

"Vindictive ex?" She smiled at him.

"You could say that." He knew he was blushing. And dying.

Eve pulled off the *Momma's boy.* note and flipped it over. She produced a pen from her bag and wrote an address on it. "Hate to see all this wasted paper," she said.

"Yeah." He had nothing to say. Anything he'd ever confided to Trish was probably written behind him.

Eve stepped closer and tucked the Post-it in his jacket pocket. He couldn't breathe. "In my experience, women get insane when they realize their ex was epic in bed. They'll do anything to get him back." She patted his pocket before walking back to her Audi.

Ryan watched her every step—the heels, the skirt, the flowing hair—as she turned and winked at him. He engraved it on his man brain. The wind picked up, and he could smell her perfume as she got in her car and pulled away. She even drove sexy.

Once Eve was out of sight, he turned and faced his truck. Nothing to do but shake his head and start peeling. If he didn't let his dick do the thinking—and that was proving to be tough—he'd suspect Eve of being a little bit too nice and her iPhone explosion a little too convenient.

"Fuck." He punched to hood of his truck, and a Post-it stuck to his hand. Ryan hated that he couldn't turn his cop brain off. And that it was probably right.

Eve waited at the stoplight. Ryan was a good cop. She could tell after meeting him, and she'd assumed as much from the reports she'd seen. He hadn't started hanging around crap joints until after her father had been beaten down. It was obvious Ryan had been assigned to appear like a creepy asswipe.

Bringing him to her father was a test. But she really didn't need it. The kindness in his eyes was not a lie. He might still prove useful, though. She tapped her hands on the steering wheel until the light turned green. A few minutes later she pulled to a stop in front of her dad's building. After freshening her lipstick, she got out of the Audi just as Ryan's defiled truck came to a stop behind her.

He hopped out and gave her an embarrassed smile. "Sorry about that."

"It's okay. You missed one though." Eve pointed to the bright yellow corner sticking out of his grill.

Ryan pulled it off, read it, and grumbled before sticking it in his pocket. "I feel so cool right now. I mean, stand back and take notes."

"I'll do that. Listen, I didn't tell him you're coming so..." She shrugged.

"So he's going to think we're dating?" Ryan finished her thought.

"Is that okay? I mean, crazy lady lures you to her dad's just because you're nice to her. Does that happen a lot?" Eve put her sunglasses on her head.

"No. No, this is a first. But I'll endure the thought of dating you if that's what justice requires." Ryan offered his elbow.

Eve didn't miss him taking a glance into her car. She met his eyes when he felt her attention.

"Shall we?" He took a step forward.

Eve led him upstairs to her dad's door on the top floor, above all the apartments he rented beneath him. Once upon a time, Blake had been the building's handyman, but now the position belonged to a single mom.

"Dad?" Eve knocked and spoke close to the door. "I'm here, and I have company with me."

After a moment, her father answered the door with tremendous suspicion. "Eve. Everything okay?"

"Yes, Dad. This is Ryan. We were in the area having coffee, and I wanted you to meet him." Eve stepped inside and Ryan offered his hand. "Ryan, this is my dad, Dr. Ted Hartt."

Her father looked even more bewildered. After shaking hands, Ryan stepped past them into the apartment. Eve threw up her hands and mouthed to her father: "Be nice. I like him."

Despite his yellowing bruises and scabbed cuts, her dad looked downright pleased. Eve sighed. She'd never brought anyone home to meet him before. Perhaps he'd begun to worry she might never find a match.

Ryan looked at the pictures on the table in front of Ted's sofa with great interest. It took a few seconds and a fake cough to get him to put down the picture of her and Blake that her father had framed.

"Right. Sir, I don't mean to be rude, but are you okay? I'm a police officer." Ryan shifted his full attention to her dad.

"I sure am. It was a nasty night, but I'll go back to work tomorrow." He motioned to his couch. The coffee table was stacked high with patient files.

"You're supposed to start work *tomorrow*." Eve gestured to the giant pile of paperwork he had obviously squirreled home.

"Eve, sweetheart, the paperwork doesn't involve anything more taxing than thinking. And despite my age, I can still do that without hurting myself. So Ryan, how did you meet my Eve?" He sat back, wincing as his skin touched the couch.

"Well, sir, she dropped her phone and things sort of went from there." Ryan looked relaxed, but Eve noticed him cataloging the pictures in the room as they sat in matching chairs.

"She's usually not clumsy. You must have really impressed her," her father said.

"Hey, is it time for pain meds?" Eve stood, ready to get the pill bottle.

"I can't take them at work, so I've been doing without them for a while."

She exhaled in annoyance. "Dad, I don't think you should have to—"

"So what'd the guys look like?" Ryan leaned forward, patting her hand as he did so, urging her back into her seat.

He was handsome. Ryan was a walking advertisement for fitness. Dark hair and dark eyes were matched with high cheekbones and a strong jaw. No doubt his vindictive ex was hating their break up more with every passing day.

"The guys? Oh, ahhh…" Her father seemed to struggle internally for a moment. "You know I just fell, right?"

Eve held her breath, wondering what Ryan would do in the face of such a lie. He said nothing, just waited.

Finally her father sighed and looked at the floor. "I was so surprised and caught off guard, I really couldn't tell." He crossed and uncrossed his legs.

Eve closed her eyes briefly. The urge to murder passed through her, and she physically had to stop herself from making a fist. Hearing her father made her reason crumble. Somewhere someone had hurt him so much and they hadn't paid for it yet. She opened her eyes and saw Ryan looking at her. Chills shook her from head to toe. It was as if he could read her mind, feel her intentions. She refused to look away. Finally, he moved the inquisition along.

"With all due respect, sir, I'm wondering if a meticulous surgeon wouldn't be a bit more observant." Ryan clasped his hands and touched his nose with a knuckle.

Ted gave Eve a sharp glance.

"Maybe if you think of your attackers as prospective patients you might come back with more," Ryan suggested. "You know, that first assessment you make when you have someone in front of you at work."

Eve stood and moved to the couch, her heels sounding loud in the awkwardness in the room. "Dad, you can trust Ryan."

Her father stood, and Ryan did the same, reaching a hand to steady the man when he teetered.

"What is this? Am I meeting a new boyfriend or being interrogated?"

Silence crowded into the room. Eve walked back over to Ryan and put her hands on his cheeks. She kissed him gently on the lips. He responded just enough to let her know the kiss was welcome.

"I care about him. And he cares about me. You're safe to tell him what happened, Dad. He's very good at what he does." Eve turned to face her father, and Ryan slipped his arm around her waist. She smiled gratefully. He seemed to want an answer from her father as well.

"I might want to let it just be a memory, Eve. I mean, they weren't after money. I still have my wallet and phone. Maybe I just pissed someone off?" He gave a cough of embarrassment.

Eve bit her tongue.

"Sir, that actually brings up more questions than it solves. Do you have anyone in your life who's been angry with you?" Ryan leaned forward.

"Of course he doesn't. My dad is the best man there is." Eve narrowed her eyes at the cop.

Ryan winked at her. "Listen, I'm sure you're a little biased. All I'd like is for Dr. Hartt to think about this with me for a moment. I won't file a report, but I can check to make sure there haven't been similar crimes in the area."

Eve sat back and let the Ryan do his job. The man was good, she had to give him that. His careful questioning revealed that two of the three attackers smelled like smokers, and one had a surgery scar on his hand. All three were over six feet tall and fit. It was more than she'd had to go on before.

Ryan closed his notepad and put it in his pocket. "When I have a quiet moment at the station I'll see what I can do to put this all together."

"I'll find them," Eve mumbled before she could stop herself. The tone she'd used was not one her dad would recognize. He had no idea she was a stone-cold killer. And she needed to keep it that way.

Her father sighed. "I was coming out of the hospital. It was late. In the parking garage I saw a man collapse. As I ran over to help him, I was hit from behind. They knocked me unconscious. When I woke up, I was in a room I didn't recognize. They proceeded to ask me all kinds of questions about who had been treated at the hospital—what kinds of injuries. I honestly don't remember everything they asked me about. I have some holes in my memory that night. What I can piece together would have fit in about fifteen minutes, but I know I was with them much longer than that." He looked at the floor. "I do know they said that if I got a call from anyone with the last name Barker I was to follow their directions immediately. One of the last things they told me was that people I loved would die if I *squealed*." He made the air quotes around the word. "I was instructed to say I fell. The next time I woke up, I was in a gutter."

Eve covered her face with her hands, squirming. She felt as if she might burst into flame. It took some deep breaths before she could actually hear Ryan questioning her father again.

"So they never took off their masks?" Ryan jotted down the negative answer. "And did you investigate the surveillance video from that morning?"

Her father watched her. "They got me in a blind spot."

"Do you have an approximate time the attack began?" Ryan was being sweet with her dad, despite the tough questions.

"About two thirty in the morning. My surgery had run long. It was a heart transplant that was delayed because the organ transport had difficulty." He looked spooked.

All the things she'd done in her past, the way she could make a man cry for his own death, nothing had prepared her to see *this* man diminished. He'd been scared, and he was still upset.

Eve walked over and sat with her father, gently pulling him into a hug. "Did they mention any other names? Or people?" She looked into his face.

"No. They just generally threatened the people I love if I did the very thing I just did for you." He hugged her back.

"Okay. Ryan's going to investigate this quietly. He knows how to do undercover work, and he'd never do anything that would hurt me. You did the right thing, Dad. I love you."

Eve looked at Ryan's now-suspicious face as she relished her father's hug. They never really showed this type of emotion. It wasn't her style, despite his attempts. She vowed to hug him more in the future.

"Rest," she told him as she stood. "And you *can* take Tylenol and Motrin." She went into his kitchen, and her hands shook as she got the pills and a glass of water.

He accepted the Tylenol. "I'm okay, Eve. Please don't worry. I know it will be hard after all you've heard here."

She patted his hand. "Dad, Ryan's going to help us both. I'll be in touch again soon."

Eve held out her hand and walked Ryan out the front door, taking the time to use her key to lock the door behind them. As she headed for the elevator, all pretense of being Ryan's loving partner dropped. They were silent on the ride down, and he jogged to keep up as she slipped out of the building and into her driver's seat. He caught her door before she could close it, but she avoided his eyes and slid on her glasses.

"What the hell is this?" Ryan crouched and stopped her from putting her keys in the ignition.

"Nothing. Great. Thanks for your help." Eve turned and faced him, her dark glasses preventing him from seeing pure death in her eyes.

"You don't just get to leave. I need to know why I was just used in there. Talk to me, Eve." Ryan was imposing now, his form blocking her whole doorway.

"Everything's fine. Here, give me a piece of paper, I'll give you my number. We can get together." She nodded encouragingly.

Ryan didn't look convinced. But he slowly stood, reaching into his pocket for his notebook. Eve jammed the key in the ignition and took off without closing her door.

It was stupid. She knew she was coming unraveled. Using Ryan was supposed to extend her knowledge—look what he'd been able to do with her father. If she'd played her cards right she could've worked him and gotten every bit of knowledge he had about Mary Ellen and what the hell was going on around here. Now she was driving like an asshole, narrowly missing cars at the intersection, and Ryan was not even four car lengths behind her.

She wasn't going to outrun him. After four quick lefts, she parked at a dead end. The road turned into dirt and rocks that fell off into the Hudson River. She sat back in her seat and rolled down her window. Ryan parked his truck behind her car as if it was a police stop. He followed the same procedure he would have if he'd pulled her over for speeding.

"Ms. Hartt? Driver's license and registration." He stood off to the side, watching her hands.

"This is a hell of a first date." Eve opened her door and stepped out.

"I do believe I asked you for your information. I did not ask you to step out of the vehicle." Ryan wore sunglasses now too.

She faced him, and the wind blew over the Hudson, whipping her black hair around her face.

"And I haven't asked you why the hell you're creeping around the shittiest parts of town looking to get bought." Eve crossed her arms.

Ryan rocked back on his heels. "So the lady works for the enemy?"

Eve shook her head and walked closer to the edge of the water. "I don't work for anyone."

"I'm confused." Ryan stood next to her.

"That makes two of us." She bent down and picked up a handful of rocks, tossing them at the river.

"Do you have no clue how to skip a rock?" He reached down and got his own handful, then skipped one after another in a spectacular show of gravity defiance.

She tried, and her rock sank.

"It's all in the wrist. Watch." He showed her again, slowing down the movements.

After a few more fails, Ryan wrapped his arms around her and helped her throw the rock. She did one more on her own, and it hopped twice before sinking.

"So this is weird." Ryan stood in front of her when she was out of rocks. "You did take me to your actual father's place. And I do believe he got the crap kicked out of him, gangster style. And then you take off driving like your tailpipe is on fire, and now we're skipping rocks. I think I'm going to need some explanations so I don't drag your ass down to the station."

Eve grabbed her head, trying to make sense of what to do. "Those men that hurt my father? I want to kill them. They should feel every bit of pain he felt." She felt tears coming to her eyes.

"I'm sure that's the way anyone would feel."

Ryan didn't see it coming. She disarmed him so thoroughly he was at the business end of his own gun before he could even reach for it. Her heel was on his throat. He stilled.

"What are you?" His sunglasses and hers were victims of the tussle, lying nearby.

"I'm angry." She exhaled and turned his gun around, handing the butt to him.

He took it and stood, holstering his weapon. "I can tell."

He was a good cop, she realized once again. The exact kind of man who did what he had to so regular citizens could stay safe from each other and themselves. She hoped she wouldn't regret what she was going to do so much that she'd have to kill him.

"I'm here to stop people from stirring up trouble in Poughkeepsie. I've been in and out of that work for a while now. My family lives here. I should've been paying attention. But I was off licking my wounds in the city, and my father paid for that." Eve looked into his dark eyes.

"That's some dramatic shit right there. Why'd you throw your iPhone at my feet this morning?" Ryan leaned against the Audi, watching her carefully.

"I'm working for the woman who's trying to claim this place. And she wants to buy you. I'm here to facilitate that. Which I'm sucking at." Eve pulled her hair out of her face and held it in a ponytail.

"Well, my job is to get bought. Maybe we can work something out." Ryan crossed his arms and looked her up and down.

She bent down to retrieve her sunglasses and tossed his to him. She used her glasses to hold her hair like a headband.

"But if you ever point a gun at me again, woman or no woman, I will kill you." Ryan smiled.

Eve smiled back sweetly, until her phone sounded an incoming text. Then she nodded at Ryan and turned her back on him completely to look at her phone's screen. "This might take a minute," she said.

Ryan took the opportunity to step a few paces away and adjust. He could pretend he wasn't hard as a rock, but his pants were not helping him a bit. He now knew she'd been a plant, but she'd twirled real life into the pretend version of herself. That sucked. Black and white was so much easier to see than gray. And damned if he could trust her. He didn't know. He scanned the water and turned to scan the rocky horizon behind him. Nothing. Then he sensed Eve's movement and found her appraising him coolly. Her phone had disappeared.

"So we're clear, you screw me over and I'll get your dad involved on every damn level," he told her. He watched as her eyes sharpened to attention. She was a fucking tiger. Still hard.

"You have your leverage, what's mine?" she asked. Her black hair was all over, making it hard to read her expression. He reached in her car and found a hair tie. He tossed it to her and she twirled her unruly tresses into a ponytail.

"Well, if you really work for some kind of organized crime outfit, there's that." He hoped he was playing it cool, even as he listened for car tires and footsteps. This girl could have lured him here for her boss.

"Trust is hard to come by." She looked at his fucking crotch, emphasizing the word *hard*.

"Eve, we were strangers this morning, and I think we'll die strangers, but I need information, and you're in a good place to get it. And I *can* help find who played piñata with your dad."

For now that was all he was willing to share. The most important thing about this woman was the picture of her in her dad's apartment. The cross, knife, and music clef had damn near sang to him from the picture of a blonde Eve standing next to a man with Beckett's tattoo on his forearm.

"Okay. I won't point your gun at you again," she agreed. "Mary Ellen will want me to date you, so that can be the ruse for now—unless it'll drive your ex up a tree." She turned and looked at the river again.

"My ex can drive off a cliff, for all I care." Ryan kept his hand near his holster. "So when do we meet next?"

"How about here in two days? Same time as right now." Hugging herself, she suddenly looked slight.

"If we're supposed to be dating, how about I treat you to a decent dinner? We don't have to keep meeting down here by the river. It's a little too Mark Twain for my style."

Eve didn't meet his eyes, but her smile curved on one side. "The gentleman reads. Ten points for Gryffindor."

"Hey." Ryan took a step toward her. "I wish you'd been a regular girl."

A humorless laugh accompanied her turning around again. "You and me both."

16

Two Lines

The two lines appeared. Pink and pink. *Pink and pink.* Kyle's hand shook. She couldn't believe her eyes. Pregnant. For the love of everything holy, she was knocked up! She jumped and shouted and cried and screamed. She'd promised to wait to test until Cole came home. But she couldn't friggin' wait.

"Hairy moat of desire! I've got a bun in the oven! Motherfucker!" She clamped her hand over her evil mouth, then switched to cover her stomach. "Sorry, baby!"

And then she realized those were the first words she'd spoken to her child. She sat down slowly, folding her legs crisscross, and lifted her shirt.

Her stomach looked the same. She gently touched the skin, still marred with bruises from the fertility shots. *It worked. My God, it worked.*

She hadn't heard him coming home, and when Cole's hand covered hers, she gasped. Her tears were unchecked as she met his serious eyes.

"Really?" he whispered.

She held up the positive pregnancy test and nodded, freeing more of her tears to flow.

"May I pray?" Cole copied her sitting position.

"Of course." Kyle touched his face while he spoke.

"Lord, you've blessed this womb with our love. In it, guarded by a mother's protection, our child will come to us. We ask that you bless this baby and see fit to give us our very own angel."

They said "Amen" together, and their Saturday evening was spent on the floor—dinner forgotten, housework left undone. They were finally allowed to hope, allowed to predict. The baby would have his eyes, of course. And Kyle's fire because there was no dodging that bullet. And she'd have to clean up her mouth, that went without saying. Their baby would be loved. Epically, unfailingly. That went without saying as well.

As promised, on Sunday evening Eve met Ryan for their first official/fake/undercover date. They'd already argued. When they'd made plans the day before, he insisted on picking her up. She'd said it was ridiculous for him to drive to Mahopac. No one wants to date a girl living in a hotel, which, sadly, was her at the moment. But she'd also refused to wait for him at her father's place. In the end he'd picked her up at the mall. It felt very high school.

Now, as she rode with him in the truck, she found him in a ridiculously good mood. Trying to snap him back to business, as they pulled up at the restaurant, she told him to get ready because they needed to show some affection in public.

"Should I take off my pants?" He pretended to unbutton his jeans.

"Not that fast, Trigger." After they got out of the car, she grabbed his hand and smiled up at him.

"Is this okay?"

"My body is ready." He wiggled his eyebrows at her.

After the hostess took their name, Eve pulled him into the corner of the restaurant's foyer to wait for their table. She touched his chin and leaned in to place a gentle kiss on his lips. She pulled back immediately and swallowed, because cop man was a good kisser. His lips were soft, and he bit one after she pulled away.

"That did *not* suck." He squeezed her hand and reached around her waist to pull her closer. "If you were really mine? Well…never mind."

She hugged him and whispered in his ear. "Careful. I'm fatal." He needed to remember that warning.

He whispered back, holding her hair so she couldn't squirm away. "Jesus. It's like you said that directly to my balls."

She laughed so hard at his unexpected reply. He smiled down at her and ran his hand through his hair.

"I wish I knew if that was a real laugh or not." He tilted his head.

Just then she had a flash: standing in a restaurant, hugging a handsome man, a good man. This could have been her future, her now. She grimaced and looked away. The hostess called their names, and Eve deliberately turned her back on Ryan as she followed her through the restaurant.

At their table, Ryan pulled out her chair and Eve sat, rolling her eyes. He waited until they'd ordered their drinks before commenting.

"Rolling your eyes? What, a man can't treat his date like a lady?" He snapped his napkin open and set it on his lap.

"It just seems out of date. A little sexist." Eve opened her menu.

"So that's how it is for you? No problem. I'll dude-bro you until you bust out with some fluffy chest hair." He pointed at her chest.

"Anything important you need to share?" Accepting her drink from the waitress, Eve tried to not see his crestfallen face. Reality was clearly not a welcome guest at the table.

"After some digging I found a guy who's on parole who had some extensive surgery on his hand. His favorite genre of shit seems to be harassment and racketeering. Son of a bitch was in an altercation in jail too, so I'm sure it's just a matter of time before we can pick him up for something again."

"Does he hang out with anyone in particular?" A lead on the men who hurt her father would be personally, as well as professionally, useful.

"He's running with a few different crowds." Ryan seemed reluctant to say more. Perhaps he could sense her penchant for vigilante justice. "I'll keep an eye out for him." He smiled encouragingly. "Also, I was approached yesterday and offered payment in exchange for delivering information. I wanted to slap some cuffs on that slimy bastard." Ryan licked his lips as the bread basket arrived.

"Describe the contact."

As soon as he got to the part about "kind of fishy eyes," Eve knew Shark was the messenger. They spent the rest of the meal speculating and plotting. Damned if they weren't starting to make a great team.

On Friday evening, an approximately five-weeks-pregnant Kyle burped her nephew as Livia stirred her homemade sauce. They were about to partake in a nice plate of spaghetti and a glass of wine, and Kyle felt ready to explode. She'd been dying to tell Livia her news, but part of her was also afraid to talk about it. It barely seemed real. Their men were arranging a clandestine casserole drop-off for Ted and then popping in at Blake's old bar for a drink. He made only guest appearances there now that his studio work paid the bills. The plain-clothes cop parked outside the house seemed silly, but since Emme had been approached at school, it made everyone more comfortable.

Livia pantomimed a sleeping baby, and Kyle smiled. Kellan had fallen asleep on her shoulder. She patted him and took him into the living room. Her niece was already sleeping on the couch, cuddling her favorite stuffed frog. Livia came in and rearranged her covers, kissing her forehead. Kyle set Kellan in his playpen and pulled a similar maneuver. She sniffed his sweet head and smiled. That was new. How many times had she tried to help her sister—or just spend time with her family—and felt so, so empty.

The sisters tiptoed back into the kitchen. Livia turned on the baby monitor and double-checked that the alarm was set. Finally they each grabbed a plate and filled it. Livia poured one glass of wine and went to fill the other glass, but Kyle put her hand over it and shook her head. In that moment, she knew she couldn't wait another moment to tell her sister.

"What? Are you wussing out on me? We are drinking at least one glass. Kellan had three diaper blowouts today. How can so much poop come from such a small tush?" She tapped Kyle's hands with the mouth of the bottle.

Kyle's eyes filled. "I can't."

Livia searched her sister's face until she put it together.

Kyle sobbed the rest, despite her intent to speak clearly. "N-N-Not good for the baaaaa-by."

But her sister didn't need the words.

"What?" Livia said this louder than she ever spoke while the kids were sleeping.

Kyle set her plate down and Livia grabbed her, squeezing. They both sobbed, and Livia pulled her sister away and looked in her eyes. When she spoke, her voice was strong. "You are going to be an amazing mother. Without a doubt."

Kyle opened her mouth to speak, to rush in with her fear she'd leave her child like their mother had done, but Livia was already shaking her head.

"Don't. You. Dare. We do this. We love. We stay. We do this. Understand?" Livia held her sister close with one arm and reached up to wipe her face.

"I'm not supposed to say—you know, three months and stuff." Kyle shrugged.

"I'm surprised you lasted this long. Crap, I called you after Kellan's pregnancy test with my underwear still around my ankles!" Livia giggled and sobbed a little more.

"That image really changes that memory for me." Kyle smiled.

"Shut up, you knocked-up nightmare." Livia hugged her again.

"We don't need her for this." Kyle hugged her sister back.

"We don't. We can thank her for having us, but we don't need her for this." Livia tilted her sister's face to hers.

"Am I selfish for wanting this baby to be twins so we can have the same number of kids?" Kyle put her hands on her stomach.

"No." Livia laughed. "I'd love to see you with twins. Or more. But they don't run in the family."

"Well, we had help. It was really hard for this to happen." Kyle looked at the floor, feeling a tinge of shame.

"Hey! Don't you do that looking-down, I-hate-myself shit. Pregnant or not, I will make you smell my armpit." Livia pulled her by the face back into the conversation.

"Please, God no. Seriously, have you showered recently?" Kyle smiled.

"How you get the miracle does not affect the results. A baby *is* a baby *is* a baby." Livia hugged her hard one more time before grabbing the plates. "Okay, let's eat this cold because I'm not sure I would even be able to get hot food down, it's been so long. And you can start developing a taste for congealed sauce. Prepare yourself—Mommy food sucks."

It was the perfect way to spend an evening: eating spaghetti and dreaming of babies in bathing suits, plus John McHugh buying everything in Toys"R"Us because he just loved toys.

"He seems good." Blake closed the passenger door as Cole started his car outside Ted Hartt's building.

"He does—I mean, physically." Cole flipped on the lights and pulled out onto the road.

The men were quiet for a few minutes. Ted had returned to work, but he still tired easily. Now his fridge had a week's worth of homemade food in it, so he could just rest once he got home.

"I felt bad lying about Eve." Blake looked at his brother's profile.

Cole exhaled. "Yeah, that's never the right choice. But she seems to know what she's doing."

"Do you think we should find him?" Blake cracked the window a bit despite the chill in the air. He wouldn't call it claustrophobia exactly, just a preference for being outdoors.

"I don't know. Part of me wants Beckett here. Does that make me less manly?" Cole laughed a bit.

"Well, we can be girls together because I wouldn't mind having him here either. Part of me misses the days when he was so damn scary you knew people would steer clear of you and yours." Blake turned on the radio for background music. "It's kind of how we entered the world, you know? Even though it was tremendously screwed up, he was kind of like a dad."

"Probably the best example either one of us ever had—murdering aside, of course." Cole turned into a grocery store's parking lot. He put the car in park and turned to face his brother.

Blake glanced around. Surely this was a safe place to talk. "But I hope he's not that person anymore. I hope he was able to change the way he wanted to. I just can't imagine what he's up to. I knew he was in a bad place, but I'm just hoping, ya know? I never thought it would be this long."

"My concern is that he's dead. Could you possibly imagine him not coming back?" Cole ran his hands across the steering wheel.

"Not for this long. I mean a year, maybe two. He did really want to figure things out. But five years?" Blake drummed his fingers on the dashboard. "I don't think he's dead, though. He's larger than life, right?"

"I don't even know how to start to find him. I never was interested in that part of his business—if that's even still his business. And we can't ask Eve." Cole pulled out his cell phone and looked at it for a moment.

"We might know someone—if you want to see if Beck is still alive." Blake met Cole's gaze. "Chaos is out of jail. I saw him walking the other day."

"What if Beckett's got a good thing going and we break it? He might be done with this. With us." Cole replied.

"Never." Blake shook his head.

Cole nodded. "True."

Silence settled over the car again. Neither brother sprang into action.

"Kyle's pregnant." Cole blurted.

"What? No way! Congratulations!" Blake pulled Cole into the brother's handshake and pounded him on the back. It was a reflex, but then they both jumped as if zapped by electricity. They seemed to realize simultaneously that they'd abandoned that particular greeting when Beckett left. Blake patted their intertwined forearms before letting go—the punch in the heart was no doubt present for the both of them.

"That's awesome. How're you holding up?" Blake sat back in his seat.

"Scared."

"Right? I cried after Emme was born but, like, not from happiness. I was so scared—that baby was so little." He chuckled a bit. "But it really *is* amazing. Like nothing else."

"Well, she's just pregnant. We're not supposed to say anything, really. But damn." Cole sighed.

"Livia and I told everyone right away. Remember the phone call from Disney World?" Blake raised his eyebrows.

"Do *you?* As I remember it you were about four mai tais into celebrating." Cole laughed.

"Yeah, I think I was scared for nine months straight until she was born. Then I was actually petrified." Blake put his hand on his forehead.

"We were having trouble, you know. We've been trying for a while." Cole shrugged.

"Really? Wow, that makes this news even better." Blake watched as Cole's smile fell a bit.

"I just want her healthy and happy, right? That's all that matters. And she needs this right now." Cole looked at his phone again.

"I'll think good thoughts. And honestly? I can't wait to be an uncle. I promise I'll tell you if you're holding the kid upside down." Blake winked.

Cole punched his arm. "Thanks. You're a prince."

"So do you want to go see Chaos or should we leave well enough alone?"

"Let's go see him. Crap, I just want to know if Beckett's alive. You know he'd find us if the situation was reversed."

"We've got an hour or so." Blake put his window down a little lower, taking a deep breath. He couldn't define it, and sure hoped Livia would understand, but he couldn't just ignore his brother's absence anymore. Cole followed the directions he gave, and in just ten minutes they were in a completely different part of town. "Turn here," Blake said. "This should be the street."

"Are you sure? Lots of these houses look abandoned."

"It's not fabulous, but at least it's not the shed in his parents' backyard," Blake offered. "The guy's actually making progress. He's been here a while now."

"Oh yeah." Cole pointed when he spotted Chaos sitting on a porch. As they parked on the street, all the men sitting around assumed a suspicious attentiveness.

When they stepped out of the car, Blake nodded at Chaos like they'd planned the meeting, silently hoping the man wasn't drugged out of his mind and would remember them without Beckett to make the connection. His question was answered when Chaos pushed off the porch and ambled toward him.

"Can you give me a lift?" Chaos opened the back door to Cole's car and slid in without waiting for an answer. "I need some smokes."

Cole shrugged at Blake before sliding back into the driver's seat. Blake sat in front as they pulled away from the curb and headed to the nearest gas station.

Once they were moving, Blake turned completely in his seat to look back at the man responsible for all the ink on his body. "Nice to see you out walking around," he commented. In the past Chaos had had trouble leaving his home. The trips to jail seemed to have left him with a version of agoraphobia.

"I'm on anxiety meds, bro. Helping a lot." Chaos' eyes sparkled. "Thanks for wondering."

Blake nodded before turning back around.

After a moment Chaos leaned forward and put his tattooed hands on the back of Cole and Blake's seats. "Your brother back?"

Blake looked again at Chaos. The time in jail really had aged him. "No. We were hoping you might know where he is."

The man shook his head. "I've heard rumors, but with all the poking around lately, I thought for sure he was here."

Cole glanced in the rearview mirror. "Like how do you mean?"

"All the old places are getting tapped and taxed. Soldiers we don't recognize. Asking lots of questions about what's happening and who's in charge. We'll be sucking someone else's dick soon if Taylor doesn't show." Chaos pulled out a switchblade and tossed it from hand to hand. His frantic movements made Blake wonder if he was high on something.

Cole put the car in park, and in the same smooth motion turned and grabbed the knife in midair. "You want to keep this, put it away."

Blake hadn't seen Cole deadly in a long damn time.

"Sure thing, priest man." Chaos took the weapon back and slid it in his pocket.

"So what are the rumors?" Blake prompted.

"About Beckett? That he's holed up in some town in Maryland. About the soldiers? That they're really his. That he's coming back after getting tons more territory, and he's scarier than he's ever been."

Chaos paused for a moment and seemed at a loss for what to do with his hands. He settled for stuffing them in his pockets. "I don't believe that second one. These people don't operate the way he did. They're getting kids involved and threatening women and shit. Damn, there was an old surgeon who had the crap kicked out of him. That's not Taylor's style. So what are we doing? You buying me smokes? Getting a tat?" Chaos hopped out of the car.

Cole rolled down his window and passed him a few twenties. "Thanks. Appreciate it."

Chaos nodded. "Welcome." He turned to walk away, but suddenly turned around. "Just so you know, the soldiers have been flashing pics of your tats."

With that, he headed into the gas station and Cole threw the car into reverse. They were halfway home before they both exhaled audibly.

"We need to think about how we're going to attack this," Blake said. He looked at Cole as the streetlights flashed over his face. "I think we should start looking in to what might be happening with Beck."

Cole nodded. "He'd never threaten a kid. What the hell is happening here?"

"I do not know, brother. But I don't like it."

17

Mouse

Eve waited for Mary Ellen on the balcony. No trace remained of the blood bath that had taken place here the night of the auditions. That was some thorough cleaning, but a chill snaked its way through Eve anyway. Despite the horrors she'd experienced in her days, the memory of those women being exterminated, their screams as they were picked off one by one, had stayed with her. Maybe it was the exuberance they'd had just moments before—no sense of what was coming. Whatever it was, it sucked.

Mary Ellen's approach was quiet—she'd selected sensible pumps today for her version of weekend relaxed—but Eve could still feel her arrival as she stepped out onto the balcony. Yet another chill passed through her.

"January. A pleasure to have you arrive on time and as requested... for once." She came to stand next to Eve, looking out over the reservoir.

Eve tried not to picture snapping her neck, clean and quick. Mary Ellen smoothed her pale lavender pants. Her matching top was paired with white cardigan with pearl buttons.

As if the woman could tell Eve was appraising her attire, she wrinkled her nose at Eve's jeans. "We do have a dress code, even on Saturdays."

"Morales has agreed to take the money you offered." She ignored the comment.

Mary Ellen nodded. "Has he made you as mine?"

Eve's temper flared at the idea of belonging to this woman. She bit her tongue while she lied. "No. Not a clue."

"Men. So typical." Mary Ellen patted her hair. "The minute they get the milk from the cow, they're blind."

"Am I the cow?" Eve hated talking to her.

"Well, I guess it's an old-fashioned saying. Girls are so free with their privates nowadays, you have to keep on top of the game. Never let his male needs go unattended!"

Eve sighed. "Anything else, or are we done here?"

Mary Ellen's fake smile masked a simmering rage. "You know what? How about you go with Bart and enter your information about Ryan into the database. He'll show you the ropes. I think it's time we initiated you into our organized way of handling business."

Eve suppressed urge to laugh and nodded. Mary Ellen turned quickly, taking tiny, feminine steps into the ballroom, calling for Bart the whole time. He was soon at Eve's elbow.

"Bart, please set Miss January up with the database so she can enter the information she's collected for us." She smiled sweetly and waggled her fingers as she departed. "Tootle-oo!"

Bart directed Eve to a library that contained a lot more decorations than books and sat in front of a computer terminal. "I'll log you in, and I have to monitor your work. Boss lady wants everything you have so far."

After he opened the proper window and stepped aside, she made a show of typing her information very slowly.

"Guess you've never been a secretary."

Eve gave him the middle finger. She took her time until Bart was bored to the tips of his balls. Finally, he pulled out his phone and began playing a game, glancing at her less and less. After a while his looks stretched far enough apart that she could survey the database system a bit. There were dated files for different "actions," as well as biography files for both staff and persons of interest. Bart glanced up, and she winked at him. He looked back at his phone. She navigated back to her original screen, erased the history, and finished typing in some half-assed bullshit before Bart could get to the next level of his game, according to the annoying music he left on.

"All done, asshead."

Bart slipped his phone into his pocket and perused her information before labeling it with January and the date. "Check it out, your name *is* a date." He laughed at his own hilarity.

"I'm out. Tell the old bitch I'm going to suck dick hard enough to make her proud."

Beckett rolled over and shoved Gandhi back over to his three-quarters of the bed. As he settled back into his pillow, his dream changed, and he was alone with Eve. She wore a simple white sundress, and they were in his old office in Poughkeepsie. His confusion evaporated when she began unbuttoning the front of her dress. His entire being focused on the slow slipping of the material away from her breasts. She laughed and held it playfully, refusing to grant his eyes what they demanded.

"I love when you laugh." Beckett took his gaze from her chest to her smile.

"I laugh all the time now, you know that." She dropped the sundress all at once.

And Eve was his—her soft skin, her tight muscles. He felt like he was stepping through quicksand, but finally he got to her. She held her hands out for him.

"I love when you're *naked* and laughing." Beckett fell to his knees, pulling her tight stomach close to his lips. He began to rim her bellybutton with his tongue, and dream Eve started laughing again. She was ticklish here, right in her center.

She moved slowly to her knees, tantalizing him by brushing her nipples across his cheek on the way down. When they were face to face, Beckett wanted to get down to business. Eve put one finger to his lips, stopping him.

"We've done so much. We should be dead—you do know that."

Her face was serious, but her lips were so pink. He bet she tasted just like she was supposed to. He strained against her finger, wanting.

His voice wasn't working anymore, so he thought: *Inside you I can find everything I need.*

She leaned her head back, taking her finger away. Permission.

Yes! He grabbed handfuls of her blond hair as his mouth found her breast. She moaned loudly. He looked frantically for a soft surface, where he would fuck Eve like the queen she was. No chapped-ass rug burn for his girl. But when he took his eyes off of her, she disappeared. In his hands, instead of her hair, he now held sand. He was on a beach. He knew he was waiting for someone. *Who was it?*

"Hey, boss."

He recognized the squeaky voice immediately. Beckett whirled and walking toward him was Mouse. *Fucking Mouse!* He ran to him: his bodyguard, his dead friend. He gave Mouse a walloping hug. He was so solid.

"How are you here?" Beckett kept one hand on the man's thick shoulder.

"It's a dream, Beckett. Remember? You're at your house. You had some seriously funky cocktails trying to cheer Ms. Chery up this evening." Mouse was so vital. His eyes sparkled with the surprise he'd managed to pull off.

"I miss the piss outta you. I've done some things. You shoulda seen me. I wish you coulda seen me." Beckett's regret washed over him like the waves that crashed close by.

Mouse put his hand on Beckett's shoulder as well. "What makes you think I missed any of it? I'm still with you, boss. Don't worry."

Beckett wanted to sit and talk to Mouse for just ever. "That night, you saved my brother, but I failed you. I fucking failed you."

Mouse smiled and waved, like he saw someone on the beach he knew. "You never failed me. Don't you remember me, Beckett? You changed it all for me. Don't you remember when you punched the asshole that pulled my pants down in grade school? Don't you remember me, Beckett?"

Mouse raised his eyebrows, and is if it had been tethered in Beckett's mind, the memory floated to the top. Beckett could smell the cafeteria food in the new school he'd been assigned to. He fucking hated change. He hated the pity he saw in the teachers' faces. The orphan was always either pitied or feared. Never once was he accepted. Fuck them all. Fucking bastards.

He walked back to claim his free lunch. The school knew he had nothing. All the adults knew he had nothing. Fuck them. Someday he would have everything. All of it. And he would piss on a million free lunches. But he was hungry today, so he'd pissed in the urinal and now went to eat the fucking food. He couldn't believe what he saw when he got back to his lunch tray: a bunch of motherfucking assholes taunting some poor, pale bastard.

Bullies. Beckett hated bullies. He stomped over to their circle of stupidity to put an end to it. He took off his jacket and covered the lily-white ass cheeks that had no place in a lunch room. The boy looked so relieved. The kid was just a baby-faced, squeaky-voiced nightmare dressed in thrift-store clothes. The snickering assholes were proud of themselves. They shouldn't be.

Beckett decided to make them pay. As he grabbed the loudest one by the throat, he knew he was going to go down in flames. His fist hit the kid's face, and he pounded at the system that gave him free lunches. As blood splattered on his face, he hit his AWOL parents who didn't have enough sense to love him. He hit the pity over and over. Fuck them all. He tossed insults and threats like candy from a parade float. And when it was over, he went to juvie. He never regretted it a day in his life.

And then it clicked. It just hit him. *The kid was just a baby-faced, squeaky-voiced nightmare dressed in thrift-store clothes.* "It was you. You were the kid on the ground?" Beckett shook his head in disbelief.

Mouse nodded.

"You never told me? Why did you never tell me?"

Mouse seemed distracted. He waved again at someone Beckett couldn't see.

Mouse made a motion as if to leave, and Beckett did the first thing that came to mind: he put up his arm like he did with his brothers.

Mouse smiled with his whole body and stepped forward. He took great care in wrapping his forearm around Beckett's. Beckett held on tight to his friend's hand.

The lumbering bodyguard disappeared as quickly as Eve had, and Beckett startled himself awake. "Mouse!"

He looked around his darkened bedroom as his life clicked into order. *Mouse.* The dream was only a dream, though his hand was still curled in the handshake. That guy must have had one hell of a puberty to have sprouted up like he did. *Mouse.*

It felt real, seeing his friend like that. It was like a gift. He wasn't into spiritual bullshit, but damn. *Damn.* That Mouse had become his friend was a gift, but a curse as well. If he'd left that whole situation alone, would Mouse—would James—have had a better life? A different outcome?

He exhaled. Gandhi rolled over and farted. Beckett knew it would be awful, so he took the opportunity to take a piss. First he splashed his face with cold water. The dream had been so clear. Realizing Mouse had been in his life since they were kids was a taint punch. He couldn't decide if it made him more evil or less. Or did it even matter anymore?

The first part of his dream had given him a rock-hard boner. Making love to Eve would make sense right now. She'd loved Mouse. Damn it, she was so fucking mysterious…Mouse probably told her all about the school-kid drama. In his dream she'd said she was happy all the time. And it was just a dream. For fuck's sake, his brain was farting out memories and pretend information at the same damn time with the regularity of his dog's ass.

He looked in the mirror, which he rarely did. Well, okay, he did it all the damn time but never while thinking deep motherfucking thoughts. He looked just like any other handsome bastard with a huge dick. The reflection's mouth pulled up in a half smirk. He'd been flopping around in Maryland for years, and all he'd really done was become a priest and parole officer for a collection of down-on-their-luck assholes.

He was supposed to be dead, like dream Eve had said. So maybe helping anyone was better than breathing dirt. He shook his head and his mirror-self mimicked him. As of right now, Chery and Vere were upstairs. His place had been transformed into a safe place for Vere to be. Her sensory shit was tossed around, task charts were posted, everything was ordered. He was blown away at all that was entailed in keeping Vere present in her everyday. Half the time it was like Chery was pulling teeth just to get a response, never mind any opinion, from Vere. Though the woman surely had preferences. She would play with Gandhi every second of the day if she could. And Vere's diet was wicked restricted. Apparently Chery got good results from taking the gluten and various other shit out of Vere's system. The more Beckett watched, the more he saw. Vere always made sure Chery's shoes were face up and by the door. And every once in a great while, he would catch Vere looking Chery in the eyes without being prompted. Chery would light up, and he now knew why. The first time Vere made eye contact with Beckett, he'd felt a zing. It was almost like a sacred moment.

It was a high-maintenance lifestyle he'd had no idea some people lived everyday. When he found Chery doing her best to soothe a compulsively rocking Vere in the living room crazy-early one morning, he saw them both clearly: Chery was an amazing sister, and Vere was a hero—battling every day to get to Chery somehow.

Jared hadn't come to the store or come snooping around his house since their encounter two weeks ago, so Beckett was fairly certain he'd scared the ever-fucking shit out of him. But he was also fairly certain his foray into acting like his old self had been like advertising where in the world he was. If Jared told the right people, he could be a dangerous motherfucker.

But maybe he wanted to be found. Why did it have to be one or the other? He wanted these two ladies safe, but he also wanted to beat the shit out of assholes until they started doing the right thing for the right reasons. Mouse and Eve. Chery and Vere. Blake and Cole. Emme and Kellan Beckett. Kyle and Whitebread. Mouse and Eve.

His heart overflowed with good intentions but his fists felt best covered in blood.

18

Recovery

After two weeks of near silence, Mary Ellen summoned Eve to her compound again. This time Eve decided to make the visit count. After the drive to Somers, she waited twenty minutes for her majesty to be ready—and while she waited she ran through all the possible ways Mary Ellen could be on to her by now.

But when she was finally ushered into the ballroom, the woman practically skipped over to join her. She sat delicately and crossed her ankles. "So tell me, did he take the money?" She leaned forward like they were girls at a sleepover.

"Yes. I watched him pick it up at the post office box." Eve listened carefully to her surroundings, wanting to hear anything out of the ordinary.

"Very good. And of course he has no idea about you?" Mary Ellen smiled again. It was so hollow, like she'd rehearsed exactly how to set her face so it would appeal to people.

"No, no idea. We've been on a few dates, and I can tell he's falling for me. He's close to his mother, and she approves of me. I let him know I like jewelry and money. And that my last boyfriend knew how to treat a lady—although that's pretty much a lie." Eve snorted a little laugh, and Mary Ellen looked intrigued.

"Do tell," she said, batting her eyes.

"Well, I get the sense you already know," Eve offered, looking down and playing the role as best she could. "You've mentioned him a couple times—Sevan Harmon?"

Mary Ellen's face remained impassive, but her body jolted visibly, as if electricity had passed through.

"It was more than a year ago, and not even for very long, but he certainly left a mark." Eve sighed, as if the whole thing were too painful to discuss. "I was of use to him, and then I wasn't, and then he was gone. So yes, as I've mentioned before, you and I seem to have a common enemy."

"Do you hate him very much?" Mary Ellen asked after a moment, her voice trembling slightly.

Eve knew then that Shark had been right. It wasn't just business; this crazy vendetta was personal. Mary Ellen and Sevan Harmon had been romantically involved. "If he was on fire, I wouldn't stop what I was doing to put him out." She met Mary Ellen's gaze.

"Mmmm…precisely." The woman nodded. "I always sensed you and I had a lot in common." She smiled an ugly little smile, and Eve suppressed a barf. "Well, don't you worry. He's going to be sorry he took from me. Just as soon as I have everyone in Poughkeepsie's attention, I'm going to be the one who fans the flames." She seemed about to finish with an evil laugh, but suddenly stopped herself, straightening her suit and smoothing her hair. "Anyway, I'm very busy. I don't have all day to chat, so please finish your report."

Just then Mary Ellen's phone rang. "Oh, just a moment. I need to take this."

Eve stood and looked out one of the huge windows. The truth was she and Ryan had been sharing information tentatively. He had yet to pin down exactly what she'd been involved with years ago, but he knew it was illegal, and he'd been treading carefully with her since the beginning. But he'd let her know where the cops were on following up with the harassments and escalating crimes in Poughkeepsie, and she'd helped him determine what sorts of information he could pass on to Mary Ellen without actually equipping her enough to be any more dangerous. And stupidly, they'd been getting along. He had a great sense of humor and kept her laughing, something she'd almost forgotten how to do. Just last night she'd caught him staring at her bottom lip longingly. It had taken her a second to realize she was doing the same thing to him.

Snapping back to her current dilemma, Eve paid attention to the bitch. She should have been listening to her phone call.

"All right, Eve, it seems I have some urgent business to attend to, but what you've told me is wonderful. I'm sure Ryan will love to spend his new money on you. Well done. And of course, you know where his mother is, in case I need to exterminate her?"

Eve turned and faced her. "Of course."

"Let's put that in the database, shall we?"

Mary Ellen motioned for another guard, and Eve noted a mass of angry scar tissue on his hand. She memorized his face.

Nearly a week later, Mary Ellen had finally mustered the courage she needed. She stood outside her father's room and checked her lipstick in her compact before taking a deep breath. She'd been to visit Daddy a few times since he'd moved from the hospital to the rehab facility, and each time it was a little harder not to tell him everything. But she couldn't. She needed to have everything back in place so she could speak from a place of strength when she finally laid out her hand. Her original goal remained unchanged: show her father she was worth her salt, not someone he could ignore or push aside. So he could know nothing of her current difficulties. She'd learned from her misstep with Sevan, and that was that. Besides, based on what January told her, she hadn't been the first woman mistreated by him. Clearly he was a professional, so it was no wonder this had spiraled into such a mess. She could hardly be blamed at all. Her mind set straight, she opened the door.

Until this experience with her father, *recovery* had been a word that conjured images of rest and relaxation. This was anything but. Today Daddy was again working the arm weakened by his stroke, with his good arm strapped to his body to prevent him from using it. Sweat poured off him, and he concentrated so hard he barely looked up to see her enter. The therapist was a hard bitch, but that's the way Daddy liked them.

The stroke had pissed her father off. He hated the idea that there was anyone—let alone parts of his own body—that would refuse to listen to him. He was used to making people jump with a glance, and now one of his hands was too lazy to grip a Vitullo-made pistol. Mary Ellen hoped the humbling of the stroke would soften him to her proposals, when it was time for them. If she could just keep the lost money off his radar until it had been returned…

"Dad! Look at you go, you prickly old bastard! Soon you'll be able to hold your dick with your dominant hand again." Primo strolled around the room like he was paying Rodolfo and not the other way around.

Mary Ellen's mouth fell open.

"Insubordinate." Rodolfo gave Primo a dark stare as he attempted to grip a plastic water glass. After a few moments, as if his anger had propelled him, he closed his hand around the cup and brought it to his lips for a sip. It took him a few tries to set it back down on the table, but he managed.

"Well done, Mr. Vitullo. Lunch will be along shortly, so let's leave your other hand strapped until that's finished." The therapist made some notes on her iPad before passing Mary Ellen and Primo and disappearing through the doorway without a word.

How dare Primo show up? He never visited Daddy. Someone must have tipped him off about her plans to be here. Now she had two mouths to keep in safe territory.

Their father leaned back and sighed. "You both want money? That why you're here?"

Primo snorted. "Dad, don't be silly. I came to see you."

Mary Ellen narrowed her eyes. As far as she knew, Primo had just gotten back from gambling his face off in Vegas. Which probably also explained his presence.

"There's nothing to worry about," she said soothingly. "I've been working hard to keep things running until you're back to full speed. You're working so hard, I bet it'll be soon." She willed herself to make confident eye contact with her father, but she was only brave enough to look at his forehead.

"Really, Mary Ellen? How is it that I can't get into the main luxury account?" Primo tried to look threatening, but his hand shook a bit.

"Well, I'm sure I don't know," she offered sweetly.

"She's been doing all kinds of crazy things, Dad. She had a party last month and— "

"How much you on the line for, son?" Rodolfo's voice was a bit slurred, but strong. Primo pretended not to understand him for two rounds of "what?" before Mary Ellen interpreted.

"He's asking how much money you squandered in Vegas this time." Both men gave her a sharp look. She always took a risk when she asserted her opinion.

"I didn't lose anything. I just needed to refill so I could get into a higher-stakes game. It was a sure thing. Dad, you know I can make money double its worth. I was on a great run. That why I needed more, and I couldn't get any. An opportunity totally lost! Care to explain that, Ms. Keeping Everything Running?"

Mary Ellen put her hand to her stiff forehead, trying to think quickly. Failing to plan for her brother's insatiable need for cash had been an oversight. "I'm sorry you experienced a disruption in flushing Daddy's money down the toilet. I just tightened the belt on you a bit. I'm focusing on our business, our more productive ventures, right now. I want to make sure those endeavors have all the capital they need." She crossed her hands and ankles demurely.

Primo kept rubbing the back of his neck over and over. He was a classic picture of the addict he was, yet her father never seemed to see it.

"Mary Ellen, get Primo his funds by tomorrow. I'll top you off, son. Don't worry."

Primo understood that perfectly. He made a big show of thanking their father and giving him a big hug. "Get better, Dad!" He flipped her off as he turned to exit, like a petulant teenager.

Mary Ellen waited until the door to the room closed, but before she could speak, her father did.

"Mary Ellen, why was he unable to get to the money? I pay DiMonso plenty to keep the accounts fluid."

"Well, DiMonso doesn't work for us anymore. I had some information that pointed to him being less than forthcoming." She tried to remain calm. Firing DiMonso had been Sevan's suggestion. Getting him out of the way would make it easier for her to move money on her own, he'd reasoned. *Bastard.*

"DiMonso has been with me since before you were born. He'd never cross me. Did he quit for some reason? What did you do to him?" Her father clearly had trouble pronouncing the letter S.

"I'm sure you're right. I'll get him back. But in the meantime I was trying to keep the money safe. Primo's habit has me concerned. I didn't want him betting your fortune away." She felt sick because she was the sensible one, and really, she'd already committed that exact atrocity with quite a chunk of her father's money.

Rodolfo's mouth began to droop a bit and his left eye started to close on him as the lunch cart was wheeled in. "Primo is more dangerous without money. I look at it as a payment I make for my peace of mind."

Mary Ellen was shocked. Her father had confided in her, given her a tip on how to run things. Even if it was a tiny one, it felt like a gold star.

"Of course, Daddy. That makes perfect sense. I'll have everything righted soon. Thank you for telling me." She stood and leaned down to kiss his cheek. "I hope lunch goes well."

He nodded again, dismissing her.

If there hadn't still been the matter of the missing money and her not-exactly-clear plan for getting it back, she'd be walking on a cloud. Instead, she wanted to throw up a little. On her way back to the car, her phone rang—Sevan's tone. She hated herself for the thrill that shot through her body. She hated him. Sliding the phone to answer, she tried to collect herself.

She said nothing, just waited to see why he would call. In the background she could hear crashing surf and laughing women. She could picture his body stretched out on white sand, surrounded by models in bikini bottoms.

"Darling, nice of you to take my call. I just wanted to thank you for the bottle of 1907 Heidsieck & Co. Monopole Diamant bleu champagne. Do you know it cost two hundred seventy five thousand dollars? It's almost mythical. The bottles sat in the hull of a ship that sank in nineteen sixteen. They had to recover it from the bottom of the sea. I had a small sip, and it was fantastic. Of course Natalia let me lick it out of her tender navel as well." He paused for a moment. "Do you miss me, luscious? Care for me to send a plane? You could be where I am in less than ten hours. Oh—now Luana is using the champagne to wash the salt from her hair." He laughed robustly. "I'll order another, dear. No, Mary Ellen insists. Don't you, love? Of course you do, because otherwise I'd have to talk with your father regarding my concerns about you."

"Please. Order two. I'd hate for the whores to have salty hair." Mary Ellen gritted her teeth and quickly pressed the end button. He was splashing her father's money on the sand. But she had her own funds—though nothing compared to what Sevan took—and it was time to take more decisive action. Clearly he didn't understand that she meant business, that she'd never accept this. She needed to grind Sevan's testicles into mincemeat until he begged her to let him return the money.

No more working systematically to put him out of business. No more waiting for information and hoping Beckett Taylor might just reappear on his own. The flow needed to stop. Now. No more of Sevan's drugs would be smuggled through Poughkeepsie, even if she had to kill all his employees herself.

19

Yellow Blanket

Livia answered the door with her finger on her lips.

Kyle walked in quietly and took off her shoes. "Don't want little man sucking on dirt from these soles."

"See, you're already way ahead of other moms-to-be. I've been training you all this time, and you didn't even know it." Livia hugged her sister and patted her nonexistent belly.

"I'm almost nine weeks. But aren't you supposed to ask before you touch a baby bump?" Kyle spanked her sister.

"Pretty sure you're not supposed to touch people's butts without asking, blister popper." Livia sat on the carpet in the living room to fold laundry.

Kyle sat with her. "I'll help, but if I see anyone over age five's drawers, I'm tapping out."

"That'll be easy. We don't wear any." Livia kept her face straight.

"You're lying your balls off right now. There's no way you two rock it commando." Kyle shivered. "Gives me the chills just thinking about it."

"No, truly, we've come to believe in letting our genitals breathe." Livia fanned her crotch.

"That's why it smells like day-old tuna in here." Kyle covered her nose.

"Tuna is better than Chef Boyardee or whatever you're rocking in your pants right now. Or you will be. I'm just saying, get ready for some serious funk." Livia deftly folded Kellen's little onesies.

"Oh my God? Really? I can't deal. I have to have my snatch smelling right. Seriously, what's going to happen?" Kyle gave her sister a hard stare.

Livia broke into laughter. "Nothing, dumbass. Your cooter will smell like it normally does. And this is a batch of kid clothes. They need expensive detergent or they get rashes. Blake and I use the cheap stuff for our clothes, including underwear."

"You had me going for a minute." Kyle slapped her sister's knee. "I swear everywhere I turn I'm hearing weird crap about pregnancy. I mean, it's happened since the beginning of time. Shouldn't it be pretty cut and dried?"

"Well, each birth is different, but don't listen to the weirdos. I swear they crawled out of the woodwork to try to scare me." Livia began turning the little socks into balls.

"Okay, so I've heard your bringing-life-into-the-world stories before, but now I'm really listening. Tell me again." Kyle gave up folding and scooted back to lean against the couch. Livia checked the monitors before launching into her birth stories.

Emme had been a dream. Livia had been loaded to the top with an epidural, and even now she was damn near euphoric detailing how easy her birth had been. "They told me I was the best pusher ever. I had nurses holding my legs, cooling my neck, and then it was a soap opera birth. I held her and cried and took lots of pictures with my lady business hanging out. It was amazing." Livia shook her head. "But your nephew? So many things went wrong in the communication. I wanted an epidural—expected one, actually—but you remember how he was a few weeks early?"

Kyle nodded. It had been a scary night. Kellan had come not crazy early, but far enough in advance of his due date that everyone held their breath.

"Well, no one told me I wasn't allowed to have the medicine, so I kept expecting it. Then the doctor walks in and refuses, and I was pissed. I found out later that they were worried about the effects of the epidural on the baby, but nobody told me! So I'm all exorcist, screaming like a monkey. I actually shouted, 'Get this thing fucking out of me!' Blake told me later that that's when he knew I was out of my mind. I hadn't called the baby 'it' since we'd learned his gender. Anyway, they begged me to quiet down, said I was scaring the other mothers."

Livia smiled at the memory, but Kyle felt herself pale.

"I'd do it ten times a day every day for that little boy if I had to." She finished lining up the little piles she'd made and finally looked up at Kyle. "Oh, now I'm the weirdo trying to scare you. I'm sorry. Really, you will be so okay. You're a tough nugget. You'll be popping that kid out like a vending machine. They are going to need a catcher's mitt in the delivery room."

"I'm afraid to think that far ahead." Kyle bit her lip. "I mean, it hardly seems real sometimes."

"That's totally normal. Until the baby starts moving, it's sort of like a theory. Though with Kellen my tummy was showing sooner. I swear, Emme made my uterus baggy for her brother." Livia patted her stomach.

"You got huge." Kyle stuffed a throw pillow from the couch under her shirt.

"Shut up. Wait until you get the hemorrhoids. Yeah, that wipes the smile right off your face." Livia tossed one of the balled up pairs of socks at her sister.

"I can't even think about that. Wow." Kyle took the pillow out from under her shirt and tossed it in retaliation.

"I still have the cream upstairs for when your special moment arrives." Livia gave Kyle an elaborate pout.

"I'm not using second-hand ass cream. You're disgusting." Kyle laughed. "I'm the gross one. Where's this coming from?"

"I'm just messing with your head. Hey, you know what? I've got something to show you. I'll be right back." Livia got up off the carpet. "You watch the munchkins."

"If you bring me your hemorrhoid cream, I will make you eat it. Just saying." Kyle warned.

Livia ignored the threat and went to the basement. Kyle watched her niece and nephew on their separate screens. They looked like little angels asleep, though she was surprised to see Emme napping. Last she'd heard the girl was all done with midday rests.

Livia came up the stairs with a box and resumed her place on the floor.

"Why's little pants sleeping? Usually she'd be tearing through this place." Kyle pointed at Emme's screen.

"She was up late last night, but I'm watching her. Sometimes they both nap more before they catch a cold." Livia lifted the lid on the box. She removed a few plastic bags that had all the air sucked out of them. When she opened them, the material puffed up.

"Cool trick, bro." Kyle reached for a now-open bag and removed a bright yellow blanket with tiny pink flowers on it. "What's this? Emme's receiving blanket?"

"You have a good memory. Yes, Emme was brought home in it. And so was Kellan." Livia waited a few seconds before adding, "And so was I, and so were you."

Kyle tossed the blanket like it was hot. "Oh."

"I was wondering if you'd want this stuff. And I don't want you to flip out or anything." Livia spread out the clothes and folded the blanket neatly. It was like she had an automatic fold setting.

"That's a loaded pile of clothes, sister." Kyle didn't want to touch any of it. She looked at the pictures on the walls instead. There were pictures of both kids in the hospital, ready to go home as infants. Both were swaddled in the yellow blanket and wore a combination of the clothes in front of her now.

Livia patted each of the little outfits. "Dad was going to throw these out. He's like you sometimes, you know? He was going through the basement one day when you were at Jessica's house. He wanted to get through the stuff so you didn't have to see it, and he didn't want it in the house anymore. When he was loading the car to take the stuff to Goodwill, I snagged the baby clothes box and put it in the back of my closet. Just to save it, you know?"

Kyle smirked. "You were probably eleven. Such a sentimental chick. Remember when we had to have a funeral for the moth you accidentally killed when you were trying to take him outside? Even though you hated moths?"

"They are horror movie staples. But I did feel bad." Livia tilted her head, smiling at the memory. "Listen, you don't have to use any of it, and you certainly don't need to make a choice right now. I just wanted you to know it existed. It's clean, it's here, and I want to make it a tradition, if you're game. Yes, she left, but I don't think she should get to take our history. I like the thought of something that gets passed from one generation to the next. And we have to be the ones to make traditions. But if this isn't the one for you, don't worry. We can do something else." Livia shrugged.

Kyle had to appreciate the sentiment. She was fiercely proud of her sister and her father for making their little family work. They were unconventional, and they'd had to figure some lady shit out for themselves, but they'd gotten it done. "You're something else, Livia Hartt. I promise to think about it. And thank you for being so goddamn thoughtful."

She helped her sister pack up the potential heirlooms and gave her a hug to boot. As they stood, Emme pounded down the stairs.

"Aunt Kyle! You came to play with me! You make the best fart noise for my frogs!" She ran into Kyle's open arms.

Kyle shrugged at Livia as she patted Emme's back. "I learned everything I know about farts from your mom's butt."

20

Welcome to Your Vag

Eve closed her laptop after helping her replacement at Silver Force Systems organize his transactions and make sense of their system remotely—again. Once it had become clear this crap with Mary Ellen was going to take as much time as she could give it, she'd resigned from her import-export job. But she'd agreed to help the new guy for a month or so in lieu of two weeks' notice. It was a little gratifying how much the company had offered her to stay, and given the way the system seemed to blow the new guy's mind repeatedly, she bet they might offer her even more now. But his wasn't ever about money. She'd lit Mary Ellen's money on fire, for crap's sake. She laughed a bit, thinking how much Mouse would have loved that move, then thanked him silently for putting her in a position where she no longer required an income.

Her cell phone rang: Ryan. His ringtone was a siren, which had made him laugh when she told him. As she reached for her phone, she looked forward to the deep timbre of his voice despite her damn self.

"Hey, pretty."

"Yeah?" She stood and went to the window, laughing when she saw his truck parked outside her dinky Mahopac hotel.

"You busy?" He smiled from the front seat, sunglasses in place and huge shoulders shrugging as he gave her a wave.

"Not anymore. I was just doing some work, but I'm happy to see you, sweet thang." She was always careful to play her part on the phone, never trusting that Ryan was the only listener.

"I know it's April, but put on a warm jacket and gloves. I want to show you something." He flashed the headlights and honked the horn.

"Keep your pants on, Morales. I'm on my way." She hung up and gathered her things, locking the door on the way out.

He revved the engine as she rounded to the passenger side, his music bleeding out around the closed windows. As she opened the door, Ryan leaned toward her, lip-synching an old Lady Gaga song. She laughed and punched his arm when he refused to drive, but instead mimicked dance moves.

"You have problems." She tried to grab his arms and make him stop.

"I have eighty-four issues but my lady is not among them," he said matter-of-factly, then wiggled free and reached past her to grab the seatbelt, which he pulled across her body.

"Are you sure about that? Is that your version of Jay-Z? I can't even find the words for how cheesy you are," she said, lips almost touching his. He smelled good—just the right amount of cologne.

He paused, Lady Gaga still singing her heart out, as he clipped the belt in. "It's not too tight, is it?"

Eve swallowed, biting her bottom lip. "You've got some game, copper."

He leaned closer and whispered in her ear. "We got one in that old Impala down the street. A little romance is appropriate."

She turned her head just enough to see they were indeed being watched. It was Wren from Mary Ellen's crew.

"He's an asshole and can't track for shit," she breathed.

"That's the truth. Can I give him an eyeful?" Ryan raised one eyebrow and puckered a bit.

"Make it worth my while." She winked as she touched his jaw, letting her hand drift to his neck and follow his bulky muscles to his bicep. He flexed.

"If the guns make you swoon, I'll understand." He kissed her lips.

She grabbed two handfuls of his leather jacket to keep him close. "More."

"Gladly." Then she let his scent and the feel of his arms rain into her psyche. Later she would tell herself this was for Wren's benefit, but right this second, being kissed by Ryan Morales was pretty freaking good.

Finally he pulled away, kissing the end of her nose quickly before putting his own seatbelt on. Eve cracked the window a bit, getting some fresh air in the cab to clear her head. Time to get back to business.

"You check the truck?" She ran her hand along the rubber edging of the window. He drove the stick shift in the way she tried not to watch. *Business*, she told herself. *Not sexy forearms.*

"Clean as a whistle." He punctuated his statement by whistling along with the music.

She took a peek at him, trying to gauge whether he was as affected by their play-acting as she was. He smiled at her, cool as could be. Evidently his confusion about real and fake had evaporated.

"Good to know. So have you done the latest the old bitch asked?" Eve crossed her ankles.

"Well, she wanted any police records related to Sevan Harmon, but of course there's crap. The guy's not an amateur. So then she wanted all our records on drug-related arrests for the past five years."

Eve laughed out loud. "What? That's not a reasonable request? Who would notice you pulling that?"

"Yeah." Ryan grimaced. "I don't think she believes me when I tell her I can't do it, but so far she's not beating my ass, so I feel lucky."

"Mmmm...yes, you're lucky for sure."

"Anyway, her last request was something about fraud charges related to weapons, so McHugh and I dug up some old reports on a few long-dead criminals. We tweaked the dates and gave her enough to keep her busy for a while."

"Good God. Who knows what that woman is playing at. She hates Sevan Harmon, though. Definitely wants to see him fry." Eve grabbed a pack of gum from his cup holder and treated herself to a piece. "Want one?"

"Do I need one? Is this your super-pleasant way of saying my mouth tastes like a monkey's tit?" He lowered his sunglasses and gave her a hard stare.

"Monkey's tit? For serious? You're one weird guy." She unwrapped a piece and popped it in his mouth. "And you tasted fine."

He smirked as he pulled into a parking lot. The Impala pulled in a few spots down.

"He's such an amateur. I can't even deal with her morons." Eve sighed. "They're going to get themselves and me killed."

"Can't let that happen." He pulled his sunglasses off. "Fuck knuckle is walking by in three, two…"

Eve kissed him before he could say one, unbuckling her belt and straddling him so she could get a look at Wren. He was taking video with his phone in a fairly inconspicuous way. She tossed her hair around while Ryan let his hands wander on her back. Finally Wren passed them, and Eve shook her head. "He was videoing it. You ready for a show?"

Ryan blew a bubble with his gum. He spoke out of the corner of his mouth, "I've got the biggest bubble."

"You are such a child." With that, Eve blew her own bubble and twisted in his lap to sit next to him. She slapped down the sun visor and opened the mirror. They compared bubbles, putting their cheeks together to measure. His bubble touched hers, and then they were stuck.

Ryan puffed out his cheeks like a blowfish and crossed his eyes. Eve burst out laughing, launching their stuck-together bubbles at the windshield. The gum landed with a splat, and they laughed so hard they couldn't breathe for a few seconds.

"Are we actually this hilarious, or are we both freaking out a little about the tail?" Eve finally asked.

"Crazy lady, I'm not worried about the tail." Ryan smiled at her.

The warmth crashed into her chest. She shook her head and twisted, opening her door to get away from the moment.

"I'm sorry?" He scrambled to follow, locking his truck with the remote. "Did I do something wrong?" He pulled up next to her and spoke softly. "Are you really concerned? There's been no change in the way she deals with me."

Eve pulled her gloves out of her jacket pocket, tugging them onto her hands. "No. Not at all. You're perfect." She turned and stole his sunglasses, slipping them on.

He caught her and spun her into a hug. "Seriously, I never want to offend you. I know it's all pretend," he said softly. "I don't want to accidently touch your boob or do something you're not ready for."

His words hurt when they shouldn't have. Of course it was all pretend. She knew that. Ryan was a means to an end. That was all. She forced a smile. "You're all good, Lady Gaga. No worries."

"Okay. Shall we?" He held out his hand.

Eve took it and walked with him toward the Walkway Over the Hudson.

"Ever do this before?" He looked only at her, never once letting on that there was now a man videoing them just a few feet away.

"No, sir. Looks pretty from the Mid-Hudson, but I never made the time." They set an easy pace as they stepped out on the concrete.

"It was an old, burned-out train bridge for the longest time. Then they made it into this."

As trees dropped out of the way, the view of the Hudson River was spectacular. The mountains in the distance even had white caps. "Is that snow? Holy crap!" Eve shivered as the wind picked up.

"A little bit. Too cold?" Ryan held open his arms.

Eve backed up to him as he snuggled her inside his jacket. She took off his glasses and slipped them into her jacket pocket. "Thanks."

He rested his head on top of hers. "Any time."

"It's really gorgeous up here. Look, a train!" She watched as it snaked its way through the trees and blew its whistle on the way into the station. "My cousin was married there."

Wren had resorted to just watching them, or at least that's how it seemed.

"At the train station? That's unique. I'm surprised it was allowed." Ryan let her rest her weight against him. He was like a wall.

She hummed noncommittally, not wanting to say too much in case Wren had a listening device.

"So, January, how about you stay the night with me instead of that hotel?" He'd chosen her fake name, so she knew he was being careful.

"It's actually charming." His jacket buffered the wind, staving off the chill.

Wren's jacket was not nearly thick enough and while they lingered, he crept back down the walkway, for sure going to warm up in the Impala.

"He's gone." Ryan had done a wonderful job of being observant without getting caught.

She told him as much after turning in her spot to warm her front against his chest. "You're a freaking furnace."

He pulled her tighter. She set her head against his shoulder and inhaled. He still smelled great. His phone began vibrating in his inside pocket, so Eve fished it out for him.

"Dude, says The Red Room of Pain is calling?" She showed him the screen.

"Hit ignore. It's my mom."

Eve hit answer it and put it to his ear. He gave her a dirty look, but kept his arms around her.

"Hi, Mom."

"Son, I love you."

"I love you too, Mom."

Eve mouthed, "Aww…"

His eyes never left hers as his mom prattled on.

"I need you to come home. I promised Trish I wouldn't tell you, and I know she's excited, but I didn't think it was fair to spring this on you."

Eve mouthed, "Trish? Insane Trish?"

Ryan nodded. "Whatever she said, Mom, it's not true. She and I broke up—"

"Of course you broke up," his mom interrupted. "But she's super supportive and has been helping me understand what's happening. And she's been wonderful about explaining the procedure to me and the rest of the neighbors. We are now fully ready to accept you as you are. I love you no matter what equipment you have."

Eve narrowed her eyes with suspicion to match Ryan's.

"Equipment? The whole neighborhood? What's going on?" He began shaking his head, so Eve had to work to keep the phone in position. He squeezed her tighter.

"We're throwing a surprise Welcome to Your New Vagina party tomorrow. And I'm so proud of you, my daughter." His mother sounded teary now. "I just want you to know I accept you, and I'm ready to make this change with you and support whatever you need to do. I didn't want you to have one second where you thought I wasn't with you. I love you so much."

Eve watched Ryan turn red with rage. She winced at his face but responded with another mouthed, "Awww…be nice to Mom."

"I love you too, Mom. I appreciate the…support. But this, what Trish is saying, it isn't true." Eve began to giggle silently, burying her head in his chest. "I can't come right now—I have plans—but I'll come over soon to talk through this with you. I'm still a man, though. Just not the man for Trish."

"Sweetheart, I know this is hard. But we're having a block party. There's going to be a banner and all your old friends from high school. Please, allow us to welcome you into your second birth."

Ryan swatted Eve's bottom as she squirmed and pulled free. She trotted a few feet away, not getting to hear how exactly Ryan extricated himself from the festivities.

"Fine. Fine. Yes. Glad you were able to get a cake on short notice, but I really…I'll be there in a little bit to talk about this. And hey, tell Trish to stay right there. Oh, she left? What a surprise. I love you too, Mom. Thanks for calling." Ryan ended the call and tucked his phone away before rubbing his hands down his face. "I'm going to kill her."

"Your mom? Don't even think about it. That's the sweetest thing in the world. How amazing of her." Eve hugged herself, trying to warm up.

"No Trish. I'm going to kill Trish. Twice." He pointed at Eve. "And if I remember correctly, I told you to not answer that call."

"Sweetheart, then you would've missed hearing about your vagina's coming-out party." She made a face at him.

He took off after her, and she was laughing too hard to get away. He backed her against the railing, nothing but a sheer drop behind her.

"This is hilarious to you?" His eyes sparkled. "My own mother remains unconvinced of my gender."

"It's actually, like, funnier than hilarious." She tried to duck under his arm, but he restrained her.

"Are you ticklish, laughing girl?" Ryan had a threat in his voice.

"No. Don't even try it. I'd have to toss you off this bridge. And then the vagina party wouldn't have its princess." She struggled, but not too hard.

Ryan went for her ribs first, and she collapsed as he mercilessly followed her down to the cement, laughing as he tickled her.

When he let her catch her breath, she said, "I'm freaking freezing."

"I'll warm you up even if you're mean to me." He helped her stand and opened his arms. She cuddled against him and took a glance around. No sign of Wren.

He held her face, warming her cheeks with his hands. "You laughing? Damn. That's a beautiful sound."

It was a gorgeous setting, and he was an amazing guy. She felt like someone else. Someone she'd once been, maybe. Or might have been. She stood on her tiptoes to kiss him. This job was going to hurt like a bitch when it was over.

Beckett tossed the slimy tennis ball for Gandhi at the local beach. It was a gorgeous slice of the world. Technically he was at a riverbed, but damn it—it had sand and water so it was a goddamn beach. In the distance was that huge, impractical bridge, set there obviously to scare the shit out of drivers, but also to make his view stunning. Gandhi farted and snorfeled his way back over.

"You're so damn ugly, buddy." He took out his phone and snapped a proof of life picture—and a freaking fantastic life at that—and sent it to Kristen. "You know that lady likes to keep tabs on you." After five years, however, he knew her concerns for Gandhi's wellbeing had pretty much been put to rest. But he kept in touch anyway. He liked being Mouse to somebody, somewhere in Poughkeepsie.

Gandhi spit the ball out at his feet. Beckett picked it up, trying to touch it as little as possible. Still the sand stuck between his fingers. The dog loved it when he chucked the ball close to the edge of the water so he could splash a bit in the surf.

Beckett loved this freaking dog so much. He brought him to the liquor store, out on little fucking errands, just anywhere he could. How an animal could have so much personality, he didn't know. This self-imposed seclusion was only bearable because of the damned dog. But sure as shit, he missed his brothers. He missed *her*. He'd Google-stalked her a few times, but of course he found nothing.

A high-pitched squeal from the dog snapped his attention back to the present. Gandhi dropped his beloved ball and ran as fast as he could to Beckett, hurling his dumpy body at his shins. Beckett crouched and checked G for seizure symptoms. The best the vet could come up with was that a previous dogfighting head injury set G's mind on fire a few times a year. Both Beckett and the dog hated the seizures. He'd wrap Gandhi in a towel or blanket and ride out the spasms with him, petting him and sitting on the floor for up to an hour if he had to.

But this was different. And then he knew. Beckett scanned the beach and sure enough, here came a huge Doberman, off leash, with a jogging owner not far behind. The animal was well trained and ignored the whimpering Gandhi, trotting by at a dignified pace. But Gandhi was shaking so hard his whines were almost yodels. Beckett waited for the jogger to pass before scooping the dog up like a baby. Between whines, Gandhi used his big sloppy tongue on Beckett's face. He shook his head. He could only guess, but it'd happened a few times at the dog park and once on a walk—certain breeds of dogs set Gandhi off. He became a shaking wreck.

After grabbing the tennis ball, Beckett carried the nervous dog up through the steep woods to the parking lot. He didn't put him down, just juggled the dead weight while he found his keys in his pocket. He got the car started and the air conditioning on. With it at full blast, he eased back the driver's seat, took a deep breath, and sang Gandhi the only lullaby that ever settled him down in times like these, channeling his inner Eminem.

It took ten minutes of cuddle-hugging before the dog went boneless in his arms. Gandhi's huge tongue lolled to the side as he fell asleep. Beckett shuffled his pet to the passenger seat before throwing the car in reverse. He almost smiled as his blood boiled. He knew he'd never know, but if he ever found out who fought his dog and scared him to his soul, it'd be real tough not to kill the shit out of him.

21

Good Ones

Cole helped Kyle back into the apartment. She could see dishes in the sink—and bloody pajamas in the center of their living room floor.

"Do you want a shower?" he asked in a whisper, but it still seemed like he was shouting into her nervous system with a megaphone.

She wished she could be numb. An epidural to the brain. She didn't answer him. Irrationally she wanted to hit him. She wanted to hit Cole until she couldn't do it any more, even if he was smart enough not to mention all the things she didn't want to hear:

"It's okay."

"You're young."

"You can get pregnant again."

He propped her up in the bathroom, leaning her against the sink. He set the water temperature and removed his clothes.

"You don't have to stay." Her voice cracked, and she couldn't look at him.

"If you don't mind, I'd like to." Cole undressed her carefully.

As he slid off her yoga pants, she looked at her thighs. They were still stained red.

He led her into the shower and stood behind her, wrapping his arms around her. All the times she'd cried in here, it seemed somehow he knew, because he was braced for her collapse. He knew how the water did something to her—made her safe to cry or released her firm grip on hope. Either. Both.

She sobbed and screamed and half drowned in the spray of the shower. He pulled her backward so she could take a breath. He didn't say anything, just held her. She turned and began hitting him. She slapped his face and punched his chest.

Tears rolled down his face, and she had to stop.

"I'm so sorry. I'm so sorry. I'm so sorry."

He shook his head. "You're so brave."

"Don't say that to me. I didn't even finish the first trimester. I killed our baby. *I killed our baby.*"

"No. God needed the baby."

"Fuck God and fuck you. He can't have my baby. I know she was a girl, and I want her back. I had so many plans for her, for us. I want her back. I didn't even get three months. Please make her come back? Help me." She bent over, hugging her traitorous middle. "I think I want to die."

Though she flinched when Cole reached for her, she allowed him to pull her to standing. He was angry now. This man, so beautiful. So broken. Naked in front of her.

"No. You look at me," he said, his voice rock solid. "Kyle, damn it, look at me. What we did, what we made was beautiful. And loved. So much. Has a baby ever been loved so much?" He was yelling to her now, determined to be heard over the pounding water, the blood in her ears, the crashing sound of her world falling apart.

"I loved the baby. I promise. I loved her." She could hear how desperate her voice sounded.

He held her face close, kissing her lips as she tried to shake her head.

"The baby we made will make us stronger. You're a mother, and I'm a father. You are a mother, and I am a father. And we're good ones."

She crawled onto him, hearing his words and trying to get closer to them.

"And we're good ones."

Kyle petted his face, touched his lips as he kept saying it.

"And we're good ones."

He hugged her hard, mouth moving on her hair. "And we're good ones."

Livia handed the baby to Blake and stretched her back. Kellan had wanted to be held all day. Emme wanted an elaborate fort built for all of her stuffed animals. And now Blake was hungry. She closed her eyes briefly. If she didn't get four freaking minutes to cut her toenails and throw in a load of laundry, she was actually going to cry.

"I think there's burgers in the freezer. Want me to start the grill?" Blake tickled Kellan's belly with his nose, his messy hair flopping in the baby's face.

Livia nodded distractedly, in the midst of making a list now that her hands were free. Blake and Emme could go for haircuts together if she got a second to book an appointment…Then Kellan giggled.

Blake looked at her, delight all over his face. The day Emme first laughed had been one of his favorite days on the planet. He repeated the motion with his hair and four-month-old Kellan definitely giggled.

"Oh my God. Do it again. Wait. Emme! Wait. Where's my phone?" Livia looked around her messy house, not seeing her pink iPhone case anywhere.

"Emme! Come see. Come look at Kelly!"

Livia was searching under junk mail when Emme came around the corner holding the iPhone. She'd likely been deep into one of her animal apps.

"Make it do the video, please!" Livia scooped up her daughter and sat her on the counter. Emme deftly flipped the phone's camera to video and handed it to her.

"Okay. Do it again. Today is Friday, April nineteenth." Livia held her breath.

Blake snuggled Kellan and waited. The baby started in with the giggle. It almost sounded like he was crying, but the gummy smile gave his emotion away.

"What's he doing?" Emme gently touched her brother's foot.

"He's laughing, gorgeous. Kellan's life is so awesome right now he's laughing. You try." Blake held the baby closer to his daughter.

Emme recreated his motion and Kellan laughed again, kicking his feet. "He's laughing!"

Livia sighed in relief when she saw that Emme had also pressed record for her, because she would have missed the moment otherwise.

"You try, Mommy!" Emme clapped her hands while Blake shifted Kellan to Livia's arms.

Kellan's eyes focused to her, and he smiled at the sight of her face. She mimicked Blake's maneuver and at first got nothing. But the second time Kellan busted out and she hugged him to her chest and kissed his sweet face. Cluttered kitchen or no, they had their moment. And Livia knew this would be one of Blake's favorite days as well. She stopped the video and handed the phone to Emme, who wanted a replay.

"So he's a person now, Daddy? He laughs?"

Blake tried a few more times for a giggle but Kellan was busy watching the pattern of his shirt now. "Yes, pumpkin. He's been a person this whole time, but now he's a laughing person."

"Well, I'm not surprised. You're hilarious." Emme pressed play on the video again.

Livia and Blake's eyes met and they mouthed, "hilarious?" Emme had a fantastic vocabulary. They loved it when she slid a whopper of a word into casual conversation.

"Okay, listen, I'll take Kellan, and you start the grill," Livia announced, back to business once again. "I have to do things to my body so I'll be considered a human woman again, and then I'll make a salad." She took the baby in one hand and grabbed his bouncy seat with the other. As long as Kellan could see her, she could get five or six minutes out of him for a brief beauty session.

"I'll make the salad. Do what you have to, but you're gorgeous no matter what." Blake winked at her.

"I smell like a dinosaur puked on me, and my toenails might have to be classified as weapons in some states." Livia puckered a kiss in his direction. "Pumpkin, can you stuff my phone in my pants? I'm going to play that music Kelly likes."

"Do not call my son Kelly." Blake gave her a glowering stare.

Emme popped the phone in Livia's pocket before she climbed Blake like a tree and grabbed his face. "Mommy says Kelly is a boy's name."

Blake growled at Livia before focusing on Emme. "Well, I guess I'll call Mommy Fred from now on."

Emme's huge green eyes got serious. "No. Mommy's name is Mommy and also Livia. And sometimes Hot Stuff. Not Fred."

Livia left the room laughing, and Blake sputtered a bit before tickling Emme, judging from her laughs. Thanks to playing Elmo at a stupid high volume—and maybe the white noise of the shower—Livia got to treat herself to the deluxe. She felt like she'd touched the face of God in that shower.

Kellan smiled when she appeared from behind the curtain, and her text message tone for Cole interrupted Elmo, which was odd. She and Cole did not have a big texting relationship. She looked at the screen, and her gasp was audible.

We lost the baby.

"No. Oh, Kyle. Noooo." Tears crowded the message from her field of vision as she willed it to change. Four years of trying. Eleven weeks of joy. No.

She dressed quickly, hands shaking. After twisting her hair into a bun, she pulled a fussing Kellan from his bouncy seat to nurse. He was full and sleeping not fifteen minutes later. Laughing had taken all his energy. Livia rocked him even though he was clearly relaxed. She felt guilty for having him, for not knowing what it was like to want. The second Blake had mentioned children, she was pregnant—both times. It had been so easy.

Blake knocked at the door, and she told him to enter. "Princess couldn't wait for a burger, so she's having microwave popcorn. And I'm boiling water instead of starting the grill because we're out of propane." He finally looked at her face. "What's up?"

She handed him her phone. He glanced at the text and shook his head before taking Kellan from her and setting him in his bassinet. He held out a hand, helping her out of the chair. "Come here."

"It's just…She wanted it so bad." Livia set her head on his chest as he rubbed her back.

"He was really excited too." Blake pointed at the monitor. Emme watched her favorite show in her room while eating popcorn.

"Is the alarm set?"

Blake nodded.

"Can we? Could you?" She leaned up to kiss his lips.

"I always can. Can you?" Blake clicked the lock on the door.

Livia nodded. "Is that disrespectful? I just need you."

"Me too." Blake smiled. "I think it's okay to be grateful. Any chance we get."

As his arms came around her, Livia realized it had been a million years since she'd hugged him chest to chest. She hummed. They made out like two horny teenagers, almost stupid about it. But when he slid his hand in her pants, she flinched. "You sure we have time for this?"

He kissed her lips again. "I would make time for this if the world was falling apart around us, and we were in public, and a hungry T-Rex was sniffing our butts and— "

"I get it, I get it!" She laughed but stopped when he began working his long, strong, piano-playing fingers. She was damn near growling when he finally let up. "Your hands are like sexual Swiss Army knives. You can do so much at once," she gasped.

He laughed, and they both looked at the monitor. Emme was singing along to her show.

"Well, I'm so inspired in this romantic setting." Blake kissed her again.

"Will you make love to me before something cries or craps? Please?" Livia grabbed a handful of him.

"Mrs. Hartt, you are such a sweet talker."

They each took off their own pants before settling down on the carpet. He crawled at her, nipping and licking until she lay back.

"Lego!" Livia stiffened as she felt a square-shaped pain in her back.

"For fuck's sake." Blake tossed the Lego out of the way then turned back to her, looking determined.

Livia smiled at his profanity. She used her legs to pull him into her. And then they locked eyes. They seemed to remember at the same moment the sad news that had made them long for this comfort. Livia kissed Blake again, holding the back of his neck and putting her hand on his chest's scar. They were fast and needy, both speeding to the resolution. She saw stars when he added his delicious hand to their movements. Both came as quietly as possible, breathing deeply.

Quickly they cleaned up and put their bottoms back on, ready to parent again, before pausing to hug.

"Thank you." She patted his cheek. "Should I go see her now? Do you think?"

Blake stroked her hair as the farewell music of Emme's show filtered through the monitor.

"How about tomorrow? Let them have tonight to each other. Tomorrow's Saturday, your dad and Kathy will be off, so maybe they could take the kids for a little while." He kissed her again.

"Daddy! My popcorn is cold!" Emme came bustling down the hall, and Blake got to the door and unlocked it just before she burst in. "Can you heated it up for me?"

"I'm not sure we can heat up cold popcorn. How about some carrots?" Blake picked up their daughter. "I think we have ranch dressing."

The two left to go downstairs and Livia grabbed her phone.

Tell her I love her. And love you too. I'll be by tomorrow.

She sent the text and lay back on the bed, looking at Kellan's sweet pucker. She couldn't imagine losing him. Her mind created a niece's face and then a nephew's. Her tears escaped, drawing wet lines into her hair. Kyle had always blamed herself for every damn thing. This would be no exception.

22

Just Breathe

The next day, mid-morning, Livia knocked on the door to Cole and Kyle's place. After a few moments Cole answered, eyes red and face sullen. "She's just out of the shower. If you need anything..."

Livia reached up and hugged him hard, not saying anything. She didn't have any words. He slipped past her, locking the door behind him, and she heard the alarm setting itself—the robotic lady's voice was the same as at her house. Cole was going to meet Blake, and John and Kathy were on childcare duty. It was the only way they felt comfortable leaving the kids. No one was getting past John, and Kathy was like a baby whisperer. The kids just went boneless when she was around.

"Slutenstein! I'm here," she called.

"I'm up here, cock dribble."

Livia's heart hurt hearing the hollowness in her sister's insult. She took the stairs two at a time. Kyle sat in the center of her bed, her legs folded under her. She held a pair of scissors and around her were clippings of her long red hair. What remained on her head was a chopped, soaking wet mess.

"Hey." Livia took the scissors from her sister's hand and pulled her into a hug. Out of habit, her comforting hug included rocking. They sat like that for a while before Livia made her sister look her in the face. "Did you have to punish your hair?"

Kyle shook her head. "Do you even realize you're a mother all the time? Like, even when the kids aren't around?"

Livia shrugged, not sure what her sister was getting at.

"It's natural. Maybe because it was supposed to happen to you."

Livia waited, remembering the words of her old professor Dr. Lavender. "*In the center of someone's mourning, the best you can do is listen.*" This had once applied to Blake. But today it seemed equally appropriate for Kyle. Grabbing one of her sister's hands, she waited.

"I mean, I didn't even ask what they did with the baby. Who doesn't ask that? Cole called this morning to find out. She was treated as medical waste. *Medical waste.*" Kyle wasn't crying, but Livia's eyes filled up. "You have babies with five fingers and toes, and I have a baby who was tossed out with the trash, not even looking like a human. They incinerate it." She shook her head. "I feel numb now. Like maybe the baby was better off not having to be mine."

Livia pulled Kyle to her chest, hard, and willed her to stop talking. "You don't get to say that. I know you. All my life I've known you. You're a gift to those who love you."

"You know, Cole's been great. But I find myself blaming him too." Kyle continued as if Livia hadn't spoken. "What if his sperm isn't good enough? How unfair. I just don't know how to pick myself up from this." Kyle hugged her sister back.

"Don't focus on up. Maybe just focus on breathing?" Livia looked out the window.

The day did not match the mood: sun drenched Poughkeepsie. Livia contemplated how to walk the fine line between comfort and pity when she swore she saw movement in Kyle's backyard. But when she focused and looked more closely, she saw nothing.

"Listen, come into the bathroom. Let's fix this hair. It looks like it was cut by a weed whacker. You should know by now you can only trim your cooter with the power tools." Livia pulled on her sister until she came with her. After dragging the laundry basket over to function as a makeshift chair, she pushed Kyle onto it.

"Dude." She had trouble determining where to start.

Kyle rolled her eyes. "Yeah."

"You might have to go to the salon or something." She ran her hands through her sister's uneven locks.

"Just fix it like you fixed your damn Barbie's hair."

"I'm still pissed about that." Threading a chunk of hair through her fingers, Livia cut on an angle to try to make a layer.

As a child, Kyle had stolen Livia's Barbie doll and treated her to a safety-scissor hair adjustment. In the aftermath, Livia had been able to trim the hair in such a way that it fell in a tapered bob. The victimized Barbie wound up being a favorite in all their subsequent doll games because her hair was so unique.

"That was synthetic hair." Livia concentrated harder.

"Mine'll grow back. No pressure." Kyle sighed. "I wish I knew how to stop hating myself for a few fucking minutes."

She looked at her sister's reflection. "Me too. The minute I heard I knew this would be hard. I wish I could fix this."

"Keep cutting. I need to look human by the time Cole gets home." She pulled a blush brush from the counter and added peach to her cheeks.

"I want to tell you this, but I don't want you to think I'm trying to put you down or hurt your feelings." Livia moved around to work on Kyle's brand-new bangs.

"Just say it." Kyle stopped and waited, clutching her brush.

"I just…If it's hard—and I'm not saying you can't or won't—but if it's an option, I'd carry your baby for you." Livia swallowed.

Kyle reached out and pulled her sister against her. They hugged hard for a few minutes before Kyle nodded. "Thanks. I hope it doesn't come to that, but thanks." She almost smiled. "Of course that would mean you'd get your vagina snot all over my kid."

"Bitch." Livia laughed. "Only you could turn the gift of life into something that makes me want to gag."

Kyle slapped her sister on the ass.

"Ow! You hit like a drunk trucker." Livia stepped away from her sister's hair. "What do you think?" The mirror showed more than Kyle would ever see. She was stunning and wholesome and worthy. And her hair looked pretty kick ass too.

"Not too fucking horrible." Kyle stood and shook her hair out. It spiked up, and she ran her hands through it. "Let me rinse off quick. I'm getting hair splinters."

Livia nodded. "Sure, I'll clean up your other grooming station."

She got the vacuum and sucked up the hair before replacing the sheets and laying out a fresh comforter. She wandered to the window, trying to think of ways to keep Kyle busy for the next few months when she saw a man walking casually out of the backyard. After a spike of fear, she pulled out her phone and snapped a picture. Since Emme was approached, she couldn't be too careful. Falling prey to her concerns, she dialed her dad.

"Yup. Hey, kiddo."

She breathed a sigh of relief when she heard Emme's happy chatter and Kellan's baby blabber in the background. "Everyone okay?" Livia turned and watched her sister go from the bathroom into her walk-in closet.

"Sure thing. My granddaughter is painting my toenails. Got to say—that's a first."

Livia busted out laughing. "Wow, I think Kyle and I need a picture of that."

"Don't worry, Kathy's taken a ton of blackmail pictures. And Kellan just had a bath." John paused, listening before adding, "And I guess he's about to have his bottle. Everything okay there?" His concern slipped into his voice.

Her sister came out of her closet in comfy clothes.

"Yes. We're doing makeovers here too. I just wanted to give you a heads up that I saw someone walking through Kyle's backyard. Keep an eye out." Kyle pushed Livia out of the way so she could look out the bedroom window. Livia switched to speakerphone and gave her father a complete rundown of what she'd seen as Kyle examined the picture on her phone.

"I really think this my neighbor from down the road. His dog is always coming over here." Kyle shrugged.

Livia listened to her father's warnings while she mouthed to her sister, "That's because you're a filthy bitch."

Kyle responded by giving Livia creative variations on the middle finger.

After promising their father they'd stay put until the men returned, Livia finally hung up. Her sister had moved on to spanking her own butt with two proud middle fingers, which gave Livia hope that Kyle might be able to work through the sadness. Laughter always made the girls stronger.

"Can I make you something to eat?" Livia kicked her sister's rump gently.

"Ugh. I'm cramping. Everything makes me nauseous." Kyle headed for the door, walking slowly. "I need to get a fresh ice pack for my sin muffin."

Just as they stepped into the hallway, the alarm system sounded. First a beeping, but then sliding into a high, piercing, and unrelenting wail.

Kyle had just moved to disarm it at the panel in the bedroom when Livia pulled her back inside the room and shook her head. They locked the door and worked quickly to push Cole's dresser in front of it.

Someone was breaking into the house.

Cole was driving again, and Blake wished they had a better plan. Chaos had texted, saying he wanted to see him for some tattoo maintenance, which they assumed meant an update on their brother.

"Should we contact Beckett? Even if we figure out how?" Cole made a right onto Chaos's street.

After scanning the area for Chaos, Blake responded. "I'm not sure. I think he'd kick our asses if he knew we had questions for him and didn't at least try." He nodded to the left. "Here he comes."

Chaos opened the back door and slid in. "Gentlemen."

Cole looked in the rearview mirror. "You staying out of trouble?"

The man smiled, and Blake noticed the inside of his lip was tattooed. He ignored the question. "I've got a lead on your brother. I'm a little tight on cash, though. Makes it hard to think."

Cole started the car and headed to his bank for an ATM. True to his word, Chaos said nothing until they arrived.

"How much?" Cole asked as they pulled into the parking lot.

"Forty thousand dollars." Chaos appeared to be about half kidding.

Cole turned in his chair and slid his sunglasses down, giving Chaos a very male stare.

"A thousand, if possible. My anxiety meds are expensive as fuck."

Blake passed his ATM card to Cole. "I'll do half. That work for you?"

After the two transactions were complete, the cash disappeared into Chaos's jacket. "There's a little town in Maryland, and the rumor is Beckett's all over it. Some assbag got the shit kicked out of him boss style a couple months ago. He's been looking for a hit on Beckett. Now, I can't be sure. These are just rumors." Chaos cracked the back window.

"Where you getting these rumors from?" Cole made a few more turns, and they looked out over the choppy Hudson River.

"Around." Chaos opened the door and got out.

Cole rolled down the window. "That's not even a hundred dollars' worth of information."

Chaos pulled out a pair of sunglasses and covered his dark eyes. "Rockvale. It's by the water. He's supposedly living with two ladies."

Blake lifted an eyebrow. There had to be more.

"He's got a liquor store. There's only four in that town. You see him, you tell him everybody's getting jumpy. This place will be a shitfest soon." Chaos nodded at them. "See ya around."

The brothers watched the tattoo artist's receding form.

"Well, that's helpful." Blake shook his head.

"I guess we make some calls. But crap—if he's started a life with a woman, should we really drag him back here?" Cole locked eyes with Blake.

"I don't know. I don't like that someone knows who Emme is. And I think I want Beckett's advice, at the very least." Looking out on the dark river, Blake thought of all the things that could go wrong. He couldn't keep Emme out of school forever. Right now they were living on lockdown. His kids needed to be able to go to the park, be kids.

Cole looked at his phone. He spent some time staring at it before finally dialing. His eyes were worried when he looked at Blake as he listened. "The alarm went off at my house a few minutes ago. Back door. Kyle hasn't turned it off yet."

Blake pulled out his phone as Cole switched to speaker so he could drive at top speed. After three rings it switched to voicemail.

"This is Kyle. This is my phone. Tell it what you think!"

Cole hit redial. The phone went straight to voicemail again. Blake listened on his to the sound of Livia's voicemail. "Sorry, my phone's at the bottom of my purse. I'll call you back as soon as I find it."

"Shit."

Cole took the turns like racecar driver and sped through intersections, barely stopping to make sure they were clear.

Blake called John on his phone and texted Kyle "you okay?" on Cole's.

"Sir, have you heard from the girls?" Blake could hear his daughter singing in the background.

"A little while ago. They were doing makeovers. What's up?" Blake could almost hear John sitting up.

Cole shook his head. "The alarm still isn't reset. Ah, here's the alarm company calling." He went through the process of notifying the alarm company that he did, in fact, have a problem. "Send the cops."

"John, please take Kathy and the kids upstairs," Blake finally continued. "We have no idea what's happening, but bring your gun. We're sending the police to Cole's, and we're almost there. It's probably just the girls forgot it was on and went out somewhere. That happens." Blake ended his call as Cole pulled into the driveway.

Cole reached under his seat and recovered a pistol. Blake had no idea his brother kept a handgun, but at this second he was grateful. From the front, the house looked fine. Livia's car sat in the driveway next to Kyle's. It was such a sunny day, the windows glinted with an almost blinding reflection of the sun. The house alarm pierced through the quiet. If they'd had any close neighbors, they would surely have come running by now—or called to report a noise complaint.

Cole and Blake ran to the front door. "Go through the back," Cole ordered. "Grab a hammer or something."

Blake sprinted around the house, and his stomach dropped. The back door was wide open. He ran through it and slipped. As he landed hard on the floor, he registered the moisture. He lifted his hand and saw it stained red. *Blood. Oh God.* He turned and scanned the woods behind the house. No movement. He pulled a knife from the block in the kitchen, the alarm blaring in his ears. It was so loud it felt like he was going crazy. He swept the rooms visually and noted the red drops of blood continuing up the stairs.

His heart pounded, and it took him a second to realize there was another pounding noise—apart from the alarm filling his ears. He found Cole in his bathroom, pulling a flat iron out from between the handles of the linen closet as someone kicked from the inside.

When the flat iron pulled free, Kyle fell out, tears streaming down her face. She rushed to get past Cole, screaming, "They took her! They took her!"

Cole went to the nearest alarm panel and finally silenced the noise. Incoming sirens replaced the alarm's wail.

"The place is clear," Blake said before approaching Kyle. He set the knife on the dresser. "Who took her? What happened, Kyle?" Blake watched her mouth as she delivered the worst news.

"Livia. They took Livia. She and I came in here, and she was going to get in the cabinet. But when I got in this closet, she locked me in. I could hear her fighting. I heard a gunshot." Kyle wiped her nose, tears choking her.

Cole had secured his gun when the police burst into the room, hollering, "Get down! Put your hands up! Get down!"

John McHugh pushed past the other officers. "Where's Livvie? Put the guns down. These are my kids." His hands were two fists.

"There was a blood trail out the back door," Blake blurted. "Let me follow it." He could barely verbalize anything, but John nodded. Blake pushed through the officers and ran down the steps. People along the way told him not to touch anything, but he ran at top speed anyway. No one was better than he was in the woods.

Blake slowed a bit as he followed the drops of blood through the backyard and into the trees. He tracked the crushed foliage and broken branches. All of the sudden the path was clear to him. He began to run again, hopping and ducking around the nature that ruled the place.

The blood was tapering off, which was good, he hoped. Branches slapped at him, thorns catching on his pants. He saw where there'd been scuffles. He prayed Livia had fought—fought so hard they left her here. But the dread was solid in his lungs. When he made it to the road that ran behind the woods at Cole's place, it was deserted in both directions. He closed his eyes and waited. After a time he thought he heard some crunching gravel to the east. *My wife was taken. Taken.*

John came up behind him, and they shared a look of complete desperation.

The sun crashed in on Blake, fracturing and turning into shards, embedding itself and tearing him apart. *Livia. Livia.* He could hear John issuing commands over the racket of his mind imploding. *Livia.* He bit his fist, and blood filled his mouth. Blake felt two hands shaking him.

"Son. I need you. The kids need you. I'm not sure what the hell kind of fancy bullshit my daughter used to make you into a stand-up man, but I don't have any of that."

Blake tried to focus on John's face. He felt like his pupils were too large to actually see with. He made his eyes wider.

"Ah, shit. Snap together, Blake." John walked away, leaving him standing in the horror and pain of the sun.

He should never have left her alone. He knew better. Damn it. He knew better. The second Emme was approached. *Emme! Kellan!* He ran to catch up with John, stopping the man with his hand. "The kids? Where are the kids?" He was asking for information, but it felt dramatic. Too much. *Oh God, she was taken.*

John turned from issuing orders. "The kids are with two patrolmen and Kathy at your house. She just called to say they're fine. Here, call her."

Blake looked at John's phone for a moment before hitting redial.

He had to do this. He had to fight for his mind. Livia needed him to focus. Kathy picked up on the first ring. "Kids?" he asked.

"Kellan's napping, and Emme is watching her favorite show. The boys from the station will keep us safe."

"Okay. I'll…be in touch." Blake ended the call and handed the phone back to John.

They walked carefully through the woods. Should he be taking the car and going to hunt her down? He didn't know. Cole came from the front yard with his arm around Kyle. Blake walked close to his brother. "You guys staying with us?" *Me. Just me and the kids. Livia. Oh God.*

Cole nodded. "They need our place for evidence."

Kyle refused the paramedics as they approached. "She stuffed me in the linen closet. I couldn't get out. The hinges were on the other side. I tried so hard to break the door down. Where is my sister? Where is my sister?"

Blake walked away from his frantic sister-in-law. He took out his phone and Googled Riverdale liquor stores. He called two in a row, each responding negatively to his request for Beckett. Then he called a third.

"Liquor store. We get you hammered quicker store. How can your day be more awesome?" His brother's familiar voice rang true in his mind.

"Beckett. They took her. Someone took Livia. I don't know—"

"Brother, I'll be there in four hours. Keep your phone close. Call Eve."

The call disconnected, and Blake stared at the phone. Beckett couldn't be any help—he was still wanted for questioning about Chris Simmer's murder. But he just didn't know how to find his wife. Beckett would burn Poughkeepsie to the ground to find her.

Blake dialed Eve's number.

"What?"

"Eve, someone kidnapped Livia from Kyle's house. There's blood everywhere." He started to sob.

"I already know. You take a deep breath. I will find her." She hung up.

Between John, Beckett, and Eve he'd released the worst he could on whoever took his wife. He tried to stop shuddering. He wanted to punch everyone. He wanted to find his kids, his wife and take them into the woods where he could keep them safe. *Livia. Oh God. Where are you?*

Eve ended her call and slipped her cell phone in her back pocket. She looked up at the entrance to Mary Ellen's mansion. There was a decided lack of activity. After Ryan had bolted from lunch, she'd known she was doomed to go back to the bitch's place today.

Ryan had been shocked when the call came in. "What the hell? She was taken in the middle of the day? What the hell? Yeah, okay. I know. I'll check in at the station in just a few."

He shook his head at his phone. "Shit. I got to run. You okay?"

Eve had nodded. "Who?"

"My captain's daughter. Keep your eyes wide open?"

Ryan had run to the parking lot, and Eve went to pay the bill. She got to her own car just in time to see a tidal wave of shaving cream fly out of Ryan's truck as he drove away. Someone, most likely the illustrious Trish, had filled the bed with what had to be an entire store's supply.

Then Blake had called on her way to Mary Ellen's, and she'd decided to fabricate a story involving progress with Ryan and see if Livia's name came up. Hopefully her timing was good. The kidnapping must have happened within the hour.

She observed as much of the property as she could before entering. No speeding cars or yelling. Just peaceful. A bodyguard opened the door for Eve. She nodded at him.

"Quiet day." She waited for his reply, hoping for something.

"So far." He locked the door behind her.

"The boss home? I have an update." Eve kept her sunglasses on so she could inspect the inside of the mansion as well.

"Yup. I'll let her know you're here. She was getting her nails done, so it might be a while." The bodyguard hit a button near his earpiece and relayed the news to someone else. "Go ahead into the ballroom. She says she'll see you."

It was a maddening wait, and Eve wondered several times if this had been the best place to come. This first few hours were critical. But this had to be Mary Ellen's work. She seemed to be throwing everything she had at Poughkeepsie, rather than waiting for any one of her efforts to pay off. *Why the big hurry?* Eve wondered. *Just impatience and inexperience, or something more?* But Livia was connected to both the police and the brothers, so Mary Ellen was escalating—whether the irrational bitch realized it or not. Eve kicked herself for not seeing how vulnerable Livia and Kyle were. She'd focused on the kids.

Mary Ellen's arrival broke her concentration. The woman smiled as she waved her hands dramatically. "My manicure refuses to dry! You know how it is..." Mary Ellen looked at Eve's hands and made a face of displeasure at her unpainted nails. "I do hold my girls to a certain level of expectation."

Eve stopped herself from sighing. "Ryan likes his lady unadorned. Makeup pisses him off."

"Very well. But that would never work for something like the party I'm throwing this evening." Mary Ellen gasped as her phone started to vibrate. "Oh no. Could you please, January? I don't want to ruin my nails."

Eve approached her and lifted her little pastel blue jacket. Her tailored skirt had a small pocket, and she lifted the phone out and held it for Mary Ellen. As the woman swiped her unlock, Eve read her text message upside down.

Package secured. Delivery now?

She glanced up and met Mary Ellen's eyes.

"Did you like my message?" the woman asked.

Eve shrugged, kicking herself for getting caught.

"Well, you already have your nose in my affairs, type this back to him..." She turned her back on Eve. "Take the package to the safe house, and send me pictures for the database."

Eve typed the message to Wren. While doing so, she glanced at the preceding messages and noted the time of "Package acquired"—about ninety minutes ago—before offering the phone back.

She patted her pocket, so Eve pulled up Mary Ellen's jacket to slide the phone back in place.

"So tell me, January. What do you think of my plans?" Mary Ellen waved her fingers and blew on the nails.

"Which ones? Going to a safe house? That sounds like a good idea. Throwing a party? I think you just want to jerk yourself off to some sort of Cinderella fetish you have. It's stupid and will probably get you killed, based on the last meeting you put on like an asshole. Or the Database of Moron-it-tude? Never write crap down. That's all the feds need to nail your ass to the wall." Eve crossed her arms.

Mary Ellen's face went from deadly to that hollow smile again in an instant. "You know what? You're going to bring Ryan tonight. I'll secure you an invitation. You might as well stay here, and I'll dress you. Then you can travel over with the girls. Have him meet you there. It's on Long Island."

Eve sighed. "Really? You think bringing a cop to one of your gatherings is a good idea?"

Mary Ellen looked at her sharply. "I think my party will be the perfect place for a dirty cop."

"So what's this package? Is it anything you'll need me to protect your ass from?" Eve knew this pushed the boundary, but she had to have something.

"No, I'm quite capable of knowing what I'm doing. She's in no shape to hurt anyone." Mary Ellen made her lips into a convincing duck face. "You can just enjoy being a guest this evening."

"You murdered her?" Eve used everything she had to stay neutral, bored.

"I really don't see how the matter is any of your business. Should I be concerned that you're asking so many questions?" She peered at Eve for a moment, eyes wide.

"I just like to know what the hell's going on." Eve sighed. "Things have gotten out of hand in the past." She waited for a moment, praying for a response. None came. "Whatever. I need to go tell Ryan about this party thing. I'll come back after that." Eve stood. She needed to be out looking for Livia.

"Also, tell your boyfriend to bring the information I requested in exchange for the money I paid him." Mary Ellen followed Eve to the door.

"Wouldn't that break my cover? Bad enough I have to think of a reason we're going to this stupid thing." This woman was literally insane.

"True. Just testing you. No worries. You can be my brother Primo's niece for the evening. It's likely the closest he'll ever get. This will be a big night for him." She cackled to herself. "Anyway, I'll find another way to get my hands on Ryan's information. And since you're so interested in details, you should know he's bringing me anything and everything the police have on Beckett Taylor." Mary Ellen paused for a split-second, as if gauging Eve's response. Then she opened the ballroom door and waved a guard over.

Eve did her best to compose herself before she turned and looked down at the woman. "And why do you want information on a dead man?"

Mary Ellen snapped in Eve's face. "Because sometimes dead people aren't dead enough until you kill everyone who knew them. You're a smart girl. I would have thought you'd see that coming."

Eve nodded. "You're badass all right."

"Enough of your sarcasm." Mary Ellen instructed her man to show January out and clicked her way back up the winding staircase.

As she left the mansion, Eve pulled out her phone and began looking for more information on Livia. She jumped a mile when someone tapped her shoulder.

"Yes?" She looked up to see Shark standing in front of her.

"The lady of the house requests that you call your boyfriend from here and remain. Actually, she demands it." Shark allowed no emotion or recognition into his eyes. He just waited with his arms crossed.

Eve dialed Ryan's number. When he answered, he sounded distracted.

"Hey. Remember my super-important uncle? He's having a party at his house tonight, and I just found out we need to attend."

Ryan was silent for a few moments. "Really?"

"Really. Drop everything tonight and come to Long Island with me or we're breaking up. Wear a tux."

"Where is it?" she mouthed to Shark who retrieved an invitation from his jacket and held it out to her. She rattled off the address and time. "I'll meet you there." Eve dropped her phone and stomped on it.

"That was dramatic." Shark shook his head at the carnage.

"I do this to a lot of phones." She kicked it with the toe of her shoe and located the SIM card. She crushed that with her heel. "Because, let me guess, she wanted it taken from me?"

Shark gave her a nod and motioned her back toward the mansion. Eve closed her eyes. Tonight she could tell Ryan about the latest update and maybe get his people on Mary Ellen's computer. She had a sinking feeling the bitch was on to her. She just hoped she lived long enough to help Livia.

23

Boss

Beckett had the whole situation on lockdown within fifteen minutes. Chery was with him at the store, and he explained as loosely as he could that he had a "family emergency" and had to go home immediately. Vere was safe at her day program for the next several hours, and Gandhi snored in the corner. After their brief discussion, Beckett went to the back and called two of his ex-employees — they were into shady shit now, but they were loyal.

They agreed to live at Beckett's house and stay alert while he was away. Gandhi was to stay there with Chery and Vere. When the dog woke up and realized Beckett was gone, there would be hell to pay, but he was sure Vere would keep him settled. One more phone call and Chaos was on his way down from Poughkeepsie to provide backup. The dude was more than likely on his way back to jail anyway, so leaving the state was right up his fucking alley.

Beckett gassed up the Challenger and was on his way. *Whitebread.* If he didn't have a soft spot for Livia…well, damn it, that didn't matter because he did. She loved him even though she shouldn't, believed good things about his heart when his hands had been murderous bastards. Coming back from the dead and arriving in Poughkeepsie was not what he'd had planned for this day, but hearing Blake's voice had blown his mind. And he was flying blind. He had no idea who was pulling the strings in Poughkeepsie now.

On the way up, in the fast lane the whole time, he made phone calls. He tracked down as many of his old douchebags as he could and pumped them for information. He called Chaos again, and while they both went in different directions on the same road, he asked him questions. Chaos confirmed there was trouble in the air, but he didn't know who was causing it. He seemed genuinely surprised to learn Beckett wasn't involved.

Whatever these people wanted, taking Whitebread was uncalled for, and in Beckett's opinion it escalated the Poughkeepsie situation considerably. She was a cop's daughter. Snatching her was almost an amateur move—or a batshit crazy one. But if the goal was to get him home, it was fucking working.

As stupid as he was driving, he was shocked he hadn't been pulled over, but three hours and forty-eight minutes later, he took the exit for Poughkeepsie without police involvement. He drove straight to John McHugh's old house, Blake and Livia's now. He refused to think of his brother alone with his kids, because he would find her.

Beckett parked the car as the sun began packing up for the day. A uniformed cop instantly materialized and opened his car door as another approached from the other side.

"I'm here to see McHugh and my brother," Beckett explained as he stepped out. "And yes, you should arrest me. But let me talk to the men in that house first."

Blake threw open the front door and jogged down the steps to grab his brother in a desperate hug.

"I'm here. I'll get her. I promise." Beckett held Blake's shoulders. He didn't like how unsettled Blake's eyes were. "You know I'll find her."

"I had to call you. I just had to." Blake held out his arm for the brothers' shake. Cole stepped into the circle and held his arm out as well.

Beckett was solemn about the greeting, pounding Cole on the back. "I'll find her."

Cole and Blake thanked the officers and led Beckett toward the house. John McHugh now stood at the door.

"Hey, can I talk to your father-in-law alone for a minute?" Beckett didn't drop his eyes from John's intense stare.

Blake looked reluctant, but disappeared into the living room. Cole followed.

McHugh said nothing, so Beckett gave him a quick summary. "She's been taken by some sort of crime organization. I know of no motive yet. I've been in touch with every douchebag I still have here, and I know where I need to go to get more information."

John shook his head. "I'm not putting my daughter's fate in your hands."

Beckett sighed. "Listen, you want to put me in jail, yes? To get Livia from these people alive will take a lot of lawlessness—things I'm more than willing to do to get your girl back in this house where she fucking belongs." McHugh still said nothing, but he didn't slam the door, so Beckett kept talking. "You do your thing. You get the cops where they need to be, and I will keep you posted. You'll know everything I do. But I can't do jack shit if your boys are going to snap me up. After I have her, fine. But right now, Blake needs me. This is something I can do." He waited, praying the father part of McHugh would buy in to his plan.

"If she dies I can't promise I won't kill you."

McHugh was out of his mind too, Beckett realized. His eyes reminded him of Blake's when he looked closely. "As long as she's okay? I don't give a fuck what happens to me. That's a promise."

McHugh rubbed his forehead. "Fine. *Fine*. Last time I trusted you, you ran out on me." He gave him a look of disgust. "I've got a man in there. He was invited to some sort of party tonight with individuals who might be involved. That might be a place to start. I've got to get down to the station. They're getting some information on the blood found at the scene."

He pushed past Beckett and into the yard. As Beckett went in to talk to his brothers he could hear McHugh passing on the command that Beckett was to be left alone. That was one miracle. Not having the cops after his ass would make this so much easier. Well, not that it was going to be easy. Chances were he was going to have to kill a lot of people to get Whitebread home.

He came into the living room and found Blake holding a small bundle. He knew he couldn't stay long, but he just wanted a peek at his namesake.

"I'm coming," Blake declared immediately. "We'll do this together."

Beckett came close enough to see the baby. He was adorable and very asleep.

From the stairs, Emme gave him the once-over. "You're new. My mommy is missing. Are you helping her come home?" She walked up to Beckett without fear.

He squatted down. "I will." She looked so much like Livia, except with Blake's green eyes. This little girl was braver than she should be. Just like her mom.

Emme reached out to his forearm and touched the brothers' tattoo. "My daddy and Uncle Cole have that same thing." Her touch was gentle. He nodded. "That means you're family. My mommy will make you hot dogs when she comes home. And then you can see my frog puppet."

"I can't wait to meet that puppet. I need you to do me a favor. Your dad has to stay here with you. Your brother and you need your dad to make you hot dogs until your mom comes home. Okay?" Beckett smiled as the girl nodded solemnly.

Just then a flying weight pounded him on the back and kicked him in the butt. Beckett stood and turned, accepting a full-body hug from Kyle. Then she punched him in the arm.

"Seriously. I'll bring her back. You have to make sure your man stays put. Okay?" Beckett set her on her feet and looked at his brothers.

"I'm only asking because I might need one of you to drive somewhere. I need people I can count on. Otherwise I'd bring you both in a heartbeat." Beckett tussled Emme's hair and reached out to squeeze Kyle's hand.

Blake looked like he was standing in full sunlight ten years ago. "I can't do *nothing*."

"Whitebread needs you here." He didn't say it out loud, but he knew Blake got it: If he failed, the kids needed a parent.

"Anyone talk to Eve?" He had to have her on his team tonight. He just had to.

Blake sighed. "A few hours ago. She's working on something, trying to help. She hasn't texted me back since we spoke."

Beckett's stomach flipped thinking of her. Hearing her name in conversation flashed him back to the way things used to be. He wanted her. He handed Cole his phone. "Can you put John's number in here? Does he text?"

Before he could focus any part of himself on Eve, Whitebread needed to get back home. He nodded at his brothers, collected his phone, and left without saying goodbye.

He had McHugh on the line before he even got in the car. "Sir, I need your men to stay off of anyone who's been associated with me in the past for a few hours."

John didn't pretend to be cordial. "No. I'd never issue that order. Anyone doing something illegal is fair game."

Beckett turned the car toward to his old stomping grounds. "With all due respect, I came out of foster care and ruled this town in less than a year. I can find one girl in a few hours. But in order to do that? I'm going to be busting this place up. With or without you, my brother gets his wife back tonight. There are no other options."

Beckett sped into the parking lot that had once held his strip mall office. It was just rubble now.

"All I can say is I won't arrest you until after Livia's home." John disconnected the call.

"Fuck him." Beckett exited his car and nodded at the gathered douchebags. There were only nine. He didn't ask about the others. He didn't address his long absence. "Anyone hear anything about a girl? Woman? Brown hair?" Beckett crossed his arms and waited. The streets were liquid with information if the right people had their ears open. No one said anything. "You will be compensated. And if I find out you knew something and didn't 'fess up, you will live the rest of your life without your dick." Beckett scanned the crowd.

"Boss, I heard of one of the abandoned houses on the east side has some movement around it tonight, a few cars there." One of his old drug runners offered the first bit of information.

"I heard Joey Fantone was making good money now. Bought himself a new Cadillac. Ain't nobody I know giving Joey any money—unless it was you. Never imagined you were still on this side of your grave." This guy used to run a pawn shop. Maybe he still did.

"Anybody offer you money lately?" Beckett gave the man a cold stare.

"A cop's been nosing around. Named Ryan Morales." The pawn owner shifted on his feet. "And some other guy came a few weeks ago asking about the cop. Swear he was looking to buy him out—like old-school you."

Beckett absorbed the information, tried to put all the pieces together.

"Saw Eve yesterday."

Beckett's eyes found the man like heat-seeking missiles. This butterball used to keep the hookers in check. "She was with some pig. All over him. They were sucking tonsils at that diner on route nine. She has her hair black. Funny though, 'cause I know she went out for a call to be a girl for an organization." He smirked. "She'd go for some good money. Bet she fucks like an animal." He looked around with a snicker, searching for another man to corroborate his slimy point of view.

The parking lot was silent. Butterball looked nervously back at Beckett. "Just kidding. God, I was just kidding. I'm sorry. I'm an asshole."

"What organization?" Beckett made a fist, wanting to crumble the man's face.

"Some crazy lady down in the city. Big league. Her daddy's in weapons—of *all* varieties. Couple of my girls went to the call as well. They haven't come back, so I guess they got scooped up. Fuckers. I should be getting compensated." He stretched and Beckett could see he'd added a new neck tattoo.

A tall, quiet man he remembered as Milton Conts cleared his throat. He'd procured hard-to-get things for Beckett back in the day. Mouse had trusted him. "There's an event this evening on Long Island that's been generating quite a bit of buzz. The woman seems to have sent summonses more than invites, but she's still billing it as a party. Might be a good place to get information. I could possibly manufacture you an invitation if you want to get in."

Beckett nodded. "Okay. I need you four to suit up and get a few cars between you. Arm yourself to the teeth of your balls." He nodded at the tall man. "I'll need that invite. Text me when it's ready. Butterball, call Joey Fantone and offer him a job with a shit ton of money. Have him meet you here."

First, Beckett would be checking out the abandoned house. Second, he was going to torture Joey until he had every bit of information the man knew. Third, he was going to that motherfucking party and killing them one by one until someone who knew something about Livia spoke. Adrenaline flooded his heart. It beat as if it could power a hundred men. Damn it all if it didn't feel fantastic.

24

Night Walk

Livia took a deep breath as someone removed the scarf around her head. She sat on the floor with her wrists bound in front of her—at least her legs were free. She found herself in a rather well-appointed house. The room was decorated nicely, but with all the cold personality of a hotel. She could count five men in the room.

Her breasts were leaking. She was wearing a black shirt, but it was still obvious. Tears slipped down her cheeks, not because of all she faced, but because she knew her baby was hungry. They were all out of frozen breast milk. Blake would have to buy formula. And what if Kellan didn't tolerate it? *Blake.* She was terrified for him. If he'd been taken this way, she'd be a mess.

"Please let me call home and tell them I'm okay. Just a quick call." She was about to get into how she needed to feed the baby when a harsh look from the man closest to her curled her tongue quiet.

They went back to what they were doing, which seemed mostly like consulting their phones. Hopelessness swamped her, staggering her mind. This was obviously planned. She thought back to the abduction, running through it to see if the outcome could've been different:

She'd heard the alarm and dragged Kyle into the bedroom. They'd blocked the door as best they could and gone into the bathroom. Livia had pushed her sister into the linen closet and closed it. She'd whispered she was going to hide in the cabinet, but after a peek, she knew she wouldn't fit. She'd spied Kyle's flat iron and stuck it through the handles on the linen closet to keep her sister inside, keep her safe. Livia had exited the bathroom and shut the door, barely hearing her sister's complaints over the alarm's piercing din.

When she'd looked up, the sight of the men made her mouth go dry. They'd grabbed her roughly and lifted her over the now-broken dresser. Everything had happened so fast. She'd clawed at them and managed to disarm the one holding her waist. While he wrestled it back from her, the gun had discharged. She'd waited to feel the searing pain, but when the man carrying her yelled, she realized he'd been struck instead. She was passed to one of the other men and restrained by a third until she quit struggling.

There'd been so many men in Kyle's house, and they seemed intent on taking her. She'd decided that if she let them, they might leave her sister here. So she cooperated. That might have been stupid. Maybe a whole different crew took Kyle. She might be in another place entirely.

One of the men now growled in her direction, still nursing the gunshot wound on his leg. He'd been able to walk, so she assumed he'd just been grazed by the bullet.

She took calculated deep breaths, trying to settle her pulse. She had to think clearly. How many times had her father told her, *Never let them take you to a second location?* But they had, and now she wasn't sure what the hell to do.

Her father would find her. He would not rest until she was found. She knew that as sure as she knew her name. Until then, her job would be to stay alive, to keep thinking. To not let her absolute ache to be with Blake and the kids take away her common sense, not let the choking fear steal her focus. Stay alive. No matter what it took. Her kids weren't growing up without a mother like she had.

No way in hell.

In her room at Mary Ellen's mansion, Eve slipped on her pale blue high heels as she watched the news. Livia was plastered all over it. The newscaster was damn near orgasming while she delivered the heartbreaking news.

Shark knocked on her door before letting himself in. The room was wired and video-monitored, so they said nothing of the news story.

"Got your accessories here. You and Micki and three others have the same necklace." Shark opened a velvet box that held a gorgeous diamond string with a huge topaz teardrop at its center.

She held still as Shark draped it on her, clasping the chain together. She nodded. Information received. She wouldn't be alone. Micki had been chosen to attend this evening as well. Mary Ellen liked to be flanked by women. Eve swore the chick had been a big, hat-wearing pimp in a previous life.

"I'm your security tonight, just so you know." He stepped away from her and she took in his monochromatic ensemble. It consisted entirely of the color gray.

Eve took one last look in the mirror. She was unarmed, so she couldn't touch anything deadly on her body reassuringly. Instead she looked like a dark-haired version of Birthday Barbie. Mary Ellen had picked a pale blue ball gown for Eve. It would do for Cinderella in a pinch. Her hair had been swept into an elaborate updo and adorned with more diamonds. Eve picked up her clutch, and Shark held out his hand. He rooted through it before handing it back to her.

"I'm to search you as well." He lifted an eyebrow.

Eve's purse felt a tiny bit heavier. Either Shark had given her a weapon or planted a bomb. She couldn't look now. His hands were extremely thorough as he searched, but she didn't flinch when he slipped a finger inside her panties. With one quick thrust, he inserted an object into her vagina. He smiled when he returned to standing in front of her, his pants straining from his adventures under her full skirt.

She had to smile and walk through the door as if she hadn't just accepted something into her body. It was comfortable, so at least she could relax a bit. The asshole hadn't slipped her an uncovered blade.

He held out an arm, and she took it for their trip down the stairs. Halfway down she turned to him. "Usually a man has to buy me a drink first."

He smirked. "Usually a man who did that would come back with a stump."

Eve acknowledged the truth with a nod as they proceeded down the stairs. Mary Ellen was flanked by Micki and two other girls at the bottom, each dressed like a colorful cupcake. Eve left Shark and took her place. It was as if they were flock of geese with Mary Ellen at the point of the V.

Unlike the other women, Mary Ellen had on a simple, white gown. But her accessories took the prize, easily tripling the copious jewels on the women behind her.

"As always, be ladies. Be available. We'll be looking to entice, to distract certain gentlemen." Mary Ellen had the demeanor of a strict schoolteacher. "With the exception of January, who has a gentleman caller this evening, you are all to seek one of the powerful men you've been studying."

Eve wished she'd been in on those meetings. Had she been purposely excluded from the plans for this evening, or just not around? Her duties with Ryan did give her a much longer leash than the other girls had. Either way, no further instructions were given, and the drill from the first disastrous event began again. Each girl had a driver and her own car, but only Eve had security too. Shark was patted down before leaving, which also struck her as odd.

When they settled themselves in the car, she met his eyes. He motioned for her purse. She looked inside first, spying a Beretta Nano before handing her bag to him. He discreetly palmed the weapon and it disappeared into his jacket. With the divider up, Shark and Eve were as alone as they were going to get. She raised an eyebrow, asking him every question she had without saying a word.

"There are no ears in here, just cameras, so mind yourself."

Eve crossed her legs and looked at her crotch.

"You've got a small blade in a waterproof container. Couldn't let you get caught without something." He stretched his arms above his head.

She covered her mouth with her hand. "And you're not allowed to carry because?"

Shark smiled at her. "Apparently you're dangerous. They were afraid you might get a hold of my gun."

"I will." She looked at her pale pink nails. "You know anything about a lady getting bagged tonight?"

Shark looked out the window, covering his mouth as well. "Heard some noise about luring Taylor back from his supposed death. That woman has a hard-on for him. Not sure why. You've gotten pretty fucking far without her knowing who you are, considering you murdered Taylor how long ago now?"

Eve ignored his barb and shrugged. "She could know. Cagey bitch. Where'd they take the lady?"

"Somewhere down by a river, so I heard. Planning some sick shit. Televised nonsense here tonight. I didn't catch it all." Shark scratched the back of his neck.

Eve's stomach dropped. If she was televising shit, what the hell was she going to do to Livia? Was Mary Ellen expecting Beckett?

"Just make sure Micki gets out alive if any shit goes down. I have a few other things I have to do tonight." Shark sat back against the seat, putting on the sham of a relaxed man.

She took the warning for what it was worth: Things were going to get wild. Again. She wasn't a huge fan of parties in general, but the ones that involved Mary Ellen sucked the hardest.

"I'll do what I can, but you have to give me more than 'down by a river.'" Eve wished she had a phone to tell Ryan to stay home.

The car pulled up at another gorgeous mansion. The façade resembled the White House. Shark held out an elbow for Eve as she exited. She followed the other girls behind Mary Ellen up the steps.

Shark leaned closer. "You look too smart. Get vacant."

She shook her head and pinched him.

As they promenaded up the marble steps he added, "The place isn't vacant like the others. Someone lives there, at least some of the time."

Someone inside announced Mary Ellen as if she were a visiting queen. Eve took in the scene as she descended the stairs into a huge room. The Long Island Sound furnished the backdrop.

Primo stood reluctantly and joined his sister in the center of the dance floor. At least he had pants on this time. A strange jumble of emotions seemed to bubble just below Primo's almost-handsome surface. Eve spotted Ryan across the room, and he nodded. He looked ridiculously good in a tuxedo, though his bowtie was undone. The orchestra began with a slow waltz, and Eve motioned for him to come closer.

He traversed the dance floor until he was in front of her. "May I have this dance?" He looked suspiciously at Shark.

Eve let go of Shark's arm and took Ryan's hand. "Please."

He led her to the corner of the floor and pulled her close. "This is one hell of a dress. Jesus."

"Right? It's like a prop from *Gone with the Wind*." She grabbed his bowtie. "And is this a stylistic choice?"

"I'm lucky I know it belongs around my neck. You know how to do this up?" He winked at her.

He smelled great. He looked devastatingly good. Eve wanted him out of this house with a visceral need. Damn it if she didn't want to protect him.

"No. I don't. Leave it. It's got flair." She held on to him as he assumed a dance position.

"I don't have a freaking clue how to dance. So I'll follow you." Ryan looked lost.

Eve touched his face, pulling him down for a kiss. She spoke while their lips touched. "I never learned. We'll just stand here and wiggle."

He smiled into their kiss, eyes lighting up a bit. She got a lump in her throat. To be looked at the way he looked at her…"Trish is an asshole for dumping you." Eve scanned the room.

"She's an asshole for a lot of reasons. One being ordering four hundred pizzas on my credit card. 'Just leave them in front of the door, don't knock.'" He shook his head, and Eve smiled. "I had to climb through the boxes to get out of my place today. I can't even…"

Eve snuggled into his chest and began to whisper the information she'd gathered from Shark. "I need you out of here and soon." She looked into his eyes.

"No way, baby. This place is filled with shitbags and fucksores. We can both go." Ryan looked determined as they swayed.

"I need a drink." Eve pulled him toward a huge bar.

"That's my girl." Ryan squeezed her hand.

Eve fought the chill that went down her spine. She couldn't stop thinking. Ryan was a good guy. A cop. A dream come true, if she was still a dreamer. But she needed not to be. Instead she scanned the room for anything that might offer insight into Livia's predicament. And if she was being honest, for anything that even vaguely resembled Beckett.

After a lengthy battle, and long after their usual bedtimes had passed, Blake finally had both kids asleep—in his bed. Kellan had been fussy, and he hadn't consumed much of any of the bottle of formula Kathy had prepared. Emme had required her favorite lullaby six times before she closed her eyes.

Now he paced in the bedroom. It just wasn't fair. They'd been through enough. He'd truly believed the worst was far, far behind them. But that isn't how life works. He should've known there was no quota of shit. He took more deep breaths. Every instinct he had as a man told him to be out looking for her, but he also needed to stay with his kids. Surely Beckett had been right. The kids needed him to stay safe so they would have a parent—always.

He set up the baby monitor and aimed it at the bed. Leaving the door open a crack, he tiptoed down the hall to knock softly on Livia's old bedroom door, now Kellan's nursery and a guestroom. Cole opened the door almost instantly, a question in his eyes. Kyle lay on the pullout bed, eyes wide open.

"Can I talk to you?" He stepped backward so Cole could exit the room.

Blake handed him the baby monitor. "Listen, I know you won't like this—"

Cole shook his head. "Don't. I know you're going after her. Kyle and I will watch the kids."

"No matter what?" Blake waited.

"I'll get you my gun." Cole turned to go back into the room.

Blake touched his arm. "No, I'm good. I'm just going to find her and bring her back."

Cole closed the door, and he went downstairs. Sitting on the mantel was Livia's paper rose bouquet from their wedding. He touched it briefly. She would come for him if the situation were reversed. She *had* come when he was in the woods, and she'd stood between him and a man set on violence. Blake slipped on his jacket and some gloves, tucking his messy hair into a knit cap. He had no good plan as he exited his house, and the cop on duty came over to greet him.

"You guys need something? I can have it brought for you." He looked at Blake briefly before scanning the area again.

"Thanks. No, I'm going for a walk." Blake moved past him.

"Blake? Really? Did you talk to John about this?" The cop matched his stride.

"No. Turns out I'm a grown man. But thanks for watching my house and keeping those kids safe. My wife…I can't sit here. She needs to know I'm looking for her, even if I'm not the one to find her." Blake turned to face the cop. He was a young one. Probably didn't have kids yet. "You can tell John I was belligerent if you want. Don't get in trouble on account of me."

"Okay…I think this is a bad idea. You at least got a phone on you?" The cop stopped following him.

He nodded. "Thanks again." Blake stepped it up to a jog, the night air filling his ears with its quiet. He would go back to the blood spots in the woods and track the car if he could—though it was probably pointless. But he wouldn't think about anything other than bringing her home. *Not* that she was taken by multiple men. Men who still had her, who could do anything they wanted to his wife.

He wiped the angry tears from his eyes, letting his inner tramp take over. This was no time to let his mind feel fragile. He was going to find Livia. He began to compose a song to her, and it was joyful and triumphant. He would play it for her when he brought her home.

25

Pretty Little Thing

Beckett busted into the abandoned house with enough gun power to level a small village. Every single teenager in the place probably wet their pants. After kicking in all the doors to make sure they weren't a front, with Livia hidden somewhere, Beckett cursed his way back out.

He dialed his phone and was soon talking to a douchebag. "You got Joey?"

"He and his Cadillac are here right now. Where you want him?" Beckett could hear Joey whining in the background.

"Put him on the fucking phone." Beckett put his car in gear and drove toward the strip mall parking lot.

"I'm not talking. Tell that cocksucker to eat shit." Joey sounded full of himself.

"He doesn't want to talk, boss." The douchebag sounded perplexed.

"No kidding. Put me on speakerphone." Beckett needed to avoid the time it would take to torture answers out of Joey. "Hey, sweetheart. You hear me?"

"No. Fuck you." Joey was all riled up. Which wasn't good. He was a slippery bastard with little loyalty. Whoever had him by the shorthairs had a good grip.

"You've been with me in the past when I needed answers from people. You remember how that turns out, babycakes?" Beckett listened to the silence for a second. "Now you're thinking. Don't do that. It gets you in trouble."

"I can't." Joey sounded less sure of his anger.

"Asshole, I'll turn your taint into a hand puppet. You know I will. You can bet your virginity on it." He listened again, only a few miles from the parking lot now.

"Fuck you," Joey said, with little conviction. "You don't know her. How this chick works. It's personal. She's got a guy on my mom. *My mom.*"

Beckett pulled into the parking lot and almost ran over Joey's toes. He opened the door hard and slammed it into Joey's kneecaps. He grabbed him by the hair and forced the man to look at him. "Your mom?"

Joey tried to nod, but winced and seemed to think better of it when his head didn't move. "Yeah."

"Isn't she in the nursing home?" Beckett slapped Joey's face.

"Fuck you. Yeah, she's there. Doesn't even know who she is anymore. The fucker sent me this."

Joey struggled to pull out his phone, and Beckett released him so he could scroll through the pictures. He found a video and hit play. Beckett took the phone from his hand.

A frail old woman sat in a dimly lit room when a man's voice startled her. "Annie! You're on fire! You're on fire!"

The confusion in the woman's face was heartbreaking. Beckett could almost see when the word *fire* surfaced from within the fog she lived in. All of the sudden she was petrified. The man kept telling her she was on fire until she started crying and swatting at her nightgown.

"Jump out the window! Jump. You've got to jump, Annie. You're on fire!" The man unlocked the window's safety latch. There was a brief shot of the ground, stories below. Then he swung back to the woman, who was pulling herself to her feet.

She staggered and fell, all while the man kept encouraging her to jump. She stood again, her face that of a wild animal scared out of its mind. Just before she could pull herself onto the sill, the man closed the window and relocked it. The video cut out.

"It's from a disposable cell. Mom's okay, other than her knees are all banged up. She couldn't tell me anything about the guy. She couldn't remember any of it — not surprising since she can't remember my name." Joey took the phone back and touched the screen before slipping it into his pocket.

"That's some freaky shit." Beckett waited for more information. Joey's body language had completely transformed. It now seemed like talking was about to happen.

"She's a sociopath. I've never met anyone made of such crap." Joey shook his head. "I've had to do jobs for her. A few jobs—like similar shit to what you just saw in that video. Scare the fuck out of people. But, you know, she's got someone on my mom." Joey lit a cigarette.

"Why not pack up mom and leave?" That's what Beckett would've done.

"Yeah, you know what kind of care my mom needs? She flips out if her slippers aren't in the right spot. I'm a complete stranger to her. The place, though—the colors and the uniforms—it seems to make her happy." Joey exhaled a cloud of smoke.

"Tell me everything you know."

"Fuck that shit. She's got eyes everywhere. She'll not only kill my mom but make it hurt the whole damn time she's dying. I can't. I can't take the risk." Joey shook his head. "You kill me. You can taint puppet me. I know you'd never touch my mother."

Beckett shook his head. "I'm looking for a kidnapped lady. You have any information that can help?"

Joey's hand shook as he took his next drag. "She's not the only one. I've had to help them bag two other girls in the last week."

"Dead?" Beckett's stomach was in knots.

"Not yet. They're related to people, so she's using them. Like the shit she's doing to me." Joey rolled his head on his neck. "They got someone you know? They're probably after you."

"Where did you take the women?" Beckett felt his anger boiling.

"We took them to houses, like with For Sale signs on them and shit." He thought a moment. "Yeah, they all had For Sale signs on them—Baker's Realty. All over New York. And one in Connecticut. They're going to do some sick shit."

"I need all your contacts." Beckett pulled out his phone and began texting John and Blake the Baker's information.

"That's just it. We all don't even fucking work for her. She's getting us all to fuck with each other." He tossed his cigarette on the ground before grinding it with his shoe.

"Who is she?" Beckett knew of no female bosses in the area. The closest thing this place ever had to that was Eve.

"Her name's Mary Ellen. She's not shy about sharing that." Joey looked nervous.

"Is this everything you know?" Beckett looked deep into the other man's eyes.

"I can give you the addresses where we took those girls. They were both blondes. Well, and one little boy." Joey made a motion as if he was writing with a pen and paper.

Beckett turned to the douchebag closest to him. "Text me his information. Hold him until I say let him go. I want the address for the little boy too."

He had to move. This shit was going to get evil fast.

Eve sipped on pink champagne and made what appeared to be very flirty small talk with Ryan. They did so to cover the cell phone communication Ryan was having with Captain McHugh. Pictures were snapped and sent, gathered information passed along, and they'd full-on made out several times, hiding texting and spying.

When Mary Ellen stepped onto the dance floor and tapped her glass, Eve shook her head. "This isn't going to be good. Buckle up, cowboy."

She stood with the crowd as three different video screens were projected on a large, blank wall. Eve leaned against Ryan and wrapped her arms around his neck. He now had plenty of cover for his cell phone. He nipped at her neck, and she smiled.

"Gentlemen, please direct your attention to the screens. I know some of you are quite anxious for an update on missing family members."

A sudden wave of silence settled over the crowd.

"Does this chick ever learn?" someone whispered near Eve and Ryan.

"Can someone please shoot her?" another voice replied.

"As many of you know from our last little gathering—and the rest of you know from the messages I've kindly sent you in the interim—I've politely requested that business dealings with Sevan Harmon be suspended. His business will soon end its operations in our area, and I'm pleased to note that many of you have been able to restrain yourselves quite appropriately. However…" She paused and made a little *tsking* sound. "Others of you have not been so wise." Mary Ellen nodded and each of the three blank video screens came alive with real-time footage of a frightened hostage.

A collective gasp escaped the crowd, and Eve could feel Ryan moving his cell phone around to try to catch every image. After a quick scan, Eve determined that Livia was not among the captives. She cursed and cheered at the same. The last screen held a heartbreakingly small boy.

"You're going to die!" came a voice from the crowd.

"Kill her."

"That's my child!"

"Wait." She was using her schoolteacher voice again, which made Eve furious. "You have no way of communicating with the gentlemen in charge of the fate of your loved ones. If you kill me, they die. Totally up to you." She shrugged.

The noise died down a bit. Thugs of all sizes and levels of refinement looked at each other blankly. None seemed quite sure what to do. None knew who to trust.

"I'm assuming you'll want these ladies and the small gentleman back," Mary Ellen continued. "If we can just come to a formal agreement regarding Mr. Harmon, I'll make sure your loved ones have every amenity."

A man approached Mary Ellen, gun drawn. She smiled.

"You'll let me because otherwise—"

She looked away and nodded. One of the screens burst into movement. The woman bound to the chair began shaking as a man reached out with an electrical probe, barely touching her arm. She couldn't scream because of the tape over her mouth, but she made noise anyway.

The whole time, Mary Ellen smiled at the man who'd threatened her. After a few moments she raised her hand and motioned for the attacker to stop. The woman slumped.

"That's your niece, if I'm correct?"

"You *know* who she is." The man stepped closer.

"She's a pretty little thing." She waved her hand. "The others haven't been touched. You caused that pain for your niece. Why don't you have a seat?" Mary Ellen motioned to his chair.

Eve turned in to Ryan's chest. He kissed her forehead.

"She's not going to let you leave. This is too much." She looked in his eyes.

"I'm figuring." Ryan shrugged.

"They're going to need you, though. They might try to take me or your mom to be sure you cooperate. I gave them a false address for her."

His jaw tensed. "Yeah."

"They can take me. If they do, don't worry. I'll be fine." Eve touched his face and smiled. "You armed?"

He gave the slightest shake of his head.

"I've got something for you." Eve spun around to face forward, hugging his arms tight to her middle. "Give me a second."

As discreetly as possible, and taking full advantage of the chaotic crowd, she reached up her dress and removed the weapon Shark had given her from its hiding spot. Straightening and smoothing her skirt, she passed it to Ryan. In turn, he slipped his cell phone down the front of her bodice.

Beckett could see a video monitor from where he stood, and on it, just behind the ranting old chick, he could also see Eve. Her hair was dark and her dress was bizarre, but it was Eve. It felt like a punch as he watched her twirl in a man's arms, whispering and touching him.

Why the hell she was at that crazy woman's party, Beckett didn't fucking know. But she'd moved on, clearly. He looked over his shoulder and nodded. Behind him four douchebags pulled down their ski masks along with him. They slammed into the structure like the fist of God.

Beckett went low and knocked over the chair the little boy was strapped to. He quickly dismantled it and scooped the boy up. The rest of the douchebags eliminated the kidnappers gruesomely, since they knew they had an audience.

Beckett put the boy down when they were good distance away from the house. He sliced through the bindings and comforted the kid as best he could.

"Listen, I'm going to get you to a policeman, and he will take you to your parents. Are you okay?"

The boy just nodded, eyes wide. Beckett remembered his mask and lifted it up. The kid was so fucking little. He pulled out his phone and tried to call McHugh. A different cop answered the phone and told him the captain was in the middle of a raid. Beckett's heart soared. "Is it Livia?" he asked. But the officer had no further details available—or so the bastard said. Nonetheless, after a brief conversation, Beckett met a patrol car in a nearby parking lot. The rescued child seemed to relax when he saw the uniform. Beckett couldn't have picked a better delivery system. The cop immediately called the kid's mom while buckling him in the backseat, and Beckett departed before the policeman got a chance to ask questions. His douchebags were supposed to burn down the house where they'd found the kid to the ground.

Back in his car, he got a text from McHugh saying a kidnapped lady had been freed a few towns over. And no, she wasn't Livia. Beckett sighed, his pulse racing. That party was going to turn into a shitstorm. What would Mary Ellen do after he or the cops released all her hostages and took down—one way or another—all her kidnappers?

McHugh had extra officers from surrounding counties and SWAT teams scoping out all the Baker's Realty properties they could find. He was damn happy he'd found the kid and McHugh had gotten a girl, but neither had been Livia, and she was his ultimate goal.

He called the tall man who procured items. "Milton, you got an invite for me? And how about a tux? Looks like I'm headed to a party."

He needed his hands around that bitch's throat to get her to talk.

26

Thank You

Just like the last damn party Mary Ellen had insisted on, this one had turned to spectacular disaster. The crowd had nearly rioted as they watched the little boy freed, and only quick action by Mary Ellen's people and several in the crowd who evidently still had loved ones in play had prevented the boy's father from taking Mary Ellen out immediately. When one of the women was freed half an hour later, Mary Ellen had blanched, and Primo had hustled her over to a safe corner for what looked like a decidedly unpleasant discussion. And, as Eve had predicted, after the second melee Mary Ellen's people had come for Ryan. They offered her no explanation, but seemed to snatch him up simply for being there, watching her all the while. She played along, making her face impassive and letting him be carted off. She waggled her fingers in goodbye as they dragged him away.

No one was allowed to leave, so the crowd was now glued to the screens, waiting to see if the remaining woman would be freed. She joined them in studying the last captive. She couldn't shake the feeling that the first man to bust into the room with the little kid had been Beckett. As she watched, Mary Ellen stepped away from Primo to look anxiously around the ballroom. Eve couldn't believe she was going to have to save this chick's ass. Again. But damn it, until she knew where Livia was, she needed her.

Eve tapped Micki as she walked by and motioned with her head for her to follow. Shark's friend had stayed alive this long, and Eve hoped she could be trusted. Micki followed Eve until they flanked Mary Ellen. Eve put her hand on the woman's shoulder, leaning down to whisper behind her cupped fingers. "You need to get the upper hand. This is turning to shit."

Mary Ellen whirled to face Eve, rage filling her eyes. "I have complete control. *Why does everyone doubt me?"* She cleared her throat and turned her back on them to return to the microphone. "Everyone! Everyone! Please. You think these events are a surprise to me? I was never actually going to keep your people. Like that was ever an option. It would be a death sentence." The group quieted down. "These kidnappings are for display only. I'm trying to show you that as individuals, we *are* vulnerable. That's why we need to work together. Clearly Mr. Harmon won't protect you—or can't protect you—so why not do things my way? My family's business is long-standing and well-respected. I'm certain we can accommodate your needs."

Mary Ellen held out her hand, and Eve helped her up on a table. She had to hand it to her: this woman was going to put icing on a pile of shit and call it cake.

"These tactics I've used to bring you together are not the ones I like. I prefer things to be much more dignified. And I see no reason they can't be, going forward. I just need you to understand how deadly serious I am about this."

She stopped and let the crowd talk among themselves for a few beats. Eve held out a hand to help her down and tried to avoid rolling her eyes.

"Thank you," Mary Ellen said demurely. "And thanks for bringing Ryan. He's going to be very helpful in ensuring I've made my point. Hope you're not too fond of him." Mary Ellen nodded to one of her guards, and he spoke into an earpiece. Moments later, Ryan appeared on the dance floor, hands bound.

Mary Ellen snapped her fingers and cleared her throat into the microphone to get everyone's attention. There'd been no rescue for the remaining hostage, so some remained focused on that screen. "Poughkeepsie Police Officer Ryan Morales is here to show you what happens to those who pledge their cooperation, accept my offer of employment, but don't follow through adequately."

She ran a finger along Ryan's jaw. He spat in her face.

She stumbled backward, gasping. Micki hurried over with a napkin. One of the guards punched Ryan in the stomach and collapsed his knees with a swift kick. Eve worked to show she was unmoved. She was being watched for sure. Mary Ellen waved her arms angrily, and her men got into position. Ryan caught her eye and shook his head almost imperceptibly as they pulled him to his feet. She knew he was right. There was nothing she could do.

So she just watched. The men who went to town on him now were clearly seasoned at this sport. Ryan flinched in pain as one hit his kidney and the other punched the center of his chest. Eve looked at the floor. She couldn't even find her fancy shoes hidden under all the damn skirts. She needed a second to arrange her face in the appropriate reaction. She opened her hands, which had balled into fists, and exhaled. When she was finally able to look up, a bemused smile placed on her lips, Ryan was facedown on the floor. Mary Ellen nodded at her and raised her glass, toasting Ryan's pain.

Eve suppressed the scream building within her. She added Ryan's beating to the list of wrongs she needed to right—along with Livia, her father, and probably all of Poughkeepsie.

Cole watched as Kyle tried the bottle again, but Kellan just let the formula spill out of his mouth. She shook her head.

Kellan had awakened, hungry, barely half an hour after his father's departure, and his cries had roused his sister. The initial mayhem was now under control, but the situation was testing their skills. And Kyle wasn't even convinced she had any to test.

"He takes bottles—Livia pumps all the time. This is bad." She put the bottle down and tried burping Kellan, swaying gently.

Cole rocked in the rocking chair, his niece asleep on his chest. "Maybe Kathy can find a different formula?"

"I don't know. I mean, all I have is this one job and I can't even get the baby fed?"

Cole watched her face. "Maybe you should sit. How's the cramping?"

"The cramping's fine. I've been on the rag since I was thirteen. Cramping is what girls do." She did sit, though. Still patting Kellan's back, she plopped onto the ottoman in Blake and Livia's bedroom.

Cole checked his phone behind Emme's back. No news from Blake or Beckett or John. He wanted to help, but Kyle came first. And he wasn't handing her solo child-watching duties while she recovered from a miscarriage.

It was like she could hear his thoughts. "Maybe I suck at babies." Her eyes glistened.

"You don't. This is hard on him, and he's used to something else. We'll get it right. Don't worry." He watched as she was rewarded with a burp from Kellan.

Cradling him in her arms, she offered the bottle again. Both she and Cole were surprised when he finally started to suck.

"There you go, buddy. Fill up that belly." Kyle readjusted her hold.

Kellan kicked his feet and smiled around the bottle.

"You do not suck. But he does now, so woo!" Cole winked at her.

"You're cheesy. Anything?" She nodded at his phone.

"Not yet. I want to text them, but I don't want to interrupt. The most important job we can do is be right here." Cole kept rocking his niece, who seemed so small in his arms.

"I wish I knew where she was. It should have been me. Seriously. Then she would be here with the kids where she belongs." Kyle kept looking at Kellan.

"As your big sister, I bet she wouldn't have it any other way. She's as stubborn as you. Do you want to pray?"

Kyle nodded.

Cole took a deep breath and thought of one of his favorites. The words of St. Theresa…Rather than closing his eyes, he smiled warmly at Kyle as he spoke the words that called for God's peace, even in difficult situations, and asked for faith and unbridled dreams as the means to overcome any obstacle. "Tonight is testing our family in ways we never expected," he concluded. "But in your infinite wisdom you blessed the McHugh ladies with tremendous strength of character and will. We thank you for their courage and ask that we might draw from their strength. Lord, help us find Livia. Surround her with your love and guidance and please see fit to return her to her children, to all of us. Amen."

Kyle nodded again. "Thanks. You always make me feel hopeful when you do that."

They stayed like this, each looking at the other—with children and worry between them—for hours.

Blake crouched low and looked at the crushed weeds off the road. He'd walked and jogged for miles.

It felt like a fool's errand, but he truly believed he knew these woods better than anyone else. Maybe his arrogance was manufacturing clues, but he felt compelled to follow the trampled plants and continued down a long dirt driveway. There was an old house on the water back here. A few years ago, it had been for sale. Now it was a seasonal home, used only a few weeks a year. The rest of the time it was vacant, save for an occasional cleaning crew.

He couldn't remember if it had been a Baker's Realty property or not, but when he drew close enough, he could see two cars. A few drops of blood were revealed in the dry grass next to them, thanks to the full moon, and Blake's adrenaline soared. He stilled when he heard the squeak of shoes on the porch. He slipped into the trees soundlessly and heard the flick of a lighter, smelled smoke, as the men lit cigarettes.

"Some crazy shit's going down. Bitch has lost her mind. You ever think of leaving?"

"Tell you what, this thing is getting too damn big for her. She has these giant fucking plans, but it's the details that bite her in the ass. Can't believe nobody's capped her yet."

There was manly guffaw. "I hear that. She's made of some slimy shit…That South American dude—the one she hates—offered me a spot. You get that call?"

They continued to talk, but Blake tuned out. Inside the house, almost every damn light was on. As he made his way around toward the water, he saw two men in the den playing pool. He scanned the windows farther down the side of the house and saw movement. He watched for a moment and sure enough, a man looked out. Just past him, Blake could see Livia.

The rush of relief almost took him to his knees, but a swirl of rage—seeing her imprisoned by people who'd taken her—soon followed. He had to focus. He had to decide what to do. Call John? Call Beckett?

The porch smokers came around the side of the house. "No shit? What are they saying?"

"Apparently two of the houses have blown their covers. Un-fucking-believable."

"Do they want us to move her? Shit, this place has a hot tub. I don't want to leave yet. Did you see that flat screen? It's bigger than my actual apartment."

Blake watched as the kidnapper with Livia looked at his phone, then grabbed her by the face. Things inside were escalating.

"I don't know. Wait—no, somebody just texted to sit tight. The bitch is fixing it somehow? Fuck this shit. Maybe we should call Harmon and tell him who we got. Maybe we can get a signing bonus."

Blake watched as the man in the room with Livia came close to her again. He clenched his fist, then touched her face. She tried to bite him. *God, I love you.*

The two smokers walked back into the house, still plotting to rat out the woman they worked for. Blake pulled out his utility knife and trotted over to the first vehicle. He slid underneath and sliced through the fuel line. He piled up dry leaves under the car to catch the dripping gasoline. Their slow, smoky burn would give him a few seconds' head start once he lit the nature and ran.

After the vehicle was destined to be a fiery distraction, Blake sprinted. He was almost to Livia's window when the car exploded and he could just see her as the sound ripped through the trees. She looked so scared, and he hoped she would be okay enough to do what he was about to ask. The kidnapper with her ran from the room and headed toward the sound. Blake tried the window, which was locked, of course, so he rapped on the pane with his wedding band. She found his eyes and her mouth dropped open.

After a frozen moment she seemed to remember how to move. She ran to the nightstand and grabbed what looked like an antique fire hose nozzle—some sort of decoration. When the man who'd been guarding her came back down the hall, Livia cold-clocked him. She dropped the nozzle as soon as he hit the floor and wrestled open the window. In a moment, she was through it and into Blake's arms. He pulled her to him and whispered, "Shhhh..." into her hair as he cut the rope off her wrists.

She was his now. Time to get into the woods. He listened, tuning in to hear footsteps over the roiling flames in the driveway. He pulled Livia across the porch and jumped off the edge, showing her what to do. She looked over her shoulder for a moment as Blake's heart dropped. If they got caught now…She threw herself off the porch, and he stepped under her just in time to absorb the impact.

"Run." He pointed to the nearest patch of woods, and Livia listened. They were a bit slower than he wanted them to be as she crashed into the woods with no grace at all. He had just taken her hand when the gunshot rang out, just a bit louder than the flames.

Livia turned and gasped.

"I'm fine. Run." Blake worked hard to listen to the footfalls behind him as he moved. He overtook Livia and grabbed her hand, pulling her through the woods. With the bright moonlight, they needed cover and quickly. He tried to settle his pulse and picture the forest around him like a map. There was an old barn to his left a few hundred feet away, and beyond that a car that was almost completely obscured with overgrowth. In the days before Livia he'd slept in that car plenty of times—whenever he was out this far past the railroad after dark. He kicked at a large rock, and instead of going down the incline after it, he pulled Livia to the left. The rock rolled down the hill for longer than Blake could listen, which was fantastic.

He stopped for a second and had Livia jump on his back. Picking the quietest path, he went past the barn and around the back of what looked like an overgrown bush. He lifted the tailgate just enough and let Livia slide off his back and into the old Volkswagen Rabbit. He waited, listening as Livia pulled on his shirt. He held up a finger. The footsteps following them had taken the bait and gone after the rolling rock. He looked back at the path they'd traveled and saw no broken branches, no telltale marks for a tracker to follow.

He would give the men about twenty minutes before he made a move. If needed, he could take Livia deeper into the woods. He ducked under the tailgate and assessed the inside as he closed it quietly behind him. It was holding up well. Livia was on him in a heartbeat, kissing him and stroking his hair. He finally felt the shudders through his body as his adrenaline left in a rush of gratefulness. *Her.* Sitting with his back against the rusted-out metal, he pulled her between his legs. He tilted her face so she could see his mouth in the moonlight seeping through what was left of the windows.

He mouthed, "You okay?"

She nodded, eyes wide and rimmed in tears. "The kids?" she mouthed back.

"They're fine. Kyle is fine." Blake pulled out his phone, and Livia covered the light from the screen with her hands.

He texted their location to his father-in-law with the joyous news that Livia was safe. He sent the same message to Cole and Beckett, trusting that they'd relay it to everyone else, before closing the phone and powering it down. Livia gave him a questioning look. "In case they can track it," he breathed. He was being overly cautious, but damned if he wasn't getting her home to her kids.

She touched his face and smiled. She didn't need to say it. It was all over her face: She loved him. He was her hero. She kissed him again and again. He ran his hands all over her body, feeling for injuries but finding only her softness.

She cuddled into him and took a deep breath. Blake wrapped his arms around her and felt primal. Here in the woods he could protect her forever. If they just got the kids and lived in the woods…

His wife. He had her.

Livia breathed in the smell of the woods on him, his strong arms wrapped around her. She'd never felt so saved, so protected.

She'd been terrified when they took her, but she should've known Blake would rap on the window of some fancy house in the middle of nowhere like it was nothing. He would make them disappear in the forest effortlessly.

She had a lot to tell him: that she was okay, that she hadn't been hurt, that he had rescued her so many times. But now, here…the silence was enough. His heart thumped her favorite steady rhythm. She looked up at him as the moonlight trickled in, leaving some of his handsome, intense face in shadow. His green eyes gazed back, calm and assured. He was so sure they were safe.

She touched his lips, and then his neck and chest. Mouthing it, because they were still in hiding, she told him what had to be said, "Thank you."

"Always." Blake kissed her forehead.

She cuddled back into him and listened to their breathing. Eventually it was in sync. In the distance came sirens. Blake rubbed her arms. Soon enough there were the sounds of dogs, and flashlight beams competing with the moonlight. Blake opened the hatchback carefully.

Her father pulled her out of the car and hugged her tight.

"Thank God." His voice broke, and she could feel him shivering. She patted his back. "You hurt? Do you need a doctor? What did they do to you?" His eyes were frantic, but Livia shook her head.

"I'm fine. Really. It was just scary. I want to go home." She hugged her father again while the other officers tried to look busy.

"That's what you'll get then." Her father grabbed her hand and Blake grabbed the other. She didn't even laugh at her two guys. When they reached the road, her father ordered an officer to drive them home.

"Thanks, Dad." She gave him a huge hug.

He slapped Blake on the shoulder. "I always knew I liked you."

Blake laughed before patting him on the back.

Blake held the door open and slid in next to her, holding her hand and kissing her knuckles as the car started. She sat with her back straight, eyes combing the passing landscape, the whole way home, and she barely let the car stop in front of their house before she was out. Cole flung open the front door as Livia ran up, Blake coming behind her.

She hugged her brother-in-law and took the stairs two at a time. She hit the door to her bedroom and busted out crying when she saw her sister sitting in the center of her bed, Emme curled up next to her and Kellan in her arms.

Tears ran down Kyle's face too. "You bitch. How dare you lock me in a closet?"

Emme woke, startled by the talking and crying. She started to cry, which woke up Kellan. Livia climbed into her bed, holding her daughter to her and hugging her sister and her baby with the other arm.

Blake and Cole appeared in the doorway, laughing and wiping their own escaping tears.

27

Guy Fieri

Beckett rolled up to the address—a giant house in Eastport on Long Island—in a tuxedo and a fedora. Dark sunglasses gave him a bit of privacy. He was sure he looked crazy and eccentric in the fucking ridiculous dead-skunk—make that a dead blond skunk—wig Milton had insisted on. But considering who was likely at this party, he'd fit right in. He'd stationed three douchebags on the perimeter. As they knew, his style was grandiose and messy most of the damn time. He might need backup.

He passed the guards his invitation and waited, music blasting from the sweet Nissan GT-R that had also come from Milton with the invite. He did appreciate the man's attention to detail. OnCue spilled forth with another verse, and Beckett smiled.

"Sir, we need to search you and the car."

"Sure you do." He held his hand out through the open window and passed the guard a wad of bills.

"You know what? We're good. Go ahead. You can just park yourself." The guard patted the hood of the car.

Beckett nodded and drove off, selecting a rock-star spot in the circle driveway. He checked his wig, straightened his glasses, and pimp-walked in the front door. It seemed security had left their posts. There were people everywhere and music poured from the sound system. Typical of these fucking shows, everyone pretended to be safe when they were all packing heat. Jeez. Had security *ever* been at their posts? And this was a bizarre group—pretty much all dudes. Some looked like they'd come straight from Wall Street, while others channeled Tony Soprano, and still others looked like they'd crawled out from under a rock. This bitch was asking for trouble. He grabbed a glass from a passing waiter.

He stepped to the side of the huge, over-decorated room and rested his back against the wall, leaving his glasses on. The air was electric, and he knew one spark would set the whole thing off. He felt her looking at him before he saw her. Like a whip straight to his balls, he just fucking knew. And then she was there, across the room. She was furious. And she was stunning. She blinked quickly and looked to the left of him, hiding the feelings—like she would. The lump in his chest felt like a heart attack. He put his glass down on a table as she turned and opened the door to the balcony. She stepped outside, and he knew he had to get there—she could disappear like a fucking ghost. Beckett skirted the room and left through the same glass door she had. It was freezing, the wind off the Sound stealing all the warmth from his body. She didn't turn when he approached.

"We're being watched." Her voice offered nothing welcoming, and not a hint of surprise. She continued to look at the water below. She was so close he could touch her, see the goose bumps on her arms from the chill.

"Figured." He stepped up next to her and peeked at her face. She was so beautiful he closed his eyes and exhaled audibly. The familiar curve of her neck and slope of her shoulder stole his common sense, his swagger.

Eve turned slowly to face him. She'd changed her hair color, but it just made her blue eyes more vibrant. She took his sunglasses carefully from his face, not touching his skin at all.

He gulped. Her stern gaze revealed nothing. "Where's your boyfriend?" He lifted his eyebrow, hating himself for asking her that first. Of all the damn things…

Eve slapped him. Beckett turned his face and felt the burn on his skin.

"Fuck you," she growled.

Beckett bit his lip and resisted the urge to rub his face.

She handed him his sunglasses back. "Livia's been taken," she reported. "But then I guess that's why you're here."

"She's been found. I got a text just a few minutes ago—Blake brought her home." Beckett stepped closer, invading her personal space.

She leaned close to his ear and whispered. "And you came anyway? Did this just sound like a good time to fucking resurrect yourself? Crappy wig and all?"

Beckett smiled, trying to get past her venom. "Livia's back, but that bitch is still loose. She seemed worth a talking to, and..." He stepped impossibly closer.

"And nothing," she said. "I have work to do." She stepped away from his arms and went to leave.

"Hold on." He grabbed her wrist.

She faced him again, chin up and proud.

"I'm happy to see you." He had to force the words out. She was so angry, and he felt utterly exposed.

"Are you?" She bit her lip.

"Of course I am." Beckett traced the inside of her forearm gently.

Eve shook her head. "Don't. You. Dare." She twisted and yanked her wrist free.

She was still strong as fuck.

"Tell me why *you're* here." He watched as she seemed to teeter between leaving and staying.

"Because my family—your family—needed me." Her gaze ripped through him.

"I was trying to be a better man." He held her stare, trying to convey his intentions.

"I don't have time for this. People are depending on me." Eve seemed primed to run. "Are you back or what?"

"I don't know what I am." He put his hands in his pockets, not trusting them around her.

"I think that's been your problem for a while." She turned and opened the balcony door, leaving him to the view of the water.

God, he wanted her.

Eve almost tripped coming back inside. The fucking ball gown was pissing her off. She checked Ryan, who was still slumped in his chair. Her heart hurt for him. And then there was Beckett standing outside on the balcony. Beckett. Right behind her—after all these damn years. Her heart hurt *because* of him.

She approached Mary Ellen, who was remarkably still alive and talking to Primo, and tried to focus. Beckett had rocked Eve off her foundation. She could still taste the anticipation his body brought to hers. It was chemical. She needed a few minutes to collect herself, but that was time she didn't have. Ryan had to get out of here.

"You should know better than to doubt me by now," Mary Ellen told her brother as Eve joined them. "I've been following Daddy's example all these years. Unlike copper over there," she added, shifting her eyes over to Eve. "He was too *busy* to follow my instructions." She looked like the cat that ate the canary.

Eve watched as Ryan came to a little. He coughed and hung his head again.

"I've got just a few more insights to share with the crowd," Mary Ellen said, batting her eyes at each of them. "Would you excuse me for a moment?" She signaled the closest guard and headed back over to the podium in front of her video screens, which had all gone black.

"Okay, everyone." Mary Ellen tapped the microphone. "Time to have a feel-better moment. I need you to understand, I'm here to help. I'm not heartless—at all."

She snapped her fingers and grinned for a few seconds while nothing happened. Preparation for the moment took an extra-long time that reduced the "magic" quality she was clearly hoping for. By the time the last remaining kidnapped girl was revealed on the screen again, Mary Ellen's smile must have been drying out her porcelain veneers. Her lips stuck around her next words:

"Pam Bookbinder may be released!"

A collective question rose up from the crowd, but sure enough, on the screen the guards freed the woman. She staggered to her feet.

"Sam Bookbinder? Your niece will be available for pickup at the flower shop in Oyster Bay in ten minutes. You may leave to collect her in just a moment. There's just one other thing I'd like you to see…"

Mary Ellen remained at the podium, but the crowd had begun to rustle, clearly wondering what the hell was next. She tapped the microphone and kept tapping it long after everyone in the room had quieted down. Eve had to hold in her exasperated sigh.

"Thank you. Finally. I assure you, becoming quiet when I ask is the best choice." Mary Ellen added a fake Marilyn Monroe-style giggle. "I think we all know at this point that I'm ready to take charge. And I'd like to add that there's no one out of my reach. How about a police captain's daughter? Much too risky, right? Not for me. You'll recall my interest in Poughkeepsie from the beginning. You've been less than forthcoming about the whereabouts of Beckett Taylor, so I just had to test the waters myself. This lovely girl is not only a captain's daughter, but someone close to Mr. Taylor…"

Eve used Beckett's terrible wig as a way to track him in the crowd. When they locked eyes, he shook his head, standing by his earlier news on Livia.

"Believe me—" Mary Ellen seemed to be getting into her pontificating now "—I can say with absolute certainty that Beckett Taylor is dead, or at the very least he's never coming back. Please turn your attention to the screen…"

A single screen took over for the three smaller ones, but when its image appeared, there was nothing but an empty chair—no woman and no kidnappers present.

The reaction was almost immediate as the crowd surged toward Mary Ellen. With no leverage left, and apparently not even much sense of what was going on, she no longer seemed scary in the least. Primo barked orders to his men, and Eve melted into the swirling crowd. Nearly as many seemed headed for the exits as were now calling for Mary Ellen's head.

Eve crossed to the back of the room and marched straight up to the guard with Ryan. "I've got to get him to a safer place. The cops will be swarming this place soon." She put her hand under Ryan's arm.

"Wait, what?" The guard seemed confused.

"Don't make a scene. We're trying to get him out quiet." Eve stepped forward aggressively, forgetting she was done up like a southern debutante.

"Not without Mary Ellen's say so. And she told us to watch out for you." He eyed her suspiciously.

"I just came from Mary Ellen," Eve countered. "She's a little busy right now, as you may have noticed."

"I've got him." Beckett swooped in and pulled Ryan to his feet.

"Ben, you best make sure you're tuned into the local stations." Eve forced a cocky smirk to her face. "Have you even noticed what's going on here—or are you too busy jacking off?"

"Come on, baby. I'm going to need your help interrogating him." Beckett nodded, and she slipped her arm around Ryan's waist.

Before Ben could formulate a response, Beckett was moving toward the exit, with Ryan and Eve in tow. She caught Shark's eye on the way across the room. "You got Micki?" she mouthed.

He nodded once and continued walking, as if he'd looked right through her.

Beckett yanked open a door and pulled Ryan into the hallway. He opened his phone, leaving Eve to settle Ryan on a fancy chair in what looked to be a reading room.

She checked his pupils and un-tucked his shirt, pushing his coat aside. She felt his hard abs and then an odd bump on his left rib cage. He winced.

"I think they broke your rib. Can you tell me your name?" Eve felt his arms and legs, which all seemed in working order.

"Still Ryan." He managed a smile and squeezed her hand.

"It's Ryan Morales, isn't it?" Beckett was suddenly off the phone. "You're a cop."

Eve ignored him, focused on Ryan.

"You need to leave. Get out of here. I've got this." Ryan looked into her eyes as he pulled out the container in his pocket.

"You're going to take on this clusterfuck with my vagina knife?" She almost smiled.

Beckett shook his head. "They're on lockdown. And this place is well guarded right now. I'll go out there and distract them. Eve, you get him to my car. It's a red Nissan GT-R." He tossed the keys to her.

She caught them and stuffed them down her bodice. "Gimmie." Eve took the tiny knife from Ryan and began hacking at her dress's huge skirt.

Rather than leaving, Beckett put his hand over hers. "Let me." He took the blade and grabbed a handful of her blue taffeta skirt. "Spin."

She couldn't see his eyes, but she recognized the smirk. This wasn't the first time he'd cut clothes off her body. After a couple circles, he tossed a giant blob of material in the corner. Now Eve wore her blue bodice and the tight bottoms of her spandex slip. The heels were a pain in the ass, but there was nothing to be done about that now.

"Fuck that plan," she said. "Get douchebags on the exits. I'm betting you didn't come alone. Have them do some flash bangs all around." Eve slipped her hands under Beckett's jacket, freeing the gun she knew she'd find there. He grabbed her by the hair.

"You're wasting time," she told him. "This place is going to be lit up pretty soon, and Mary Ellen's going to realize I'm not there to protect her—and that no one's protecting Ryan anymore. We all need to go *now*."

Beckett let go of her hair, and she stuffed the gun in her bosom on her way to the window. Although they were on the first floor, it was quite a drop. The music ground to a halt in the main room just as she opened the latch and swung the window out. It was so huge she could stand in it. She could see party guests scurrying to their cars.

Ryan had staggered to his feet. "Go. Take Guy Fieri with you. I'm fine."

Eve gave him a dirty look.

Beckett finished texting and scoped out the terrain below. "You get down there, and I'll lower the pansy to you."

She shook her head. "No. Too far."

Beckett grabbed the curtain and ripped. Eve ducked just as the entire window treatment came off the wall. He used the knife to slice a long portion from the rod. "Go. I got it."

She turned and slid down, then let herself dangle from the end of the fabric, her knees scraping against the stone façade. She let go and bent her knees as she hit the ground. After a brief scuffle above her, Ryan emerged with a curtain wrapped around his back. He walked rappel-style down the side of the mansion for few feet before Beckett obviously ran out of material to feed him. Ryan slipped out from under the curtain and hit the ground with a groan. "Aw, fuck. That hurt."

Eve pulled him to his feet and waited. Beckett peered over the edge of the window. "Get out here," she hissed.

Beckett turned and pulled the same maneuver Eve had, but without the curtain to aid him. They all crouched behind the bushes until the first grenade popped and the screams began. Eve stood and pushed Ryan at Beckett.

"I'll get the car." She trotted over to Beckett's ride, which was an easy find in candy apple red and parked like an asshole as usual. She pulled it off the driveway and onto the grass as the valet followed, hollering.

Beckett opened the door and slid Ryan into the backseat, slamming the door just as the man's feet cleared the frame. He banged on the car and pointed for Eve to leave without him.

She shot the ground where the valet stood and growled at Beckett. "Get in the fucking car, fuckhead."

He pulled open the passenger door and Eve took off, the force of gravity seating him and closing the door on his legs. He cursed and pushed it open, pulling his feet inside.

Eve passed him the gun, and he pulled out two more, handing one to Ryan. "You know how to work one of these, son?"

Ryan took the gun as Eve hit the button to slide her window down. More flash-bang grenades detonated, and the front gates began their motorized procedure to close. They would be hell to bust through once they shut.

"Get the gate men." Eve put her high heel to the gas and slammed it to the floorboard.

Beckett and Ryan fired right up until the second they ducked. The car didn't even slow, just plowed through the narrowing gate, metal-on-metal screeching down the sides.

Beckett was on the phone almost as soon as the Nissan got free, telling the douchebags to evacuate, and fast.

Eve checked the rearview mirror. Ryan slumped in the backseat. "Hey. You okay?"

"I'm fine."

Eve would've believed him if his eyes hadn't rolled back in his head right after he said it.

Ninety minutes later, she pulled up to her father's apartment building and knew she had to stop ignoring Beckett. Not like she was really ignoring him anyway. She'd never met someone so fucking present in the world. He took up all the space in the damn car, and he'd determined Ryan had a pulse and was breathing on their way back from Long Island, which is why Eve decided to bring him to her father first.

Given what had happened to her dad just outside his place of work, she didn't entirely trust the hospital to keep someone safe. If Ryan needed surgery, that'd be another thing. Eve called her father again to let him know they'd actually arrived and she didn't want to move Ryan unless she had to. After a few minutes he stumbled out the front door, wearing pajamas and completely confused.

"Why are you dressed like that? What's going on? It's the middle of the night!"

"Dad, Ryan's hurt. I can't tell you more. Can you check him out and decide if we need to go to the hospital?" Eve watched the streets for any activity.

Ted tossed up his hands but eased into the car. After a few minutes of examination, he reemerged. "I'd like to take him in and get a CAT scan and few x-rays. He needs to be monitored at the very least. Hydrated, some pain meds. This looks very familiar."

"Tell me what you need from the hospital." Eve slipped past her father and expertly moved Ryan's unconscious body toward the vehicle's door. Her father raised his eyebrows. Beckett shrugged and reached for Ryan. Eve worked around him and together they got him in the front door of the building in one smooth motion. Then they started on the stairs. It helped that he woke up enough to move his legs.

Finally, they set him down on the couch inside Eve's dad's apartment. Eve went into the kitchen and wet a hand towel. She wiped his face clean and his eyes opened again.

"How you doing?" Eve gently tried to remove the blood caked in his hairline. "That was quite a work-over. Those bastards were experienced."

"Did you kidnap me? From that woman?" Ryan tried to sit up, but gasped and groaned before lying back.

Eve could see her father was furious. But he was a professional. He rearranged Ryan and went to the closet, where he pulled out an alarming number of medical supplies. As he prepared an IV, he met Eve's eyes. "Now you're glad I bring my work home with me, aren't you?"

Beckett pointed to his chest and back at Ted, silently asking if he should step in. She shook her head. As her father slid in the IV, she tried to find the words to explain. "Dad, when I lost David and the baby..." She looked the floor. God, it hurt. "I did some stuff to survive."

Scarcely acknowledging he'd heard her, her father briskly assessed his patient. He opened Ryan's shirt to reveal a pretty spectacular chest. "To survive? Eve, you are the privileged child of a doctor. What the hell are you talking about?"

"Can we talk about this later, when we're alone?" Eve headed for the door. "Do you have to work today?"

Clearly exasperated, he followed her. "No, I don't have to work and no, we can't talk about this later."

"Keep Ryan here. Call me if you need anything." She reached for the door handle and Beckett came to her side.

Her dad touched her shoulder. "Wait. I can't understand what's going on."

She looked into her father's face—so trusted, so comfortable. She didn't want to break his heart. "I love you." She hugged him.

He got it, she was leaving. He raised his palms and sighed.

Beckett nodded. "Sir."

The evil look her father dropped on Beckett was the last thing Eve saw as she closed the door. Beckett wisely kept his mouth shut as they retraced their steps to the car.

A cold burst of night air slapped her face as soon as the building's door opened, and it snapped her mind to attention. Beckett's car was still sitting in front of her father's house. *How could I be this stupid?* "Shit."

Beckett trotted in front of her and jumped in the driver's seat. She had no choice but to get in the passenger side.

"How come I didn't dump this?" Eve punched the dashboard. "Mary Ellen *loooves* to track her party guests."

"I didn't do it either." He shrugged.

"I don't make mistakes. What's your excuse? Gotta dump it in the river or something." She opened the glove department, looking for a tracking device. She'd never put it in there. Under the car or tucked in the upholstery was best. She began searching. Beckett wasn't driving nearly fast enough. She opened her mouth to tell him so, but he spoke first.

"I'm stunned you're here with me."

She stopped searching to look at him, her anger unleashed by his words. "Really? I feel the same way. Where have *you* been? Five years I waited for you. Five fucking years."

She kicked off her heels and climbed over into the backseat to continue her search as her emotions came crashing. She was losing it. Needing to harden, hating that she was out of control and sloppy, she punched the leather. He needed to apologize. He needed to stop the fucking car and kiss her. She had to slap him. Eve didn't realize how badly she'd been craving this man. She could still remember how he'd made love to her that morning so many years ago, how devoted he'd been.

Beckett was silent.

She lifted the armrest and found a tracker. Rolling down the window, she threw it out and met his eyes in the rearview mirror. He rolled his window down and threw out his wig. He held her stare so long it was amazing he kept the car on the road.

He broke the connection first and turned his attention to his phone, hitting speaker on the call he made. "Milton, I want you to notify Police Captain John McHugh that Ted Hartt's house needs protection. Tell him Ryan Morales is there and has ticked off a crazy lady who may be able to track him. Try to keep him out of any public places for a few damn days. If that man is going to stay alive, they need to be fucking vigilant. His cover has been blown. Leave me a car in the parking lot and be ready to dump one." He ended the call.

The silence was thick. Eve sighed. She wished she had normal clothes on. She wished she wasn't tits deep in a crazy-dangerous situation.

"You love him?" Beckett asked quietly.

Of all the things he could be asking, those were the words out of his mouth? "He's a good guy." She dug her nails into her palm, trying to clear her head.

Beckett pulled into his old parking lot and switched vehicles with little fanfare. He handed Eve her shoes and pointed to the SUV Milton had left running. She got in the passenger side. "Give me a few minutes to get some fucking things settled." He took off driving to no place in particular.

Eve shook her head. He was so used to barking out commands and directions. She could kick him. Instead she tilted her chair back and took a deep breath. She was so tired. And as much as she hated to admit it, in Beckett's presence she could turn off. No need to try and rest on the edge of sleep. She went out like a light for the first time in years.

28

Only You

Blake was waiting outside the bathroom when Livia emerged, wrapped in a towel.

And he'd been there a while. After their initial adrenaline rush had subsided and Cole and Kyle had gone to bed in the guestroom, she'd fed Kellan until he was full and then slipped into the hot water what seemed like ages ago. To be home, to know her children were safe, she was safe—she'd relaxed in a way she'd almost forgotten was possible.

Livia smiled at Blake, and she knew he counted. Past his shoulder, through the window, the sun was coming up, and a horrible stretch of time was coming to an end. He stood and pulled her to him, tracing the water droplets on her shoulder. She looked up with a question, but when she saw his eyes she knew. They had to connect. Just be together. He needed to be inside of her.

Livia touched his face, and he leaned into her hand. He opened his mouth as if to speak, but he said nothing as she touched him. She pulled his shirt off and touched the scar on his chest. "I know." She could almost hear his thoughts. He was so thankful, so full of love. "I know." She leaned up and kissed his lips. He was warm and real and here. "I was coming back to you. The whole time."

He tugged at her towel until it fell to the floor. He took her hand and turned her in a circle.

"They hurt you," he said, tracing fingers over bruises on her arms and legs. She could hear the cold fury in his voice.

She shook her head. "I'm okay." She hugged him, her breasts leaking a bit.

Blake ghosted her shape, honoring her. Instead of her usual shyness, today she felt proud. He touched her breasts, traced the small stretch marks, and grabbed two handfuls of her bottom.

"No one takes you from us." Blake kissed her neck and nipped her ear.

She unbuckled his jeans. "You saved me, Blake Hartt. Only you." The way he looked at her was breathtaking. His eyes were a soft green in the rising sunlight. She ran her hand through his hair.

"I cherish you." She kissed his cheek.

He looked at her lips. "If I didn't find you…" He was a lion for her, fierce in his devotion.

"You always will." She hugged him tight.

He kissed the top of her head as she reached into his briefs. She loved his groan as she touched him, hot and velvet. She felt his long ridges and twirled her finger at the very top. He grabbed her face and kissed her, slipping his tongue in her mouth like when they were first dating. When he picked her up, she wrapped her legs around him. She could feel the muscles in his back flexing as he walked her to their bed.

He put her down and smiled. "You okay? Anything hurting?"

She shook her head no before Blake began. He kissed her shoulders, her breasts, and worked his way lower. He was gentle at first, but responded more vigorously when her groans demanded it. He knew her body so well. After all these years, he could be terribly wicked between her legs. She finally pulled him up and pushed him onto the bed.

He tried to pull away but she refused. He would receive as well. Livia twisted her hair and tucked it to one side as she decided where to start. Little licks teased the length of him. She put her hands all over him, pressing his favorite parts and stroking him slowly. She was not in a rush at all. She took a moment to watch him watch her. His smile was carnal and possessive.

"Lick. Bite. Blow." She winked at him as he covered his face with a pillow.

She proceeded with their torturous pattern as Blake managed a muffled, "You're going to kill me dead. Right here."

At that point she wrapped her lips around him. She used every bit of knowledge she had to make him gasp.

"Whoa. Stop. I've got a little more to do yet." He pulled her onto him, kneeling while she straddled him.

She slid him inside and waited, squeezing the whole time. "I love you."

Blake nodded and pulled her hair away from her face, gathering it in a ponytail. "So much," he answered.

He helped her rock on top of him. His strength allowing her to go faster than she could have on her own. And when she was full of him and concentrating on her pleasure, Blake added the perfect amount of friction with his thumb. His eyes flared as she began moaning his name.

He flipped her over in a genius move that—if she hadn't been in a blurry orgasmic state—she would've applauded. His lips captured her mouth as he fixed her legs to his liking, going even deeper than before. She summoned the strength to squeeze again when he had his release, laughing as he tensed up and panted.

Blake collapsed next to her. "Thank you. I thought my balls were going to die."

She swatted him. "Blake Hartt. How dare you? I'm scandalized."

He grinned and tickled her. "Seriously? You're going to play that card? You do know how often I hear you and Kyle's witty banter?"

Livia found her favorite place: with her head on his chest. It was slightly damp from their exertions. She pinched his nipple before he trapped her hands, kissing her nose. They snuggled for a bit before she sat up with wide eyes. "Was I too loud? Oh, God."

"You were fine." He gave her a slightly guilty smirk.

"Was it bad?" Livia covered her mouth.

He shook his head. "A man has needs."

She rolled her eyes and felt her breasts drip like faucets. She pointed at her nipples. "Dinnertime again."

He ran a hand over his chest. "Yeah. Sticky."

She slipped into the bathroom to clean off their passion. "Come shower then," she called. "I'm like a beverage machine. I can't stop it."

Blake came to her, and they kissed a little more before Livia heard the baby start to wake. With a final kiss on her forehead, he released her and turned toward the shower. On her way out she stripped the sheets and set out a folded pile of clean ones for Blake to finish. Their sex had been wonderful, but breast milk was everywhere. She dressed quickly as Kellan went from fussing in his crib to all-out crying and stepped into the hall, only to find Kyle bringing Kellan.

"You better feed this kid or I think Cole might start lactating."

Livia took her son from Kyle and walked him back to his bedroom, where she settled in the sliding glider. He quickly latched on as Livia found a breast pad for her other boob.

"Was the sweaty Twister good for you?" Kyle eased down to Kellan's plush carpet.

"Seriously, I'm so mortified." Livia tucked her boy into his favorite position and relished the release of her milk.

"Oh, Blake. Right there. Yes! Yes!" Kyle fluttered her hands to accompany her high-pitched voice.

"When I put this baby down I'm going to kick your ass." Livia tossed a stuffed monkey at her sister's head.

Kyle laughed. "No, I know for a fact that after-kidnapping sex is fucking wonderful."

"Really? You were in the hospital." Livia watched as Kyle yawned.

"Bitch, please. I'm a sexpert. I can be a sperm jockey anywhere." She stretched out on the floor.

"I should have raised you better." Livia lifted Kellan and burped him. "How're you feeling?" She set him to her other breast.

Cole walked into the room, spotted the breastfeeding, and did an about face. "Just wanted to ask about breakfast! You guys want pancakes? That's Emme's pick. Everyone's wide awake now!"

"She feeding the baby?" Blake called from the hallway.

"Yes, sir," Cole reported.

Blake pounded his brother on the back. "Don't worry, we won't use the breast milk in the pancakes you're about to make us." They disappeared down the hallway together.

"Anyway," Livia prodded gently. "How are you?"

"I'm sucking at life, I guess?" Kyle managed a laugh. "But I was really glad to be here when you needed me." She made circular patterns in the carpet with her finger.

"I knew you'd be here if they hadn't taken you too. I'm so glad they didn't. Blake said you agreed to watch the kids if he and I didn't make it back." Her voice grew soft. Saying the words hurt. "So thanks for that."

"Any time. Well, don't go anywhere, but you know I'll always be here for them. You're doing a great job, so you know. Emme is a pisser. And Kellan is so happy."

"They get a lot of awesome from their aunt." Livia watched as her son fell asleep, little lips still working from time to time. She covered up and carried him to his crib. Once he was settled she put out a hand and pulled Kyle off the floor.

"Thanks."

She wanted to tell her sister she was wonderful and would make a great mother as well, but Livia could tell she was on the edge of crying.

Emme appeared in the doorway, and Livia pulled her daughter into her arms. Kyle turned on the monitor as Livia put a finger to her lips to tell Emme to stay quiet. When Kyle had closed the door behind her, Livia kissed her daughter nosily. "So you want pancakes for breakfast?"

"Mommy, who took you?" Her daughter's giant green eyes were somber, her hand twirling in Livia's hair.

"Jerks. I'm back, and I'm not going anywhere." Livia sniffed Emme's hair.

"I don't like jerks. And yes, I want pancakes, please." Emme laid her head on Livia's shoulder.

Gratefulness surrounded her like a warm blanket.

Eve felt years younger who knows how long later when Beckett slid back into the driver's seat and jarred her awake. "What time is it?" she asked as he sped back onto the road.

"It's almost nine a.m. — on Sunday, that is — and I'm pleased to report I've got more loyal assholes than I thought I did."

"People have no trouble being devoted to you." She didn't look at him. "It's that reciprocal shit you suck at."

Beckett's jaw tensed, and she could see him grip the steering wheel. But instead of responding, he asked, "You got a place with clothes?"

She shook her head. "Not close."

"Let's handle that. Fairy Princess still in the fashion business?"

Eve shivered a bit. "She's managing the new branch of Mode in the mall."

"I'll call Cole. I bet she can open up the store for us." Beckett pulled out his phone and began a quick back and forth with Cole. "Hey, brother…"

It was surreal being in a vehicle with him. It fit like a murderer's glove. After a few moments he confirmed the plan and hung up, and minutes after that they pulled into the parking lot at the mall.

While they waited, Eve thought she best hand him all she could about her current situation. "Listen, Mary Ellen's in up to her imitation forehead in crap. You remember the name Sevan Harmon from back in the day?"

Beckett nodded. "Yeah…handsome motherfucker. Runs pharmaceuticals, as I recall. Likes to move his shit through Poughkeepsie."

"Yeah, well, he's taken Mary Ellen for a ride. Started out getting some weapons from her daddy and moved right on into her pants after that. He somehow convinced her she oughta move some money around while her dad was out of commission—the old guy had a stroke a few months ago. And then after that Sevan disappeared and moved the money again. He's trying to blackmail her, but she's more concerned with covering her mistake so her daddy doesn't find out. And she's determined to ruin Sevan in the process—hence her obsession with Poughkeepsie. She's out there on the ragged edge of batshit crazy over this stuff."

"No shit?"

Eve shrugged. "Isn't that pretty clear?"

"Well, true. But the Sevan angle is good to know. Thanks for the debrief." He shook his head and scanned the parking lot. "I see Cole's car. Let's go."

Beckett climbed out and took off his jacket so Eve could wrap it around her waist as they walked. "I'm not sure nine o'clock in the morning is ready for how fabulous your ass looks in those fake pants."

"They're Spanx." She took the jacket and headed toward the mall entrance.

"If they're spanking your ass, they're lucky." Beckett gave her a forced wink.

Cole's old man car came to a stop in the front row of spaces. He hopped out and slapped Beckett on the back. Kyle emerged from the passenger seat and enveloped him in a full-body hug.

"Fairy Princess, look at fucking you. Gorgeous. Love the hair. And the tight ass."

He laughed when she slapped his butt in response. "You cock-wrangling testicle pimple. I swear I thought you died in a hooker's meat drapes years ago."

"I tried. I promise."

"C'mon, you two. We've got clothes to find," Cole urged. He slapped Beckett's back again and the two fell in step.

Kyle looked Eve up and down. "Rough night?"

"One of many." Eve shook her head. "Listen, it's better if you're not seen with us. I'll pay you back for whatever we get. When does the mall open?"

"Not for a couple hours, but it's fine. I'm going to work on stock while we're here."

Inside, Eve picked out jeans, a T-shirt, bra, and new undies before realizing she had no money on her. In an instant Beckett was next to her. "I got this."

Kyle cut off the tags and sent Eve into the fitting room to change. Wearing her new ensemble, Eve felt a strange shyness as she handed Beckett back his jacket. Five years had been good to him: his dimples a bit deeper, his intense eyes even clearer. Seemed he hadn't taken drugs in a while.

He tossed her old clothes in the store's trash can, and they retraced their steps to the mall's entrance. Keys in hand, Kyle let them slip out, giving them both a hug.

"You gonna stay here all day, Cole?" Beckett teased.

"I actually might. I help her with the heavy boxes and whatnot." He smiled as he and Beckett parted in their time-honored way.

"Hungry?" Beckett asked when they were back in the car.

She nodded. She was actually famished. "We've got to get out of here, though. The bitch will be after me. You need to get out."

He ignored her and drove over to Starbucks in the mall parking lot. He disappeared inside and returned with two coffees and a sack of food. Setting them on one of the outdoor tables, he opened her car door and boldly invited her to sit. When she hesitated, he set out her favorite sandwich. Maybe she'd forgotten how reckless he was. And how much it turned her on. Fucker. She joined him at the table. The hot cocoa was a gift from God, and she was done eating in five seconds flat. Damn him for remembering she didn't like coffee.

He laughed at her. "Let me guess? It's been about twelve hours since you've eaten?" He took a sip of his coffee.

She gave him the finger.

"You always slip into sign language when you're turned on." Beckett grabbed her trash and crumpled it into a ball. "Ready?"

She felt slightly human again and decided to follow him. They should at least talk about what the hell was happening next. Was he leaving? Would she be cleaning up this mess with him or alone?

As a lazy afternoon settled over the house, Blake's view from his bedroom doorway took the cake: Livia had settled in the bed to nurse Kellan, and Emme had crawled in next to her. Livia looked up and smiled as he came in the room. He made sure she had a nice pillow to prop the baby on and a tall glass of ice water, because she got so thirsty. His daughter sucked her thumb, which she hadn't done in at least a year, but he got it. Comforting, normal things felt like a miracle right now.

Within minutes, Livia and Kellan were asleep, the untouched ice water forming condensation. Emme looked all around for a few minutes, but the afternoon light was softened by the drawn blinds, and she was clearly sleepy as well. Emme put her little hand on Livia's cheek and patted gently.

"Good mommy."

Blake felt his eyes rim with tears. This whole damn thing had him at the edge of his emotions. Emme's blinks got longer and longer until she too was asleep. He turned the sound off on his phone before snapping a few pictures of the serene moment, then he stood and tucked a blanket around all three of them.

He'd kill to keep them safe, tear the world apart to make sure they never felt anything but joy, no matter how unrealistic that was. Damned if he wouldn't try. He turned on the fan so they'd have some white noise and aimed the monitor at them. There were about five hundred songs in his head, waiting to be written down. Really he should snuggle with his family, but at the tips of his fingers he had a way to memorialize this quiet, grateful moment. So he carried the monitor down the hall, noticing that Kyle and Cole had closed themselves in Kellan's room after coming back from Mode. It was stupid—they were full-grown adults, but he was happy they were here as well. Their presence added to his inspiration. If only Beckett and Eve had been able to come home with them.

He sat down in his soundproofed basement studio and put the monitor in front of him where he sometimes placed music to read. With a fresh notebook and a sharp pencil, Blake began to create. Lately he'd been designing mood music for movies and television shows, but right now he could only think of his family. A song began to form, first in his heart, then in his mind.

It was about peace—the peace that came after stunning worry. It was about being strong enough to fix and powerful enough to keep things that way. The melody sang of a love so intense it changed how he was made. Loving Livia had changed his DNA. There was only her and him. There wasn't one without the other anymore. And then the children. He added them to the song as the bass line, the steady and most important part of their love. He added forever to the song, because he would lose everything if forever wasn't there.

Over and over he played, pausing to draw notes on the paper and stare at the monitor, watching his family sleep peacefully. He didn't even realize Cole had entered the basement until he saw him coming down the stairs. He finished up the last bit, nodding at his notes on the page before turning toward his brother.

"That's amazing—maybe the best song I've ever heard you play," Cole announced as he sat on the couch.

"Thanks, brother. I'm motivated." Blake nodded at the image.

"Yeah. I get that." Cole touched his tattoo. "Wonder where he is."

Blake shook his head. "That was a shock. Damn nice seeing him, hated the circumstances."

"For sure." Cole put his hands behind his head. "There's a lot of days I wish he could just be around. You know?"

"He's got so much counting against him." Blake turned on his piano bench and fingered the keys.

"Can you play that one again? I really loved it." Cole reclined completely.

"Sure. I'll record it this time." Blake looked at the monitor again, flipped a switch on the computer, and the song poured forth once again.

29

Tattoo

It was Sunday afternoon, and after more than three months, Rodolfo Vitullo sat in his own chair, in his own house on 59th Street, gratefully. Although he would still have daily visits from his OT, he'd been discharged from the hell on earth known as rehab. Coming back from this stroke had hurt every damn minute, and it was a fight he'd never expected. His whole life he'd battled others—for money, for market share, for power—but the worst he ever had it was from his own damned body.

Truly, it was good to be home, even though a visit from DiMonso a few hours earlier had damn near given him another stroke. It seemed Mary Ellen—senseless, worthless Mary Ellen—had somehow handed a nice chunk of his fortune to Sevan Harmon. Every time he began to think she showed a bit of real potential, something slapped him across the face and reminded him that she was crazy. If he hadn't been so busy relearning to use his limbs, he might have noticed she was being less than forthcoming during her visits. DiMonso had apologized profusely, but given that he was not employed at the time the transactions had evidently occurred, his ability to sort them out was greatly impaired.

Hmmm…and what else was making his first day back a veritable bowl of cocktail weenies? One of the tails he'd placed on Primo had spotted him betting on digital horse racing in a gas station all morning. And this was his best option to run the company after he died? This freaking kid was still living his teenage years as he approached his fifties. Speaking of the devil, Primo walked in the front door, looking haggard. Rodolfo wondered for a moment if he even knew he was home—or had he just stopped in for cash and booze?

"Son, I've had it up to here with you slaving to your vice," he barked, causing Primo to jump and very nearly turn around and run from the room. Guess that answered his question. "I'm going to have to put my foot down." Rodolfo watched as panic overwhelmed his son. So weak. So predictable.

"Dad, Mary Ellen had an event last night that blew up in her face and makes us all look like shit. She dragged your reputation through the mud, and she's out of control. I heard people saying you were probably dead. Everyone knows something's up. Rumors are flying about money being missing, and Mary Ellen never got the cash to me that she was supposed to."

Rodolfo listened as Primo's complaints and confessions circled inevitably back to his addiction.

"Hofstra." He signaled the man waiting just outside the door. "Find my daughter and have her pay me a visit. Tell her I know about her indiscretions, and it's time to pay the piper."

Primo's grin dissolved into a huge yawn as he made himself comfortable on the couch. Rodolfo looked away, trying to focus on the nature outside the window. An hour later his daughter appeared with her hands clasped. When she was tired or guilty her face regained a shade of its pre-surgery look. Rodolfo looked at her from a distance and remembered her mother's beauty before waving her forward. Primo sat up on the couch, seemingly eager to witness the show.

"Leave us, Primo." Rodolfo put his hand up to ward off his son's protests. "Don't make me say it twice."

Primo stomped out of the room but knew better than to question Rodolfo. The king was back in his castle.

"I know how much is missing. Tell me everything. What else did Harmon take?"

Mary Ellen went to the couch and draped herself across it. "I thought I was in love, Daddy. I thought he was the one."

"Don't. You could have *loved* him without filling his pockets with my money." Rodolfo gripped the arms of his chair. He had to focus to make his weak hand respond, but he forced himself to do it.

Mary Ellen began the tale from the beginning, telling him how scary his stroke had been for her and how Sevan had seemed so capable, so eager help her succeed. She promised her revenge and swore she'd taken decisive action. Not only would she recover the money, she'd ruin Sevan's business by taking Poughkeepsie off the table. She spoke at length of her parties and her trained women and her threats to just about everyone, though she was a little light on the details where costs and collateral damage were concerned. Even so, after a time he could not listen for another minute while she babbled on about ball gowns and diamonds, and he held up a hand to silence her. She stopped her full-body dancing demonstration and returned to the couch, but her eyes never left his.

He had to hand it to her—at least a little. She did have confidence, and she did have a plan. It would never work in a million years, and it would likely land her in jail or worse, but at least it involved a coherent thought pattern—unlike Primo's gas station gambling. Perhaps he hadn't given her quite enough credit, or quite enough attention. Something was out of whack with this one for sure. For now the best approach seemed to be containment.

"Let me think on this, dear," he told her sweetly. "This certainly causes a bit of trouble, but it's nothing we can't recover from in time, don't you think?"

She nodded so vigorously he feared her head might fly off.

"All right, then. I need to rest now. I have therapy in the morning, but perhaps you could come back tomorrow afternoon to discuss the best strategy for the future."

"Of course, Daddy. Oh, thank you. I feel so much better now that you know. I'm sorry I kept it from you, but I just didn't want to upset your recovery and—"

"Nonsense, you were covering your own ass. No need to blow smoke up mine. Come back tomorrow, and try not to get us any deeper into this clusterfuck between now and then."

She stood, saying nothing more, and curtsied on her way out.

Ryan looked around and was startled to discover he had no freaking idea where he was. His ribs hurt, he had to take a massive piss, and he was pretty sure his headache was eating his brain. His eyes focused on Eve's dad, who sat nearby, watching him, and he gradually recognized the room around him as Dr. Hartt's apartment. "Sir?"

"Get up slowly, son. You've taken quite a blow to the head." The man took the stethoscope from around his neck and placed it in his ears.

"Eve?" Ryan sat up and felt his whole body wince.

"She went with the other guy. Do you know who he was?" Dr. Hartt listened to Ryan's chest and checked his pupils.

"No. He helped her last night. What'd she tell you?" His throat felt like he'd given a cactus a blowjob.

"Nothing." The man was pissed. And worried.

"I got to call in." Ryan rubbed his eyes. His vision was blurry.

"McHugh already knows you're here. And he wants you to stay."

Dr. Hartt handed him a glass of tepid water. After gulping it down, Ryan hoped desperately he could have more. It tasted so damn good.

"That's not going to work until I know where Eve is." Ryan stood and swayed.

"You have a concussion. And I'm pretty sure you have a few fractured ribs. And have you seen your face?" Ted pointed toward the decorative mirror on the wall.

Ryan took tentative steps. His vision was sharpening, but he wished it wasn't. He looked like a human canker sore. "Jesus."

"I've been trying to find out about Eve too." The doctor's cell phone rang. "Yeah. He's come to. He's standing at least." He turned his back on Ryan.

It hit him again how much he had to take a piss. He guessed correctly and found the bathroom. When he came out, Dr. Hartt was waiting.

"McHugh's swinging by to pick you up. He said to be ready. I'm going to give you some painkillers, but you really should be in bed. A concussion is a brain injury."

Ryan took the second glass of water gratefully. "Thanks." He tucked the envelope of pills in his tux pants pocket. "Do I have shirt?" He didn't remember taking it off. "I have to feed my fish, find Eve."

The doctor went into the bedroom, and Ryan's gaze fell on his collection of pictures again. Eve was blonde in each of them—even when she was younger. And then there was the picture that had caught his eye the first time through. He focused again on the tattoo on the man's arm as he posed with an unsmiling Eve.

Dr. Hartt returned and handed Ryan a plain white T-shirt. "You can keep this. I'm going to have to toss the other one—too much blood, and it was all torn up."

"Figures. It was rented." He slipped the T-shirt over his head and gasped. "Seriously! Hamster fucks, that hurts."

Dr. Hartt helped him get the shirt over his body. "Sorry, I should've gotten you a button down. This is usually stuff the nurses handle." He looked at the pictures Ryan had been examining.

"I miss her hair. The black's too harsh." Ted picked up the very image Ryan had fixated on.

"Who's that? He looks familiar." Ryan pointed with his pinky.

"That's my nephew, Blake." Ted replaced the picture.

"I feel like I've seen that tattoo before…" He was being obvious, but he didn't care. He hurt too much to care.

"Yeah, a few guys have it. His brothers." Dr. Hartt went to the window. "Up, the captain's here. I'll help you down the stairs."

Ryan probably would've pushed more, but his brain was freaking exhausted. After getting down the stairs in as manly a way as he could with Eve's dad's help, Ryan met Captain McHugh at the door.

"Can't thank you enough, Ted. It's been a crazy night," the captain said. He took note of Dr. Hartt's instructions for Ryan's care, then responded to the man's questions about his family. "Yeah, we got her home. It's good. Blake's doing okay. I think it messed with all of us."

Carefully he walked Ryan to the unmarked police car and watched him flop in. Ryan knew grace was not his strong point right now.

McHugh turned back to Dr. Hartt. "Hey, if you're up to it I think Blake and Livia'd love to have you drop by—and just observe Livvie for me. She says she's okay, but I want to make sure from a medical point of view."

Hartt agreed as McHugh got in the driver's side.

"Your daughter's married to Blake? Blake with the tattoo on his arm?" Ryan put his head against the headrest.

"He's got a few tattoos. So you want to go back to your place and get changed?" John put the car in drive and started off.

Ryan's fuzzy brain made the connections slowly. "Blake's brother is Beckett Taylor?" Ryan turned his head to see his boss.

McHugh nodded. "Not blood. But they're devoted."

The pictures from his files at the office swam before Ryan's eyes. He replaced the blond skunk hair with plain dark hair...The guy from last night was Beckett Taylor. Beckett Taylor who killed Nikko and Wade. Beckett Taylor who'd taken the joy right out of his mother's eyes.

"Did you know he's in town?" Ryan felt panicked, then betrayed.

"Spoke with him yesterday. He...was a necessary evil." McHugh was obviously tortured by his involvement.

"You know he got off easy. Seven years ago he killed two men—just claimed self-defense and got off." Nikko and Wade had mattered. It wasn't fair no one was fighting for them.

"We had nothing good on him. I went over that case a million times. You know as well as I do that once a case leaves our desks any damn thing can happen—and usually does. Christ, you can get more time for holding bag of dope than beating a baby to death. We can only do our jobs the best we can." McHugh pulled into the parking lot of Ryan's apartment complex. "You need help up there?"

Hearing that McHugh had looked into the case made Ryan feel a tiny bit better, justified a little. He'd always liked his boss, and the man did things by the book. Having to work with Beckett Taylor—and feeling like he *needed* to work with Beckett Taylor—probably sucked.

"I got it. There's an elevator." Ryan pulled himself awkwardly out of the car. "My truck is still at that place. The key's with the valet." Ryan pulled his house keys out of his pocket, somewhat surprised to see them considering everything he'd been through.

"I'll see if we can get Tommy out to tow it, and I'll get a patrol car over here. Clean up and then you can ride over to the station. I know you must feel terrible, and you do need to rest, but I need you to explain as much as you can from the video we pulled off your phone."

Ryan nodded and winced at the movement. "Okay, later."

He trudged to the front door of the building and punched in the code. After a trip in the creaky elevator that always smelled vaguely like piss, he stumbled to his door. He needed to swallow some of those pills Eve's dad had given him and drink about five gallons of water. He opened the door and an entire wall of balloons fell on top of him.

"Trish."

She'd somehow rigged his front door with tape and balloons so he had an avalanche of the things to deal with. Oddly, they weren't laced with something evil. He stomped and popped his way through the entryway. He went to the fridge and a frosty twelve-pack of water waited for him. He guzzled two and looked around. Based on the balloon setup, Trish should still be here in his fucking apartment. A huge banner that said *I love you!* was taped to his big-screen TV. There were balloons and flowers and what looked like an entire aisle of a Target store's Valentine display.

Motion-activated dancing animals damn near gave him a heart attack when they all started singing and playing fake instruments as he headed into the bathroom. His mirror was covered with lipstick kisses and hearts. "Trish? Are you here?"

He turned to the toilet and lifted the lid—a sure sign a woman had been in his place—and got his answer a few seconds too late. His bladder had been completely full thanks to all the damn hydrating, and as his pee hit the plastic-wrap barrier and splashed off and down the sides of the bowl, he cursed.

"Ahhhh, crap." There was another lipstick message on the inverse of the lid: *Where were you all night???*

He immediately checked on Poseidon, who was alive but hungry. And he examined the food carefully before feeding it to the fish. "At least she's smart enough to leave you alone, buddy. I am so frisking her ass and stealing back my key."

Upon further examination, he found his apartment to be littered with the remnants of her evening, and she'd once again liberated of a number of key items. No more towels, no more bedding. Interspersed with the decorations and proclamations of adoration were further signs of her meltdown and disappointment. She'd switched from lipstick to Sharpie at some point, and *Where were you?* was a recurring theme. On his stripped bed he found scraps of lingerie, probably hacked from her body with the kitchen knife lying next to them. She'd written on his bare mattress: I'LL BE WATCHING YOU WHILE YOU'RE FUCKING HER!!!!

"Wow." He noticed his open bedroom window and saw that the ladder for the fire escape was engaged. He closed the window, noting that the lock was now busted, and went to his bathroom. He stepped over the puddle of his own urine and took a long, hot shower.

As he steamed, his thoughts shifted from Trish to Eve and turned over the ridiculous events of the last twenty four hours. He had a horrible feeling. If Beckett Taylor had hurt her, there was yet another reason to kill the man.

30

The Saddest Thing

Chery heard the now-familiar buzz from the nightstand and looked at her phone. Jared had texted her fifteen times since Beckett left town yesterday. One of the store patrons had let it slip that the boss was gone. Word traveled fast in this town.

She hated herself for even looking at the words. But she'd never left him before, and for a time she felt powerful. And yet she missed him. He had a way of making her feel electric. It was so stupid. She knew, in her mind, that he was never going to change. But in her heart? She hoped she could change him. Back in the day, when they first got together, he'd been nice to Vere. He'd whistled at Chery loud and long, always giving her a compliment. Feeling that desired made her seem important, protected. Again, she was a dumbass. So that's where the guilt came from.

Jared's first texts had been filled with anger and rage. But now he texted her pictures of flowers and teddy bears. And this very latest text was an apology. She'd never heard those types of words from his mouth. They made her feel strong again, powerful enough to grant him her presence. The house was full of men: one weird guy from Poughkeepsie and two she'd once worked with at the store. Vere was exhausted and sleeping after a day of playing with Gandhi, as always.

She texted Jared back for the first time since she left:

Ur getting sweet on me. Don't recognize u.

His text back was almost instant:

U should. Sorry. I'll be better.

She waited, turning on the bedside light.

Look! I miss you so much. Just talking to you did this to me.

His next text was a picture of his erect penis. She blushed looking at it, and jumped when her phone flashed with an incoming call from him.

She quickly hit the button to ignore it. *What the hell am I thinking? Beckett would be so disappointed.*

He texted right after the phone beeped with the voicemail he left.

Don't b scared. U know I need u.

She got up and closed the bedroom door completely before texting back:

U don't need me.

I do. U know this time of year is ruff 4 me.

His parents had told him they were getting a divorce in the spring. This time of the year always got him down.

I no.

U know or u no? Be specific. My dick is hard.

She waited a little longer. He texted another picture of his penis.

I know.

I been missing u a lot. Ur so pretty. Miss ur mouth.

U lie.

I won't lie anymore. I need u. Bought u a present.

She shook her head at her phone. Her hands were shaking and, damn, her heart was beating fast. It felt like she was falling in love with him all over again.

Look!

The next picture was thong underwear. She hated that style.

Ur ass will look so hot in this.

The next text was a video of him getting himself off, whispering her name. She snorted. He was going to every extreme. She saw herself in the mirror and flushed red. Her eyes were wild with the excitement of it, the danger of him. She was supposed to be good. Stay here and take care of Vere. But Vere was sleeping now, and just a few moments with Jared would make her feel different. She held her breath as she texted:

U handle that by urself?

Meet me on the road out back. U can handle it.

Chery bit her lip and put down her phone. Quickly she put on a dress and left off the panties. This made her like a heroine in a romance novel—being sexy, meeting her lover. She brushed out her hair and swished with mouthwash.

Here.

He was right outside. Just a few minutes with him, then she'd leave again to prove she could. Chery slipped out the window of her bedroom in Beckett's house. She walked carefully out onto the garage. Jared was on the blind side of the house, waiting for her. As she turned and dropped down from the roof, his hands slid up her legs and under her dress. She faced flat against the wall as he ravished her. She'd never felt so sexy in her whole life. His hands were everywhere at once.

"I'm seriously going to come in my jeans. You are so hot."

She turned and kissed him deeply. He palmed her breasts and pinched her nipples, hard. She gasped.

"You'll remember who your daddy is by the end of the night." His breath was laced with whiskey, and his callused fingertips caressed her stomach.

She smiled in his strong arms. "That's what they all say."

His eyes flashed with jealousy, and their sliver of meanness gave her a rush. She'd never been so turned on in her entire life. This man did things to her she couldn't explain. He was toxic, yet she smiled up at him.

He yanked her arm and dragged her back to the car. Halfway there he tossed her over his shoulder and jammed two fingers inside her and his pinkie in her ass.

Chery almost came.

Nighttime settled over the neighborhood as Beckett stopped the car about four blocks from Blake's house and made the call. He couldn't stop the smile that spread over his face when his brother answered the phone. "Just wanted an update. Everything still cool?"

"Yeah. House full of sleepers. Me and Cole just opened a beer. You want in?"

He could hear the bottles toasting in the background. Beckett wanted to have a beer with his brothers so bad he could taste it. But he couldn't risk it. "Yeah, bro, I got to pass. Last thing you guys need is this fucking bastard knocking on your door."

"Come around to the basement. We're waiting for you." Blake hung up, taking the choice out of his hands.

Beckett left the car where it was and jogged through yards until he got to Blake's back door. Blake was waiting, and he must have told the cops this was authorized, because he pulled open the door and grabbed Beckett's shoulder without any interference.

Blake already had an extra beer open and pushed it into his hand. With his tattooed arm, he wrapped Beckett in a welcome. Cole joined, and they toasted their drinks above their braided forearms.

"You fuckers. God, I missed you." Beckett let his common sense fall away and drained the beer in as few gulps as possible.

Soon enough they all put the empties on the floor, and Blake pulled out three more, tossing two in the right direction.

Cole laughed. "This is number three and— " He pulled out his phone and looked at the time. "It's only been an hour."

"That sounds like a good damn day." They toasted again, and Beckett clapped his brothers on the back. He knew he hadn't stopped smiling since he walked in the door. "Motherfuckers." He shook his head.

Years had passed, and he loved being able to sit with them, instantly at ease—not a beat had been missed. They were the best company. Always would be. In a perfect world, he would talk to both of them every damn day.

Cole hopped up and hit play on Blake's iPad. A song poured over them, and they sat in stunned silence while it played.

Beckett began clapping as it ended. "Honey, you've got talent blooming out of your damn asshole. I love you like a fucker."

"I feel the same way about you." Blake laughed and Cole groaned.

Cole leaned forward after taking another pull from his beer. "So what the hell have you been up to?"

Beckett shook his head. "What about you guys? Blake's cranking out babies like a Mormon. What are you and Fairy Princess doing?"

Cole's smile turned sober. "Kyle just had a miscarriage. We've tried for a long time, and pretty much we just can't…It's hard to put in the day right now."

"Whoa. No shit. I'm so, so sorry. You must be wrecked." Beckett shook his head. That kind of devastation must be crumpling Kyle. Such a sensitive, caring chick, with a filthy fucking mouth.

Cole shrugged. "Everything's relative, you know? It's been a crazy bunch of hours. Eve okay?"

Beckett took a long swallow of his beer before answering. The truth was, he had no fucking clue how she was. After getting back in the car, all full of coffee and sandwiches, he'd kind of lost his mind. He'd had no right to do it, but he'd grilled her about the cop. The way she'd been all over him at the party was one thing, but the way she tended to him at her dad's was a kick in the pee hole. He could tell she cared about the guy, wanted him safe.

But it made sense. After so much damn time, she was doing exactly what a normal girl should. But when he'd congratulated her on finding a good man, repeating her own words back to her, she shook her head.

The argument that followed was not a proud moment. All these years he'd been training himself not to react with anger, instant and vicious, but his discipline had evaporated. He'd done the right thing by having the asshole protected, but that was about it. The last words he remembered launching at her were, "I asked you to not fuck anyone else! That's all I asked. It's too hard to keep your goddamn legs closed?"

"Five fucking years, asshole," she'd shot back as she slammed the car door, weaved through the parking lot, and disappeared.

Beckett winced at the memory. He'd been anything but charming. Not the least bit complimentary. She'd looked fantastic. But he was afraid to say so because maybe she'd attribute that to her happiness with the cop.

He'd decided to give them both some time to cool down. Then he'd catch up with her and fix it. The beer was already settling his frayed nerves.

"She looks good. Not sure how things are going to work out though," he finally answered Cole. He got up and pressed play on the iPad, wanting to hear Blake's hopeful song again. On the baby monitor, he could see Whitebread all safe with her kids tucked in around her. "You did good, sweet pea. Did I tell you that? I was duly impressed with your kick-ass Die Hard rescue."

"I was scared the whole damn time." Blake's eyes drifted to the monitor. The song matched the picture.

"That's because you were amazing. It hurts, and it can be scary. Happens to me all day, every day." Beckett raised his beer in Blake's direction.

Cole snorted, and Blake threw a pillow. Beckett ducked and laughed. If he could keep these two men in his pocket for the rest of his days, he would.

Chery hid in the bathroom back at Jared's. Well, hiding wasn't exactly right. He knew where she was. But this was the safest spot she could find while he raged outside. She sat on the closed toilet, head in her hands. The blood from her lip dripped onto the floor, ironically making a puddle that resembled a heart.

She wouldn't make it out alive. She knew this now, and she said a prayer for Vere. In these last minutes of her life, she felt a stunning regret for abandoning her sister. Maybe Beckett would step up and watch out for her. Her tears joined the heart on the floor. This wasn't love. Now she had clarity—when it wouldn't do any damn good. Love shouldn't hurt. Love doesn't hurt.

The door vibrated with his fists, and her entire body shivered. This bathroom didn't have a window. Any time she'd taken a shower, the mirror had fogged up for half an hour. The door vibrated again, and Chery turned on the shower, hoping to buy some time. After a few minutes, tendrils of steam seeped from behind the curtain.

He'd stopped pounding, and that gave her a small glimmer of hope. Maybe he'd passed out. Lord knows he drank everything in the house tonight. But then the door handle began to jiggle. She rushed forward and held the knob, the moist air making the metal slippery. He'd remembered there was a key to this flimsy lock. She'd had to use it a million times when Vere had locked herself in this very bathroom while Chery and Jared fought. She'd use the key and force her way in, closing the door behind her and cuddling her sister. She always sang her sister's favorite lullaby then, trying to bring her back around, grounding her by reminding her of their mother's love.

The knob twisted in her hands, and terror shot through her. He was so wiry and strong, pushing the door in even though she had all her weight against it. His angry face was filled with victory as he shoved his shoulder through the opening, like in a horror movie.

Chery quivered as she sank to the floor, but she stared to sing—just a whisper, really. "Rock-a-bye baby, in the treetop." Jared pulled her up, his face so close to hers. She sang so quietly, she doubted he could hear her. "When the wind blows, the cradle will rock. When the bough breaks, the cradle will fall…" Her arms were useless, his hands full of venom as they squeezed so hard.

The saddest thing was, with just a few more sips of anything—beer, whiskey—he would pass out. But there was nothing she could do. Chery closed her eyes, singing the last line of the song in her head because he'd wrapped his hands around her throat: *And down will come baby, cradle and all.*

The evening became a haze of old times, and the brothers had a blast as the beers flowed. In the wee hours of the morning, Beckett wished he could stay awake, but eventually his body gave out, and Blake tucked him in on the basement couch like a baby. He hadn't even been smart enough to protest, and when his phone buzzed, it was already Monday morning. He rubbed his eyes and took a look at the screen—a text from Chaos.

You know where Chery is?

"Shit." Beckett called him immediately. "What the hell are you asking *me* for. I'm in New York."

"Boss, we thought she was sleeping in. But she's not here. Her window's unlocked, and I think she crawled out."

"What happened when Vere woke up?" Beckett stared at his feet.

"I did the shit Chery does in the morning, and I took her to the place she goes to. I looked at the store, but nothing. No one knows where she is." Chaos was frazzled.

"Fuck." Beckett needed a minute to think, but Chaos kept talking.

"She with the assbag, you think? I mean, we set the alarm. She went to bed before I walked Gandhi, so I set it after he took his dump. I don't know. Tell me where the ex-boyfriend lives."

"You call the number I'm about to text you—it's the place you dropped off Vere—and tell them Vere's sister Chery is missing. Ask them if Vere can stay the night. Tell 'em Chery might be in trouble. Then you pack heat and take my employees with you to check out the asshole's house. I'll send you that address too. Keep me posted. I'm on my fucking way."

Beckett ended the call just as his brothers came down the stairs, questions all over their faces.

"Sorry—was I too loud? What the hell happened last night? Ahhh, remember when I was trying to be a better fucker?" He texted Chaos the information while he talked. "Well, I wound up being the king of the misfits down in Maryland. Like, my congregation is assholes and down-on-their-luck bastards. My employees are bottom of the barrel, un-hireable twat hairs. But it worked. A lot of them got on their feet for a while."

Cole clapped Beckett on the back, pride blooming on his face.

"Yeah, but, you see, I pictured, like, I don't know, doing something huge. Saving the world." Beckett shrugged.

Blake shook his head. "Sometimes you can save someone's whole world just by smiling at them. Kindness is one of those things that has immense value to the person experiencing it."

"Well, anyway, Chery's like that—or she was. She works for me at the liquor store, and I've been helping her out. She's got a shitty resume because she's got a sister who needs her help and a boyfriend who kicks the crap out of her. Now she's missing. I got to get down there and see what the hell's happening." Beckett ran his hand through his hair. "I've got a horrible feeling."

Cole squeezed his shoulder. "You need help, brother?"

"Thanks. No. This is one asshole—up here we got a ton of them. I'll be back soon. Won't take me too long to sort this out. Eve and I had a fight-ish thing. So I'll text her, but if you could keep an eye on her…" Beckett held up his arm, and his brothers' arms met him in the middle.

"We can try our best," Blake said. "But she's like protecting a shark."

"Don't I know it." Beckett shook his head.

He'd already stayed too long, but he hated leaving. What the hell had Chery gotten into? He knew it was Jared. Motherfucker.

"Should've killed him," Beckett said as he jogged back to his car.

31

Mine

Mary Ellen took a nice bowl of cereal in the morning because it was good for her digestion. She would never admit it to anyone, but in the recent years, things had become dire if she didn't have her morning fiber. Officially, she was fifty three. According to all paperwork, she was thirty eight and holding. Her fourth face lift had gone a little bit awry, and her eyes didn't completely close. She sipped from her orange juice glass and tried to ignore the flashback to her juice cleanse last month. Her lips were still numb from the injections a few days ago.

They weren't typical, the reasons for her grip on her youth. She just wanted to remain daddy's little girl for as long as possible. He was starting to forgive her for the Sevan thing, she could tell. Of course he needed the money back, but they'd work together to make that happen. They'd work *together*, just as she'd always wanted. Perhaps she'd mail Sevan a thank-you note in the end.

Her brother had looked simply murderous when she passed him on the way out of Daddy's house yesterday, of course with a smile on her face. Those were the perks of fighting like a woman. Her brother could most likely maintain status quo with the business—at least for a while before he gambled the whole thing away—but she knew her father wanted more for his legacy. Soon she'd have an opportunity to show him what she could provide. The man was eighty three. Time was a villain who couldn't be forgotten, but infamy would last forever.

She just liked his approval. And that wasn't so wrong.

Now January was an issue. She'd known the woman was more than she claimed, and yet she'd never expected such blatant disrespect. To leave the party, leave her protection duties when things were clearly falling apart, *and* take a hostage with her? Mary Ellen touched the linen napkin to where she was almost positive her perfectly plumped lips were. Seems January had a weakness after all. Or at least she hoped she did. Mary Ellen stood and tucked her satin robe around her.

She jumped at an unexpected knock on the door to her suite. Her staff knew she needed private time after her cereal. What on earth could this be? She signaled the interruption to enter with a stern voice.

Instead of Bart, January waltzed in wearing jeans and a T-shirt like a common house painter headed to a picnic. Mary Ellen was already angry, but this sloppy attire and unannounced entrance was a slap in the face. What the hell were her people thinking?

"You have some nerve. My orders were for you to be killed. Can you explain why you're still looking at me?" She tapped her fingers on her satin robe.

"You're insane. That stunt you pulled last night was a giant ass fuck to so many people. You think that's the way to build trust? To get co-operation? Seriously? I will hand it to you, though. You can improvise the fuck out of a disaster." January closed the door behind her and put her hands on her hips. "But trotting out Ryan? Kidnapping women and children, including a police captain's daughter? I'm shocked you're still looking at me, to be honest. You've pissed off a crapload of people. And they're not going to forget." January looked her up and down.

Mary Ellen hated the way the girl seemed to catalogue her with just a glance. "They way I conduct my business has *nothing* to do with you. As far as I'm concerned, you're Miracle Grow for my roses now. Bart?" She smiled pleasantly.

January advanced and stopped just short of the woman's face. "Here's what you need to know: Poughkeepsie is mine. The people. The shops. The cops. I decide what happens to them."

"You can talk whatever type of gibberish you want. You're just an animated dead body right now. Bart?" Mary Ellen stood.

A loud thump hit the door, and January bent down to look in her eyes. "That would be Bart dropping dead."

A trickle of fear almost made Mary Ellen gasp, but she stayed silent.

"I killed my way in here, motherfucker. The dude with the hand surgery? Gone. His smoking friends? Corpses. The pedophile with the eye scar? Spectacularly dead. You messed with my family. That's not allowed." January pulled a knife from her hair.

Finally the fear was given a voice. Mary Ellen shrieked as she realized her closest weapon was in the bedside table drawer. January grabbed her hair and yanked, revealing her throat.

"Kill me now and my father will hunt down every one you've ever met and turn them into dog food," Mary Ellen spat.

January shrugged before smiling. "Poughkeepsie's mine."

The blade was so sharp Mary Ellen couldn't even feel it as it entered her windpipe.

Eve stood over Mary Ellen's body and knew she'd made an epic mistake, a horrible miscalculation. These situations were what she was good at fixing, but instead she'd created one. Her mind was like Jell-O between seeing Beckett and managing her feelings for Ryan, which had no place. Both seemed stupid, but the mess at her feet left her no doubts that she was more than a little out of her head.

Shark burst through the door and into the suite. "What the hell did you do?"

Acted like a hotheaded pussy. "Get Micki and get out of here." Eve turned to face him. Bart's dead body was lumped in the doorway. The poison she'd injected had paralyzed him standing and stopped his heart shortly thereafter. The sight of him made her want to puke a little. He'd been nice to her. Shark was still standing there, frozen. "Go!" She wiped her knife off on Mary Ellen's body and slid it back into her hair.

"You're staying? 'Cause I didn't press the panic button—you're fucking lucky I was on security this morning—but that shit still gets transmitted." Shark shook his head.

"Is it still on?" Eve looked at Shark. He was wasting time.

"Yeah." He nodded. "I disabled the audio though…You're just going stay?" He seemed completely confused.

"Her father would look in to me if I ran. He'd find my family, people I care about. I can't let that happen." She inhaled deeply and exhaled, knowing she was doing so without pain for a precious few more minutes.

"This was some Kamikaze shit." Shark advanced on her. "You want me to tell anyone anything?"

She took a swing and hit only his shoulder. "You find my father and Ryan and tell them I'm dead."

He swung back and twisted her into a hold she didn't fight. "Shit. I can't kill you, you know that." Shark absorbed her less-than-spectacular blows.

"Just knock me out, for Christ's sake." Eve managed to twist and meet his eyes.

Shark looked a little sad. "Good luck."

He was excellent at the maneuver. The black claimed Eve just as she realized he'd choked her out.

The old man paused at the top of the steps. He'd been napping in his favorite chair when he was shaken awake. One of his best bodyguards looked nervous, and that never happened. Apparently Mary Ellen was in a bad way. According to the men on the scene, it had been an assassination.

His people watched him carefully to see how he would react. They were probably all waiting for him to keel over again. But if he'd survived three months of the most ridiculous rehab, he could certainly get through this. He showed no emotion. After all, he was too old to not see this coming. Mary Ellen had made too many rash decisions while he was away, let her emotions get the better of her.

He retraced his steps through her growing-up years on the ride over to her residence. He'd tried to teach her, but she just showed limited capacity for the nuances of their business. She was one of his only two children, and her mother, his darling Diane, had been the one woman he'd ever really loved. Primo was his only boy, so he'd done his best to make him into something even though he came from the loins of the housemaid. Diane had passed more than ten years ago, but every day he wished she were still here. Mary Ellen had been her mother's spitting image until she began messing with her face.

Once inside her home, he pulled himself up her ridiculously long steps. She was so dramatic, fancied herself a Scarlett O'Hara as she traipsed down this grand staircase every day. His path was littered with dead bodies—men expertly killed. In his business he'd developed an eye for craftsmanship, and this assassin was the Picasso of murder. He held the doorframe at the entrance to her suite and caught his breath from the exertion. His daughter had been covered with a duvet, and a gorgeous woman in jeans lay close by.

"Let me see Mary Ellen." He nodded at the covered lump.

His bodyguard reverently removed the cover from her face.

"All the way." He came closer.

Mary Ellen's eyes were wide open and her mouth a circle. All her color was gone, and the gash on her neck was more of an incision. An expert crime of passion. There was hate in this room with these two women.

"Take a picture of my daughter. Bring the other one to my guest house here." He turned to leave.

"That's it? You're sure?" The mouthy guard was one of hers.

He turned slowly until he found the one who spoke. "My men know what Mary Ellen needs now."

The man shook his head. "Wow, I expected more."

Rodolfo looked at his hands. They were old and that still surprised him, even after his body's recent betrayal. How many men had he killed using only his thumb and forefinger? So many.

"What's your name?" The man answered a few times before Rodolfo heard him.

"Anthony."

"Anthony. You're never to talk to me. Ever. And as far as that one?" He pointed with his cane. "I'll make pain her god. As a matter of fact, we're going bring you too and teach you some respect." He nodded to one of his men and turned away from his daughter's body. He wished he felt more loss, but her face looked nothing like her mother's anymore.

32

Unbreakable

A little after noon, Beckett pulled into Jared's driveway. Chaos met him with a shaking head.

"Still singing the same tune?"

"Says he hasn't seen her. The whole place smells like bleach." Chaos gestured to the house. "Vere is still at the place. I spoke to Florence, the director. And your dog is fine."

"Anyone call the cops yet?" Beckett pulled on fingerless leather gloves. They were the style he used to buy all the time when he was busting skulls.

"No. Right now she's not even missing. She's a grown-ass woman. She can go where she wants." Chaos looked pissed.

"You got a thing for Chery?" Beckett went to the front door and "knocked" with his shit-kicking boots, splintering the shitty door.

The tattoo artist shifted from foot to foot. "Nah. Just seems like a nice girl."

Jared didn't answer, so Beckett kicked the door in the sweet spot as hard as he could. It flew open, bouncing off the wall inside. "Knock, knock, twat taffy. I'm here to murder your goddamn ass." He inspected the house while Chaos crowded in behind him. "He's still here, right?"

"Yeah. Should be in the back bedroom cuddling a gun." Chaos sounded fired up.

Beckett kicked in a second door, and there was Jared: sitting on the bed, cuddling his gun.

"Where's Chery?" Beckett scanned the room. It was neat and tidy, unlike the rest of the shithole he'd just walked through.

"I ain't seen her. Go look at the store." Jared sniffed and tried to look manlier, aiming the firearm at Beckett's chest.

"Point that gun at me, and I'll shove it up your fucking ass." Beckett opened the bathroom door and the smell of fresh bleach was strong enough to make him gag. "You motherfucker. Where's her body?"

Beckett's heart sank. He knew. He'd known as soon as he heard from Chaos in Poughkeepsie—she was dead. He'd known since he decided not to kill Jared weeks ago that it was the wrong choice. Maybe that was his only gift: knowing when a murder *should* be committed.

He spied a toothpick on the bedside table. "Chaos, go get me a handful of toothpicks from the kitchen."

"What the hell do you want? Get out of my house!" Jared scrambled to the other side of the bed and stood.

"Do you know who I am?" Beckett crossed his arms in front of him.

"No. But I heard stories. And I told a shit-ton of people all about you." Jared was obviously used to setting the tone of the fear in a room.

"Where's her body?" Beckett acknowledged Chaos and took a handful of toothpicks.

"You got to the count of three to get out of here. And take the fucking toothpicks with you." Jared settled into a stance, holding the gun in front of him.

"You'll answer my goddamn question. You can do it now, or you can wait until I get creative. Do you remember how I almost killed you with a motherfucking hamburger? Imagine what I can do with these." He fanned the little splinters of wood in his fingers like Edward Scissorhands. "Never mind, don't hurt yourself. I'll let you find out."

Chaos relieved Jared of his gun. The man had spent so much time in jail, stealing shanks from murderous bastards, disarming this still-drunk was a cakewalk.

"Tell me where you put her body." Beckett nodded at Chaos, and the man threw Jared to the bed. There was some serious anger in his movements.

"Give me your hand." Beckett nodded at Jared.

"Fuck you!"

Beckett smiled. "You'd like that too much."

When Beckett was done with Jared, the whimpering man was willing to tell him every secret he'd ever had. They went to the backyard, and Jared opened the combination lock to his shed with bloody hands, some fingers missing nails entirely.

Beckett took a breath before stepping inside. All the things ahead of him flashed in his mind: telling Vere, figuring out how to make her comfortable—it was mind-boggling. Thinking of taking on her needs sent a new wave of respect for Chery flowing through him.

Chaos began slamming at a huge wooden storage crate with a sledgehammer. Jared tried slipping out the door. Beckett caught him by the nape of his neck and squeezed.

"The only reason you're still alive is because I need to see how much pain you caused her. I'll multiply it by a million before I kill you."

Jared still looked shifty, despite the pain he'd endured.

The storage crate had been soldered closed—the hinges now nothing but melted lumps. But Chaos busted into it, forcing the lid open and cracking the wood. Inside, wrapped in a bedspread covered in blood, was the small shape of a woman. Chaos reached into his pocket and pulled out a switchblade. He cut the ropes around the neck and body.

The gasp from the form made them all jump. Chaos reacted quickly, slicing carefully though the blanket until he got to her.

"No. No. No. That's not right," Jared murmured.

Chery's eyes flew open, and she began to cry when she saw Jared's face.

Chaos stepped in front of her line of sight. "It's okay. You're okay. Beckett's here, and Vere's okay, yeah? Don't fear him. You have help."

Beckett turned and smiled at Jared, throwing a punch that would put his lights out for a long time.

Eve didn't open her eyes when she woke. Instead she focused on her breathing, maintaining a slow, regular rhythm. Her head hung at an uncomfortable angle, but she let it remain.

She used all her other senses to assess: her arms were bound behind her and her ankles fastened to the chair she sat in. Judging from the thin, cutting pain, her restraints were plastic zip ties.

The room was remarkably quiet. She thought she might be alone until she heard a person shift, clothes rustling. She'd marched right in and killed Mary Ellen in her own home. Stupid. A crime of passion. Since when did she have more passion than brains? Maybe for a long time now, actually…

As far as she could tell, nothing had been done to her—yet. She'd have to open her eyes to get a full understanding of the situation. And when she opened her eyes, she'd also open herself to the pain that was surely headed her way. She lifted her head and found a man sitting at a table some distance away. She didn't make a noise, just matched his gaze.

He did as she'd expected: alerting various people that she'd finally roused. They certainly had ways of waking her, so this was either poorly planned or part of the experience. The room had a single door, two electrical outlets, and one small vent for heat and air. The lack of windows meant it was either custom designed or remodeled to be a prison.

Her chair was fairly comfortable, with some padding, but her hands and feet were totally secured. Her clothes were still on. The door opened and an elderly gentleman she suspected to be Rodolfo Vitullo, along with five other men, came through it.

"Well, I have to commend you," the geezer in charge said. "After seeing your work at my daughter's house, my men insisted we bind you. They're rarely this cautious. You are skilled." He waved the guard away from the table and took his place, using his cane to balance himself. "Why don't we start with your name? I'm Rodolfo Vitullo. I've been indisposed for a period of months, but I'm sure my reputation precedes me. I understand you and my daughter were quite close."

Eve said nothing. She catalogued the weapons the men had brought into the room so she'd know what she wanted when she got the opportunity to use them.

"No? Nothing to say? I'm not surprised. I must confess, I'm an old man but you have piqued my interest. And not much peaks anymore, if you know what I mean." He gave her a knowing look.

"I'm actually trying not to think about your ancient balls, if that's okay with you." Eve smiled at him.

"Feisty. Respect would suit you." Rodolfo began coughing and hacked up something he spit in his employee's coffee cup.

The man closest to Eve produced a Taser and stepped closer to her. Eve refused to look at him, instead keeping her eyes on Rodolfo.

"No fear? Impressive. Wasted effort, but good. Hmm." He shifted in the chair, the metal legs screeching on the cement floor. "Don't use that, Rogers. Go get her the one that plugs in—with the insertable attachments."

Eve knew then that it was going to be bad, worse than she could imagine, because this guy was old school. "You should have them get a thank-you card for me. Your daughter was a crackpot. She was going to drive your business into the ground. So soon, actually, that you'd probably live to see it." She tried to shift her hands, and the plastic bit into bone. Whoever put the ties on had used all his strength to close them. The nerves in her wrist were on fire.

"You know I'll have you cry. You'll beg for death." Rodolfo stood and made his way slowly over to her.

"Wouldn't be the first time." Eve returned his steely gaze.

"Tell me your name, precious."

The man returned with a device that looked as old as the man. He plugged it in and untangled the cord.

Rodolfo propped his cane against his hip and dusted off the device. He twisted a long, pointy cone onto it. The top, like the star on a Christmas tree, was a single, rusty barb.

Jesus.

"The insertable. Where do you think we should put it, boys? It can go anywhere." Rodolfo grabbed Eve's chin and handed the device back to the man who'd brought it. "Tell me your name."

The device made an audible hum, charging and warming when he switched it on. Its very tip began turning red. Eve refused to look directly at it, instead staring into Rodolfo's cataract-filmed eyes.

"Name?" He wrinkled his nose, and she could see the long hairs in it.

Her voice was strong, but quieter than she'd intended: "Unbreakable."

33

PAINKILLERS

Kyle waited for Cole in the hotel room. Rather than wear out their welcome at Blake and Livia's, Cole had suggested they get a little spot of their own for the next couple days while the police finished up at their house. In a further show of chivalry, he was now buying her dinner downstairs, and she was starving. She looked at her chopped hair in the mirror, thinking back to the moment when she decided to cut it. It had been the hair or her wrists. Had that been just days ago?

So much had happened since. She'd faced the very real possibility of her sister's murder. She and Cole had been in charge of her niece and nephew while their parents were gone, maybe permanently. And then she'd helped a lady on the lam clothe herself. She snickered remembering that one, but it was a lot. All of it was a lot.

Cole opened the door, juggling their food, and she went to help him. They made small talk: *Was the line long? Oh, they were out of Coke?* Simple stuff. Easy stuff.

After they ate, Kyle finally decided to ask, because he hadn't mentioned it. "Is my hair okay?"

Cole regarded her and bit his lip. "I like it."

"You hate it. I look like boy. You want a divorce." Kyle stood from the table and sat on the bed.

"No. No. And no." Cole came and sat next to her. "I think it's nice."

"You won't touch me. I look like a fucking mushroom." Kyle covered her face.

"I didn't know touching you was an option." Cole ran his fingers through her hair, trailing them along the back of her neck. "This part? So sexy. Getting to see it all the time? It's almost like an obscenity—a delicious obscenity." He gently licked her skin and spoke against her neck. "You never, ever have to worry that I'm not attracted to you. I would be having sex with you as often as I breathe if you'd let me. I dream about you. When I dream of anything, it's always you. And sometimes, you even have short hair in those dreams. How lucky am I? You're my dream girl."

Kyle turned and buried her face in his chest. He smelled so good. How he could have skin that smelled like perfection, she didn't know. She pushed him back on the bed and cuddled against him more.

He continued to stroke her hair. "This has been a crazy couple of days. I've been praying so much."

She lifted her head. *Damn it.* She'd done it again: thinking about herself so much that she'd forgotten he was more than just her stable, comforting guy. He had brothers involved, he was worried about her, and he'd lost his baby too. Plus he'd had to figure out how to diaper Kellan. It had all been hard for him.

"So what did Beckett say? Will he be back?" She looked into his eyes. They were a miracle, the color of prayers.

"I don't know. He was really thrown for a loop, worrying about those two girls in Maryland. I haven't heard from him since he left." Cole looked back at her and touched her cheek. "Love you."

"Back at ya, handsome." She flopped against his arm and settled in. "So is it like a *Big Love* thing? Eve's gonna be pissed."

"I didn't get that impression. Chery was more just someone he wanted to help. They both were. He said he got a dog too." Cole rolled onto his side and laid his hand on her stomach. Kyle readjusted it to rest on her left breast.

"The girls have been lonely without you." She smiled.

"We're only doing what you're ready for." He looked at her tenderly.

"How about kissing and snuggling? Is that too blue-balltastic?" She kissed his lips.

He smiled in between kisses. "It's perfect."

They kissed and kissed, and Kyle felt herself relax. She boldly touched her husband everywhere until a cramp reminded her she was healing.

"Wow." She lay back on the pillows.

"Pain?" He got up and found her purse, getting out two Advil.

She swallowed them with the last of her dinner drink. "It's like my body has to remind me I suck."

Cole exhaled. "I think your body needs an attitude adjustment. Seriously. Everything you have to do with that body makes me feel like a chump."

Kyle raised her eyebrow.

"No, really. All of this is on you. I'm totally wishing I was a seahorse so I could carry a baby. You have periods, bring life into the world, secrete milk...I don't know. All I can do is open jars and kill spiders." He reached for her hand. "I wish there was more I could do. I mean, when will it be okay to tell you we *will* laugh again? We'll never forget our baby, but we have to be on this planet. We owe it to each other, right?"

"Yeah. I don't know. I've got such guilt—about my mom, about how I lived, about stealing you from the church."

"I'm grateful to your mom every day. Does that make me a bad guy?"

She pulled her hand out of Cole's grasp. He shook his head and very purposefully took it back.

"Because without her, there would be no you. And why do you have to feel bad about having had some sex along the way? So that's how you handled sexuality: in excess. That's who you are. You do stuff big. You love big. Your mistakes can be big. It's this reckless girl who had the guts to make me fall in love with her at first sight. You willed that into existence. Tell me something." He pulled her into his arms and tilted her face until she was looking in his eyes. "How does this feel? This. Right here."

She closed her eyes so she could gather the words. "Right. Soothing. Exciting." She opened her eyes, and he was nodding.

"As long as this feels right? We're doing okay. I'm selfish enough to think all those other things happened so we could be right for each other." He kissed her.

"I like when you're selfish." Kyle nodded as the painkillers kicked in, and she relaxed in his arms. She was going to try harder to think positive. She'd force herself if she had to.

The sun was sinking, and Beckett was almost finished driving back to Poughkeepsie. He slurped a Red Bull and did his best to stay awake. Gandhi, however, snored so loud he just about drowned out the music. The damn dog had been so happy to see him, it was hilarious. He'd headed at him like a freshly shot cannon ball and hit him in the nuts at a hundred miles an hour. He'd been tempted to leave the dog with Vere, but damn it if he wasn't attached to his ugly mug. His phone rang as he merged onto the New York State Throughway. It was a douchebag.

"What?" Beckett put the phone on speaker.

"Boss, I just heard from Shark. You remember him?" This was Harris, kind of a shifty douchebag.

"Barely." Beckett petted G's head.

"Yeah, well, he just called and wanted me to get a message to you. It's not good fucking news." Harris sounded nervous.

"Waiting." Beckett's knuckles went white. Shark was an asshole from back in the day—had his dick in every pot he could to stir it. He'd never liked or trusted him.

"Eve killed Mary Ellen Vitullo."

"Shit." Beckett nearly swerved off the road. "Where's the body?" He hated these kinds of conversations on cell phones, but he needed to know how to cover Eve's ass.

"That's the thing. The body's at Mary Ellen's house. She just murdered her way into the woman's room and slashed her throat. The woman's father, Rodolfo, he's got Eve now. She just waited there. Shark forwarded the security tape to me. I'll send it to your phone." The douchebag paused.

"Rodolfo has her?" Beckett was hoping he'd heard wrong.

"That's what Shark said. They're still at the house. If I hadn't seen the video, I'd never believe she'd get caught like that."

"Okay, get me a crew with wheels and the nicest fucking suit you can find. Get Milton on it." He cast a glance at Gandhi. He'd have to leave the dog with one of his brothers. No way he'd get his pooch involved with this shit. Sucked. He wanted to show him off to Eve. After a quick texting back and forth, Cole was the first taker. Fortunately they were at a dog-friendly hotel.

Rodolfo Vitullo was a fucking legend. The fact that the man was in his eighties and still going strong—and not in prison—was a testament to how ridiculous he was at the weapons business. If something was likely to irritate that man, you left that shit alone.

Beckett made some more calls and soon enough he was back where he'd started—barely twelve hours after he'd left. Despite the fact that it made him queasy, he called John McHugh, who sounded somewhere between disgusted and intrigued when he answered the phone.

"All the victims have been recovered, as near as we can tell. And we now have a very nice, long list of people of interest." McHugh's voice was icy. Beckett knew the man hated him, and he respected that. "And I'm grateful for Ryan's retrieval," McHugh added. "He's a good officer."

"Yeah, that was all Eve. She wouldn't leave without him. Insisted on it." Beckett waited for some sounds of surprise, but it seemed McHugh had already processed that Eve was more than she seemed. "Speaking of Eve, she's currently an unwilling visitor of Roldolfo Vitullo's at Mary Ellen Vitullo's compound in Somers. At least, that's the intel I can gather so far."

"You don't say. Rodolfo's a coward and a monster." Judging from the clicking, McHugh was pulling up files. "So are you filing a missing person's report? Do you want to come in and report it as a kidnapping?"

Beckett sighed. "No offense, sir, but no one in your department is going to be able to help her. I just wanted to let you know where I am and what I'm doing. As of now, my plan is to stop in over there. I've got nothing after that." Beckett petted the dog again as he drove toward the gas station where he'd agreed to meet Cole.

"Well, I'm giving you as much space as I can, but this can't last forever, Taylor." McHugh sighed heavily into the phone. "And I'll have to tell my contacts in Somers what's happening. Their move is their call, but I think it's good to have the police on Vitullo."

"He's probably got more cops on the payroll than you do. But whatever you think. I'm getting Eve out no matter what. I know your concern is for your girls, but resolving this situation increases everyone's chance at a bright future. And I can't say I won't blow shit up." Beckett put the car in park and clipped a leash on Gandhi. The dog seemed reluctant to get out. There was silence on the other end of the phone. Beckett understood. The man couldn't condone anything he was planning. Kyle and Cole pulled in as Beckett thanked McHugh—or rather the continued silence where McHugh had been—and hung up.

Beckett strolled over Cole's car, and Kyle was out the door in a shot. Gandhi was too surprised to even bark as the redhead wrapped Beckett in a hug. He kept an arm around her as Cole got down to let Gandhi sniff his hand.

"This dog is so ugly." Cole laughed.

"What happened to all God's creatures and all that shit?" Beckett held up his arm again. He knew they'd done it too much in the last handful of hours, but damn it, seeing these faces just made Beckett need to acknowledge his family.

Cole stood and wrapped his arm around Beckett's, patting his shoulder solidly. Kyle got low so she could get to know the dog.

"So, it's cool for you guys to watch him? I've got his food in the trunk. He's super easygoing. Loves belly rubs." Beckett slapped Cole on the back again and went to retrieve the food.

"Why can't he stay with you? You afraid to have something prettier than you in the car?" Kyle stroked G from head to tail.

"Eve's in trouble. You got any prayers left in you, brother?" Beckett handed the bag of food to Cole.

"Yeah. She all right?" Cole transferred the bag to his backseat.

"Just pray. Having this guy's ugly mug taken care of was last on my list. Now I gotta fill up the tank and run. I'll keep you posted. Lay low if you can. Keep an eye on those kids, your sister and my brothers, okay, Fairy Princess?" Beckett held open the old-man car's door for Kyle and picked up his dog. He petted him and kissed his crazy face before putting him on Kyle's lap. G immediately tried to kiss her face.

"You flirt," he chastised his dog.

Kyle laughed and rolled down her window. "Be careful and bring her back."

"No worries. I got this." Beckett thanked his brother and got into his car. He couldn't waste another second getting to Eve.

After six minutes of erratic driving, he pulled into his old parking lot. Waiting next to a nondescript white van were three well-dressed and impressively armed douchebags. Beckett stripped and changed into the Italian suit Milton had selected, stepping into his shoes while his men piled in the van. He tied his shoes and stood to assess their faces. They were decent douchebags—hungry for power and not afraid to kill. He was lucky to get them on short notice.

"Okay, anyone find out shit?" Beckett slipped the tie around his neck and began to do it up.

After the brief rundown, he'd learned that Eve was taken to Rodolfo's guesthouse on the premises, and they were treating her like the motherfucking kick-ass assassin she was. He pulled out his phone and played the surveillance camera footage. The scenes were spliced together into a flawless Eve show. One after another she eliminated her obstacles, culminating in the poisoning of the last doorman. Then after a brief chat, she sliced Mary Ellen's throat.

He hit pause and looked at Eve's face right after the murders were complete. The vacancy there was chilling. The douchebags, however, were complimentary, asking to see the video again. If killing were choreography, Eve was Bob Fosse.

"Get me someone who's done business with Vitullo before. I've stayed out of his crotchety old hair until now." The guys with him began making calls and texting. "And one of you ride with me. We gotta move."

Dell O'Neal slid in next to him in the Challenger and kept the line of communication open with the van. Dell was out of jail and hungry, but Beckett knew he was loyal. He'd been around five years ago, and Milton had vouched for him. Dell handed him a burner phone. Beckett made a quick phone call to assbag Sevan Harmon's organization to tighten up the freaking mental ammunition he was preparing. By the time they pulled up to the guesthouse, which really was just another fucking mansion behind the one Mary Ellen had lived in, Beckett knew at least some of what Sevan knew, and he had a few tricks up his sleeve.

The driver hit the intercom, and Beckett introduced himself to the video camera. "Beckett Taylor. Make sure your gates can open wide enough to fit my giant balls. You're torturing a woman in there who's mine."

He sat back and was pleasantly surprised when they were buzzed through.

"Ritzy-titzy Somers likes us, boys. You ready to ride again?" Beckett heard the roar from the van through O'Neal's phone.

"Hell yeah."

"Giddy up."

"Nuts of Wrath!"

As they pulled up at the guesthouse, an army of blood soldiers stood waiting.

"We're not expecting you."

Beckett straightened his tie and stepped out of the car. "No one does. You've got one of my assets in there, and I need her back."

"You'll excuse us if we're unmoved to help. We recently had a death in the family." The man's eyes were hidden behind dark sunglasses.

"You tell Rodolfo I helped expedite the death in your motherfucking family. And if he doesn't talk to me right now, I'm going to blow his ass cheeks wide open. Anywhere he's ever taken a shit will be razed to the ground."

Beckett waited as the goons spoke into their earpieces.

"Follow me—just you, though." The one who appeared to be in charge frisked Beckett and, piece by piece, pulled out an almost hilarious amount of weaponry. It was all for show, though. Beckett had known he would be walking in barehanded.

"Boys, stay put. I'll be in touch." He saluted the douches and followed the guard inside.

After meandering deeper and deeper into the labyrinth of the guesthouse, Beckett finally found himself in front of a metal door. He settled his mind, knowing he could see just about anything on the other side. To get them out of here alive, he'd have to wear his game face. No matter what.

The door swung open, and he forced himself to search for Rodolfo, not Eve. Every second, every breath was going to be weighed and measured. He met Rodolfo's thickly glazed eyes. Crinkly old bastard. Eve was tied to a chair and, based on his peripheral vision, looked alive.

"Rodolfo." Beckett nodded. "I'm here to collect my weapon."

Eve offered a barking laugh. "I don't even know him. Kick him out." Her voice was harsh and ragged, like she'd been through hell.

"Beckett Taylor, please come in. Quite the reputation you once had. Such promise until you decided to nancy out. I thought you were dead. That would've been braver." Rodolfo shook his head.

"Congratulations on the death of your daughter." Beckett tipped his hat at the old man.

"Cut out his tongue." Rodolfo pointed at Beckett with his cane. "His common sense must have fallen off. It's the only remedy."

The man who'd walked him in pulled a switchblade, and Beckett disarmed him without looking. "Homeslice, put this away before you hurt someone." Beckett closed the blade and handed it back to the attacker handle first.

"You *do* know you're surrounded." Rodolfo nodded at his men, who pulled out handguns.

Beckett shook his head. "Do you think I'm stupid enough to waltz in here without insurance? You're seconds away from getting bombed like a college freshman."

"I hear no helicopters, homeslice." Rodolfo raised an eyebrow. "I'm calling your bluff."

Now that he'd stepped completely into the room, Beckett could see a man lying on the floor, holding what looked like the devil's dildo, which plugged into the wall. There was a slight electric crackle, and the body twitched — the man was frying on the floor.

"He try to steal your ass toy, Rodolfo?" Beckett nodded at the electrocuted man as he strolled casually toward Eve.

"No. He's just warming it up for you. Too bad your ladyfriend here didn't get to enjoy it." Rodolfo let out a forced cackle. His men joined in with laughter.

"That's how you treat the people who work for you? That's shit. My men know where they stand with me." Beckett finally let his eyes meet Eve's.

She was pure fury. Thank fuck. Because that shit the guy was flopping around on the floor with was ancient craziness. And they'd had her a long damn time. Fury meant she was still home.

"Okay, cut the bullshit." Rodolfo was done humoring him. "Why are you here, baby mobster. Tell me your story before I make it so you can tell no more."

"I ordered the hit on your daughter. I saw what you couldn't. She was out of control."

"That's a lie, and I know my daughter better than anyone. You think you get to be eighty without seeing every trick in the book? No matter what you tell me, I'll know the truth. You're here because you love this girl. You want to save her." Rodolfo took a pistol from the table and hobbled over to Eve. He held the gun to her temple. "You cannot."

She turned her head, positioning the gun on her forehead instead. "Do it."

Beckett's stomach dropped. "You're right. I do love her. More than you loved your daughter."

"And you know this how?" Rodolfo threw up the hand not holding the gun.

"Because this lady's still breathing. Your rage should have overcome you. You knew Mary Ellen was rotten. Do any of your kids love you? Would Primo change your shitty diaper if you didn't have a dime?" Beckett stepped closer.

"You tire me." Rodolfo turned his attention back to Eve. "Shame. You are talented."

"I know about Sevan Harmon." Beckett took his hat off.

"Speak more." Rodolfo released the safety on the gun.

"I've had some dealings with him—helped him out a bit here and there, back in the day. I'm sure you're aware that Poughkeepsie is essential to his operation." Beckett kept his voice even, although inside his entire being was made of jelly.

Eve grinned at Rodolfo and his gun. "Your daughter was a vapid asshole, and she gave a bunch of your money away. I enjoyed killing her."

Beckett threw his hat at Eve. "Shut up. Seriously. I'm here to pledge my allegiance to this old fart so you can leave. Don't make it worse."

Rodolfo stood silent for so long, Beckett was afraid he'd fallen asleep. Finally the old man spoke. "What exactly is it you think you have to offer me?"

"I understand your accounts are not exactly in order. Your daughter and Sevan misplaced some money, it seems."

"Yes, thank you for reminding me of that. But I don't believe insolvency is on the horizon. It's nothing, truly. And I still fail to see your relevance."

"If the money were gone, that might be true," Beckett countered, his voice like honey. "But it's still there. You just can't get to it. And you've got Sevan Harmon in your business until this matter is resolved. Perhaps I could persuade him to help you clear things up."

Rodolfo again said nothing for a very long while. Beckett swore he could hear himself sweating.

"You will wear my brand," Rodolfo finally announced. "Get the brand, Boston." He put the safety back on the gun and nodded toward Eve. "This weapon you have, she's unpredictable. Can you keep her under control?" Rodolfo waved Boston back in and the man set up his tools: a blowtorch and million-year-old iron brand.

"She'll listen to me, but she leaves." Beckett had no idea if Rodolfo would let her live. This whole scene was a crapshoot.

"She leaves, but you do not." Rodolfo countered. "I need to discern whether you actually have any value. I fear I already know the answer." He took the heated brand from Boston. "Hold out your arm."

Beckett braced himself, and the old man pressed the red-hot metal to the skin just below his *Sorry* tattoo.

When Rodolfo pulled it off, Boston followed with a handful of salt. Beckett didn't flinch, but his balls crawled into his stomach. He looked into Eve's blue eyes. For her he would die. For her he would take any pain. Boston followed the salt with lemon juice straight from a fresh-cut wedge. When the searing aggravation was completed, Beckett looked at his arm. Although bloody, he could make out the shape—some sort of twirly letter V, kind of like a tree.

Rodolfo nodded at his men. "Bring him in tomorrow after I've had some sleep. I'm going to bed."

The old man hobbled out the door, and all guns remained trained on Eve, except for Boston's, which honed in on Beckett. A guard stepped over and sawed through the plastic on Eve's ankles.

She stood with her hands still bound and refused to look at Beckett.

"Hey!" he called. "She gets to take my car. And I want to see her get in it. I need to know you let her leave with my men."

The guards conferred among themselves and finally came to agreement. One of them outfitted Beckett with his own set of tight plastic bracelets and relieved him of his car keys. Under heavy guard, they let him walk by Eve's side until she went out the front door. They cut her wrists free and handed her the keys skittishly, moving away from her as quickly as possible as if she might explode.

His men looked shocked when she came carefully down the steps and sat in the Challenger.

"I'm staying. Take her home." Milton nodded, and Beckett could feel Eve's intense glare on his back as he turned and went back into the house. Finally he heard the gravel kicking up as his car and the van pulled away.

34

Underestimate

He hadn't been able to sleep for two nights now, and they weren't letting him come in to work, so while Ryan waited for a call from McHugh about Eve, about Beckett Taylor, about *anything*, he made a big pile of all the weirdness Trish had brought into his apartment and Windex-ed the lipstick off the mirrors.

He groaned when the intercom buzzer sounded—what the hell time was it, anyway? Not even eight a.m. He ambled over and paused for a deep breath before he hit the button. "Trish, you're an insane cow udder. Go away. Actually, you know what? Never mind, I'm coming down. I want my damn key."

Ryan yanked open the door, but instead of him walking out, Eve walked in, blood all over her hands.

"Sorry, I came up when someone opened the door. I'm sorry I came here." She staggered a bit, and Ryan grabbed her.

"Whoa. Wait, what the hell happened?" He eased her inside and onto his couch. He reached for one of her hands, and she hissed. Her wounds completely encircled her wrists.

"Jesus. We need to take you to the hospital. Let's go."

She shook her head. "I just need to bandage them up. I'm going to be fine. I—I can't go to the hospital. My dad works there...I'm undercover...this is a huge mess...Please. I just need a few minutes."

"Holy shit." Ryan waited for more of a response. "I'll be right back. Don't go anywhere." Ryan pointed at her. She looked like crap. Her face was gray.

"Don't worry, copper. Even you could catch me if I tried to run now. You do what you gotta do." She attempted a smile.

He slammed the front door behind him and double-timed it downstairs, returning with the first aid kit from his truck. It was the expensive one from Target, and he hoped to hell it had what he needed. Her eyes were closed when he returned.

He'd never seen her so…unaware. Broken. He cleared his throat, and she opened one eye. He knew some basic first aid, but he didn't like the look of the deep wounds in her wrists.

"Can you feel your fingers?" He wet a paper towel and sat next to her.

"I've got swelling and nerve damage. It'll be fine."

"You sound like a lady with a lot of handcuff experience."

She didn't respond. He took her right hand and set it on his lap. He gently wiped as much of the blood as he could from the wound before slathering her wrist with antibiotic cream and winding gauze into place. He repeated this process with her left wrist.

"Are you hurt anywhere else?" He looked at her skeptically.

"Nothing that'll kill me." She closed her eyes again. "Do you need me to leave? I don't have a car. They were going to drop me off at my dad's, but I didn't want to burden him with this."

"Ahh…okay…" Ryan couldn't come up with anything intelligent to say, and he had even less idea what to do.

"How are you feeling? Were the ribs broken?" She looked him up and down.

"I'm fine." Ryan replied dismissively.

"That's good. Your face looks better. Can I shower?" Eve pulled herself to standing.

"Well, that'll get your bandages wet."

"It'ssssss okay." Eve slurred a bit, but she moved determinedly down the hall.

"Listen, I don't have towels at the moment, so there's some of my clean laundry in there…" Ryan listened for a reply, but heard none, just the water starting in the shower.

He sat for a moment, paralyzed, before his police protocol kicked him in the ass. He pulled out his phone and dialed his boss.

"McHugh," he answered gruffly.

"Captain, I have Eve Hartt here at my place. She looks like shit, but she's safe. I'm not sure where she came from or what's happened." Ryan waited for more direction.

"That's good. Ahh, for now listen to what she says and report back. She's been with the Vitullos, I believe." McHugh sounded distracted. "I haven't heard from Taylor, so I'd really like the know what the hell he's up to."

"Okay, of course, sir. I'll be in touch." Ryan was about to ask whether he should contact Eve's father—or the hospital—when the captain hung up.

He threw the phone on the dresser and straightened up his place some more, cursing Trish for stealing all his crap—again. He didn't even have sheets now, or a blanket to cover her Sharpie message on his mattress. After it'd been a stupid long time, he knocked on the bathroom door. Everything he'd ever learned about women told him you never, ever open the bathroom door on them. Ever. So he waited a bit longer. The steam from inside the room seeped under the door.

Finally, he tested the knob. It turned easily. She hadn't locked it. He opened it a crack and called her name a few times. No response. His heart leapt to his throat when he saw her curled up naked in his tub, water pounding down on top of her. He twisted the knob to the off position and climbed in, quickly confirming that she was breathing.

Her body was bruised in strategically horrible places. And it looked like she'd been Tasered quite a few goddamn times. His anger got the best of him for a few seconds. In repose she looked so serene, so peaceful. But he knew she was like a tranquilized panther. Carefully he positioned himself and lifted her, shocked at how heavy she was. Pure muscle. His pants tightened, and he cursed his body's reaction. She was helpless, for fuck's sake. She was also slippery, and he had to concentrate.

Her eyes fluttered open. "I'm sorry," she mumbled before closing her eyes again. She was fucking exhausted.

After laying her on his bed, he examined her injuries. Someone had Tasered the crap out of her. All over her body: her breasts, her stomach, the bottoms of her feet. *Jesus.* He'd needed a nap after one shot from one of those things as a rookie. And here she'd dragged herself all the way to his place. Her wrist wounds were bleeding through the sopping wet bandages, and now he noticed her ankles didn't look so good either. He gently covered her with a brown robe his mother had bought him for Christmas, but he never wore.

He pushed her wet hair out of her face and spread it out on the mattress to dry. He removed the bandages, and she stirred a bit, but didn't fully wake. He reapplied the cream and used the rest of what the Target first aid kit had to offer. While Ryan made her a pillow out of a sweatshirt, he remembered the prescription painkillers he'd gotten for strained back muscles a few months ago. They'd been some strong shit. He found them under the sink and grabbed a water bottle.

It took a lot to rouse her, but she took the pill and swallowed it without asking what it was, thanking him before falling asleep in his arms.

He held her like that for a while—to make sure the pill didn't fucking kill her. He felt a powerful need to protect her while she was unconscious. She was so goddamn capable when she was awake. He wondered if she ever let her mind completely turn off. Finally able to stare at her unabashedly, he admired her beauty. When she was awake, her attractiveness was like a costume—seemed like it pissed her off that men were drawn to her. But like this? Christ. Men would fight wars over this kind of gorgeous.

Ryan stroked her hair, trying to help it dry. His buzzer sounded. Hating to do it, he lay Eve back on the mattress.

"Yeah?" He really hoped it wasn't Trish this time.

"This is Ted Hartt. You have my daughter?" Dr. Hartt sounded frantic down below.

He hit the buzzer and opened his apartment door, waiting. After a few moments the elevator dinged, and Eve's father practically burst through the doors.

"McHugh told me she was here. Is she hurt?" He pushed into the apartment.

"Yes, sir. But she says she'll live." It sounded so hollow, repeating Eve's lame-ass diagnoses to her doctor father.

Sure enough, he gave Ryan a withering look, so he just took him to the bedroom. Ryan stood in the doorway while Dr. Hartt examined his daughter. He gently prodded her awake.

Eve groaned but allowed her father to look in her eyes and mouth.

"What the hell happened, Eve?" He adjusted the bandages and noted the Taser marks.

"I fell." Eve struggled to keep her eyelids open. "And I can't go to the hospital. You know how that is."

Her father shook his head. "Is she on anything?" He lifted the pill bottle from the nightstand.

"I gave her one of those." Ryan confirmed. He was second-guessing the shit out of himself now.

"She was tortured. *Tortured.*" Dr. Hartt dug through his bag some more before finding an injectable drug. "This will help with the swelling," he said more to himself than to Ryan.

"Thanks for coming. She wanted to stay here…is that an option?" Ryan hated to press, her father was still reeling.

"Yes. At least until I'm out of work tonight." He touched Eve's face gently. "Baby girl, what have you gotten yourself into?"

Eve was not conscious enough to answer.

"Listen, you have a few minutes? Or are you leaving?" Ryan put his feet in shoes.

"I can stay for an hour or so, then I have to get back for surgery, assuming she's stable." Dr. Hartt's eyes never left Eve.

"Let me run to the store and grab her some clothes, and some blankets and stuff. Anything else I should get? You need anything?" He put his wallet in his pocket.

Her dad wrote a list of things on the back of a drug advertisement pad he had in his bag. "Get these things."

Ryan left in a hurry and went to Target. Four hundred and fifty dollars later, his cart looked like he was getting married to Martha Stewart. He had the essential medical stuff at the bottom, then clothes for Eve, then blankets and pillows and towels out the ying-yang.

He made two trips up and down, piling the things outside his door. Dr. Hartt opened his door before he could insert the key after the last trip.

"I have to go. They've paged me twice. I'll check in as soon as my surgery is over. Here are the phone numbers I can be reached at, but if there's anything, anything at all, you call the ambulance. I don't care what she says."

"Of course, sir. Sure thing." Ryan nodded vigorously as the man left.

After Dr. Hartt went out, Ryan dragged all the stuff into the apartment. First he selected some clothes and set them near the bed for Eve. When she woke, she could put them on. Maybe his huge case of perma-boner would settle down when his dick knew she had clothes on. He ripped the tags off the towels and tucked them into the cabinet in the bathroom. All his new bedding was ready for the bed as soon as it was empty.

He sat at his desk and tried to make himself useful, reviewing case files and looking again at the video on his phone. He made notes about everything he'd seen that might possibly be helpful. The hours ticked by until mid-afternoon, when a woman's shriek and a loud thump sent Ryan running into his bedroom.

Trish—dressed in a teddy and an open trench coat—was on the floor with her eyes bugging out and her lips turning blue. Naked Eve had her pinned to the floor. His perma-boner took off like a rocket. Again.

"Trish! What the hell are you doing here?" He grabbed the discarded robe and pulled gently on Eve's shoulder until she released her grip on Trish's neck.

Eve staggered a bit, eyes hazy. Ryan slipped the robe over her shoulders. She put it on.

"She's wearing your mother's dookie-colored robe?" Trish scrambled to her feet, gasping. "You hate that thing!"

"How did you get in here?" Ryan looked at the open window. "Did you climb up the escape? You are an insane person."

"You're sleeping with slutty whores? I'm here to get my stuff." Trish stomped into the living room as Eve leaned against his bedroom wall. "I heard all over town you've been running around with a tramp."

She came back into the bedroom. "After I leave, Ryan, you'll never have another woman like me."

Eve's hand was so quick around Trish's neck she was like a rattlesnake. "Drop it." Trish hesitated, and Ryan watched as Eve tightened her hold, inching her thumb closer to Trish's ear. "Take off the trench coat too."

Trish opened her mouth with indignation before dropping the bedding he'd just bought. When she made no move with the coat, Eve pulled her into a restraint that was much more complicated than she made it look. "Take off your trench coat."

It wasn't what she said, it was the way she said it—steel in her voice. The energy coming off of her was so, so dangerous.

Even irrational Trish heard the warning in the words. She slipped off the coat.

"Now you're going to leave the way you came." Eve pushed Trish toward the window.

Trish gave Ryan a look. "This is your new girlfriend? She's charming."

Eve propped herself against the wall again and waited.

Ryan shrugged and pointed to the window.

"I can't believe this. I'm suing." Trish climbed back out the window, heels clicking against the metal while she proceeded to curse a blue streak.

Ryan smiled a little before retrieving the coat from the floor and tossing it out the window. "Leave my truck alone, Trish. Or I'll sic my girlfriend on you."

He turned as Eve slid down the wall to sit on the floor. "Had to give her the coat. She's got a lot of walking to do."

Eve closed her eyes. "I'm sorry."

"You say that a lot lately." Ryan grabbed the sheets and dragged them over the mattress. It looked like Eve was asleep. Her bandages were starting to bleed through again. He put the blankets on and added pillows before crouching down next to her. "You want to put clothes on? I got some stuff."

"Please. That'd be great." She opened one eye.

He set out pajamas and three packages of different underwear. "I could not figure out how the sizing works for these. Boy shorts, high cut, thong…"

"You did fine." Eve pulled herself off the floor.

"Can you manage this?" Ryan half hoped she'd say no.

"As long as no more ex-girlfriend terrorists crawl through your window, it'll be okay." Eve began untying her robe.

Ryan left her and tried to imagine a meal. Breakfast seemed simplest, so he started pancakes and bacon.

Eve came into the living room and tucked herself on the couch, wrapped in a blanket. From a quick peek at her wrists, he could see she'd re-bandaged herself.

He plated food and cut the pancakes up for her, adding syrup. She took it without a word and plowed through. He made his own plate and sat in the recliner.

After they finished, Eve set her plate next to his on the living room table.

"I love somebody else." She met his gaze, her eyes soft and much more focused now.

"He's a lucky guy." Ryan hoped his face didn't show his disappointment. "That's not why I made you pancakes." He'd bought her pale pink pajamas. They were so soft in the store. He'd thought they would be comfortable and warm. But he hadn't counted on her looking so vulnerable and huggable, the pink giving her face a little extra color.

"No, he's not. Lucky would never describe his lot in life." She sighed. He didn't know what to say. "I think in a different world? I'd be all over you. You know that? Handsome, strong, funny, and smart. I bet you'll make a great dad someday." She closed her eyes.

He'd seen a similar look on the faces of retiring cops. They'd seen too much. They were left jaded and unimpressed with just how evil people could be. She was way too young for that look.

"If that's the way he makes you feel? He's not the guy for you." Ryan gathered their plates and got her another pain pill.

"Really? With what I am?" She took the pill from his hand and swallowed it with orange juice.

"Actually, with *who* you are, I do feel that way." He sat back down.

They were quiet for a while as the tension in Eve's shoulders relaxed. Ryan guessed the pills were hitting the spot.

"Keep drinking." He pointed at the glass she'd put down. "I think you lost some blood."

"I've lost a lot more than blood." She shook her head and picked up the glass.

"Why don't you tell me? Consider me your fake boyfriend slash priest." He put his feet up on the coffee table.

After a swallow she gave him a skeptical look. "Man, you're on the wrong side of the law for confessions. I couldn't do that to you."

"You know, a million years ago two guys who were my only father figures were murdered. Ever since then, I've had this burning revenge thing going on. I feel like no one gets that. It's why I fuck insane chicks like Trish. That's so much easier than explaining that I have this..." He looked for the right word for a few breaths. "...mission. It's been more important than anything else normal. But meeting you has put it on the back burner. I find myself thinking about you instead of plotting. It's like a relief. And I know you're not mine. And I know you're fucking deadly. But I just want to, like, hug you."

He stood and paced. "What I'm saying is, I have no pure intentions. Not as cop. Not as a man. Not as a friend. I've got secrets of my own. So confess, baby. You're safe with me."

She sipped from the orange juice before regarding him with eyes hazy with drugs again. "Let's speak hypothetically. How's that?"

"Works." Ryan sat next to her on the couch.

"I'll tell you a story. You ready?" She nodded as he nodded.

Eve was bombed off her ass.

"There was a girl. She was raised by her father because her mother's new marriage was much more exciting than her kid. This girl dreamed of becoming a mom. After she met the man of her dreams, she was pregnant." Her words slurred into one another, and it took her longer and longer to recover from her blinks. "And then a murderer killed her love and her baby." A tear slipped from the corner of one eye as she squeezed them shut.

"The noise that the car wreck made? It broke that girl. She died that day. And right then, she decided she'd never love again. All her pain was funneled into becoming a machine. Revenge was the only setting she had. And she became better at killing than the murderer." She took the last sip of her juice.

He took the glass from her. She hugged her knees to her chest.

"But even though she could kill *anyone*, when she finally found him, she couldn't kill him. Even if he deserved it." She exhaled and looked at the floor.

"Who was it? Taylor?" Ryan's rage was contained, but only because he'd had so much practice.

Eve shook her head, her hair falling around her shoulders. She looked him in the eye. "I killed Mary Ellen. I butchered my way through her house, murdered her guards, and slit her throat. I'm not girlfriend material, Ryan."

He whistled. Getting through to the head honcho was ridiculous, action-movie-type stuff.

"And Taylor found me and volunteered his services to Rodolfo so I could be free." She touched her forearm, a bruise there getting more and more colorful. "So here I am."

"So you hate him and you love him." Ryan cut right to the center of the story.

Eve had a sad smile. "And I'm just as bad, if not worse, than any criminal you've ever put behind bars. There's no redeeming that—no matter how many lives I live."

Ryan moved the hair away from Eve's face, looking into her beautiful, sad eyes. "I want to save you."

Her eyes brimmed with tears, which sparkled in the light before she blinked them away. "I'd never let you. Way too dangerous."

Ryan touched her cheek before sliding his hand to the nape of her neck. He leaned down and gave her the softest kiss—just tasting her before looking back at her mouth. "You underestimate me."

35

Here

Chery woke up dead. Or at least that's how she felt. Chaos was there, and he seemed relieved when her eyes opened.

"Vere?" she asked.

The small, dark man came to her side. "She's at the day house. They're going to keep her overnight."

"Everything hurts." Chery wanted to move, but pain stopped her. "Jared! Jared might try to get Vere to punish me!" Chery forced herself to sit up and look around. A hospital room. Her heart sank.

Chaos supported her back. "No. Not anymore."

The finality in his voice soothed her, and she lay back.

"Your job is to heal. Want me to call a nurse?" Chaos sat in the chair close by.

"I can't. She'll want to question me. That's what they do. I stopped coming to the hospital because of that." Chery looked at her arms. They were covered in the scars of her battle. "I thought I was done. He finally tipped over the edge."

"I'm sorry, señorita." Chaos nodded at her like she was a princess stepping off a boat. "I'm glad you weren't."

"You know how they're going to look at me? I'm here again. And I knew better. I knew better." Chery found it hard to swallow. She vaguely remembered Jared choking her. And then being in the blanket…the banging of being sealed in.

"You are here. But that's better than other places you could be. No one can judge you, except you. A person makes their destiny." Chaos folded his arms across his chest.

"You wouldn't understand. It makes no sense now." Chery grabbed the flimsy hospital blanket and squeezed.

"I've been in prison for more days than I've been out of it. No worries, though, I've never touched a woman in anger in all my days," he added quickly. "But you see, when I get out? I do things that could put me back in. It's like I can't live without the thrill of being caught. It's hard…the pull. And then you're so used to the doors being locked, when you're finally allowed to walk through, you stumble." Chaos shrugged. "Is it like that? For you, with him?"

Chery didn't respond, but looked at the IV snaking fluids into her body. It *was* sort of like that: a jail term—one willingly and not so willingly sought.

A nurse walked in and seemed pleased to see Chery awake. She made chipper small talk while she checked Chery's vitals. "How's your pain from one to ten?"

Chery shrugged and the pain made her wince. "About a four."

"Okay, I'll have the doctor approve a painkiller that will be good for you and safe for the baby." She smiled and nodded.

Chery looked at the nurse like she was insane. "You sure you have the right patient?"

"Yes, ma'am. Says right here the blood test for pregnancy was positive. I take it this is unexpected." She patted Chery's hand. "Make sure to discuss it with your doctor. There are options."

After the nurse left, Chery looked past Chaos to the window. "Well, I guess there's no getting over him now."

Beckett was dropped off in his old parking lot on Tuesday evening. His douchebags were waiting with the Challenger.

"So?" They looked eager.

"I have agreed to work with a human being who is as close to dead as I've ever seen." Beckett took off his tie and tossed his hat on the ground. He'd also likely be relying on communication channels and contacts close to dead because he hadn't used them in so damn long. He rubbed his hand over his face. "The key to this whole thing is Sevan Harmon. He likes to move his drugs through Poughkeepsie on their way to greener pastures, and I gotta rekindle our relationship. Actually, first I gotta find him, so this isn't going to be an overnight job." Beckett wondered how to do any of this without completely reverting back to his old life. It was a fucking debacle. The whole thing made him long for his dog.

"You staying here?" one of them asked.

"Yep, I'm supposed to start working my magic. They took my phone. Can I grab a call? Where's Eve?"

The closest tossed a phone to him. "We dropped her off at that undercover cop's place."

Beckett nodded. Eve went to lick her wounds with another man. Fine.

He dialed Chaos' number. "Talk."

"Chery's awake now. I just checked on Vere, and she's okay." Chaos sounded strained.

"Anyone looking for the fartbag?" Beckett had left Jared's body in a wooded area on his way back to New York.

"No one. And I don't expect that'll happen. I'll keep you posted." Chaos cleared his throat.

"You like running a liquor store?" Beckett looked at the overgrown rubble in the parking lot: remnants of the strip mall from one of he and Eve's previous misunderstandings.

"I don't know, boss. That's a lot of responsibility."

Beckett nodded even though Chaos couldn't see him. "Chery and Vere are going to be the owners, and I'll pay you to keep everything going for them. We'll have a much longer conversation, but for now all you need to know is I have to stay in Poughkeepsie. And those two ladies need a guardian. I think you're that man." Beckett waited, the sun glinting from behind the fallen structure.

"Sir, I'd love to. It'd be…nice." Chaos sounded choked up. "We just got a few things to work out, but you handle your end. I've got Maryland on lockdown."

Beckett hung up and turned back to his men. "I'm going to need a place—something with a backyard for my dog to crap in. I'm moving back."

It took a week. Cash streamlined things considerably, and Beckett was now the proud owner of a huge house. He hadn't a clue what the hell he was going to do with it. He was also the less-than-proud confidante of Captain John McHugh. McHugh hadn't seemed wild about it either, but Beckett had decided to tackle things head on and his position working with both Rodolfo Vitullo and Sevan Harmon had proved impossible for the Poughkeepsie police to pass up. He'd set up Milton as the go-between and hoped that would keep Rodolfo off the trail. He also checked in with said bag of bones once a day, keeping him posted on progress with IDing Sevan's people and setting up a meet with the slippery son-of-a-bitch himself. Beckett didn't fucking like being under the corpse's thumb, and the bastard certainly didn't make things easy, but he had yet to come up with a better way to keep Eve alive.

Gandhi had taken well to the transition, though he seemed to miss Vere. Beckett kept busy, buying shit, keeping track of his old stomping grounds. Haunting his former places of income became his modus operandi. He held meetings at the pawn shop, gradually getting closer to Harmon by conversing with his assholes of varying importance. Sevan was apparently overseas enjoying a splendid vacation. Free money, courtesy of Mary Ellen, had given him a wildly free spirit, and he simply couldn't be troubled to meet with Beckett right now. So, Beckett hired new assholes of his own and considered opening a restaurant. He could open it odd hours and maybe collect misfits like he had in Maryland.

But mostly he waited for her to call—to say anything. He saw the back of her head from time to time as she walked through town. Her hair was blond again, and she was always with the cop they'd saved from the party. They'd been holding hands one time, and Beckett had actually reached for his gun before he stopped himself. He'd given her a life back, and damn it, she could do whatever the fuck she wanted with it.

Three weeks into his relocation, he'd video chatted with Chery, who he finally had to force to stop apologizing for going back to

Jared. He hadn't told her Jared was dead in so many words, but he suspected Chaos had hinted at it. He liked the looks he saw Chaos and Chery share, but the news they gave him was unsettling. Apparently, Chery was knocked up with Jared's kid. And she wanted nothing to do with it. She was three months along and willing to finish the pregnancy, but raising a child who would always remind her of the past wasn't an option. He'd agreed to think on it with them, and since then he'd been turning it over in his head.

In fact, a week later, that's what he was doing at this very moment in his new house. Cole knocked on the back door, casserole in hand, and Gandhi greeted him with gusto.

"Dude, Fairy Princess cooks?" Beckett took the ceramic dish and set it down before meeting his brother again for their handshake.

"Seriously? It was me. Yeah, I'm not afraid to say I like cooking." Cole opened every cabinet until he found the plates.

"She sucks at it?" Beckett called as he went to feed Gandhi in the basement and grabbed two ice-cold beers from the downstairs fridge.

"So much. But you didn't hear that from me." Cole located the forks and a knife and soon they were sitting at the table.

There were still stacks of boxes everywhere. Beckett just couldn't get motivated to put stuff away. He couldn't lose the feeling that this whole "I'm home" act would be over in a heartbeat—one way or another.

"Where is that redhead tonight?" Beckett took a bite of the dinner, and it was delicious. He told his brother so.

"Thanks. She's working. Blake would've come, but they have the flu running through the family." Cole took a swig of his beer.

"Disgusting." Beckett raised his beer. "Here's to not crapping and puking at the same time."

"Toast." Cole smiled. "The dog okay downstairs?"

Beckett nodded. "Little dude eats and then sleeps like a bear in winter."

"So are you here for good?" Cole asked. "What the hell happened? Your messages and texts have been cryptic."

"I'm working on some serious shit, and I'm kind of doing it for someone else." Beckett rolled up his sleeve to show his brother his brand.

"That doesn't seem like you at all. I thought you were out of the business." Cole pushed his chair away from the table.

"I thought I was out of the business too. I've tried to be—and I'm still trying to do things differently—but maybe there's never really a getting out, you know?" Beckett rubbed his hands over his face. "I'm wired a certain way, good at certain things…Anyway, I hope to find a way out of this situation at some point, but I can't say too much about it now. And listen, that's not why we're here. I've got something I'm thinking about, and I don't know if it's crazy or offensive and— "

Cole interrupted. "Is it illegal?"

"Nnnooooo…Not if we do it the right way. I don't think?" Beckett took another bite and started with the tale of Maryland: what he'd been doing and all about Chery and Vere. And finally, Beckett got around to the baby who might need a home.

Cole nodded, saying nothing. He was a terrific, non-judgmental listener. Beckett leaned over and slapped his brother on the back. "So glad you're here. Damn it."

Cole smiled back. "Feel the same way. This is a lot to take in. Are you suggesting we adopt this baby?"

"That was my thought. You guys want a kid, and I know a lady who has to deal with a lot of emotional stuff right now. But I'll tell you this: she and her sister are exceptional people. Good stock." He didn't expect an answer right away and told his brother so.

"And the father?" Cole looked afraid to ask.

"I killed him." Beckett had tried to think of a way he could avoid telling Cole this, but he needed the man to know every angle. "I didn't kill him at first. I tried it another way. But then I did go ahead and do it. He was a beater, and he finally tried to kill Chery. Like Rick from back in the good ol' days. She just couldn't get out of his grasp. When I found him he'd hidden her, like a body. He thought she was dead."

"Was she pregnant through this?" Cole was astonished.

"She was. Still is." Beckett peeled the label off his beer.

"This is a really stressful time for her to make this kind of decision." His brother worked on his beer label as well.

"She's just a couple months along. So there's time, but she's anxious. I know she wants to find a resolution, and I think this is one she'll like." Beckett didn't want to press the situation, but the solution seemed obvious to him. "She's clean, caring, and devoted. She'd love for this kid to have a great upbringing. I know she'd do a great job herself, but I guess she's afraid the baby will remind her too much of the father. I don't think she'll change her mind."

Cole nodded seriously. "I don't know...I like to do stuff on the up and up."

"We'll do all the paperwork. I'll make it so it's legal." Beckett had already reached out to a few contacts.

"I need to pray on this, talk to Kyle. But you tell Chery she's in my prayers."

Beckett smiled. "Just tell me when you can. I think it'd give her peace of mind to just know, either way."

Cole stood and found some foil to cover the casserole. "You can have the leftovers. Just bring back the dish or Kyle will freak."

"You really mean you though, right?" Beckett teased.

"Yeah, I do." Cole laughed.

Beckett was showing his brother out the back door when Cole turned. "You know what? You tell her we'll take the baby. I won't tell Kyle until Chery's sure, and then she'll have less time to wait. Less chance anything could change."

"Seriously?" Beckett gave his brother a huge grin and held up his arm for the handshake.

"Yeah. Yes. I want that baby for her." Cole smiled right back.

"Wow. That's awesome. Shit. I'd have given anything for a father like you." Beckett pulled Cole into a hug.

When he finally closed the door, Beckett felt like he'd done the right fucking thing. And that felt good. He was about to call Chery when the doorbell rang.

He crossed to the front of the house and peeked out the window. He saw blond hair. He yanked open the door.

Eve stood on his doorstep, her beautiful blue eyes filled with a million emotions: hate, lust, pain.

But she was here.

36

Hate Mates

The door opened, and he was there: magnetic, his dimples just a slight indent on his surprised face. Beckett exhaled her name, like it came from deep within him. Eve put her fist to her lips. She wanted to ask if she could come in. She wanted to yell that he shouldn't have rescued her from Rodolfo's. She was breaths away from telling him she'd never needed him in all the years he'd been away, and she certainly didn't need him now.

Instead she pushed herself against his chest and growled his name back at him. He gathered her hard against him, slamming his front door behind her. The smell of him, the feel of his strength—knowing he could easily take what she'd dish out flooded her with lust.

Face to face, they looked deeply into each other's eyes, and Eve knew the first to give in to the kiss would be weak, the loser. And it was every inch a war. She ripped Beckett's button-down shirt open, buttons flying like popcorn. He grabbed her wrists, and she winced, but Beckett held tight. She tilted her chin up at him, daring him to try something, anything.

He twirled her so her back was against the wall. For a second she thought he was going to bite her neck, yet he stopped just before his lips could touch her skin. He passed his mouth over her, his heated breath ragged. She felt his moist want on her chest, across the tops of her breasts, all while he held her still-healing wrists too tightly.

This man knew exactly how to grind her into an animal. With him their passion was an argument, a sexual fight. It was almost mating, wild and deadly. She was already wet for him, nipples hard. He came back up from her neck to look her in the face.

Eyes wide and basically panting, Beckett was obviously as undone by her presence as she was by his. She smiled at him, breathing erratically. She pulled her hands toward his face, working against his tight grip. Finally, she rested her palms on his cheeks. He fought against her, making her work for this intimate touch. Then he pressed himself over her, steel against her curves. She looked from his eyes to his lips, over and over, trying to make a choice. He was made of venom and primed for an attack. She came close, their lips almost touching, her nipples pressed to his hard chest. She licked her lips, and the tip of her tongue made contact with his bottom lip because they were so close.

Her tongue was his fuse. And like a bomb had been lit, he punched the wall on either side of her head. She didn't flinch. He slammed the wall again, unable to channel his emotions properly. Every strike came so near, his violence timed with her rapid heartbeat. They had such fucked-up foreplay. All she could hear was the blood rushing through her body. Finally, he stopped, and with almost superhuman effort he pushed away from her, grabbing his hair.

"Damn it, Eve. Why'd you come here? Why are you here?" His eyes raged with suspicion, hurt, and lust. He stepped behind his couch, giving them both a barrier.

"I don't know. I couldn't stop myself." She hugged her arms to her chest. Just a taste of him was crazy. Her body shuddered with want.

"How's your boyfriend, the cop? Does he know you're here? I sure as hell wouldn't want my girl at a criminal's house." Beckett threw his hands up and gave her a hard stare. "Jesus fucking Christ, you're gorgeous."

Eve walked straight to him, jumping the couch and finding his arms again. Here she couldn't think, only feel. Her voice was filled with tears. "Fuck you. I love you, and you know it. And you left me *for years*. I thought…" She gently clawed his face. He looked at the ceiling, hands jammed in his pockets. "I thought you were dead."

Beckett exhaled, still looking at the ceiling. "I was dead without you. Every day."

She tilted his face to hers and touched his lips, his chest, his gunshot wounds. She pulled his hand out of his pocket and turned it to reveal his brand. Eve put her lips against the outline, grazing the wound with her teeth, then met his gaze.

"I never wanted you to give up your freedom for mine." She let go of his hand and stepped back. Her words were out there. He knew how she felt.

He looked at his feet as her emotions began to burn from the center out.

"Did you ever…" He looked at her hard and stepped into her space. "…for *one* second…" He put his hands behind her neck. "…think I wasn't coming for you? In New York? At the Vitullos'? Here?"

"Yes." She nodded. His face was every conundrum she'd ever had. Murder and love. Vengeance and forgiveness.

"You're a fucking liar." He kissed her so hard and fast, she couldn't even take a breath. His oxygen became her nourishment. The burning center of her emotions flamed over. He tore her clothes from her body. Not for a second was he gentle, and she returned his fervor. Finally, they were naked together. Windows uncovered, lights blazing. Making every mistake in the world.

"I love you, Eve. You're the only heart I have."

The only thing that could stop him from making love to her now was a SWAT team, and that's exactly what burst into his house—through the door and the windows.

Cops screamed, "Freeze!"

"Hands in the air."

"Get on the floor right now."

Eve and Beckett went to their knees and then to their bellies. The red and blue lights reflected off their naked skin as they looked into each other's eyes.

Eve looked over to see John McHugh crunching through the broken glass. He approached her, knelt for a moment, and covered her with his jacket. She watched as he picked up her clothes scattered around the room and directed her to the bedroom. There he offered them to her and averted his eyes so she could change.

"What are you looking for?" she asked once she'd dressed.

"Taylor," he answered. "It wasn't my call to have it happen like this, but he's wanted for questioning in the murder of Chris Simmer."

She followed him back to the living room in time to watch Beckett be cuffed in the nude on the floor of his living room.

"Can you get my dog from the basement and keep him?" he called to her.

She nodded as an officer put Beckett's pants in his hands and marched him out the door.

As the house emptied, Captain McHugh lingered for a moment. "Officer Morales know you're here?"

Eve watched through the broken window as Beckett was put in the back of a cruiser. She didn't answer out loud, but in her head, as she watched a fellow murderer be driven away, the answer was no. No, Ryan didn't know. And she felt like a fraud and a cheat and a junkie.

McHugh took her silence for the answer it was. "You need to leave here tonight. There's no good way to lock up." He paused for a moment. "Actually, I should take you to the station too. There are quite a few questions you should answer. How about you and I have a quick heart-to-heart here and we spare you that?"

He didn't need to explain further, and Eve appreciated his kindness. The station would always be where her life had changed.

They sat together on Beckett's couch, and she gave him a carefully edited account of the last few weeks of her life: She'd been hired for some event work and security by Mary Ellen, who quickly proved herself completely crazy. Yes, she'd been held for a time by Mary Ellen's father after her murder. No, she did not care to press charges or discuss further what he had wanted from her. No, she was no longer employed by the Vitullos. Yes, she planned to stay out of trouble, perhaps stick closer to home and take care of her father.

When she'd finished, he was silent for a long time. "I can't promise we won't revisit all this again," he said. "But I can't bring myself to book you right now. No one's pressed charges, so let's leave it at that.

Please let me know if you find you have relevant information for me in the future." He walked out and left the door open, an obvious invitation and reminder for her.

The flashing lights faded until she was alone. After brushing the glass off Beckett's couch, Eve sat down. Her shirt had to be held together, and she just threw out her bra. She'd been so close to losing control with Beckett. Hell, it took an army to stop what was set in motion by her impulsiveness.

And where had it come from? For the past few weeks, once she'd confirmed Beckett was alive and had returned to Poughkeepsie, she'd practically lived with Ryan—cuddled into him for no other reason than to feel the comfort of his arms, laugh with him, and avoid thinking about what she'd done as they both healed. Ryan was easy. He was a good man, and he reminded her of who she'd once been, the woman she might have become. But damn it all to hell, in her heart she knew he would never be enough for her now. It was just a version of her who fit with him, never her whole self. Only Beckett understood the person she'd become, the reasons why she'd done what she'd done. They had always been a sexual tsunami. Sometimes pain felt better than nothing real at all.

But what if it was time for her to be the stronger one? Could she step away, as he'd tried to do—leave him to find his way without her misery as a burden? They loved each other, but what if that was a death wish?

She had no answers, but there was no reason for her to stay here. And yet she was powerless to move. She brought the snorting, slobbering dog up from the basement when he barked, and after a short romp in the backyard, he curled up in his dog bed like it was his job. She sat with him for hours until the sun rose, the morning breeze laden with dew. Beckett's house, and the stuff inside, had no barrier now to the weather, to strangers. She was still sitting in glass, watching the curtains blow when she heard gravel popping under tires.

She heard his mutter of thanks before he walked through the open door. Beckett was already back—now wearing his pants and a scrub shirt. He looked ridiculous. The dog hopped up from his bed and charged Beckett like a bull. As he scooped him up, he locked eyes with Eve, his face strangely vacant.

"Funniest shit. I get there, and I already have a lawyer. Super fancy. They were barely allowed to ask me shit, and it seems the evidence from the crime scene has been compromised somehow." Beckett set the dog down and picked up a piece of glass, turning it over and over in his hands. "So I'm back."

"Rodolfo. He was teaching you humility. And he may have actually been useful for once." She tied her shirt in a knot in front of her boobs as Beckett sat on the coffee table.

"True. Or maybe he gets off on body cavity searches." He put his head in his hands. "Honestly, I can hardly believe it. McHugh didn't look happy, but he didn't vow to hunt me down this time."

Eve pulled her hair from her face and twirled it like a rope, tying it in a knot.

Beckett sighed deeply. He didn't seem nearly as relieved as he should have. "Why is it I'm not a strong man? Do you have a clue?" He looked at her as if she might have an answer.

"Not sure what you mean." She stood, and there was the gentle sound of glass shards hitting the ground, like angels losing their wings.

He watched her stand but remained seated. "I promised in my head to leave you be. And when I saw you…I was supposed to be man enough to turn you away. Fuck, I'm not a horny teenager. It's just you." He finally did stand. "You break me. You break everything I think I stand for."

"I know how you feel. I'm the one who showed up here, remember?" It was this connection that bound them. Their sentence. If there was such a thing as soul mates, there must be hate mates too. Even a knock on the badly damaged door couldn't drag her eyes from his.

The dog's barking and Ryan's voice filled the room. "Eve, you ready?"

She felt a smile on her face. Ryan had read the situation and was here to save her from herself. But she reached out for Beckett, trailing her fingers down his arm. It wasn't goodbye or a promise—just a touch. Then she turned her back on him and took Ryan's outstretched hand. He stepped behind her and guided her out of Beckett's new house.

Beckett watched her leave with the cop. In him a war was raging—that she would leave. That she *could* leave. It would take a pack of rabid zombies to tear him from her. Maybe she was only in his veins, and he wasn't in hers. He clenched his fists, forgetting about the glass shard he still held until he noticed blood dripping down his forearm, covering his new brand and his old *Sorry* tattoo.

He looked despondently at the mess for a while before finding a broom. It took him hours to rectify the destruction, and all the time his mind flashed through stills of her here: opening the door, her naked breast, the way her skin goose-bumped as his fingers touched her, gasps, growls. All of it so Eve. How she could walk out his door, that she was strong enough to break the connection his body was glued into, even when she wasn't there, had stunned him stupid. He'd always figured they'd drown together in the endlessness of their attraction. He loved her so much—it was like the devil himself was squeezing his heart. And she'd said she loved him…

How could something he felt this intensely, this impossibly, be wrong? His love had to be right for her. Wasn't there a way to make it right for her? *Be a better man.* His vow from long ago echoed in his head. But although he could find a way to accomplish most tasks, that one had eluded him. And now—even more so after this latest police station stunt—he was chained to the soul-sucking Rodolfo Vitullo. Maybe his love just wasn't enough.

The suburban neighborhood he was currently occupying was full of life now, and neighbors strolled outside for a look at the house that had caused all the commotion. He needed to get a glass company in here. He needed to be a good neighbor. And if he really loved Eve—sick, twisted bastard that he was—he needed to push her toward something more than he could give her. Even if she wasn't sure she wanted it, she deserved the chance to figure her life out, no matter how long it took. Hell, he owed her five years.

So much in his life felt out of his hands now, so Beckett turned to the shit he knew he needed to get done. He needed to get the damn money back from twatbag Sevan Harmon, and he needed to check in on Chery and Vere. And probably he should've started with Rodolfo's crap, but damned if he didn't need a win first—a win he'd brought about on his own.

Chery answered her own phone, which was good.

"Hey, pretty. How's things?" Beckett slid down the wall in the hall and sat on the floor.

"Beckett, how are you?" He listened to the background noise on her call, trying to figure out if she was still in the hospital. "I'm better. I'll be checking out of this crappy hotel in a few minutes." Her voice held hesitation.

"Glad to hear it. Just so you know, the liquor store and my house are going to be put in your name. Chaos will manage the store, and he's on my payroll. But if he pisses you off in any way, I'll send someone else." He heard her exhale in relief.

"That's too much. Boss, I'm just a cashier."

"Nah. You're a fantastic person, and you're Vere's sister, so that makes you super important. And you're a hell of a cashier as well. Speaking of which, I took G, and I know Vere must be disappointed. Would it be okay if I got her a dog?" Beckett looked at the ceiling, picturing Vere's sweet face.

"Well, sure. You don't have to do that, though. You've done so much. I can't thank you en—"

Beckett interrupted her. "It was nothing. Listen, I've another offer for you, and it is what it is. No pressure—just an option. I did some thinking on your baby situation, like you asked me to."

"Okay." She sounded hesitant.

"If you want to pass that baby on to a set of parents, I know a couple that'll take him." Beckett heard the words come out of his mouth and realized it was almost too big a decision to make.

Silence was her only answer for a long while. Then Chery asked Beckett to tell her all about them. He left nothing out. By the time he was done describing his brother and sister-in-law, Chery would've been able to pick them out in a crowd without ever having seen a picture.

"They sound amazing. And real. I'd love to meet them," Chery commented before telling him she had to go. The nurse was there with her exit papers. Beckett heard Chaos's greeting in the background as he hung up, which made him smile.

The next number he hadn't called in five years, though he still texted her on occasion.

"How's Gandhi? Is there a problem?" Kristen was all business when she answered.

"He's a snoring, humping mess, and I love him." Beckett smiled. "He's actually been amazing for a friend of mine who has autism. Unfortunately, I can't even imagine parting with G, and I've had to move back to Poughkeepsie. You have anybody in the shelter who needs a get-out-of-death-free card? I'll get them all their shots and cut off their balls and shit."

"You know, you were the best wrong choice I ever made. Come by tomorrow, after hours like last time. I got a few I'd love to show you."

After hanging up with Kristen, Beckett sat in the hallway a little longer. She was correct. He was always the wrong choice.

37

Good Soul

Ryan kept looking over at Eve, but she was quiet the whole way back from that asshole's house. Her clothes were in disarray—like she'd been attacked. But he couldn't imagine anyone getting one over on her now.

He hated that he'd pussied out and gone to get her. But McHugh had a soft spot for Eve, and what was he supposed to do after his captain told him her location? Ryan definitely had a soft spot for her too.

She took a shower when they got home, leaving the whole apartment smelling like her conditioner and lotion when she was done. She came out with wet hair, in a tank top and jeans. He had brunch almost ready, so she set out plates and glasses. Still Eve said nothing. She was so damn hard to read. They sat when he'd put the food on the table.

Finally, the silence did him in. "I'm not going to get you again. Ever."

She put down her fork and regarded him.

"This isn't a threat. It's me telling you I'm never pulling you out of his house. I'm not a forgiving kind of guy." Ryan forced himself to keep eating.

"You shouldn't be. And I never asked you to come for me."

"I know we haven't been…intimate. And I have no claims on you. It's just…" He wanted to be firm, be some sort of alpha for her.

She waited, with a look in her clear blue eyes that said she already knew everything he was planning to tell her.

"You don't need to hear this." He put his fork down.

Eve stood and pulled her wet hair to one side. As a reflex, he slid his chair out as she sat in his lap. Her eyes went from sharp and clear to a faraway gaze.

She hugged his head to her chest and kissed the top of his head. He put his arms around her waist. "You're my dream guy, from a long time ago. When I was a kid? Ugh. I had the hugest crush on policemen—the uniform, the gun. I had fantasies of getting pulled over and the cop asking for my number. God, I was so naïve." She grabbed his chin and made him look in her eyes. "You deserve to find a lady who still believes in that stuff. Someone you'd be a hero to." She was soft, her whole face was easy, unguarded.

"I'll be your hero." He knew it was cheesy, but he was dead serious.

"I'm a perp, Ryan. I'm the bad guy. The worst."

She was still soft. He didn't know what the hell she was even saying. She stood and twisted so she could straddle him. Almost urgently, like she was leaving.

"I've killed people. More than I can count anymore. So much blood..."

Ryan leaned forward and placed one finger on the button of her jeans. She allowed the kiss he gave her as he used the finger to lift her tank top above her taut abs. His lust pounded in his ears, between his legs. He was barely able to hear her over the rush of his desire. For months they'd spent endless time together, pretended to be in love, yet she'd never made love to him.

"Would sex with me make it all better?" she demanded. "Could you live with who I am? Could you sleep next to a person who can torture a grown man until he cries for his mother?"

Her lips were saying words he knew he should heed. There was a warning for his heart laced in the syllables. Instead Ryan stood, lifting her, and walked her to the couch, where he lay her on her back. She looked defeated, disappointed.

"I have no idea what the fuck you want. Is this a confession? An offering? Are you having fun teasing me? Teasing my dick? Fuck, Eve, I just got you out of a murdering bastard's house."

She just lay there, like she expected as much from him. He sat on the coffee table.

"That's what I am, Ryan. And I want to make sure you hate me," she said quietly. Eve turned her face toward the cushion, her hair dripping like gold silk off his crappy couch.

"Well, that's the bitch of it. 'Cause I'm pretty damn sure I love you." The words sounded much more hollow than they'd felt in his chest.

She sat up and swung her legs around so she was sitting properly. "I used you. This hasn't been fair."

And there it was, his heart flayed open. He closed his eyes as the pain took root. She came close to him again, when she should be leaving. Eve hugged his head, pulling him to her stomach.

"I never thought I'd care if you were hurting. But damn you, Ryan, you have a way of getting inside. Do you know how numb I am? How dead I have to be to kill someone?"

She went to her knees, parting his legs to hug him around his middle. He gripped the table to keep from showing her affection. The wood protested his force with a crack. He wanted her.

"I wanted kids who chased lightning bugs and ate sticky ice pops on hot summer days. I needed the most normal stuff—snowmen and stepping on Legos. I needed a guy that bitched about his day who I could sneak into the bedroom while the kids watched a movie."

She twisted until she had him in a deadly headlock. Her voice was so different when she spoke again. "This is what I'm good at now. Snapping spines and inserting knives. Plotting and killing and committing the kind of crimes that should have me in prison forever." She slapped his own handcuffs on his wrists smoothly.

She moved around him, torturing him by rubbing her breasts across his face. Spreading her legs, she straddled him again. "Can you stomach that? To have me? Are you going to lie to everyone? What will you say when I come home covered in blood and you never find the crime scene because I'm too fucking good to get caught?"

Eve was biting him now, clawing his skin. His moan was probably heard four blocks away. His dick was trapped in his jeans, and it was going to die there soon. He stood, but she was too quick. She caught her balance and stood with him. And that's how they were: criminal and cop. He with his hands cuffed and she with tears of defeat in her eyes.

"What if I told you this is all bullshit?" He stepped toward her as he worked to dislocate his thumb. "What if I said you don't have the balls to live like a stand-up bitch? And maybe I'm twice as deadly as you?" With that he pulled his hands from behind his back. Using the chain and cuff to aid in his restraint, he had Eve facedown with his knee in her back like the felon she was claiming to be. "All I have to do is lean in and your spine cracks. You'll be paralyzed from the moneymaker down." He put weight on her. "And maybe you shouldn't be so certain that sleeping next to me is the safest fucking thing either."

He waited for her to cry uncle, to beg even a little for him to let up on her. The best she could do was sigh. He stepped off of her and gathered her against his chest. He expected the tiger fight in her eyes, not a tear escaping. He let her go, mumbling, "I'm sorry. I scared you."

She laughed then, one empty cackle before covering her mouth.

He sighed. It hurt to look at her. She was still so beautiful and vulnerable.

"You do scare me, but not in the way you think." She backhanded the tear from her face like it'd pissed her off. "You're like a ghost to me. You remind me of the man I lost, the one I pictured that perfectly, wonderfully normal future with. He was kind and amazing, but when it really came down to it? I knew he'd fight for me. He'd want to save me too." She rubbed her eyes.

Ryan walked away from her and found his handcuff key on his desk. He freed his other hand and relocated his thumb. "So is this a bad thing or a good thing?"

"Years ago I killed two men." She waited.

When she didn't go on, his cop brain jumped to conclusions. "Nikko and Wade?" He knew his eyes were wild.

Eve kept her eyes on him while she nodded almost imperceptibly.

The kick to his core shook his being. He dropped his handcuffs and keys, putting his hands in his hair, shaking his head.

"You're protecting him. I know it was him." He pointed at her.

She shook her head. "No."

Ryan could feel his skin burning. He bent forward and wanted to throw up. After all these years, he was face to face with the killer he'd sought. And all he wanted to do was make love to her.

"Wade was the second. I took him to another location." She laced her fingers together.

"Don't. I don't want to hear you." Ryan stood up and shook his head.

"I had a knife in his kidney. He thought he might survive. I let him believe that until I had him in the car. And then…" She began rocking a bit.

"Stop. Anything you say can and will be used against you—"

She kept on. "I told him he was going to die."

"No."

"And he said, 'But don't you understand? My nephew needs me.'" That tear was back, painting her cheek with the only regret she showed.

All Ryan could do was growl a warning noise at her. He was close to making her stop, and yet he couldn't form coherent thoughts.

"I killed him by twisting that knife like a key in a door. I took him to the woods and lit his body on fire. I buried the ashes." Her voice cracked at the last bit.

Ryan shook, his whole body reacting to the torture she described.

"He was one of many, but it was the nephew part that stuck with me." She glared at him, eyes blazing. "Still want to save me? Still want me to be the pretty girlfriend? This is what I am now. This is all I can be. I can't make anything I've done go away. Do you get it?" Eve held her hands out, like she was expecting judgment to be placed in them.

His voice was hoarse. "Why?"

"That's not important."

"Yes, it is. You owe me that much. Tell me fucking why!" His voice was loud, too loud. He didn't care.

"I don't remember. It's a blur." She looked at her feet and dropped her hands.

He advanced on her and grabbed her face. "Now."

"That's not how you want to remember them. It won't help you." She met his eyes only because he forced her.

"Tell me." He knew he was squeezing her too tight.

"They were meth heads about to rape a friend of mine."

It was as if she had snakes seeping from the depths of her. Ryan let go and backed up. He couldn't get away from her quickly enough, stumbling over his discarded handcuffs and sitting down hard on his ass. "Wow. Way to try and save your skin. That's a good lie." He moved until his back was against the wall.

She stood. "Okay. Am I leaving, or is there more to this?"

"Is this to protect him? Beckett?" He was having trouble breathing with her in the room.

"No."

"I don't know what to believe. They were good men. They were both good men." Ryan shook his head again.

Eve crossed the space between them. He held up a hand. "Don't come near me."

"I think they were good to *you*. But you need to go through their files. Have you done that? Did they have any priors?" She crouched down so her eyes were even with his.

Ryan swallowed. He'd checked their adult records and nothing had been too bad—unpaid parking tickets and few possession busts.

"I'm not trying to defend myself. I don't deserve forgiveness. But this wasn't their first time around. And that girl was saying no." Eve sighed.

"I can't put you in this role in my head." His nervous system was charged and wasted.

"That's okay. As long as you're not putting me in the damsel-in-distress role, you can be safe." She stood. "This puts us on opposite sides. And if revenge is what you need, you let me know. I know how that works."

She was almost to the door when he caught her. She waited, looking in his face with the steel he was used to.

"In all my life I've never known a woman like you. I've never wanted someone so badly. I don't believe a murderer is all you are. I see a part of you that you try to hide."

She shook her head. "I'm everything you think I'm not. I can't be saved. And I don't want to be." Still steel. She touched his lips with seeming regret. "I'm sorry for the loss of your uncles. If that night hadn't happened, I think the goodness of your soul would have turned them around. Shit, it's even tempted me." She took his hands from her arms.

He stepped back as she opened the door. "Where will you go?"

"Don't worry about me, copper. I always land on my feet." She looked at him for a beat too long before closing the door behind her.

Ryan stood there for at least an hour, hoping the door would stay shut and praying it would open at the same time.

38

STRONGER

Livia couldn't sleep. The quiet in the house was unnerving, though she knew it shouldn't be. She looked over at Emme and Kellan's monitors, both peaceful. After a few rough weeks, they'd returned to sleeping like champions, their little bodies awash with the relief of sameness. Blake was absent, but he'd been writing songs on and off all day. No doubt inspiration had struck again. She lay in the dark, still wide-awake when he entered about half an hour later.

"Beautiful, you're supposed to be asleep."

"I can't figure out how to make my brain shut off." He was in jeans and a T-shirt, his hair a mess from his own hands. Whenever he was composing he took it out on his head. It was endearing.

"Whatcha thinking about so much?" He sat down on the bed.

"Where to start? Just now I was wondering why Beckett lives in Poughkeepsie, but we can't see him. What is he doing? Is his life any different after all those years away? And Eve told me we don't have to worry about the man who found Emme anymore. How can she be so sure? I'm feeling bad because it calms me to think he's out of the picture, but I know it can't have been because he was arrested, you know? And where is Eve? She doesn't even call you anymore, does she?"

"Well, I'll tell you what I know. Beckett is trying to be different, but it's a long road from where he started, and the safety of his family is always at the forefront of his mind. That's why he's keeping us away.

I hope someday that will be different, but I don't know. And Eve is back in the City. I think she's processing a lot of things and needs some time to herself as well. You're right that she hasn't been calling, but she did let me know where she was." He squeezed her hand and sighed. "Now you're ready to just drop right off to sleep, aren't you?"

"Everything just seems so unsettled. How does Cole seem to you? Kyle definitely has good days and bad days, and I just don't know what's ahead for them. My heart hurts just thinking about it. And I guess the worst is that the kidnapping still makes me feel unsafe sometimes—even six weeks later." She reached for his hand again as her words came out in a rush.

"Those are things we can't solve right now. It's just going to take some time—except for the feeling safe bit. I'm here. Let me worry about the safe thing. You know what? Hold up."

Blake went into the bathroom and started the water in their bathtub. It was used mostly for Emme's "winter swimming" sessions, complete with bathing suit. Sure enough, he reappeared with an armful of tub toys. Livia laughed when he put them down on their carpet as they squirted and honked at him. He pointed an angry finger at the pile. "Shush."

She knew she should point out the wet spot that was certainly forming on the carpet, but instead she just waited to see what he was up to. He disappeared into the hallway and in a moment came back juggling candles, a light stick, and a bottle of wine.

"Your favorite." He nodded at the bottle. He disappeared into the bathroom again, and this time she had to follow. She pulled her fuzzy robe on over her penguin pajamas.

He set up the candles and lowered the lights. "You need to take your mind off all these things. Let me spoil you." He put his phone on the vanity with his own compositions playing softly.

"Wooing me with your own music?" she teased him.

"It's all I have on my phone. I was recording downstairs." He added her favorite body wash and let the foam bubble up. "And don't make fun of me."

Blake opened the wine and handed her the bottle. "Want me to get glasses? I couldn't fit them."

Livia took a swallow, spilling the wine down her robe. "Wow. I really thought I was going to pull that off. Wine's heavy."

He took the bottle and drained an impressive amount before handing it back to her. "Better? That stuff tastes like fruit punch, by the way."

"Thanks for taking some for the team." She set the bottle down and undid her robe.

He began a running commentary. "The beautiful brunette removes her wine-stained robe for her lover. And is it? Yes, dear God, yes it is. She's wearing the penguin pajamas."

Livia tossed her robe at him and hugged her body, laughing.

"Oh, how can a woman so decadently dressed be so coy? She *is* a conundrum." He wrapped one hand around her waist and pulled her to him.

Her only view was his sharp jawline with a bit of stubble and his white teeth as he smiled.

"This penguin with the ice cream cone?" He pointed to the one on her nipple. "Pure sin."

She rolled her eyes. "Such a sweet talker. The tub's about to overflow."

"Crap!" He spun and turned the water off. The bubbles were indeed almost to the edge.

"Where was I? Drink your wine." He pulled his T-shirt off and unbuttoned her flannel top while she took a gulp. "I'm naming this penguin Lucky." He pointed to the one between her legs.

She had to stop drinking so she could laugh. "Oh no, I can't keep drinking. I'm making baby food here."

"You have three non-alcoholic bottles of deliciously pumped milk in the fridge. You'll be fine until you detox." He unbuckled his belt and removed his jeans. "Plus, your mouth is going to be too busy to drink anyway."

"Blake Hartt! You filthy thing!" She play-punched him before turning her back.

"Must be why I have filthy plans." He swept her into his arms. "Now let Lucky taste the floor so I can take his place."

She struggled a bit, laughing as he tugged her pajama bottoms off.

"Take that, Lucky." Blake turned her around. She removed her own top.

"And goodbye Sin."

"Is this the foreplay? Talking dirty to my penguins?"

"Well, looks like you're just in your panties. So you may call me the master of seduction."

She covered her breasts and laughed out loud as he slid her panties off.

He growled at her through half-closed eyes. "Funny lady." He spanked her bottom, and she yelped. He put his finger on her lips. "Shhh. Don't wake the little monsters." He set the two monitors side by side so they could see the kids.

Livia sat on the edge of the tub, drinking more wine while she watched him light the candles. Gratefulness became a lump in her throat. Despite all the confusion around here and in the lives of those she loved, to be here, safe with him, was more than she could have ever asked for.

Blake kissed her forehead and got in the tub behind her. She twisted around so her feet were between his legs in the water. As she slid in, he parted her knees.

Livia took another healthy swig of the wine before scooting toward him. "Drink up, handsome." She offered him the bottle of wine.

His eyes sparkled as one hand took it and the other disappeared under the water.

After that she quickly lost the upper hand, barely remembering to set the wine bottle on the side of the tub as he handed it back to her and set to his task. She grasped the edge of the porcelain as Blake proved how well he knew her. His long fingers and warm kisses over her face and neck had her seeing stars. She swayed, about to fall backward into the water when he looked up at her.

"You're chilly. Let me help with that." Blake steadied her hips as he slid inside, drawing her closer, her legs encircling his waist.

Her mind now swirled in an entirely different way as her buzz washed over her. "Wow. Wine. This is warm. And that's…yes." She shivered: her top half cold and her bottom half toasty and engaged.

Blake traced her goose bumps with his warm finger. He used his hands to cup the soapy water and pour it over her skin, warming her with his hands. She began rocking on top of him. He wrapped his arms around her waist, and Livia bent backward until her hair was submerged, coming up slowly.

"So beautiful. Do you even have a clue?" Blake waited for her with kisses.

"I must be to catch a guy like you." She traced his jaw with her fingertips. Together they rocked until water and bubbles sloshed over the brim of the tub.

Livia turned and stood, Blake standing behind her. She turned on the water again to warm up, and out of habit she pulled the curtain and hit the shower button. Under the spray, he kissed her again, and the fine mist of water everywhere made the room a blurry gold. The candlelight flickered as Blake lifted her to his hips. She was so close, and when he slid his hand between them and pressed her against the tile wall, her orgasm was just heartbeats away.

He increased his friction and embedded himself in her hard and fast, just like she liked it when she was this close. She melted as he watched, growling and gasping, calling his name. She lost herself as she came, knowing he was so strong, holding her steady against the wall, never letting his own release stop how hard he worked for her. She touched his wet face, his stubble, the strong muscles in his chest, the scar over his heart.

Finally she slid down the tile, pulling him back down into the tub. He rearranged them so she could lie between his legs and rest her head on his chest. She heard the drain pull and knew he'd worked it out with his foot.

"You made a drunk, sloppy mess, wife." He smoothed the hair away from her face as the water poured down on them.

"Mmm…" was the only response she could muster.

The water went from lukewarm to ice as the water heater gave them its last. Livia squealed and abandoned Blake. He gallantly braved the freezing stream to turn off the water. She tossed him a towel and wrapped one around herself. The rest of the towels went to the tub overflow.

"Hope that doesn't leak through the ceiling." Livia watched as Blake arranged the towels to do the best job they could. The room was hazy with humidity as he rescued the wine bottle and took another gulp.

He brought it to her lips and tilted it so she could have a bit more too.

"Thanks." Livia ran her hands through his hair, smoothing it to look like a newscaster's. "I loved my naughty bath. It's like Vegas up in here."

He kissed her again. "Any time."

"You're a gift to me. Truly."

He hugged her again. "You as well. I almost lost it for a while. I was really close to letting go of my mind after you were gone."

"I'm sorry." She touched his lips.

"I hate that that's in me. A chance like that. It worries me." Blake rubbed her arms while he exhaled.

"Don't worry, because in there with that concern is my heart. And you know I'm too stubborn to let you go. The sun can't have you. You're mine." She traced his scar.

"I believe that. You'd actually tell the sun to go to hell, wouldn't you?" He smiled at her.

"I won't have to. You're stronger than you give yourself credit for." She touched his wedding band.

"I love you." He kissed the top of her head.

"I love you too." Livia knew she would sleep fantastically now. She could hear the bed calling to her.

They put on fresh pajamas and crawled in. They were just about settled when Kellan woke up crying.

Blake laughed. "Nice of him to wait until we were done. You sleep. I'll get him and warm up a bottle."

39

Shark Week

According to Cole's calculations, Chery had just over five months left before giving birth to her son. A son. *My son.* They'd told him the sex when he met with her and Chaos one afternoon a couple weeks ago. Not telling Kyle about this was the hardest thing he'd ever done, but he couldn't bear the thought of getting her hopes up for nothing. At least Chery had been sympathetic, rather than weirded out when he'd brought pictures of Kyle to their meeting, rather than the real thing. And by the end of their time together, everyone seemed to feel sure this was right.

Tomorrow was his next Sunday meeting with Chery, and he hoped to bring Kyle. He just had to explain it all first. The lawyer was ready to draw up the paperwork, but he didn't dare take that step without her. He adjusted the flowers on the table just as he heard her hit the alarm on her car outside. The pasta dish he had simmering was one he'd wanted to cook for a few weeks now.

He met her at the door as she inserted her key into the lock. "Hey, sexy. Welcome home. How was the early shift?"

She smiled for him, and they kissed quickly as she set down her bag and sunglasses.

"It was early. People should not be allowed to get sick. But I'm done now, hallelujah. And that means the weekend starts now! What are you making in there? Smells like the devil's balls—delicious." She licked her lips and winked.

"Did you edit that comment for me?" He locked the door and reset the alarm.

"Yes. I know you hate it when I talk about God's balls." She reached inside her shirt and unlatched her bra, ripping it out through the armhole. When she threw it at him, he caught it without comment. She did this every day. Kyle shimmied her shoulders. "Got to shake the wrinkles out of these bastards. They've been in jail all morning."

He wrapped his arms around her, eventually cupping the prisoners. "And what did they do wrong this time?"

"Please, they're criminally awesome." She nipped at his bottom lip. "Louis here stopped my purse from knocking over my coffee this morning, and Clark pressed the shift key on the keyboard."

"Impressive. Glad they do tricks. Still don't know why they're named after guys." Cole ran his thumbs over her nipples.

She feigned a frown. "Because they're travelers. Lately they've been headed south."

Cole laughed. "Never a dull day with you."

"That's the plan. Hey, why so fancy? I didn't forget an anniversary or something did I?" She slid her hand down his pants and used her thumb to mimic his movements on her breasts.

"What? No. That's my job. I just made you lunch. But if you keep that up, we won't be eating anything at all." He kissed her.

She ended the kiss by rubbing her nose on his. "Can't." She pushed away and pointed at her crotch. "Shark Week!"

"How you can tempt a man…" He tickled her as she pretended to be offended.

"Let's eat then, Iron Chef."

Cole dished out the food and felt so nervous he barely ate any. Kyle seemed to love it.

"What's up? You feel okay? You seem tense." She squinted and looked him over.

He stood and got the folder he'd prepared for her. It was now or never. He totally doubted himself now—why had he kept her out of the loop, visited Chery without her? He wanted to throw up.

She looked scared. "Is it Beckett? Is everyone okay?"

"No. It's happy stuff. Good stuff. Nothing that'll hurt us." He hoped. He prayed.

He opened the folder and removed a picture of the baby in utero. He slid it over to Kyle and let her look.

"I don't know what this means." Her hands were shaking.

He took the picture from her and held her hand. "I've waited to tell you. And I hope that was the right choice. A few weeks ago Beckett came to me with a story. And I'll tell you the whole thing, I promise. But the gist of it is he knew a woman who was pregnant with a baby she couldn't raise."

She pulled her hand from his. Her eyes filled with tears, and she covered her mouth with both hands, shaking her head back and forth.

This did nothing to bolster his confidence, but Cole powered forward. "I've been in contact with the mother for a little while. We've met. And both she and I really believe this is right for all of us—if it's something you want."

Tears fell over the tips of her fingers.

"I'm sorry I didn't tell you. I wanted to meet Chery, and I wanted to give her some time to really be sure. And I think she's as sure as anyone can be in this situation."

Kyle continued to shake her head. His stomach felt like he'd gone over the first hill on a rollercoaster.

"Say something. I'm dying here." Cole thumbed the paperwork he'd prepared to show her.

"This isn't possible. I've Googled the shit out of adoption. We have to have, like, body cavity searches and four million dollars in checking." She stared at the sonogram picture.

"Well..." Cole moved some of the papers around in his folder. "It'd be a little off the beaten path."

"Cole Bridge, is this *illegal?* Are we buying a baby?" He liked the word *we* in her sentence, but not the accusing tone with which it was delivered.

"No! Of course not. Beckett knows a lawyer who helps with this sort of thing. I don't know. I've researched it backward and forward. I've met with Chery, Beckett's guy, and a lawyer of our own. It should be okay. I've told Chery from the beginning that I'd like her in his life."

"His?" Kyle went to touch the picture again, but stopped herself like she was afraid she'd get burned.

"A boy. The baby is a boy." Cole couldn't believe how much he hoped in his own heart. He'd wanted this for Kyle, but now he knew he wanted to raise this boy too.

"I can't even look at him. Please put it away." Kyle stood from her chair and left the kitchen.

He nearly collapsed as he heard her angry stomps above him. Never had he really thought she'd be anything but happy.

He took the picture and kissed it before placing it back in the folder. He held his head, stopping his tears from coming like he did in the old days, back when he was a kid. He focused on the sound of his breathing, ignoring everything else for what seemed like an eternity.

"You want this?"

He hadn't heard her return, so her voice so close was a shock. He didn't look at her, just opened his eyes and focused on the table.

"Cole, you think getting some sort of illegal crack baby from Beckett's kid-supplier is a good idea? I can't even believe you would carry this so far. No wonder you didn't tell me anything about it." He heard the scrape of a chair as she sat back at the table. "It's actually cruel. This was mean. And you don't have a mean bone in your body. Where's this coming from, Cole?"

He looked at her now, taking in her angry, beautiful face. "You know what? You're right. Here I was thinking it's some sort of miracle. My brother just happens to be able to help me find a baby. To think that I could save a kid from the fate I had. Without us he's going to foster care—at least to start."

He watched as her anger faded. "Babies find homes really quickly," she countered.

"Really? Sometimes you're in and out your whole life. Your first memories are a jumble of people and places. Your parents just won't sign the damn papers." He inhaled and counted silently backward from ten. He'd told Kyle bits and pieces of his childhood, but he never laid it out end to end for her to examine. "It's fine. It's over. I'll call Beckett tomorrow. I never wanted to make you feel bad or criminal. That's that."

He put the folder in the drawer in the kitchen where he'd been cultivating it over the past weeks. "I'm going to mow the lawn."

As he headed toward the garage, Cole promised to pray for Chery and that boy every day for the rest of his life. Because for a few weeks, in his head at least, he'd been that baby's father.

Eve looked around her Manhattan apartment: neat, clean, organized. All evidence of the last three weeks she'd spent wandering through here had been erased. She'd run from Poughkeepsie to escape Ryan, escape Beckett, escape her past—spent some time cloaked in New York City's anonymity. She'd resigned from her job here months ago, so she'd spent her days training at the gym and walking through the streets, trying to clear her head. She couldn't go back to her pretend life again, but she couldn't quite let it go, either. Trapped, paralyzed—that's how she felt about everything, and she kicked herself for her weakness. And then finally it had come to her: she had to go. Start over someplace new. Find out who she wanted to be, who she could be, what her kick-ass skills could be used for besides actually kicking ass. Maybe that had worked for Beckett and maybe it hadn't, but this wasn't working for her at all.

She'd booked a ticket to California and packed four suitcases. The rest would stay, and the landlord could rent it as furnished. This was the last suitcase. She just needed to tie up a few loose ends and find a way to tell her dad. Exhaling, she pulled the handle out of the bag and turned it, taking one last look around her place. For years she'd waited here. For Beckett. For her life to come to her. To forgive herself. All she'd become was harder.

She wasn't expecting the knock on the door. The doorman would never have just let someone up. There were perks to the obscene price she paid for this place. She looked through the peephole: nothing. The absence of someone in her line of sight assured her it was bad news. Or the person was bad news.

She unlatched the locks and pulled open the door. He leaned against the outside wall of her place, looking at his hands. His deep blue eyes met hers and the shock of his presence coursed through her. She stepped backward and let him in.

Beckett filled the room. "Nice place." He nodded toward her suitcase. "You got a plane to catch?"

She didn't answer.

"Surprised I found you? Don't be. You saw me at the height of it, when I had plenty of people to do the little shit. But I can find anyone. And I've always known where you were." He made a show of strolling the length of her apartment.

She let go of the suitcase and crossed her arms in front of her.

"Dressed up...Going on a date? Judging from the beaten-down posture of your cop lately, I'm figuring you dumped him." He picked up an empty vase from her living room's built-in shelf.

She didn't want him making light of Ryan. She turned and looked out the window. The gray, rainy day made for a somber view of the skyscrapers.

She heard him put down the vase and continue his walk all over her soon-to-be-former residence.

"How's Rodolfo?" Her words were tight in her chest. She was the reason he worked for the bag of bones.

"He's a dickwad and a crazy person. And his son's delusional—a lot like Mary Ellen, I'm betting. Both he and Sevan are making me work for this deal, and I sense the old corpse is getting a little impatient." Beckett sat on her couch and kicked his fancy Italian shoes up on her coffee table. "So where you headed, killer?"

His old nickname for her sent a shiver through her body. She wouldn't show it. "Leaving here."

"You done with Poughkeepsie too?" He picked up an expensive piece of metal art from her end table and began tossing it from hand to hand.

"My father lives there so I'll never be done. Why are you here? Just to prove you know where I am?" Eve watched him carefully. His coat had fallen open and she could see the weapon strapped there. The art went higher and higher, almost touching the ceiling. "Don't break shit. I want my security deposit back." She tapped her foot with impatience—and excess energy, if she was being honest with herself.

He palmed the art and set it down, pulling his feet from the table. "Just checking on you, baby. Seeing if you still want to grind my balls into mulch or what."

"You can't just pop up, or pop in. That's not the way it works. I have a meeting."

He stood just as Eve went to walk past him, blocking her way. They were way too close. She looked everywhere but at him, but she could feel the heat from his chest.

"But I will. Until the day I die. Which—good news for you—should be soon." He clicked his tongue and stepped aside.

Eve shook her head, grabbed her suitcase, and left Beckett in her apartment. Everything sexual in her wanted to take him to bed. It actually hurt to close the door between them.

She drove the few miles to the warehouse where she trained, but this time she didn't change. It was a ghost town, and she headed straight to the locker room.

Shark was in a towel. "What kept you?"

Eve raised her eyebrows instead of responding.

"You're a hard bitch, you know that?" He stood, dropping his towel.

She shrugged, still silent.

"Fine. What's going on?" He walked slowly to a locker, dressing and flexing at the same time.

"Tell me everything you know about Beckett Taylor." Eve sat on a bench.

"I'd say you know more than me, pretty lady. Is he a screamer or a grunter?" Shark slipped on boxer briefs and a T-shirt.

"I'm not giving you any more jerk-off material than you already have." She gave him a hard stare.

"Fine. You're a sweetheart, by the fucking way." He tipped an imaginary hat to her.

"Suck my dick." She exhaled her frustration.

"Oh, does the princess have somewhere else to be?" He put on a pair of jeans and took his time threading a belt through.

"You have two more minutes before you know what your own ass tastes like."

"You're assuming I don't already know. Now your ass might be a nice snack."

Eve stood and stepped toward him. "Don't make this ugly. You're being a prick for no reason."

"Fine." He buttoned his shirt. "Rodolfo is set to test Beckett tonight. Thinks he's moving too slow on their deal."

"Blood in, blood out?" Eve was surprised Beckett hadn't been hazed through a beating already.

"Sort of. It's bare-knuckles, old-school fisticuffs. Beckett's men versus Rodolfo's." Shark spritzed on too much cologne.

"That'll work in Taylor's favor. His guys can hold their own." She leaned against a locker near Shark.

"Seriously? Are you too damn young to know anything? Rodolfo fights dirty. It's all a show. He's notorious. Rodolfo will take half of Beckett's men. Then Beckett will have to beg the old bastard for the lives of the rest of his guys. It's a twisted game. But Beckett gave the guy his nuts as a party favor, and evidently his negotiation skills aren't cutting it."

"He'll never take his men into that." Eve shook her head.

"No. He's not going to. That's the thing. Crazy beast is going to the fight tonight alone. Refuses to take his people. Told them he'll shoot them on sight if they show." Shark began putting on his shoes.

Beckett's visit today suddenly made more sense. He was saying goodbye. Eve turned and walked out of the locker room.

Shark rushed to catch up. "Wait, that's it? What about tit for tat?"

Eve stopped and gave him a look. "I kept Micki safe, and I didn't just make you wear your dick as a hat. That's enough tits for you."

She left the warehouse, ignoring Shark's protests. Beckett was prepared to die tonight. She got in her car and knew what she had to do. If she could get there in time…

Kyle walked upstairs slowly, clutching the folder. It had been a tense afternoon, a silent dinner. Unable to stop herself, she'd pulled Cole's research out and paged through it after he went upstairs to shower. He'd done an amazing amount of work. There was a picture of Chery and long transcriptions of their meeting and phone calls. He'd catalogued the prenatal reports by date. Cole had clearly grilled Beckett's man and seemed to have a very legal-looking route to follow for adopting the baby. He even had a page of carefully printed name choices. John McHugh Bridge seemed to be at the top.

Those details had swirled through her mind for hours, and although she still couldn't articulate her feelings, she was tired of sorting through them alone. When she got to the top of the stairs, the light from the hallway illuminated her husband where he lay in their bed.

The room itself was dark. She could see the scars of the childhood he rarely spoke about littered across his chest. They faded a little every year, she'd noticed.

Though he was perfectly still, she knew he was still awake. She came close to the bed, hugging the folder to her chest, and sat down. "Tell me what it was like—as a boy. What happened?"

There were a whole host of reasons she'd never asked that question in all the years they'd been together. For one, she knew it must have been horrible and she hadn't wanted him to relive it. It was long in the past, but now it seemed important, relevant to this situation. She could make out his shape as her eyes adjusted. His hands tucked behind his head, his feet crossed at the ankles. Wanting to lay her head on his chest, instead she sat crisscross and waited.

He cleared his throat. "It's funny. The adults told me not to tell. Now look at me—decades later and my throat still closes at the thought."

She placed a hand on his knee, and they were silent for a while.

"The lady who gave birth to me…she wasn't a nice person." He made the noise of a laugh, but there was no joy in it. "It was drugs, they said. The counselors. But she was cruel. Her eyes? There was nothing like compassion there. Like when you see a cute cat or hear a sad story? I look at your face and see the stuff affect you like it's supposed to. She was concrete—her face, her eyes. I look back on her, any memory I have, and that's all I see. Flat. Flat hair, flat eyes, flat ass."

His tone was strange, like he was sliding into those very memories as he spoke. She crawled to him and rested her head on his bare chest, petting the soft hair there.

"I was a means to an end. That's how it was for her. Anyone was a piece in a puzzle. A way to get: get more money, get more drugs, get more money again. I was a pawn for her. I remember the times the state came to get me. She'd fight so hard. But it was never for me the person, you know? It was for this body, this human body she felt entitled to."

He waved a hand over his scars. "There were things she did to me that most people wouldn't have the heart to do to an animal."

Kyle knew he could tell she was crying. He had to feel the tears that fell on his chest. She hugged him tightly.

"There was a cage. It was really a closet they'd rigged with dog crates. Anyone who gave her money…well, they got the keys to the cage."

Kyle's fury engulfed her. He had been right not to tell her, because right now she was vicious for that little boy. Thinking of her husband so helpless made her crazy.

"And then I went to Evergreen. The bitch still wouldn't sign me over, so I had to do home visits. I'd be at the school, taking classes, talking to my teachers. They'd take us to see movies or to a restaurant. It felt like another planet. And the other kids there? We were all shell-shocked, amazed that crazy crap didn't have to happen all the time. That someone would wash your clothes? Care where the fuck you were? Remember if you were in one place or another? They never forgot us in a cage for days at a time."

He was barely a shadow now—his voice, the look in his eyes. She touched his face.

"You know, I had Mrs. D. She's the closest I'd ever had to a mom. She let me know I was going to have more someday, that there would be a day I'd make my own choices. She knew it was hell when I went home. I know now she went to bat for me a billion times, and eventually that woman who birthed me signed away her rights. And that's when I made enough of a change that I could go to a foster home."

"Where you met your brothers..." Kyle added for him. Even though that foster home had been shit, at least he'd made a family for himself.

"Yes. There was Beckett. He just knew there was more to me. And Blake had an aura, you know? Like he was something special. You just wanted to help him. But Beckett, he wanted to help us both. He *did* help us both. And I know he's a criminal. I know that. He's made terrible choices, but sometimes I know he didn't really have a choice."

Cole sat up a bit, scooting up against the headboard and pulling her with him. "But whatever Beckett had done, I knew with everything in me that he'd never let anyone lock me in a damn cage again. And I'm a grown man, and this sounds ridiculous, but I trust him. I know he wouldn't hurt me with this. He'd never hurt you either."

"Not on purpose. I agree with that." Kyle nodded.

"That's it. Right there. Not on purpose. That, to me, is goodness. When you're caring by default." Cole hugged her back. "I'm sorry if this wasn't the right choice for you. Here I was thinking I'd save you worry, and I've upset you."

"I think we should do it." Kyle pulled away from him enough to see his face as his eyes went wide.

"Don't say that because you feel bad for me." Cole watched her carefully.

"No. I was going to say it before you told me what you went through. I think I was—and am—afraid to get my hopes up. If this Chery decides she wants her baby back, or to not give him to us at all…I'm just scared." Kyle sighed. "But that could happen with any adoption, and even with any pregnancy. Sometimes things don't go as planned."

Cole swallowed. "So?"

"So I'd really love to try and see if we can make this work." Kyle patted his cheek and kissed him. "I'm ready for a baby, even if my body isn't. And this—you and me and little John? Let's try. Let's hope and pray and figure it out. We'll talk to Chery, and I'll try not to curse my face off. Let's have a baby, Cole Bridge." She kissed him again with all the hope she had. With her hands she willed him new memories—just love, only caring. This body of his, which heartbreakingly had been currency for someone else, she would treasure and value.

"Will we do okay, you and me, do you think?" He kissed her before she could answer.

When they took a breath, she let him know the only thing that mattered. "Always."

40

Hell and Gasoline

Beckett was going to fight without his douchebags. He'd convinced the fuck out of them that he'd be fine, that he had a deal with Rodolfo and this was all for show.

He didn't, and it wasn't.

Yet he wasn't about to drive them to a bloody fucking death. Bad enough that he'd done it to himself, but really, what did he expect? After the life he'd lived? The choices he'd made? Perhaps this was best for everyone. To make sure of it, he'd arranged a few things: set up trust funds for his brothers and pulled a few listings for available property clear on the other side of the country. A letter detailing how they could all live there and who to call to manage their money would arrive by courier tomorrow at noon, unless he was by some miracle alive to stop it. He'd planned for everything he could think of, including a birth suite for Chery and a specialist to help Cole and Kyle with the adoption. He'd done everything he could to make it legal now, and that gave him peace.

He'd dressed like the fine motherfucker he was and didn't bother to pack heat. He'd be outnumbered a hundred to one, so what was the point? Seeing Eve had been a kick in the nuts, but a necessary one. He needed to know she was okay—moving out and moving on. It gave him a sick pleasure to know Ryan was past tense, but damn it, once he was dead he'd probably be half rooting for the bastard. She needed someone good in her life. Someone better than him.

Eve was a tough one. It took tenacity to get into her heart. Like he could say he had any claim, but fuck if he didn't love her. He hoped tonight would prove that to her once and for all, even if he weren't around to see the outcome. And if this game took everything from him, at least he'd leave with his debt paid and his family taken care of.

His fantastic black Hummer looked as pimp as it should, and he rolled up onto Rodolfo's meeting place without hesitation. Beckett planned to go out with a shit-eating grin because, well, fuck you, world. He was born to assholes, and he'd raised himself and created his family. He'd leave them enough money to be provided for. Eve would be alive and maybe with him gone, she could truly fucking heal. He exhaled as he opened the door, leaving the engine running and his music blasting.

Old-school Rodolfo was surely pissing his Depends with anger. Respect was demanded, but Beckett wasn't in the mood to play games. Or to fake anything. He found himself at the back end of yet another huge house. The man was just crapping money at this point. The front must have faced a lake or something because he could smell a moldy wetness in the air. Torches along the driveway and blazing light from the house's floor-to-ceiling windows illuminated the yard, as well as the snipers perched in the upstairs windows. Rodolfo came strolling out the French doors, cane in hand and face in obvious disapproval of Beckett's lack of an army.

The old man slowly made his way to Beckett. "Turn that off." He pointed at the Hummer. Beckett shrugged, so one of Rodolfo's men hopped into the vehicle and shut it down.

"You were to show force tonight. Prove yourself. You haven't been able to do it any other way. Your value is rapidly dwindling." Rodolfo looked furious, though he was reining it in.

"This is all I need to show you how awesome I am." Beckett winked at the old man and held out his arms. "You don't appreciate my mind, baby."

"There are ways to do things. Proper ways. How is it you can't even do this right? Go get your people, then come back."

Beckett was about to start in and tell the man how, unlike him, he had respect for his people and wouldn't use them in a chess game when the buzz of a distant motorcycle caught everyone's attention. It was traveling at a tremendous speed.

Beckett smirked. Instantly he knew who it was. She drove like a goddamn stunt person. After a few moments the motorcycle came to a stop in a spray of gravel somewhere close behind him. He didn't turn—Rodolfo could just think he'd expected her—instead he watched the reactions of the men standing before him.

Beckett pictured her in his mind's eye. She'd stunned them stupid, that's for sure. He heard the clack of her steel stiletto heel on the bike's kickstand, the sound of her pulling off her helmet. He imagined her long blond hair falling out from under it. From the way a few of the men around him adjusted their pants, he was betting on black leather that looked like it had been poured over her insane body, every curve highlighted by the unforgiving material.

She stood right behind him. He could feel her there, her hands behind her back like the amazing weapon she'd always been.

"Boss."

That was all she said, and all she needed to say. She'd let him know why she was here with one word. Somehow she'd figured out what he was doing, where he'd be. And she had the timing of Superman. Unfortunately they'd probably both die—Rodolfo knew how he felt about Eve.

"The hair is different. But that's the woman who murdered Mary Ellen." Rodolfo set his heavy gaze on Eve.

Beckett finally allowed himself to turn to her, to see what they were seeing. He had to smile. She was sheer sex and sin. The boots were old favorites with high, steel heels. And as predicted, her pants were orgasmically tight. She had a corset on, goddamn it, and her tits were so distracting it was obscene. Across her chest hung rounds of ammo like she'd just won the beauty pageant of death, and a leather jacket topped the whole fucking thing off. Well, that and the impressive automatic weapon slung over her shoulder.

She pulled her favorite knife from where it was strapped to her thigh next to another. She twirled her hair into a bun and slid the knife into it, meeting his gaze when it was set. Eve was magnificent. Every damn time.

"I'd have loved for us to live through this." Beckett shook his head and held out his hand.

She looked at his hand briefly before knocking it out of the way. Instead of walking past him or blowing his balls off, she grabbed the back of his neck and laid a kiss on him that made his knees buckle. She leaned close to his ear before pulling away. "Never say die."

Rodolfo looked on at this ridiculous display. His child's murderer put on quite a show, but he was actually grateful for a moment to take stock. The kid showing up without a crowd had been a huge speed bump. He'd not wanted to kill him. Beckett's work negotiating the Harmon deal had showed some promise. In fact, Rodolfo explicitly forbade his army from taking Taylor's head. He just needed to remind him who was in charge here, motivate him in his deal-making. When things slowed down, Rodolfo had learned to worry it was because his people were getting greedy.

He certainly hadn't expected this kind of upheaval in his golden years, this sort of betrayal from his own daughter. *She* was the one who'd gotten him into this mess. Women. He'd always suspected Mary Ellen would be an exercise in futility, but his son was a sorry sack too. Neither had children. However, Primo was just entering his fifties, so an heir might still emerge.

He regarded the woman again. She would make an excellent breeding mare—as long as she could be prevented from eating her young. A nice son from her womb with his blood in its veins...that could work.

Rodolfo cleared his throat, drawing their eyes toward him. "You've flouted my traditions here tonight. And I'd like you all to take a moment of silence to observe my restraint and understanding—this woman killed my daughter, and she's still breathing." Rodolfo waved over his closest man, who responded by pulling out a foldable chair. Getting old hurt every moment of every day. No matter how much money he had, his joints ached, and his left side was slow to cooperate. He was exhausted, honestly, and this nighttime meeting was kicking him in the ass. He'd wanted to be asleep three hours ago.

Taylor was obviously shocked to see his ladylove. She'd put herself back together since the last time he'd seen her, and this bitch with a plan was a scary scenario. Back in the day he'd have offed her a long time ago. But now, she was more. He was really warming up to the idea of her as his grandchild's mother, and he could kill her moments after a baby was born.

The cocky bastard winked at him. "Sorry for blowing air up your skirt, grandpa. I kind of suck at following rules."

"Primo, come here. Pick one of these two to live. Only half can leave a meeting with me. Those are the rules. Let's let my boy make a choice."

Rodolfo snapped over his left shoulder. There was some hustling behind him and finally his son stood next to his chair.

The blonde held up one fist. Taylor smirked.

"Hey, Primo," the woman purred. "You might want to stop breathing. Just for a fucking second." She pointed with her pinkie.

Rodolfo turned in his chair to see his son's head covered in laser dots from what had to be twenty different scopes at all kids of angles.

He turned back to face Taylor. The blonde had just finished whispering in the traitor's ear.

"You waste my time, Taylor. You think I don't have rings of men protecting this very location? Two guys with a handful of laser pointers aren't going to scare us off."

The blonde walked to the closest car, Rodolfo's midnight black Rolls Royce Ghost, and pulled the knife out of her hair. "You had twenty dropshots here, here, and here." Using the blade, she marked his car with an X and made little circles in the paint, revealing all the tactical places he'd put men. "We found fifteen of your scouts on the ground, and we easily outnumber you just beyond these trees."

His car now bore the marks of his defeat. His eyes burned like hot coals. "So what's the situation, Goldilocks? You and your boyfriend want to run my business?" Rodolfo looked to his right-hand man and Nicholas nodded, giving a hand signal he hated to see. It confirmed that his men would retreat as soon as he ordered it.

Eve gave him a onceover. "No, sir. We only want you to take your business elsewhere. No more of the crap your daughter started. Leave us and Poughkeepsie alone, and no one has to die tonight. Every single one of your men has been incapacitated, but they live. Taylor insisted on a peaceful show of force out of respect for your years." She slid the knife back in her hair, then paused, as if she'd almost forgotten something. "And I believe if you check your accounts you'll find everything in order. Due to Taylor's efforts we were successful in recovering your stolen money." She resumed a soldier's stance.

Taylor shook his head in apparent disbelief before recovering. "I gotta tell you, R, I was prepared to lay my balls on a platter for you, but she's right. This is better. Back in the day I stayed out of your way for a fucking reason. You're a legend. And all I want—all I've ever wanted—is that tiny town and my family safe."

Rodolfo stood. His son still looked like he had a case of the electric chicken pox, and the dots scarcely wavered at all. The marksmen at the other end of the weapons had steady hands, no fear, which was all the proof Rodolfo needed to know the words from the blonde were the truth.

He had no choice. "I agree to your resolution with one addendum."

Taylor nodded, showing he was listening.

"The girl comes with me."

She didn't even flinch. Just an ice-cold stare. If Rodolfo still had a working penis, it would surely be pointing at her.

Beckett scoffed. "No way, oh cadaverous one. Get your own monster bitch. She's with me till the end." The younger man's face went deadly. "Why is it you still think you hold the cards here? I've done what you asked, what I agreed to do."

"I do not hold all the cards." Rodolfo stepped in front of his son, the lights dancing on his face as they worked to re-aim on their original target. "Not here. But out there? You know I do. I can buy and sell you. You know you've been sloppy enough that I can find everyone in the world who ever muttered your name."

Silence. A stand-off as both men waited to see which way the wind would blow the conflict. Taylor looked over at the woman, who seemed to speak to him with her eyes. Eventually Rodolfo's patience was rewarded.

"I don't want a war," Beckett told him. "All I want is peace in Poughkeepsie and this woman next to me. Without them? Know that I'm crazy enough to take us all to Hell with a couple gallons of gasoline."

The kid wasn't posturing, there was no ticks or tells.

"All right, Taylor. I will release you from your allegiance." Rodolfo waited, taking a deep breath and wondering if he was doomed to miss this night's sleep. If he was awake past twelve, he'd be up until five pissing every half hour. Getting old was torturous business. "But I do hope we might prove useful to one another in the future."

Taylor nodded and crossed the distance, holding out his hand.

Rodolfo made sure to squeeze firmly. "Perhaps this is for the best. As you can see, I'd grown a bit bored with our current relationship."

Taylor chuckled. “You and me both, pal.” He raised his hand in signal and the laser dots disappeared from Primo’s head. The blonde whipped out her phone and texted furiously for a moment, then nodded at Taylor. He waited for her to get on her motorcycle and start back down the drive before pulling away in his Hummer.

Nicholas approached immediately. “You want the girl? I’ll get her now.”

Rodolfo shook his head. “Tonight we’re done. But I want the file on Taylor to have the color of his mother’s crotch hair by tomorrow. I want everything there is to know about that bastard. And now it’s time for bed.”

He turned to see that Primo had wet his pants and sighed. His legacy was a crazy dead woman and a pussy.

41

Come Here

Beckett watched her on her bike. She would be pissed to hear how fucking feminine she looked on it—amazing that she could be so hard and so soft all at once. And of course, she also looked like she'd just run away from a vampire-slaying movie or something in her getup.

At the stoplight, she angled her side mirror, and he pointed to the left, toward his house. It felt like the old times for a few more turns until they parked, and she got off the motorcycle. The look on her face when he met her in the driveway was so much more complicated than it had been back in the day.

Of course, she'd just been trying to kill him back then, not love him.

"You saved my ass back there—not that I asked for it." Beckett pointed at his front door, and she followed him inside.

The windows had all been replaced, and with a few extras he had the contractors throw in as well, this place was now a fortress. He locked the door behind them and smiled. This time no one without a Sherman tank could bust down his door or break his windows.

She took off her jacket and tossed it on the back of the couch. Gandhi snorted himself awake, and Beckett had the pleasure of finally introducing him to Eve. Sure, she'd spent the night with him once, but she hadn't even known his name. It helped that G was a shameless flirt. Eve crouched down, and he waddled his way over.

She let him snorfle at her hand before petting his head. "What happened?"

Beckett needed a moment to register what she meant, as he didn't even see the scars anymore. The dog's face was such a part of him now.

"Somebody tried to fight him." Gandhi rolled onto his back, offering her his belly. His happy, slobbery noises proved how unfit he was for anything but love.

"Dog fighting?"

"Yup. He was about an hour from death row when I busted him out. He kept me from losing my mind when I was away. Forced me to get out every day, you know?" Beckett came close and helped Eve pet the dog's middle.

She stood, stepping back as soon as Beckett was close. "What's his name?"

"Gandhi. I hope that's not rude. Never thought about it until too late." Beckett leashed the bulldog and stepped outside with him. When they returned, Eve was walking through the house, noting the improvements.

Beckett locked up and pulled out two glasses. "Thirsty?"

She answered with a quick nod and he began pouring vodka, adding a few things from the bar to make it fancy.

Beckett made sure his hand took up way too much real estate on the glass when he handed it to her, ensuring she'd have to touch him to get her drink. She did so without looking at his face. She turned to look out his living room window and took an impressive swallow before holding the glass with two hands, like it was a cup of coffee keeping her hands warm.

He stood across the room, giving her space as he forced her to face this emotional thing between them.

"I expected to lay it out tonight. Why'd you show up?" He tried his own drink, barely tasting it as he waited for her answer.

"Because Mouse would've wanted me to." Still, she wouldn't look at him.

"And if all hell had broken loose?" The tension was like a high wire, strung from his heart to hers. He could almost see it.

It was then she set her blue eyes on him. "I've got the devil on speed dial."

He took another drink, buying time. "Lucky bastard."

She was dressed like a dominatrix, but this was clearly a fragile moment for her. He had to believe that.

"All this time and here we are. Wish it was different?" He set his glass down, as if about to do battle.

She tensed. There was no response forever as she looked at her boots, then her clasped fist, and finally back at him. "When I'm not with you, I'm wishing I was."

And with that, the tension snapped and a whirlwind began.

"Come here to me," Beckett demanded in a gravelly voice. He pointed to the spot in front of him. "Come here or run, because the next choice you make will be for the rest of your life."

He felt anything but sure, but he didn't let his uncertainty seep into his demeanor. If Beckett knew anything, it was that Eve liked him to be rough, uncompromising.

She took her time walking to him, her bravado slightly false as she put the tips of her boots against the toes of his shoes. She was gorgeous enough for candles and romantic music, but that's not what he had. Beckett bit his bottom lip as he dragged his hand over her thigh, up to her stomach, and across her breasts to grab the hair at the nape of her neck. He grabbed it hard and felt the knife she kept hidden there slice into his hand. Hot blood seeped from his hand into her hair, but he watched desire surge through her. Her pupils dilated and her stance widened.

She licked her lips. "Abuse me."

"Oh, shit," Beckett breathed as he put his other hand on her ass and pulled her against him. She tilted her head back, digging the knife in deeper.

She slapped his face, and when he turned back to her, he bit her neck. He raked his teeth across her chest and bruised her skin with his fingers. He knew she'd never show weakness, but he might actually die trying to make her do just that.

And then she engaged, so needy with her hands and mouth, it damn near choked him up. She climbed him, hanging on while she kissed him like she might never stop. It felt like Eve was trying to get inside him, and he staggered backward. Regaining his balance, he started up the stairs, setting her down hard halfway up. She took the opportunity to undress him — the jacket she clawed off, and his shirt ripped as she found his chest. She looked up at him as she licked her way across his abs and twirled her tongue delicately around his nipple before biting down.

He grabbed her by the throat and pinned her against the stairs. He watched her lips go blue as he undid his belt and let his pants hit the floor. Her eyes started to widen, the lack of oxygen getting to her. When he kissed her, her blue lips had turned cold.

"I know how you like it, you sick fucking bitch. You have to be half dead to come." As he let go of her neck, he noticed his injured hand had left a bloody print. He wiped his palm across her heaving chest. "Fuck, Eve, how dare you think you could live without this? Without me?"

He yanked her quickly so she was ass up. He put his foot in the center of her back and stripped her like she was his enemy. Using the knife she had strapped to her thigh to rip through the lacing, he destroyed her corset. Next he set to work on her insanely skin-tight pants. He could hear her seething, breathing through her teeth, but when she tried to get up, he slammed her against the stairs again. He shredded the leather into pieces, finally getting her bare, though the strips hung down like a hula skirt. He pushed through them and into her with no warning. Three fingers, no waiting.

She gasped, and he loved it. "Do you know what's next? I'm going to fuck the hell out of you."

He let her up, and she was already swinging. She gave him two hard nut shots, his boxer briefs offering little protection. His anger and his lust combined in the precise way only she could make him feel. He roughhoused her up the stairs to the top. She was claws and teeth, mixed with a soft tongue on occasion. With brute force he wrestled her onto her back, spreading her legs and pinning her knees on either side of her head. Her spike heels became deadly obstacles between him and her beautiful face.

Eve was spitting mad, but after one glance at her bareness, he could see she was also wet, ready. He was fucking conquering her, and it was all she needed. He'd been ready to sink into her from the second he saw her at Rodolfo's.

Beckett pulled his briefs down just enough to release himself. He slapped her center with his dick, once and then twice before dragging himself along her. "Beg for it, Eve. Fucking beg for it." He had her bent like a damn pretzel, so he put his face close to hers, always conscious of her damn spike heels. She captured his bottom lip in her teeth, pulling enough to worry him. Then she switched to licking, slowly outlining his released lip. He let his tongue touch hers.

So close to her, he could smell the sex between them. "Beg for it," he commanded softly.

She closed her eyes, breathing shallowly before finally looking back at him. "Five years was enough begging."

Beckett let go of her legs, allowing her to change her mind. For all his brutality, he knew she was in charge. This moment was hers to choose.

"It'd take me a thousand fucking lives to be worth you."

Sitting up, topless and bloody, Eve shook her head. "You don't get it."

She stood and turned, her strips of pants swirling around her legs. His dick almost died as he saw all her amazing bare skin. Her stilettos scratched the hardwood floors, and his favorite birthmark in the world breezed by on the back of her left thigh. Slamming his bedroom door against the wall, she strolled in. As he followed, she found her way to his meticulously organized closet. After angrily removing her belt and tossing her pant remnants on the floor, she stood naked, save for the fuck-me boots, in the small room.

Beckett slipped to his knees, watching her. Besides the ridiculous horniness he had going on—which could very well become his super power right fucking now—her body was his home. Every curve, all the soft lines around her strong muscles were his. When they'd been together years ago, their bodies were their pawns, amusement parks, a way to feel something. But now...

She yanked a crisp white shirt off the hanger. It still had the tags from the dry cleaner, and she tore those off as well. Pulling the shirt on, she buttoned it up, her insane boots now at war with the simple button down.

"Tell me what I don't get. Don't be a fucking woman with the silent treatment crap. We're too old for that." Beckett had pulled his boxers back in place, but still he ached for her.

She seemed to reset herself for a beat before coming to meet him in the bedroom. She knelt as well. In the white shirt, she looked less lethal—despite the blood on her, his blood on her. Allowing her to choose him was bathing her in his sins. But if all this time between them had taught him anything, it was that they were orbiting the same fate. Together, always together, even when physically apart.

"Your time away went from you being a better man, to me not being worth coming home to." She set her hands on her lap.

"That's not true. That's not what I wanted." He needed her in his lap, or on her knees, his hands grabbing her breasts. He willed himself to focus.

"I believe that. But when were you coming back? If Livia hadn't been taken, when were you coming back?" The pinkie on her left hand began to twitch, the only sign of her internal distress.

He could only be honest. "I don't know." He needed her on top of him, sweating, tossing her hair, growling.

She nodded. "Should that be enough for me? Do you think that's enough?"

He knew Eve despised asking these questions, navigating through this. Cracks had begun to appear in her icy demeanor.

"No. Right. You know what I want *for you*, but it's different than what *I* want. I told you a million years ago: A minivan, kids, PTA mom. Making you wait for that shit ain't right. But I'll never be that guy. Even when I try to do things differently, even when I *am* doing things differently, I'm still me. Shit, I had to almost strangle myself to keep from killing a guy down in Maryland. And then I killed him anyway. Bastard deserved it." He shook his head. "I can see you in a wedding dress. I know I'll miss you every day of my life, but I don't deserve you. And you sure as shit need more than this." Beckett clenched and unclenched his hands again and again. The blood began to flow renewed from his palm. "But I won't let you say I haven't loved you, haven't tried to be right for you. You know I fucking love you."

She thought for a few minutes, this woman of few words trying to make him understand her heart. He wanted to hush her desperate search for her feelings with his mouth on hers.

"Here's the truth." She looked as sharp as when she was loading a gun. "I can't *think* like that. I'm always looking for an exit, I *never* sit with my back to a window, and I practice death skills all the time. It's the only thing that makes sense. I cracked a long time ago, died a long time ago. But I'm still here. And this— " She slapped her chest and then his over and over, back and forth. "This is all I have.

Waiting for you, loving you—if that's what this pain is—it's why I face a day instead of eating a bullet. Only you understand the me that's left." And then she exhaled.

"Eve, I don't..." Beckett was at an impasse. There was no rulebook for this, for her. What, for all the donkey punches in the world, was the right thing to do? He'd spent five years trying to answer that question, and it seemed no clearer than the day he'd moved away.

"Don't." Her voice froze him. "Don't feed me shit you make up. Just truth. Give me the truth. Telling me you love me is not an apology. It's not a future. It's not a choice. I *do* need more. You told me downstairs to come to you or run. I came to you." She stood, agitated, pointing at him. "Now I'll tell you the same thing. Come here to me or run. Truth, right?"

Beckett stood—even with her boots, he was a head taller than she was. "I don't have a choice. Don't you get it? I'm too selfish to stay away, too stupid to care what it does to you." He grabbed her again, his red palm marking the shirt she wore. She looked like a butcher, and maybe that's all she was. Maybe that's all she had the capacity for anymore, and maybe he wasn't meant to keep pushing her toward the life he'd created for her in his head. She was who she was, and her past was never going to be different. His part in making her who she'd become was never going to be different. But they were right for each other as they were now, and he was fucking kidding himself if he thought he'd let another bastard have her. He was jealous, he was dominant, and he was in love.

Two quick motions was all it took to lift her and free himself. As she slid down his body, he entered her. And she accepted him. He had the pleasure of watching her face register his presence inside her. Beckett bent his knees so he could get as deep as God would allow. She held his shoulders.

"Tell me I'm enough for you," he demanded. "Can you be with me even though I'm so wrong?" She was satin and warmth. The way she squeezed, he was desperate to move, pound, inject her.

She looked at him. "This is. You are. I can't do this any more if it's not with you. So please fuck me straight to hell."

"Jesus." Beckett was gentleman enough not to play with words at a time like this.

The bed was too far away, so he knelt again, turning her expertly so she settled on her knees. It was all about the power between his legs, the need that woke heavy for him in the mornings, every morning for years. At first it was only a complete thundering—fast, hard, and deep. He found her breasts and grabbed at them, pinching her nipples while he drowned himself in her. He dragged his hands away from her chest, scorching his way, digging his fingers into her back until he had her hips. He went faster, bringing more friction, more pressure. He was fixated on the sight of it. In and out, he watched as they became one. He found the flair of her hip, her womanly hourglass staggering him. His primal male mind made only pure noise: More. Her. His.

And at last he felt the gathering behind his dick, warning and promising of his release. Beckett sat back on his heels and pulled the knife from her hair, throwing it aside. With his other hand he found her and began the relentless friction that would make her an animal as well. He used his fingers wisely, his thumb never stopping, over and over finding the spot that he hoped made her vision dissolve into pure white. Two other fingers explored the sensitive parts, pinching a bit to make her whimper. Because of his hold around her neck, she could not flail.

"Come, Eve. You know you have to. I'm not stopping. I'm never going to stop."

A low growl began in her throat, so Beckett picked up the friction—all fingers rubbing and pressing, forcing her to forget herself.

She was sweating now, her back moist against his own sweaty chest. He looked over to the full-length mirror against the wall, and damn it, he could see her. Her body painted against his, nipples hard, breasts taut. Her hands pressed to her stomach, poised and waiting.

And then he felt her release. Liquid against his hand told him she was at absolute peak pleasure. She gasped and screamed.

"Pinch your fucking nipples or I'll cut them off."

She did as he asked. Her eyes rolled back into her head. "Pleasepleaseplease," she begged. And though he knew she had no idea what she was asking for, he did.

At that moment he resumed, fucking her from behind with everything he had. He released her neck and pushed her forward. As she continued to come he flipped her over, manipulating her legs so he stayed within her. And then she was on his floor, orgasm almost done.

Beckett heaved her legs over his shoulders and had at her. No mercy at all: pulling out completely, slamming back in. Inside her was his dick's paradise, the satin twitching and clenching, the tip of his penis engorged—the sensations took away any good sense he'd had. He knocked off her legs, spreading her wider and used both hands. One he slipped underneath her, fingering the sensitive spots there, while his other rubbed her furiously. And as her orgasm resurfaced, he released all his passion into her.

She pulled him on top of her, scratching his back before hugging him tightly.

He lay there for a few minutes before sliding to her side. She'd never been much of a cuddler, but he made her snuggle in now. "Boom, baby. How you like me now?" Beckett wanted to stroke her hair, but it was a knotty, bloody mess. He felt proud.

She laughed. "Pretty damn good, I'll give you that."

"I love your laugh. I need more of it." He pulled her closer and kissed her forehead.

Her fingers seemed to have a mind of their own: running across his chest, playing with the hair there. "Hmm," was all she managed.

Lying in his arms felt more right than wrong—even though it was depraved and dirty, it was perfect.

"It's been so long I thought I was going to have to take over Cole's old priest robes." Beckett chuckled.

"No ladies in Maryland?" Eve was surprised.

"No. We had a deal, remember? Right?" Beckett sat up, pulling her with him. He looked at her, holding her shoulders. "I know it's been a really long time for you too, right?"

"If you say so." She lifted her eyebrows.

"Are you kidding me? Who was it? I'll kill the motherfucker to death." Beckett's eyes went wild. "Was it the cop?"

Eve untangled herself and saw her reflection in his mirror. "You cut my hair!"

She stood and headed for the bathroom to inspect the damage. She shook her hair out and watched as some chunks came loose.

"Freaking hair knife amateur," she mumbled. He was still carrying on about sex with other people as she figured out how to turn on his complicated shower.

The water came from all sorts of angles, and she stepped into it, wetting her hair before he followed her, still ranting. He ran his hand over the top of his head and grabbed the bottle of soap with the other.

Stealing the soap, she poured it into a loofah, smirking at him. "Use this to keep your panties clean?"

"Are you even listening to me?" Beckett stole the sponge back and took over washing the blood off her skin.

"No. I'm too busy making fun of your totally girly shower setup." She found his shampoo and added it to her hair.

She turned to face him when she felt him stop his ministrations. Instead he looked at her feet. The bottom of the shower swirled with pink water and long blond hairs.

"Looks like a fucking crime scene." He dropped the loofa and ran his hands over her. "Bruises and marks all over. Jesus. I even cut your hair."

When she bent down to get the sponge, Beckett slipped inside her again. She yelped and laughed. "Nice prison maneuver there."

And then he pounded the laughter out of her, eventually pulling her upright and pushing her against the glass shower door. She could see through the door to the mirror in the bedroom, her refection showing soapy breasts pushing rhythmically against the glass.

He finished quickly. "Wow. Sorry about that. You naked does that to me."

She shook her head. They rinsed off again, and he didn't have any conditioner, so her newly butchered hair would be a ball of knots.

Beckett insisted on toweling her off, and she rolled her eyes but let him. He tucked the towel around her before grabbing his own. They took a few minutes to bandage and treat their various wounds.

"Hungry?" He held out his hand when they were finally done.

She looked at him for a minute: stupidly good looking with his low-slung towel and dimpled smile. "I could eat." She let him hold her hand on their way to the kitchen, both of them in their towels like a TV couple. She sat on a bar stool as he whipped up a plate of scrambled eggs and toast. Gandhi sat expectantly at his feet, long tongue lolling out. After some eggs had cooled enough, the dog was rewarded with a mouthful. He plated their eggs and sat next to her.

She loved him, really loved him. With her heart. The wave of it hit her hard.

When they'd finished, he cleared their plates, and standing at the sink, he loaded the dishwasher. Seeing this deadly guy do something so mundane in his towel was incredible.

"What?" He caught her staring.

Eve bit her tongue—she had a running practice of not saying shit. But this was something she had to do. "I like seeing you. Being here with you. The way you move turns me on."

His face registered shock before he reacted with a suggestive dance around the kitchen. "You like me now?" He dropped his towel, even though there was no music.

"Now I like you a little less."

He stopped dancing and growled. She took off before he could launch himself at her, losing her towel as she scrambled up the stairs. She almost got the door to his bedroom closed before he busted in.

"Seriously? You're powerless against my mad dancing skills. Just bow down." He began gyrating again.

"Okay, please. If it makes you stop." Eve climbed onto his bed and covered herself with blankets.

He danced over, making a huge show of his manhood bouncing around until she flat out laughed.

He crawled under the covers with her. "If that's what it takes to make you laugh, I'll become a nudist and follow you around like that wherever you go. Grocery store? Me. Bam. In line at the DMV? Me. Still there. Pow."

He was thrusting under the covers, punctuating his speech as best he could with his penis. She smacked him on the chest before he trapped her hands. She let him.

Face to face again, he wiggled his eyebrows at her. "Hey."

"Hey." Eve pulled her hands free and forced him to lay back so she could rest her head on his chest.

They listened to each other breathe for a while.

"I don't want to leave." He was being candid again.

"We've got time." She touched his face. "In fact, I should have bought us all the time we'll ever need—an insurance policy, if you will. While I was chatting with Sevan, I liberated a nice pile of evidence he'd collected about Vitullo Weapons' less-than-savory dealings. If someone comes calling, we can always threaten to leak it and tank their legitimate business. It's not perfect. But it's something."

Beckett kissed her again. "You're a genius. The best fucking weapon there is." He smiled. "But actually, I meant I don't want to leave your side. Naked or not, I want to be right next to you for the rest of the time I have on this planet." He looked from her lips to her eyes and she could see he held nothing back. Pure honesty.

"The way we do things, chances are forever is a pretty short time." She hated to think of it. Having him here, knowing he was safe gave her peace. No one could hurt him without going through her first.

"I'm sorry about that." He touched her face as well.

She smiled at the irony of two murderers being so tender with each other, so in love that the prospect of dying made them afraid.

"So what are we, Bonnie and Clyde?" He titled his head with the question.

"They were fools who got trapped and died." She straddled him.

"Romeo and Juliet?" He found his place inside her quickly, ready for her like a machine.

"Dramatic assholes. Also wound up dead." She began rocking, reaching a hand behind her to grab him.

"Oh, God." His eyes fluttered into his head briefly before he returned to their conversation. "No one gets out alive, killer."

"Then we can be Eve and Beckett." She used every muscle she had to sheath him, multiply the pleasure of his time inside her. All the while her hand manipulated him, finding ways to increase his sensations. "Because I'd like to come first."

He fought back, grabbing her breast with one hand and parting her so he could tease her release lower. Then nothing else mattered. Her voice grew hoarse from screaming his name and cursing his torture. At the tipping point of no return, at the very edge of her orgasm, he stopped.

She gasped at the loss of him, his exquisite talent. He tossed her onto her back, kissing her slowly until her breathing was under control. "You want to come first? Your wish is my command."

When he turned his back to straddle her and slipped lower, she fought him, writhing until her head hung off the edge of the bed. "Race to the finish?"

He groaned and held up a finger. "Fine, but I get power tools."

He pulled a serious-looking vibrator out of the drawer by his bed.

She mocked his voice. "I needed priest robes."

"I'll have you know this thing is brand fucking new. I bought it for you. Smell it."

She covered her face. He wrestled the latex ball close to her nose. "Inhale, damn it."

Because she had no choice, she did. Indeed it did smell overwhelmingly new. "That was nasty."

"You want nasty? My next assault between your legs will be on another fucking level."

She burst out laughing.

"You are destroying the mood. Suck my dick." He pushed her head into position.

In an instant she took him in completely, remembering when he hit the back of her throat how goddamn huge he was, though the soreness between her legs should have reminded her already.

Before he could get oriented, she did everything she remembered he liked and hated. Teeth, tongue, and a swirling hand motion started his hips pumping and his mouth cursing—every sensitive spot hit like the assassin she was. No build up, no slow seduction, she gave him everything and he responded in kind, his fingers and mouth fighting back, forcing her to release him and take a moment to gasp.

And so it began, for every sexual task she set to, he matched and bettered her, yin and yang. Sucking and biting, his fingers asked her to experience things only he could create for her. Then the vibration started at a dull roar. He dragged the vibrations from back to front, her legs twitching when he found her melting spot. And then he pressed. It was as if her body was electrically wired to his desires. Her orgasm came quickly, while he watched from inches away. She'd stopped sucking him off for fear she might actually injure him. She was flat-out screaming and growling for him now. She grabbed the backs of his thighs, clawing her desire into his skin.

"That's right. Come. I know you have more." And then he began with the fingers, punishing her body into submission. Her release was ridiculous, pouring from her and soaking his mattress. It was minutes that seemed like hours of an out-of-body experience. The heaviness gone, finally free. She was boneless and useless, but when she opened her eyes and saw the room upside down, she still remembered she'd lost the battle.

It was time to win the war. She stole his battery-powered torture stick and used it to take his balls on a joyride. He braced on the mattress and fucked her mouth for all he was worth. When his cursing filled the room, a good number of people might have been frightened, but not her.

She took liberties with this powerful man that only she had the guts to do. Fingers, hands, teeth—scraping and teasing until she knew he was full to the breaking point. And then she spread her legs so his only view was this power she had over him.

"Holy fucking shit." Beckett was about to pull free, so she grabbed his ass and locked him in her mouth, swallowing what he had to offer, killing him the entire time he came.

And she took back the win.

After yet another shower, Beckett had his girl in his arms on the couch in the living room. G was a snoring mess after a thorough belly rub from Eve.

"I won the sex—so we're clear." She gave him a kiss on the lips.

"You won the battle. For us, sex is a war, stuffin muffin. And I'm a warlord." He growled at her.

"Okay. Keep telling yourself that." She rested completely against him now.

Beckett pulled her closer as he rearranged himself to sink deeper into the couch, rubbing his foot on his dog. No enemies lurking, no fucking errands to run for His Geezerness Rodolfo, and an ace in the hole against future troubles, thanks to the cunning Ms. Eve. He was a little bit terrified by how much he loved this moment.

Sneak Peek

The Poughkeepsie Brotherhood Book 3

Eve parked her motorcycle outside Starbucks in the crisp November air and used her credit card to pay for street parking. Beckett had given her hell for not going with him to Maryland to see the new baby. But although she was thrilled that Cole and Kyle were finally getting their child, the sight of a baby still killed something in her and she could find no way to tell him that. So he was pissed, and left strict instructions for her to take douchebags with her everywhere she went until he got back.

However, at the moment, instead of accompanying assholes, she had her piece on her and a knife tucked inside her jacket. It had been months since their showdown with Rodolfo Vitullo, and neither he or anyone else from Vitullo Weapons had bothered them at all. Besides, she just needed a quick cocoa.

She got on line and ordered her usual. But when she went to pay, Ryan's voice was in her ear. "Let me."

Eve nodded, keeping her eyes on the counter. She knew having to face Ryan was coming eventually now that she was living in Poughkeepsie again. It was a miracle it had been this long, but she just wished she'd seen it coming. As they waited for their drinks, she looked him up and down—still handsome, but more rugged than last time. And he still had love for her in his eyes, which made her look away.

"Ride here on the back of someone's bike?" he asked, gesturing to her helmet.

She responded with her best not-fucking-likely glare.

"You have your own?" He grabbed her drink before the barista could call Eve's name, then took the next order right out of the lady's hand.

"I do." She tapped her foot and looked at her beverage.

"Come with me to a table, and I'll let you have it." He gave her a smile.

He was trying. She hated how deeply she'd hurt him. "Fine." She followed him to a corner spot and sat, resting her helmet on the extra chair.

"This is where it all started." He slid her cup across to her waiting hand.

She said nothing, but took a sip of the piping hot chocolate.

"Fancy meeting you here." He tried again. "I was just thinking about you."

She could see women looking at him. He made a nice package in his crisp slacks and button-down shirt. She sighed.

"Listen, I'm not trying to make this awkward for you. I just wanted you to know I looked into my uncles' records. I unearthed some buried juvie reports." He twirled his coffee in his hands. "There was some information there I wanted to address with you. You were—"

"You didn't have to do that," she interrupted. "Why change your memories of them? You should have left well enough alone."

His jaw tensed. "Because as much as I said I didn't believe you, I didn't think you'd…" He looked around before lowering his voice. "…kill people without a reason. Now Taylor, yes. I still think he's a barnacle on a dragon testicle."

Eve suppressed a laugh.

"Okay, whatever. I'm nervous."

She smiled at him and sighed. "You know you taught me to laugh. I didn't do it enough before you."

He stopped talking and took a sip of his coffee. They sat together, the distance between them so much greater than the table.

"You with him now?" Ryan stared out the window.

"Yeah." She crossed her legs and accidently brushed against his under the table. "Sorry."

"For kicking me or for throwing your life away?" He leveled his brown eyes on her.

"If you thought that was a kick, we have an issue." She tried to make light of his question, but things were getting awkward. She got to the point. "You need to move past me now."

He shook his head and frowned. "I disagree. I'm not one for giving up."

"Let's review: You're a cop. I'm the exact opposite of that." Eve touched his hand. "And besides, he's where I'll always be, even if it's just in my head. You deserve better." She stood and grabbed her helmet. "That sounds fake, but I want the best for you. I really do." She shrugged, knowing he'd never understand how much she wished they could be friends. She'd miss him.

He nodded instead of answering, and Eve tossed her cup out on the way to her bike, a thousand emotions swirling through her. By the time she looked up, it was already too late.

Ryan watched her leave, silently hating how goddamn beautiful she was. It would be a hell of a lot easier to sit rejected if he didn't have a giant hard-on. And if she wasn't driving a motorcycle.

Fuck me sideways. He hung his head. Damned if he hadn't lost her forever. And it sucked. *Son of a bitch.* He looked down at the table, running his hands through his hair until the red and blue lights reflecting off the walls of the coffee shop caught his attention.

He stood and turned, looking for the source, and he saw Eve kneeling on the sidewalk with her hands in the air.

Ryan walked briskly outside, where two policemen had their guns drawn and pointed at Eve.

"Keep your hands nice and high where we can see them," one of them admonished.

Ryan couldn't stop himself. "Hey, what's going on?"

"Step aside, sir. This is police business."

"Really? Then you won't have any trouble sharing." He pulled his badge out of his jacket and showed it to the men.

And look of panic flashed between them. Although they were in uniform, they had what appeared to be an unmarked car.

"What's your station house? Because I know this isn't a local situation." Ryan stepped closer to the armed men and looked at Eve. She was staying put, hands in the air.

"Sir, we're in process here. If you'll excuse us…" The first holstered his weapon and approached her carefully.

He pulled her hands behind her and grabbed his handcuffs. Ryan pulled out his cell phone and dialed Kathy, the receptionist at the station.

"Hey, cutie," she answered. "I'm headed out the door. What's up?"

"What's your badge number, partner?" Ryan wasn't above getting physical, but after staring for a moment, the man rattled off a number. Ryan repeated it to Kathy and asked her to run it. It was wrong, the way these guys were going about things. "What're the charges?" he asked them as he waited.

"This is our case, and now is not the time." The second man pulled Eve to her feet.

He was staring into her eyes when Kathy told him what he already knew: "There's no record of that number. You need some backup, baby?"

"Okay, sorry. I know you were leaving. Thanks for your help on that." Ryan hung up on her and turned to the men.

"I apologize—just jittery lately. You guys need any help bringing her in?"

"No, we're good. Thanks, though."

They pulled Eve along and tossed her in the back of the car in a way very unlike what any real cop would do. One jumped into the driver's seat, and the second slipped in next to Eve in the backseat as she righted herself.

She slumped again, as if she'd been hit or shot, as the car pulled away, lights and sirens blazing.

Beckett pulled into the hospital's parking lot feeling off. Something wasn't right, but damned if he could figure it out. He called Eve and it went straight to voicemail.

Though she hadn't said it, he knew she'd shied away from seeing baby John because her own scars would never actually heal. Regret swelled up as Beckett's brain reminded him again that her life was painful because of him. He shook it off and refused to be anything but joyful on his brother's big day.

He met Chaos in the lobby, and the man walked him through the visiting process so he could see Chery before the baby-meeting event. When he entered her room, she was dressed and seemed poised to leave.

"Hey, pretty. How you holding up?" Beckett embraced her gently.

"I'm all right. Tough stuff, though — this thing." She didn't seem to know where to put her hands.

"You still sure this is what you want?" Beckett sat on the empty hospital bed.

She nodded. "But I feel like I'm torn up on the inside. It hurts so much." Her eyes filled and Chaos beat Beckett to her side, rubbing her back. "But it's the right thing. He can have a clean slate. He deserves it." She shrugged as Chaos handed her a tissue.

"I can't imagine. All I know is you're fucking brave as fuck," Beckett said.

Chery laughed a little. "You're a goddamn poet."

"Where's Vere?"

Chaos answered. "She's at the day facility. We're getting her as soon as Chery's got her walking papers."

"That's cool. How's the dog working out?"

Beckett got the full story of Vere's birthday party and how much she'd loved the gift he'd sent. The dog, rescued from death row and now named Camo, had arrived by limo, complete with all the food and toys he'd ever need.

Soon enough the nurse came in with a clipboard, so Beckett gave Chery a hug and shook Chaos's hand. After asking a few questions, he was directed to a room clear on the other side of the maternity ward.

Inside, Fairy Princess was feeding baby John and beaming.

"Now that's a fucking sight. How beautiful you are." Beckett leaned against the doorframe.

"You hitting on my wife?" Cole pounded Beckett on the shoulder.

"Every chance I get. She's a sweet piece of woman." He grabbed his brother up in a hard hug. "Congratulations, Daddy. You guys getting to know each other?"

Cole held up his arm for the shake. "It's amazing. He is just… an answer to prayers."

The handshake got a third arm as Blake entered and joined in. This was magic for Beckett, pure and simple. The world slowed down, his cares melted away as he looked from face to face. He loved these men so fiercely, it'd probably scare them if they knew.

Livia came in behind Blake and busted through the boys, passing Kellan to Beckett and Emme's hand to Cole.

"Rude." Beckett teased her.

She shot him a look as she kneeled in front of her new nephew in her sister's arms. "Oh, Kyle…" was as far as she got before both women were crying.

Beckett knew he wasn't the only man now looking around the room, trying to avoid tearing up himself.

Emme pulled on Cole's hand. "Why are they crying?"

Her uncle bent down. "Well, sometimes when all your dreams come true? The best you can do is cry. It's happy, not sad."

Beckett laughed as Kellan put his little hand in his mouth.

Blake patted his shoulder. "Careful, he loves to feed people."

He was about to reply that Kellen took after Uncle Cole when the boy stuffed a wet cracker in his mouth.

After he'd gagged it down, Beckett tried not to hurt the kid's feelings. "Yummy."

Kyle passed John to Livia and snickered. "Looks like you loved it, hot shot."

"Pipe down, sweet ass…" He noted the children and quickly covered, making the word longer. "…ociated banker?"

Kyle hugged her niece and stole her nephew from Beckett's arms. "Look at that, big guy. You have some company."

Everyone started talking at once, and the kids got down to playing with the toys Blake pulled out of their bag. Pictures were taken in every possible combination.

Cole sheepishly asked Blake if he could come double-check the car seat just to be sure, and Beckett followed, leaving the women and children in the hospital room.

"Thanks so much for coming to see John. Means the world to us." Cole was every inch the proud papa. "I feel so alive when we all get to be in the same place. Doesn't happen nearly enough."

"Couldn't be anywhere else, brother." Beckett slapped Cole's back as the three stepped off the elevator and headed out to find the car.

"I had it parked in a reserved spot and totally forgot about it," he explained with a laugh. "This morning I got here just as the doctor was waiting to pull in. He was pissed until I explained I was out of my mind." Cole opened the back door and Blake checked the seat, showing Cole how the belt fastened and where it should sit on the baby's chest.

"I'll text you a picture of my handiwork before we leave," Cole promised. He and Blake slipped into daddy talk as Beckett checked his phone. Three text messages rolled in as soon as he opened it.

They were from a douchebag with bad fucking news. Word had it that Eve had been arrested. Beckett looked up, and as if the messages brought the man forth, John McHugh and Kathy approached them from down the row of cars in the parking lot.

After hearty congratulations all around, Beckett asked John for a moment. To his credit, the man squelched a look of disdain and stepped aside with him.

"I just got intel saying Eve has been arrested. You know what for?" Beckett's mind was going a million miles an hour. There'd been no movement, no threats for months. Why now? Though, of all things, getting picked up by the cops was one of the safer options for Eve.

Confusion crossed John's face. "Really? I think your intel is shit. Let me find out." He stepped aside and pulled out his cell phone.

Beckett noticed Kathy waiting, within earshot. "You know anything? Everyone knows the receptionists are really the brains of the place." He moved closer to her as John shot him a dirty look.

"No, sir. Eve's father is a friend of mine, so I think that would perk up my ears. But…" She bit her lip.

He urged her to continue.

"Just before we left—weirdest thing—I think one of our officers was investigating a possible impersonation of a police officer. I'm sure it's just a coincidence."

John rejoined the conversation with a stern face. "Ms. Eve Hartt is not being detained, nor is there any indication she has had contact with our force. I guess your shit intel was just shit. But if you hear anything further, let me know. Now, if you'll excuse me, I have a grandson to meet." John held out his hand to Kathy, who gave Beckett a shrug.

Beckett hated the scenario that had just played out in his head. Grabbing up Eve was damn hard. She'd be looking every which way for someone out of the ordinary. But if they had badges, she might be forced to go with them. This could've been the most perfectly executed kidnapping ever.

Fuck.

Acknowledgments

Readers:

I can't even begin to fit my gratefulness in simple words. Because you are so open-minded, intelligent, and wicked sexy, I can take chances and put every bit of my imagination into my books. You unleash me. XOXOXOXOXO

Family:

To Mom and Dad S and Pam: Funny is funny. Thank you for making me laugh and never being far from my heart. I love you.

To Mom and Dad D: Florida looks so good on you! Welcome to your forever. I love you.

S, E and J: You guys are amazing.

My Aunt G and M and J: Your support is crazy fun!

My Aunt J and Uncle T: From soccer games to books, you guys have always been there.

Other aunts, uncles and cousins: You know who you are! I love you.

Omnific Publishing:

The dream makers! To the ever-stunning Elizabeth: You are my fairy godmother.

Enn, we will take over the world together!

Micha (my bitch forever and cover designer to the stars) and Traci, you guys are spectacular.

Huge thanks to Coreen, CJ, and Kim. You are the wheels on this vehicle!

Jessica Royer Ocken, you are the only reason anyone can read my chicken scratch. You are a sculptor, a poet, an excellent mimic of Beckett, a visionary, and a super-accepting professional. I owe you more than thanks. The laughter, the giggle, and the understanding we get to have is my favorite part, I swear it. XO

Carol Oates, how can two people who live so far away know each other so well? You are totally selfless with Poughkeepsie and its boys. I would be lost without you. XO

My Omni sisters, you couldn't be more fantastic.

Bloggers:

I have so many of you I would like to ride like a pony while hugging your neck it's insane. On my Twitter I have a list of all my friends, so I'm thanking that list now. A special ass spank to: The Smut Club, The Sub Club, Read Love Blog, Flics2Flics, Aestas Book Blog, Dymps, StacyHgg Reads, The Pixie Reader, Sweet Spot Book Spot, Hootie and Glo, Autumn Review, Bookish Babe, The Bookish Brunette, and Supernatural Snark. Holy crap, I adore you all.

Friends:

Karen Hancock, you and me and the beach, baby. Poughkeepsie Street Team, each one of you is such an ass-kicking, stone-cold amazing rock star. My Sweet Filets! (Shalu, Erika, TK, Gin, Amanda, Kiya, Alice, and Nina, the sleepover will be epic!) My F.R.I.E.N.D.S., you are so freaking helpful! Miss TammyVoiced, your brownies are my favorite drug. I can't believe I get lucky enough to be your friend. Shannon Lumetta, I'm keeping you forever—book or no books. Silly Jilly Stein, Nise, Denise, and Alicia, touch those tats for me and the boys! And love to Midian, Andarta, GraceDZ, Sunny, Tricia, Jen M, Sarah, Noemi, Suzy, Trayce, Ambyr, Rachel F, Jennifer, Thessamari, Gitte, Jenny, Eve and Eve, Ayeisha, Lori, Jennifer, Arethea, and Clista.

About the Author

Debra Anastasia is busy, just like every other mom. There's dinner, the dogs, the two kids, and her violent IBS—which is under control thanks to medication except for occasional multi-tonal farts. Her first love and crowning achievement is her thriving career as the weirdest mom on the block.

Her writing started a decent handful of years ago when—along with the animals and humans in her house—the voices of characters started whispering stories in Debra's ear. Insomnia was the gateway to plots that wouldn't give up, wouldn't let go. Now they stalk her everywhere. Halfway through making lunches, a twist takes hold and—fingers full of peanut butter—she finds somewhere, anywhere to write it down.

She's eternally grateful to Omnific Publishing, which has now published four of her books: two in the Seraphim Series and two in the Poughkeepsie Brotherhood Series, as well as her novella, *Late Night with Andres.* That one is special because 100% of the proceeds go to breast cancer research. (So go get it right now, please!) She also very much appreciates her open-minded readers, who embrace everything she has to offer, with a focus on anti-heroes and bathroom humor.

Debra lives in Maryland with her family. You can find her at DebraAnastasia.com and on Twitter @Debra_Anastasia. But be prepared…

check out these titles from

OMNIFIC PUBLISHING

Contemporary Romance

Boycotts & Barflies and *Trust in Advertising* by Victoria Michaels
Passion Fish by Alison Oburia and Jessica McQuinn
The Small Town Girl series: *Small Town Girl* & *Corporate Affair* by Linda Cunningham
Stitches and Scars by Elizabeth A. Vincent
Take the Cake by Sandra Wright
Pieces of Us by Hannah Downing
The Way That You Play It by BJ Thornton
The Poughkeepsie Brotherhood series: *Poughkeepsie* & *Return to Poughkeepsie* by Debra Anastasia
Cocktails & Dreams by Autumn Markus
Recaptured Dreams and *All-American Girl* and *Until Next Time* by Justine Dell
Once Upon a Second Chance by Marian Vere
The Englishman by Nina Lewis
16 Marsden Place by Rachel Brimble
Sleepers, Awake by Eden Barber
The Runaway Year by Shani Struthers
Hydraulic Level Five by Sarah Latchaw
Fix You by Beck Anderson
Just Once by Julianna Keyes
The WORDS series: *The Weight of Words* by Georgina Guthrie
Theatricks by Eleanor Gwyn-Jones
The Sacrificial Lamb by Elle Fiore
The Art of Appreciation by Autumn Markus

New Adult

Three Daves by Nicki Elson
Streamline by Jennifer Lane
Shades of Atlantis by Carol Oates
The Heart series: *Beside Your Heart* & *Disclosure of the Heart* by Mary Whitney
Romancing the Bookworm by Kate Evangelista
Fighting Fate by Linda Kage
Flirting with Chaos by Kenya Wright

Young Adult

The Ember series: *Ember* & *Iridescent* by Carol Oates
Breaking Point by Jess Bowen
Life, Liberty, and Pursuit by Susan Kaye Quinn
The Embrace series: *Embrace* & *Hold Tight* by Cherie Colyer
Destiny's Fire by Trisha Wolfe
The Reaper series: *Reaping Me Softly* & *UnReap My Heart* by Kate Evangelista

Erotic Romance

The Keyhole series: *Becoming sage (book one)* by Kasi Alexander
The Keyhole series: *Saving sunni (book two)* by Kasi & Reggie Alexander
The Winemaker's Dinner: *Appetizers* & *Entrée* by Dr. Ivan Rusilko & Everly Drummond
The Winemaker's Dinner: *Dessert* by Dr. Ivan Rusilko

Paranormal Romance

The Light series: *Seers of Light, Whisper of Light,* & *Circle of Light* by Jennifer DeLucy
The Hanaford Park series: *Eve of Samhain* & *Pleasures Untold* by Lisa Sanchez
Immortal Awakening by KC Randall
The Seraphim series: *Crushed Seraphim* & *Bittersweet Seraphim* by Debra Anastasia
The Guardian's Wild Child by Feather Stone
Grave Refrain by Sarah M. Glover
Divinity by Patricia Leever
Blood Vine series: *Blood Vine* & *Blood Entangled* by Amber Belldene
Divine Temptation by Nicki Elson
Love in the Time of the Dead by Tera Shanley

Historical Romance

Cat O' Nine Tails by Patricia Leever
Burning Embers by Hannah Fielding
Good Ground by Tracy Winegar

Romantic Suspense

Whirlwind by Robin DeJarnett
The CONduct Series: *With Good Behavior* & *Bad Behavior* & *On Best Behavior* by Jennifer Lane
Indivisible by Jessica McQuinn
Between the Lies by Alison Oburia

Anthologies

A Valentine Anthology including short stories by Alice Clayton ("With a Double Oven"), Jennifer DeLucy ("Magnus of Pfelt, Conquering Viking Lord"), Nicki Elson ("I Don't Do Valentine's Day"), Jessica McQuinn ("Better Than One Dead Rose and a Monkey Card"), Victoria Michaels ("Home to Jackson"), and Alison Oburia ("The Bridge")

Singles and Novellas

It's Only Kinky the First Time (Keyhole series) by Kasi Alexander
Learning the Ropes (Keyhole series) by Kasi & Reggie Alexander
The Winemaker's Dinner: RSVP by Dr. Ivan Rusilko
The Winemaker's Dinner: No Reservations by Everly Drummond
Big Guns by Jessica McQuinn
Concessions by Robin DeJarnett
Starstruck by Lisa Sanchez
New Flame by BJ Thornton
Shackled by Debra Anastasia
Swim Recruit by Jennifer Lane
Sway by Nicki Elson
Full Speed Ahead by Susan Kaye Quinn
The Second Sunrise by Hannah Downing
The Summer Prince by Carol Oates
Whatever it Takes by Sarah M. Glover
Clarity (A *Divinity* prequel single) by Patricia Leever
A Christmas Wish (A *Cocktails & Dreams* single) by Autumn Markus
Late Night with Andres by Debra Anastasia

Young Adult

The Ember series: *Ember* & *Iridescent* by Carol Oates
Breaking Point by Jess Bowen
Life, Liberty, and Pursuit by Susan Kaye Quinn
The Embrace series: *Embrace* & *Hold Tight* by Cherie Colyer
Destiny's Fire by Trisha Wolfe
The Reaper series: *Reaping Me Softly* & *UnReap My Heart* by Kate Evangelista

Erotic Romance

The Keyhole series: *Becoming sage (book one)* by Kasi Alexander
The Keyhole series: *Saving sunni (book two)* by Kasi & Reggie Alexander
The Winemaker's Dinner: *Appetizers* & *Entrée* by Dr. Ivan Rusilko & Everly Drummond
The Winemaker's Dinner: *Dessert* by Dr. Ivan Rusilko

Paranormal Romance

The Light series: *Seers of Light, Whisper of Light,* & *Circle of Light* by Jennifer DeLucy
The Hanaford Park series: *Eve of Samhain* & *Pleasures Untold* by Lisa Sanchez
Immortal Awakening by KC Randall
The Seraphim series: *Crushed Seraphim* & *Bittersweet Seraphim* by Debra Anastasia
The Guardian's Wild Child by Feather Stone
Grave Refrain by Sarah M. Glover
Divinity by Patricia Leever
Blood Vine series: *Blood Vine* & *Blood Entangled* by Amber Belldene
Divine Temptation by Nicki Elson
Love in the Time of the Dead by Tera Shanley

Historical Romance

Cat O' Nine Tails by Patricia Leever
Burning Embers by Hannah Fielding
Good Ground by Tracy Winegar

Romantic Suspense

Whirlwind by Robin DeJarnett
The CONduct Series: *With Good Behavior* & *Bad Behavior* &
On Best Behavior by Jennifer Lane
Indivisible by Jessica McQuinn
Between the Lies by Alison Oburia

Anthologies

A Valentine Anthology including short stories by
Alice Clayton ("With a Double Oven"),
Jennifer DeLucy ("Magnus of Pfelt, Conquering Viking Lord"),
Nicki Elson ("I Don't Do Valentine's Day"),
Jessica McQuinn ("Better Than One Dead Rose and a Monkey Card"),
Victoria Michaels ("Home to Jackson"), and
Alison Oburia ("The Bridge")

Singles and Novellas

It's Only Kinky the First Time (Keyhole series) by Kasi Alexander
Learning the Ropes (Keyhole series) by Kasi & Reggie Alexander
The Winemaker's Dinner: RSVP by Dr. Ivan Rusilko
The Winemaker's Dinner: No Reservations by Everly Drummond
Big Guns by Jessica McQuinn
Concessions by Robin DeJarnett
Starstruck by Lisa Sanchez
New Flame by BJ Thornton
Shackled by Debra Anastasia
Swim Recruit by Jennifer Lane
Sway by Nicki Elson
Full Speed Ahead by Susan Kaye Quinn
The Second Sunrise by Hannah Downing
The Summer Prince by Carol Oates
Whatever it Takes by Sarah M. Glover
Clarity (A *Divinity* prequel single) by Patricia Leever
A Christmas Wish (A *Cocktails & Dreams* single) by Autumn Markus
Late Night with Andres by Debra Anastasia

coming soon from
OMNIFIC PUBLISHING

Client N° 5 by Joy Fulcher
Vice, Virtue, and Video: Revealed (book 1) by Bianca Giovanni
Blood Reunited (Blood Vine series, book 3) by Amber Belldene
Keeping the Peace (The Small Town Girl series, book 3) by Linda Cunningham
St. Kate of the Cupcake: The Dangers of Lust and Baking by L.C. Fenton
The Plan by Qwen Salsbury
Legendary by LH Nicole
Kiss Me Goodnight by Michele Zurlo
Fatal by TA Brock
Blind Man's Bargain by Tracy Winegar

CPSIA information can be obtained at www.ICGtesting.com
Printed in the USA
BVOW03s1230160114

341887BV00003B/20/P